Ptah's Travels:
KINGDOMS OF ANCIENT EGYPT

by Kathryn DeMeritt

Kathryn De Meritt

∞
Infinity Publishing

ISBN 0-7414-2728-1

Library of Congress Cataloging-in-Publication Data
        DeMeritt, Kathryn.
Copyright Registration Number: Pending

Cover illustration © 2005 by Val Paul Taylor
www.raindogcreative.com

Book design by Kathryn DeMeritt
www.ptahstravels.com

Published by:

INFI∞ITY
PUBLISHING.COM

1094 New De Haven Street, Suite 100
West Conshohocken, PA 19428-2713
Info@buybooksontheweb.com
www.buybooksontheweb.com
Toll-free (877) BUY BOOK
Local Phone (610) 941-9999
Fax (610) 941-9959

Printed in the United State of America
Printed on recycled paper
Published July 2005

This book is a novel. While many of the situations presented in this story are based upon real people and true events, the facts have often been—how shall I say?—embellished, which is every storyteller's right.

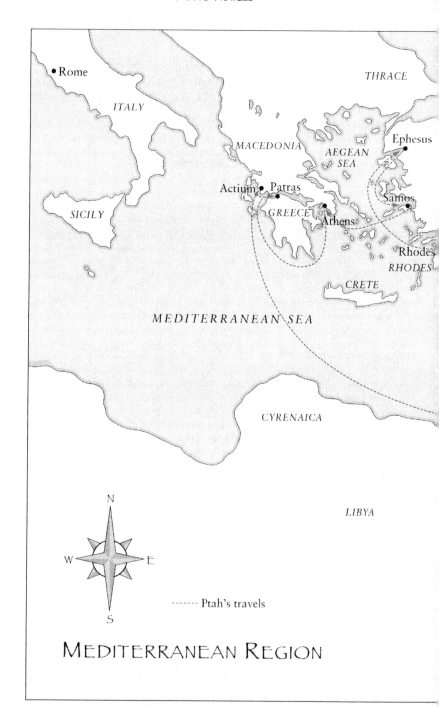

N

W ——— E

S

------- Ptah's travels

MEDITERRANEAN REGION

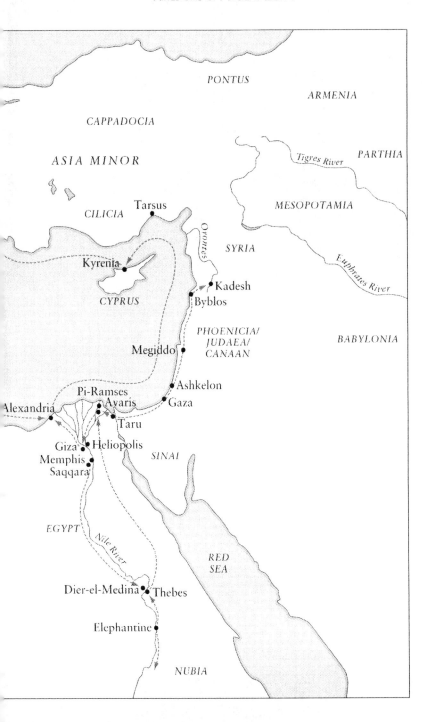

Ptah	(p-tah´)
Narmer	(nar´-mer)
Imhotep	(im´-hoh-tep)
Shabaka	(shuh-bah´-kah)
Kandake	(kan-dah´-kee)
Anubis	(uh-noo´-bis)
Maat	(maht)
Ammit	(ah´-mit)
Nebre	(ne´-bree)
Wia	(wee´-ah)
Ipuwer	(ip´-oo-wer)
Horus	(hohr´-uhs)
Smendes	(smen´-dez)
Mentuhotep	(men´-too-hoh´-tep)
Khufu	(koo´-foo)
Souti	(soo´-tee)
Baba	(bah´-bah)
Ahmose	(ah-mo´-zee)
Thutmose	(tut-mo´-zee)
Paser	(pah´-ser)
Setau	(set´-ow)
Ramses	(ram´-zeez)
Muwatallis	(muh-wuh-tal´-is)
Sashai	(sah´-shay)
Isis	(ī´-sis)
Osiris	(oh-sī´-ris)
Dionysus	(dī-uh-nī´-suhs)
Marc Antony	(mark an´-toh-nee)
Nefertiti	(ne´-fer-tee´-tee)
Cleopatra	(klee´-oh-pa´-truh)
Sphinx	(sfinks)
Ptolemy	(tol´-e-mee)
Octavian	(ok-ta´-vee-an)
Herodotus	(he-rod´-uh-tuhs)
Eros	(air´-ohs)

Prologue
The Urn

The old priest gazed pensively at the soft lump of clay sitting on the stone slab before him. Its shape, he thought, was like the first dome of earth to have risen above the sea at the time of creation. He pondered over what to make. Ideas, like tiny birds refusing to alight, flitted timidly through his mind. He heard voices, too, urging him on, telling him in garbled whispers what he ought to create. Gradually the voices grew louder and their message became clear. An urn—yes!—a very special urn, he decided. Wetting his gnarled and wrinkled fingers, the priest began to gently knead the clay, mumbling ancient incantations as he worked.

The urn being made was for an important person. Not only was he the king's highest official, this man possessed that rare sort of wisdom and intelligence Egypt sorely needed, and would need again in the future. The urn would be far more than a handsome ceremonial vase. It was intended to be a tool, equally as important as the man. In the hands of the right person, it might even reverse the fate foretold by the stars!

When the priest finished kneading, he began to roll the clay into long, thick ropes. Snakes, he always thought of when he did this, and not your harmless garden-variety type of snakes, either. His mind always turned to the most poisonous ones: cobras, asps, and the like. The snakes slithered through his fingers as he worked the clay, hissing their secrets into his ears, planting their riddles deep in his mind.

"What? What is it you want?" he cried. Sensing a power far

greater than his, the priest hastened to fix a base for the urn, then wound the ropes in circular coils to form its body, wound them higher and higher while pinching the mouths of the snakes to silence their infernal hissing. When at last the room grew quiet, the priest set about smoothing the surface of the urn to form a canvas for his art.

When he wasn't doing his yearly three-month stint at the temple, the priest was an artist. *A fine one, too,* he thought, although few people seemed able to understand his work. Most couldn't see beyond the fact that he ignored the Egyptian standards of proportion and beauty, that he drew his images as he saw them in his mind.

"Touched by the gods," were the words people used to describe him. "Crazy is more what they mean," cackled the priest softly to himself. "The fools. Let them say what they will. Time will tell whether I'm crazy or not!"

The priest began carving his delicate images into the smoothed clay. Beginning at the bottom and spiraling his way to the top, he carved slowly and carefully, mumbling more incantations as he worked. *These images will tell a story,* he mused, *a story that will provide passage to those who are willing and able to accept it.* Hours later, as the vessel neared completion, the priest's thoughts turned again to the man who would be receiving this gift, disguised as payment from the king.

True, this man had been born into the right family, had been given opportunities that others had not. As a young boy, his father, a middle-ranking official, had been able to pull enough strings to have him trained as a scribe. But the boy went on to prove himself from there. After having quickly mastered the hundreds of hieroglyphics necessary to perform his craft, he went on to study astronomy, medicine, art, and architecture—a genius, in other words.

Yes, this urn was being made for a man whose time had come, and would come again many more times in the future. For the priest knew what others did not: that this kingdom would not last! Three times it would rise and three times fall, only to be passed into the hands of foreigners who would rob the country blind. Unless . . . unless this man found passage through the urn of time.

Part I
A Wish for Adventure

The New Millennium
Year 2005

1

Ptah

The grandfather clock chimed six o'clock—time for Professor Mariette to come home from work. Waiting for him, hidden behind a wing-backed chair in the living room of his apartment, was a young black cat. The cat wasn't so much waiting for the professor to come home as he was waiting for the door of the apartment to open. And for his chance to escape.

Muffled footsteps approached from down the hallway. A key turned in the lock. The cat crouched low, muscles tense, watching while the door inched slowly open. *Now,* he thought. *This is my chance! This time I'll make it for sure!*

As the door swung wide, the cat sprang from his position and dashed across the room. Taking a running leap, he flew for the door as though the furry white "wings" on his back truly worked. *Whump!* A foot came down swiftly and wedged itself across the opening of the doorway. *Wham!* The cat hit the leg full force, crumpling into a heap on the floor. Very gently, the foot nudged the cat back inside the apartment and the professor entered the room.

Click! Dazed but unharmed, the cat looked up to see that once again the door had closed on his hopes and dreams, and on his plans for seeing the sights of Egypt.

"Ptah! What has gotten into you lately? You seem bound and determined to get out that door! How many times have I told you that it's dangerous out there?" The professor walked to the front hall closet, set down his briefcase, and hung up his coat.

Ptah, for that was the young cat's name, slunk back to the living room and over to the large picture window. Hopping onto its sill, he gazed morosely down at the city below, certain that something exciting was happening out there that very minute. He felt caged and miserable inside, and he longed to go back to the days before he'd ever heard there was going to be an Egypt exhibit, to the days when he'd been perfectly happy to be an indoor cat.

Back then, even the tiniest thought of escaping had never entered Ptah's mind. He loved his apartment high on the hill. And he loved the professor, who doted on him endlessly. He had everything a cat could ever want or need. Everything, that is, except adventure.

Ptah was a slender young cat with short black fur and sapphire blue eyes. He had very long legs, standing well over an inch taller than other cats his size, and a long ropy tail. He was an ordinary cat in most ways, although he did possess one unusual feature: the three white patches on his fur. The first, in the middle of his forehead, was shaped like a diamond, while the other two, one behind either shoulder, looked just like a pair of wings folded onto his back.

It was from these distinct markings that Ptah received his name. His owner, Professor Mariette, was a professor of ancient Egyptian history at the nearby university and had named his cat after an ancient Egyptian god. The god Ptah was thought to come down to earth from time to time in the form of a black bull with a white diamond on its forehead and a pair of white wings on its back. The Egyptians believed this god to be very powerful; among other things, Ptah gave artists the ability to turn their ideas into reality. The professor didn't think his cat was a god, of course, and he certainly didn't mistake him for a bull, but he did consider the name to be quite clever.

Ptah's "wings" were sure to bring comments from the professor's friends who visited. "Has that cat ever tried to leap out the window and fly after the birds?" they'd ask. Or, from fellow Egyptologists, "I thought Ptah was supposed to come down to earth as a *calf*, not a *cat*." But most of the comments he received were about how striking and unusual Ptah looked.

Professor Mariette took these jokes in stride because he was a good-natured sort. A tall and handsome man with dark brown eyes, bushy black hair, and coppery-colored skin, he was nevertheless the kind of person you wouldn't notice in a crowd because he always wore dark-colored clothing and kept his head bent down, deep in concentration. He was forever trying to think of a way he might contribute to his field of study. He had traveled to Egypt several times in pursuit of his quest, but as yet had found nothing of particular interest.

Egyptian blood ran deep in the professor's veins. His mother was Egyptian, and although his father was French, he was a distant relative of the famous Auguste Mariette, a man who began his career by smuggling treasures out of Egypt for France, but later felt sorry for what he'd done and returned to Egypt, determined to find a way to stop others like him. Auguste eventually became the director of Egypt's first museum, at one point having thirty-seven excavations under his direction. While the professor lacked the funds to go digging around Egypt the way Auguste had, he was still inspired to discover something any way that he could.

The professor was passionate about what he taught, believing that everyone should know about the fabulous civilization that was once ancient Egypt. Probably because he was so focused on his work, he had never married. He lived alone with Ptah, but was not lonely because he enjoyed his cat very much. As people will sometimes do, the professor treated Ptah much like a son—buying him plenty of cat toys and spending hours reading to him, mostly books about Egypt.

The apartment they shared on the twelfth floor of a rustic brick building suited them perfectly. One man's junk is another man's treasure, Ptah had once heard, and this phrase summed up their place fairly well. Their apartment was filled with all sorts of treasures the professor had collected while on his journeys—alabaster statues, bronze swords, copper pots, faience amulets, and more. It was the kind of place a person could visit a hundred times over and see something new each time. Their apartment was also blessed with a terrific view. Ptah had spent many long hours on the living room windowsill gazing out at the scenery below—the bustle of city streets, the myriad of ships coming and going on the sparkling blue waters, the islands and snow-capped mountains beckoning in the distance.

Ptah had always been a happy cat, content with his life indoors, until the day the professor had come home with some exciting news.

"Ptah, there's going to be a major exhibit of Egyptian artifacts at the museum, and I have tickets to attend the opening night!" the professor announced as he burst through the door.

"Oh, Professor, how exciting!" exclaimed Ptah, leaping down from the windowsill and scampering right over. "Are you saying the museum will be showing real treasures from ancient Egypt? I would *so* much love to go with you! The ancient Egyptians loved cats! Why, there might even be something there that belonged to my great-great-great-great-great-great . . . oh, whoever it might have been, it would be great! Can I go with you, please, can I?" Ptah danced around the professor's feet, causing him to stumble a bit.

"Ptah, settle down, kitty! What's all that meowing for? Oh, I get it—you're hungry!" The professor went into the kitchen, tossed some kitty crunchies into a bowl, and set them down at Ptah's feet.

Ptah looked at his food bowl, then up at the professor, then down at his food bowl again. "Excuse me, Professor, anybody home?" he asked. More than once he had questioned the intelligence of his owner. *It makes no sense,* he thought. *I understand every word he says, but if I ask him how his day was, he gives me a bowl of food. If I try to talk politics, he plops me into the cat box. Well, at least that one makes some sense.*

Shoulders drooping, tail dragging, Ptah slunk back to the windowsill. The more he stewed about it, the more upset he became. *I shouldn't even have to tell the professor I want to go the exhibit,* he thought. *He should know that already. I mean, how many hours have we spent together pouring over books and watching shows on ancient Egypt? I know all about the Egyptians. At one time they were the most advanced people on the face of the planet. They were building huge temples and monuments when other people were still living in caves! Anyone that loved cats as much as they did had to be intelligent!*

As it so often does, disappointment planted a seed in Ptah's mind, and that seed began to grow. Ptah began to feel trapped, stuck in a life in which nothing exciting ever seemed to happen. All at once, it seemed, it was no longer enough for him to sit on the sill and watch the world go by; he wanted to be part of it. And so right then and there, he decided that he would do something about it.

"I'm *going* to that exhibit," he vowed, "even if I have to get there myself!"

2

The Great Escape

Ptah woke early, twitched his whiskers, and pricked up his ears. He felt as though butterflies were flitting around in his stomach, but for the life of him, he couldn't remember having eaten any butterflies. A few bugs, maybe, but definitely no butterflies. Why was he so nervous?

Then it hit him: the Egypt exhibit opened tonight! This was his last chance. If he didn't find a way out of his apartment today, he'd never get to see it. Ptah ran to the living room window, jumped to the sill, and scanned the ten blocks between his apartment and the museum, trying hard to believe that everything would go smoothly this time.

The past few weeks had been difficult ones for Ptah. For the first time in his life, he had been a bad cat. He'd been testing the waters, so to speak, to see what sort of behavior might get him thrown outside. In hindsight, he had to admit that some of his tactics had been downright nasty. Climbing the curtains and clawing on the furniture were one thing, but he cringed to think of the time he had literally stooped so low as to use the professor's slipper for his cat box. Even so, he couldn't help but smile when he pictured the look on the professor's face as he felt his foot go *squish!* Despite these many capers, however, none had managed to get him the boot. All he had to show for his efforts was a cleaner cat box and one plan left.

By early afternoon, Ptah was beginning to feel a little better. As it was turning out, several things were going in his favor. For one, it was a beautiful fall day outside. For another, the professor, who normally had his head somewhere up in the clouds anyway, seemed even more distracted than usual. That morning he had actually poured kitty crunchies in his cereal bowl and had given Ptah Cheerios for breakfast! Ptah had also overheard the professor saying that everyone attending the opening ceremony would be wearing black and white. He'd be sure to blend in once he got inside the museum.

As evening approached and the time for the Professor to leave drew near, Ptah got ready to carry out his plan. Positioning himself on the kitchen counter next to a large metal canister, his plan was simply to push the canister off of the counter at the exact moment the professor opened the door, thereby creating a loud distraction and giving him the chance to slip out unnoticed.

Ptah waited for what felt like hours before the professor emerged from his bedroom dressed to the nines in a black tuxedo he'd rented especially for the occasion. Did he ever look dashing! With its shiny satin lapels and its crisp, smooth fabric, the tuxedo fit as though it had been personally made for his lanky frame. His shoes shone like polished ebony.

The professor strode merrily into the kitchen to say good-bye, then went to the front hall closet to collect his coat. As he walked to the entry door and twisted the knob, Ptah stepped back from the canister, turned his shoulder into it, and charged.

Pow! As the door swung wide, both cat and canister flew from the counter and crashed to the floor. Ptah's world turned instantly white as a plume of flour rose into the air. He had thought the canister was empty! Through the haze he saw the professor rush in.

"Ptah! What have you done?" he cried.

Covered with flour, Ptah gathered his feet up under him and took off running. Bolting past the professor, who was brushing flour dust from his elegant clothes, Ptah dashed through the apartment, out the door, and down the hallway. Racing to the elevator, he began jumping feverishly at the call button. He missed it once, he missed it twice, but on the third try, he hit it! The elevator door slid silently open, Ptah leaped inside, the door closed, and the next thing he knew he was trapped. Twelve buttons were staring him in the face. Which one to push? He had to act quickly; the professor was probably right behind him!

Suddenly the elevator began to move by itself. Heart pounding, tail twitching, Ptah crouched in the far corner of the cab vowing, *They'll never take me alive,* as the elevator went down, down, down until finally, with a lurch, it stopped. As the door slid open, out he shot like a spring-loaded cannon.

Wham! No sooner had Ptah sprung from the elevator than he skidded across the freshly waxed floor of the apartment building lobby and crashed into a plant, which promptly toppled down on him, spilling dirt all over the place. Stunned, he looked up. He had made it to the lobby! Now all he had to do was to get out the door—through the very same door the mailman was exiting that minute.

Yikes, thought Ptah. *That door might not be opened again for hours!* Pulling himself together, he dashed across the lobby, and then in one desperate motion, he flung himself toward the mailman, shouting, "Wait!" But of course all the mailman heard was a horrible screeching noise like the sound an alien might make when descending on its prey. The mailman froze in the doorway, then slowly began to turn around, at which point Ptah landed squarely in the center of his back, claws dug in deeply.

"Aiyee!" shrieked the mailman, twirling round and around while looking back over his shoulder to see what sort of demon had hit him. What he saw was a deranged cat, covered with dirt and flour, and with blue eyes as big as saucers.

Ptah was just as frightened as the mailman, and he was getting dizzy from all the twirling. But he couldn't stop now—he was halfway outside! Taking a giant breath, he released his claws and dropped to the ground. Then, leaping onto the sidewalk, he took off running.

By the time Ptah reached the museum, he was shaking and out of breath. *The professor was right,* he thought. *It is dangerous out here!*

The journey through the city had been fraught with terrors. Things were so much bigger than they had looked from the window of his apartment! Faster and noisier, too. Cars whizzing by, horns honking, people crowding the sidewalks—so much activity had left him a nervous wreck. Ptah knew he needed to rest before attempting to get to the exhibit, so he found himself a hiding place behind a tall iron sculpture and began to clean himself. A half hour later, and looking all the better for it, he was ready to go on.

The museum festivities were already well underway. Ptah waited until a large group of newcomers arrived, and then, falling in step behind them, he slipped though the door, and darted behind the ticket counter. To his left, a dozen or so people were milling about, waiting to check their coats. Ahead, a corridor led to some elevators where more people waited. To his right, a wide marble staircase rose majestically along the entire length of the museum.

And what a museum! Soaring windows and a cathedral-like ceiling produced the effect of a great hall. Festive banners depicting ancient Egyptian gods hung in colorful rows along the creamy stone walls. Ptah saw Thoth, the divine scribe, and Horus, the falcon-headed ruler of Egypt, and there was Isis, queen mother of the earth, standing next to Osiris, the god of the dead. Added to this splendid atmosphere was a gentle and exotic form of music produced by a harp, the most beloved of all Egyptian instruments.

Ptah decided at once to take the stairs. He had had enough of elevators for a while, and there were plenty of people on the stairway for him to blend in with, since wine and hors d'oeuvres were being served on the landing halfway up. Padding cautiously forward, Ptah ogled the guests. He had never seen such an elegant crowd: ladies wearing shimmering black dresses and velvet gowns, men sporting tuxedoes and black satin jackets. Jewelry sparkled from every angle.

Suddenly Ptah's heart skipped a beat, for there, not three feet away, stood the professor in his speckled gray tuxedo, talking to a lovely young Italian woman with long, wavy hair. Ptah stifled the urge to run up to him. Hadn't the professor been wearing black? He cringed, the flour incident weighing heavily on his mind.

Ptah continued upward until he reached the second floor. Strolling into the first room he came to, he took a good look around. Nothing in there but a bunch of wild paintings that looked as though the artist had been playing with a paint-ball gun. He shrugged and proceeded to the third floor, which held carved wooden masks and other fine works of African art. *At least I'm getting closer geographically,* he thought. At last he reached the fourth, and final floor. As he crossed the threshold, Ptah's heart began to soar.

The Egypt exhibit was even more fabulous than he'd imagined it would be! Passing by giant statues of ancient kings, Ptah entered room after room filled with beautiful antiques. There were golden masks and broad collared necklaces set with turquoise, carnelian, and lapis. There were cedar chests and ebony chairs inlaid with ivory and gold. There were boxes and figurines made of alabaster and blue faience. There were ostrich-feather fans and model boats and vases and jars and dishes.

Each piece was a masterwork. Living in a country with an abundance of food, the Egyptians had had the luxury of time to perfect their crafts.

When Ptah had studied ancient Egypt with the professor, it was often hard for him to grasp just how long ago these people had lived. The numbers were mind boggling. The civilization of ancient Egypt had lasted for over three thousand years before finally coming to an end over two thousand years ago. That meant that people who lived and breathed five thousand years before him could have made the beautiful objects he was now gazing at!

Roaming cautiously from room to room, Ptah lost all track of time. At one point he noticed that the crowd had thinned, but the next thing he knew, there was nobody left. Suddenly he realized that in all of his excitement he had forgotten to enact part two of his plan, which was to find the professor so he could get a ride home!

Ptah dashed down the stairs just in time to see the curator locking the museum doors as the last person went out. He stood there immobilized, not knowing what to do. At last he decided to return to the exhibit. He'd worry about getting home tomorrow.

Back on the fourth floor, Ptah roamed freely about this time. In the far corner of one room, he spied a large clay urn he hadn't noticed before. It was rather plain compared to the other pieces, and he wondered why it was even included in the exhibit at all. But on closer inspection, he was enchanted to see that the urn was covered with marvelous little images, many of which were cats! Dozens of them pranced across its surface, spiraling their way upward in a circular pattern from base to rim. *Now here is a work of art,* thought Ptah.

He turned his attention to the message posted on the plaque below:

Egyptian Urn. Experts are divided in their opinion as to when this urn was made. Though highly unusual, its artistic style places the urn's origin to be some time during the Old Kingdom, possibly during the reign of King Zoser. However, carbon dating techniques have failed to verify this theory. In fact, carbon dating has failed to provide any clue whatsoever, because the results vary each time the test is done. Therefore, this urn is one of the strangest finds to date.

How odd, thought Ptah. He circled the vessel, studying its tiny images. They seemed to be telling a story, though he couldn't quite make out what it was. Eager to get a closer look, he jumped to the rim of the urn and peered over its edge.

Suddenly, Ptah heard footsteps approach. Before he knew it, two people had entered the room. With no time left and nowhere to run, Ptah dove into the darkness of the urn. Immediately, a low hissing noise filled his ears, alarming at first, but then soothing, like the sound a seashell makes when placed close to the ear.

Ptah strained to hear what was happening outside. Above the low hiss, he could hear voices. It sounded as though a private tour was going on. Ptah settled into the base of the urn, surprisingly comfy and warm. As he lay there waiting for the tour to finish, his incredible day caught up with him. Giving in to sleep at last, he closed his eyes and let himself be carried away into dreams of Egypt.

Ptah Dreams:

Bastet

Late that night, when the moon was high and the lights were low, Ptah had a very strange dream.

He dreamed he was walking down a long, stone hallway, gloomy except where lit by oil lamps that hung at intervals from copper brackets set into the walls. There were no windows in this hall, but the light from the lamps flickered as if blown by the wind, causing Ptah's shadow to dance along the floor as he passed slowly by.

Suddenly, from out of nowhere it seemed, a mysterious cat appeared. Her lustrous fur was the same soft, dark gray as the shadows from which she emerged, and her eyes were as pale and as bright as the moon. "Greetings, young cat," she said, her voice soothing and low, like the sound of deep running water.

Ptah froze in his tracks. There was something weird about this cat. She appeared to glow, surrounded as she was by a soft pinkish light. "Who . . . who are you?" he stammered.

"I am Bastet, goddess and protector of cats," the gray cat said, smiling. "I have been watching over you, Ptah, and I've come to take you on the journey your heart so desires. Follow me!" She turned and began walking further down the long, stone hallway.

Ptah hesitated for a moment, then hurried after her. "Where are we going?" he asked. He didn't know what sort of journey she could possibly be talking about, nor did he know how it was that she came to know his name. He also didn't know whether it was wise to follow a strange cat—no matter how beautiful—down a darkened hallway. But Bastet seemed kind, and her words were much too enticing for him to ignore.

The two walked on in silence, at one point rounding a bend in the hallway, after which they began passing by a series of doorways along either side. The doors were open, and inside, Ptah was surprised to see scenes of fields and villages, or forests and mountains, or rivers and valleys going off into the distance. It was as though each doorway led to a completely different world! Curious, he asked Bastet whether he could go through some of them, but she shook her head no.

"Not now, not yet," she replied, as if that were enough in the way of explanation.

Further and further down the hallway they went, each bend that they rounded leading to yet another long series of doorways with more views of far-off places. The hallway seemed to go on forever! Finally, Bastet stopped and pointed at a particular door.

"It is time," she said.

Bursting with curiosity, Ptah rushed forward to look inside. Gazing out across the distance, he could see a sparkling river winding its way through a lush green valley beneath a crystalline blue sky. Along the river's edge he saw villages, tidy and small, and on either side of the valley there were reddish mountains and deserts made of sand. The tangy scents of cinnamon and saffron wafted up through the air, and the music of flute and harp played sweetly in his ears. It was a wondrous place, a place that most certainly looked inviting, but Ptah hesitated to go further, fearful of where it all might lead.

"Go on," encouraged Bastet.

Timidly, Ptah stepped over the threshold. Immediately, he was overcome by a strong sense of vertigo. He felt as though he was falling swiftly through space, when in fact all four of his paws were planted firmly on the ground. Frightened, he reached out a paw for Bastet to take hold of, but she merely backed away.

"Fear not," she said, "for I will always be with you. Stay with the urn! It will take you wherever you need to go." After that she melted into the shadows and was gone from sight.

Ptah panicked. The world around him was beginning to turn hazy, and he could no longer see. His vertigo made him feel dizzy and sick. A loud hissing noise, like the rush of the wind, swirled round in his ears. The terrible feeling of having been left all alone and unprotected grabbed hold of his gut. He tried to step back through the doorway but it had vanished in the haze, the hallway along with it. His senses now reeling, Ptah was encroaching upon the brink of despair, when all at once the hissing, the vertigo, and the dizziness stopped, and he found himself back inside the urn, surrounded by warmth and darkness.

Part 2
The Mountain of Gold

Old Kingdom
Saqarra, 2650 BCE

3

The Step Pyramid of Saqarra

Ptah woke slowly as if from a long, deep sleep. For a while he just lay there, enjoying that lazy-morning feeling and thinking about the strange dream he'd been having. His dream had seemed so real! He stretched, and his paws pressed against firm clay walls, reminding him where he was—the Egypt exhibit, the urn. He was still inside! *I've got to get home,* he thought. *The professor will be worried.*

Reaching up and placing his paws on the rim, Ptah poked his head outside. *That's strange,* he thought. *I must have been moved to some sort of storage room last night.* The room he was in was made completely of stone and was filled to the brim with Egyptian pottery, jars, woven baskets, wooden chests—beautiful things, all finely crafted. A narrow window high up on one wall cast a ray of sunlight into the otherwise darkened room.

Ptah hopped out of the urn and went to find his way out. A doorway led him into a long hallway, lit dimly by oil lamps that hung from copper brackets set into the walls. His fur bristled. The hallway looked similar to the one he'd just dreamed about! Nervously, Ptah glanced back over his shoulder for signs of another cat. Dust floating in the light of the storage room window danced in the air, but beyond that, both room and hall were still.

Whew! thought Ptah. Looking to his left, he could see a bright light at the end of the hallway. He was just about to head in that direction when he chanced to look to his right, where he was met with an incredible sight.

"The museum should have opened up this room last night!" he

murmured as he wandered into a magnificent space. Rows of stone pillars, carved and painted with brightly colored patterns, sprouted from the floor like trees in a magical forest. Scenes of Egyptian gods and kings, and of everyday people doing their work, decorated the walls like picture-book stories waiting to be read. Gold accents glittered in the soft light cast by oil lamps. Ptah sniffed the air. A sweet, musty fragrance tickled his nose—the scent of incense burning.

Ptah meandered through the room, marveling at its beauty. At the far end he came upon a wide stone stairway leading up to a long, low platform on which stood a huge statue carved in the likeness of a man whose body had been wrapped from neck to toe like a mummy. The man's arms were bound across his chest, but his hands were left free. In one he held a crook, in the other a flail—symbols of Egyptian royalty.

Ptah stepped back. This was no friendly looking being he was gazing at, and he wouldn't have gone near it, had he not suddenly seen what was sitting at the statue's feet. Food! Bowls filled with meat, milk, and cheese! He scampered up the stairway and dove right in.

No sooner had he started eating, however, than a voice boomed out, "Hold it right there! Get your paws off my food!"

Ptah gulped. Looking up, he saw a brown Egyptian Mau cat heading straight for him, its emerald eyes flashing. He knew this type of cat by its distinctive markings: black stripes across its head and forelegs; black spots on its middle, hind legs, and tail. The cat was big—maybe not as tall as Ptah, but strong and muscular.

"Where did you come from?" demanded the cat. He jumped onto the platform and strutted close to Ptah.

"I, um, I came from the storage room," Ptah mumbled, his mouth stuffed with cheese.

The other cat gave him a dubious look.

"What I mean is, there's this urn in there, and I fell asleep in it, and when I awoke I was here." Ptah cringed, realizing that he was sounding terribly stupid. "By the way, where exactly *is* here?" he asked.

The Mau cat ignored his question and began circling around him, talking as he went. "You must be from Memphis. You look like a city cat, you do. Led an easy life so far, I can tell. Why, look at your paws—all soft! I'll bet you've never caught a meal in your life, and here you are, feasting on the only easy grub I get around this place. A common *thief*, that's what you are!"

"Hold on a minute!" snapped Ptah. "I don't see *your* name written on these food bowls. And I'll have you know that I catch my meals all the time," he added, thinking about the way the professor would toss kitty crunchies across the kitchen floor for him to chase.

The husky cat smirked but said nothing, so Ptah continued. "Now, if you don't mind, would you please tell me where I am? And while you're at it, why don't you introduce yourself? My name is Ptah. I seem to have come here by mistake, but—"

The Mau cat burst out laughing. "You . . . *Ptah?* You've made a mistake all right, buddy! You certainly have the markings of the great god Ptah, but you can't fool me. Everyone knows he's a bull, not a cat! Listen, I think you may have been *steered* in the wrong direction, so maybe you'd just better be *moooving* along." The cat was now rolling on the floor, unable to contain his laughter.

Oh, brother, not this again, thought Ptah. "I never said I was a god," he said huffily. "I can't help it, the professor named me that. Did *you* name yourself?"

The brown cat got up, still chuckling. "Okay, okay, but you can see the joke, can't you? Why, I haven't had as good a laugh as that since my friends and I wrapped ourselves up like cat mummies and ran through town!" Shaking the dust off his fur, he said, "Pleased to meet you, Ptah. As a matter of fact, I *did* name myself, seeing how I have no owner. I'm Narmer, named after the first king of Egypt. A great warrior he was—came from the south to conquer the north; united the Two Lands! But that was long ago, must be five hundred years by now.

"Anyway, to answer your question, you're standing in the temple of Saqarra. This room here is dedicated to the great god Ptah—your namesake," Narmer added with a chuckle as he nodded in the direction of the giant figure towering over them. "Once a week the priests put out food for the statue, which is lucky for me! You should see how skinny the rats are around here. Hardly worth chasing!"

Ptah furrowed his brow. "Wait a minute, Narmer. What do you mean?" Then he said, "Oh, *I* get it. You mean that this room has been created to *look* like the temple of Saqarra. For a minute there, I thought you were talking about the real thing! But of course not. We're in the museum. And besides, everything here looks so new!"

Narmer looked quizzically at Ptah before responding. "What are *you* talking about, buddy? This *is* the real thing, and it looks new because it *is* new! In fact, the workers finished up on the pyramid just yesterday. Took them ten years to build it. The whole country's been talking about it! Where have you been?"

Ptah knotted his forehead, then threw back his head and laughed. He knew a joker when he saw one, and this cat was certainly a doozy. "Narmer, do you actually think I'm stupid enough to believe that if I marched down that hallway and out of this building into the sun, I would see a for-real Egyptian pyramid?" he asked. "I don't think so!"

"Shall we bet on it?" A wry smile spread across Narmer's face and his emerald eyes twinkled. "I show you the pyramid and the food here is mine. No pyramid and you can have it all for yourself. Deal?"

"Deal!"

The two cats hopped off the platform, crossed the temple, and then followed the hallway out of the building and into the sun. Momentarily blinded by the brilliance, Ptah squeezed shut his eyes, then slowly began to open them again. As he did, they grew wider and wider despite the bright light. Could what Narmer said be true?

"Ha! Look there! The most magnificent tomb ever built in Egypt!" Narmer tipped his spotted tail toward a colossal structure made of limestone blocks, stair-stepping their way up to the sky. The summit, capped in gold, sparkled radiantly in the early morning sun. "Never before has anything so big been built," he boasted, "and out of stone this time, too, instead of the mud bricks they usually use."

Ptah blinked, unable to speak. There was no doubt about it. The giant pyramid in front of him could be none other than the Step Pyramid of Saqarra. The thing was enormous! It had to be as wide as a football field and as tall as a skyscraper! And there were other stone buildings and statues, too. How on earth did he get here?

"Big, isn't it?" Narmer asked. "Can you believe that they built this thing just so when King Zoser kicks the bucket he can be buried somewhere deep inside? They'll keep the exact location a secret, you know, because they'll be burying him with more gold and treasures than most people earn in a lifetime. The way I've always heard it, the king needs these treasures to enjoy during his next life in the Underworld. But you can bet there are plenty of people who would like to enjoy those very same treasures right now in this world!"

Ptah's head started spinning. *King Zoser!* If everything that Narmer said was true, then not only had he somehow traveled across the world to Egypt, he had also traveled back in time nearly *five thousand years!* He was just beginning to wonder whether the urn he'd slept in the night before had anything to do with it, when Narmer's chatter caught his ear.

". . . and you sure picked the right day to show up," he was saying, "because today is the Grand Jubilee celebrating the completion of the pyramid. There's going to be one heck of a party, with music and dancing and food galore! Even the pyramid's architect, the great Imhotep himself, is going to be here!"

Ptah caught his breath. Imhotep . . . coming *here?* He remembered the professor telling him about this man, how he was one of the most important people in ancient Egyptian history. Not only was he the king's highest official, he was also a famous inventor, priest, astronomer, and scribe, as well as the architect who had designed the very first pyramid. Ptah could hardly believe his luck—much less anything else that had happened to him so far that day.

Narmer was watching Ptah closely. "Ah, I see that you've heard of Imhotep. Well, who hasn't? Say, I know of a great place where we can watch the festivities. Everybody's gathering in the main courtyard now. The royal procession should be coming through the Hall of Pillars any moment! Are you with me?"

Narmer took off scampering down a formal walkway lined with fluted pillars on either side. Without skipping a beat, Ptah scurried after him, all thoughts of returning home completely vanished.

4

Imhotep

Narmer and Ptah arrived at their lookout, high on a smooth stone ledge that jutted precariously over the courtyard below. Narmer immediately began cleaning himself; but Ptah could not sit still. He paced about, edgy with excitement. To his right, he had a clear view of the pathway the royal procession would take. Directly ahead, the courtyard bustled with activity. Dark-skinned men wearing white linen hip-cloths and short black wigs were bringing in long wooden tables and piling them high with food. Other men were rolling in barrels of beer and placing them in the shade of covered walkways. Still others appeared to be organizing the event. These men wore long white robes and had heads that were completely shaved except for a single ponytail or braid that hung down their backs.

"Who are all of these people?" Ptah asked.

"The men wearing robes are the temple priests," replied Narmer. "See that tall guy shouting out orders over there? He's the head priest, the only person who lives here year round. The others are mostly scribes who work at the temple for three months out of every year.

"The rest of the men are the workers who've been building the pyramid," Narmer continued. "Nearly all of them are farmers who've been coming here each year during the four months when the river is flooded and they can't work in their fields. They get paid, of course, but if you ask me, it's a scam. King Zoser takes a fifth of what they grow for taxes, and then pays them back using the same grain they grew themselves! You'd think the farmers would revolt, but I guess they consider Zoser to be some sort of a god on earth, one with direct connections to all the other gods."

The husky brown cat continued his preening. "At any rate," he said, "the flood is going down now, so the farmers are anxious to get back to their fields." He paused, twitching his whiskers. "Hey, look! The royal procession is coming through the Hall of Pillars!"

Ptah eagerly turned his head to see a small group of men wearing long linen kilts and colorful beaded necklaces making their way forward. Accompanying them were flag bearers waving bright banners of red and gold, and musicians sounding out a festive tune on their flutes, horns, and drums.

Ptah could tell at once who Imhotep was. Although shorter and of rounder build than the other men, he was nevertheless an imposing person due to the dignified way he carried himself and the way he was dressed. In addition to his long white kilt, Imhotep wore a leopardskin cape tied with a ribbon in front, a shimmering gold necklace set with onyx and jasper, and a pair of sandals made from papyrus plants. Tucked under his arm he carried a long papyrus scroll. Despite his formal appearance, he had a friendly-enough-looking face—round, with a pair of wide-set hazel eyes—and he laughed and chatted merrily with the others as they strolled across the courtyard. Two servants, following along on either side and slightly behind him, carried a lightweight parasol and an extra pair of sandals—signs of a wealthy man.

A podium had been set up directly beneath the ledge where the two cats were sitting, and there the royal procession came to a halt. After the men had taken their places, the musicians blew their horns, signaling the start of the ceremony. The priests and workers gathered around, and Imhotep unfurled his scroll.

"Honored priests and loyal workers," he called out, "we are gathered here today to celebrate a joyous occasion: the completion of this grand and glorious pyramid in honor of our great and powerful king—long may he live!" The crowd cheered.

Imhotep's speech continued, and soon he was droning on, thanking this person and honoring that, crediting this god or the other for making it all happen. Ptah noticed that the crowd of workers seemed more intent on staring at the feast than on listening to what this great man had to say. After a while, he complained, "You know what, Narmer? This is a terrible spot. All I can see is the top of Imhotep's head!"

"Well then," responded Narmer testily, "would you rather go someplace where you can get a better look? Maybe see Imhotep real close up and personal?"

"Anything would be better than this!" Ptah answered.

"Okay, then move over a little bit to your right . . . just a bit further. Good! Now, lean out over the courtyard . . . There! You'll be able to see him now!" With a muscular heave, Narmer shoved Ptah off of the ledge, seemingly unconcerned about the height because cats were known to land on their feet.

Taken totally by surprise, Ptah sailed down, his first thought of getting back at Narmer quickly replaced by his instinct to ready himself for landing. *Oh no,* he thought. *If I'm not mistaken, I'm going to land right on Imhotep's—*

Whump! Ptah's belly hit the top of Imhotep's bald head, his legs shooting out on all four sides, then wrapping around the great man's ears like a catskin cap. Imhotep shrieked and threw down his scroll, then hurled Ptah to the ground.

A gasp rose up from the crowd, followed by a buzz of excitement. Wincing, Ptah looked up. Hundreds of eyes were staring at him; hundreds of mouths hung open wide. *Oh, boy, I'm done for now,* he thought. *I'll probably be mummified or something!* He glared up at Narmer, who was looking down on him, smirking.

Ptah crouched, getting ready to run, as a cry began to ripple through the crowd. "Hail the great god Ptah! Hail the great god Ptah!" Before he knew it, the workers had dropped to their knees, bowing down before him.

"Look!" whispered Imhotep to the head priest beside him. "The workers all think this cat is the great god Ptah!"

Glancing up, Ptah realized that the head priest must have thought the same, for his slack-jawed face was petrified with awe.

Seizing the moment, Imhotep swept up Ptah. Lifting him high into the air, he cried, "Behold! The great god Ptah has fallen from the sky! He has come to earth in the form of a cat, bringing his blessings to King Zoser, to this pyramid, and to all of Egypt!

"Let us celebrate!" he continued. "Let us spoil our honored guest! We shall eat and drink until our hearts are merry and then dance 'til the light of Re breaks over the horizon!"

"Hor-Re!" shouted the workers, who all leaped to their feet and made a dash for the feast. As if on cue, the musicians burst into a cheerful tune while dancing girls, who up until then had been hidden in the wings, whirled onto the courtyard, their scarves flowing and their bangles jingling as they gyrated to the rhythm of flutes and drums.

Still high over Imhotep's head, Ptah eyed Narmer in triumph. The Mau cat's expression had utterly changed from one of smugness to one of complete surprise. Now it was Ptah's turn to smile.

The following morning Ptah awoke in the temple to find a pair of emerald eyes glaring at him.

"Did you get enough to eat last night?" snarled Narmer. "Don't think I didn't see you, riding high on people's shoulders, being given the best food off their plates. And what was that dance you did with the oil lampshade on your head? I don't suppose you saved one morsel for me, now did you?"

Ptah sighed and covered his face with his paw. "Not now, Narmer. I'm still sleeping. I had a big night last night."

"A big night, I'll say! I'm here to remind you who you have to thank for your big night—me! If it wasn't for me, you never would have met Imhotep."

"If it wasn't for you, I wouldn't have nearly plunged to my death!" Ptah retorted.

Narmer shrugged. "So, got any leftovers?"

"I don't know. There must be," Ptah replied with a groan. "Did you check outside in the courtyard?"

Narmer rolled his eyes. "Look, Ptah, a cat like me can't just sidle on up to the royal table and help himself to the free food. But you— you could go get me something."

"I just don't feel like doing that right now," Ptah said, yawning and beginning to stretch.

"Oh, yeah?" Narmer's eyes blazed fiercely. "Well, maybe you'd *get* to feeling like it if you knew what I heard on my way over. Now what was that again? Something about you . . . and Imhotep . . . going on a journey? You know, it's right on the tip of my tongue, but my memory gets a little foggy *when I'm hungry.*"

"A journey? Hmm. Okay, Narmer, hang on. I'll go get you some food." Ptah took one last stretch, then rose from the large, soft pillow he'd been given to sleep on and went outside.

It was just past dawn. The sun, hovering over the eastern mountains, cast a golden glow across the face of the pyramid. Long shadows streaked the ground.

The courtyard had a definite post-party look. Overturned beer barrels and drinking bowls were strewn about, and people were still sleeping in heaps where they had danced the night before. Ptah found the place where the feast had been laid and began to forage around. Most of it had been pretty well picked over, but he spied a large drumstick—from what kind of bird he had no clue—and, clutching it in his teeth, he half-dragged, half-carried it back to his room.

After Narmer had eaten his fill he was ready to talk. "Imhotep received orders last night to return to Memphis at once," he began. "King Zoser wants to see him—something to do with his traveling to Nubia far to the south."

"So, what has that got to do with me?" asked Ptah.

"Imhotep plans on taking you with him," Narmer replied, adding, "and this is not good! Rumor has it the Nubians shoot poison-tipped arrows and—" He shuddered. *"And they eat cats!"*

Brushing these warnings aside, Ptah said, "Look, Narmer, I appreciate your concern, but this news doesn't bother me in the least. I've had my fun. Now it's time for me to go back home. So, if you'll excuse me, I'll return to the storage room, climb inside my urn, and stay put until whatever it was that brought me here takes me back."

"If you say so," said Narmer, "but there's something else you should know. That urn you're referring to was part of Imhotep's payment for completing the pyramid. In fact, the entire contents of the storage room was payment, and if I'm not mistaken, it's all being loaded onto donkeys for the trip back to Memphis as we speak."

"*What?* Why didn't you say so?" Ptah leaped off his pillow, and then sprinted out from the temple, screeching to a halt near the gates of the pyramid complex. There he gazed with dismay at the activities going on around him. Just as Narmer had said, a dozen donkeys stood tethered together and were now being loaded with baskets, linens, wooden chests—things he recognized from the storage room.

And there in the hands of one of the workers was the urn—his urn!—the only possible portal back to the future he knew of, and it was about to be strapped to the rear of a donkey! Suddenly he felt himself being lifted from behind.

"There you are, Ptah. I've been looking all over for you! We need to go to the palace to meet with the king." Imhotep adjusted his leopard-skin cape, then began walking briskly toward the donkey caravan. "I wonder what he wants this time," he murmured while rubbing Ptah's ears.

Ptah wiggled and squirmed to get free. Usually a good ear rubbing had the effect of calming his nerves, but today was different. *Nubia!* He knew practically nothing about this strange and exotic land. *Cat eaters!* Where, oh where was home sweet home?

Imhotep tightened his grip and waited patiently for the caravan to finish being loaded. When all was ready to go, he carried Ptah to a pair of donkeys that had a sort of chair fastened between them with leather straps. Readying himself for mounting, he momentarily loosened his grip, upon which Ptah seized his chance and bolted. Jumping onto the rear of a donkey, he continued jumping head-to-rear, head-to-rear along the donkey line until he reached the one that held his urn. In one desperate motion, he plunged inside.

Imhotep laughed. "It looks as though our little god prefers to ride inside the urn. Well, so be it!"

Huddled at the bottom of the urn, Ptah began chanting, "There's no place like home; there's no place like home," imagining all the while Dorothy's success by doing the same.

How he wished he had a pair of ruby slippers!

5

King Zoser

The donkey caravan began to move, or so Ptah guessed, because the urn began gently rocking. Huddled at the bottom, he kept up his chanting until finally it became so unbearably hot inside that he was forced to get some air. Stretching up and placing his paws on the rim, he peered out over the edge and looked around.

The caravan was traveling north across a desert plateau. The late morning sun, already scorching down on them, melted the jagged edges of the rocky, barren landscape into blurry waves of heat. Behind them loomed the pyramid of Saqarra, looking strangely out of place and yet somehow already appearing as though it had always been there.

Ptah turned to face the direction they were heading. The road they were traveling on sloped gently downward, so his view from the donkey's back took in an entire valley, with its fertile fields and thick stands of papyrus plants, and with the lovely town of Memphis built along the muddy banks of the Nile.

The Nile! Ptah stared transfixed at the river that lay before him. Here was the river of legend and glory, the maker and breaker of kings. Bloody wars had been fought over these waters, and would continue to be fought for thousands more years to come.

Ptah knew that the Nile was a prize well worth fighting for. A constant source of water in an otherwise barren land, the river's origin lay deep in the heart of Africa, where heavy rains each summer sent water rushing northward. Far from being a disaster, this yearly flooding deposited a thick blanket of nutrient-rich mud, which enabled Egyptian farmers to grow up to five times more food than rain-fed land. As a result, the Egyptian people were freed from the burdensome task of constantly foraging for food, and they enjoyed a level of wealth and stability beyond any that had been seen in the ancient world.

"The Great River," as people called it, was deeply rooted in all Egyptians' lives. It was their hunting ground, their playground, their avenue of transportation. And whosoever ruled this land was a very powerful person indeed. As he reflected on this, Ptah spotted the king's palace, its high white walls seeming to glow in contrast to the earth-colored buildings surrounding it. Ptah knew that the Egyptian name for Memphis meant "white walls," and now he knew why.

Before long the caravan reached the palace gates, and Ptah and Imhotep were shown inside. Behind the walls, the palace courtyard was ablaze with color: the rich dark greenery of gardens; blooming flowers in pink and blue; the dazzling plumage of peacocks that roamed freely about. The people of the palace were equally stunning: beautiful women dressed in sheer linen shifts and men wearing thigh-length kilts, all with broad beaded collars and shining copper arm bands. Lazing in the sun beside a large rectangular pond Ptah saw dozens of cats, who momentarily lifted their heads to glance at him before drifting back to sleep. *Hmm,* he thought. *Life could be good in Memphis.*

Ptah and Imhotep were taken to a meeting room to wait for King Zoser. The room was simply but elegantly furnished with a long ebony table and twelve matching chairs, all intricately carved and inlaid with ivory and gold. Along the base of one wall sat three wooden chests, and across from them stood a row of pedestals on which sat alabaster statues carved in the likeness of the gods. Forming a stunning backdrop, the walls had been painted with colorful hunting and fishing scenes set in the marshes of the Nile. Giant hippos reared up from one wall, while cranes and ibises flew across another. Between them, fishermen hauled in a bounty of fish with their nets.

Amidst all this grandeur, in walked King Zoser. An older but imposing man with a solemn face and a purposeful stride, Zoser was dressed in a knee-length white tunic cinched about the waist with a golden sash. A gold-collared necklace set with red carnelian and blue lapis peeked from beneath his embroidered cape, which was clasped at the neck with a jeweled brooch. On his head he wore the kings' cloth of blue and white stripes, pulled away from his forehead and tied with two flaps. Keeping the cloth in place was a golden crown, the front of which featured a rearing cobra—a symbol of royalty. With its ruby red eyes and its sharp gold teeth, Ptah found the snake to be unnerving, and he couldn't take his eyes off of it for a single moment.

Zoser strode across the room and sat in a fanciful wooden chair carved in the shape of a falcon, with wings that extended out from his shoulders when he sat.

Imhotep bowed. "Your Highness, it is an honor to see you looking so well."

"Thank you, Imhotep, and thank you for coming so quickly. Be seated," said the king. "I hear there was quite a party at Saqarra last night. I'm sorry I couldn't have been there."

"It was a fine party indeed!" replied the architect, removing his cape and taking a seat in one of the ebony chairs. "I'm sorry you couldn't have been there, too, but you know it is bad luck for a king to set foot near his tomb before it is time."

Ptah jumped onto Imhotep's lap, the better to keep an eye on that snake. In doing so, he attracted the king's attention.

"Good heavens," Zoser exclaimed. "Is that your cat?"

Imhotep laughed. "Meet Ptah, Your Highness. He practically fell from the sky at Saqarra yesterday. Landed right on the top of my head! Because of his markings, the workers all thought he was the great god Ptah come down to earth in the form of a cat. One can understand their mistake, considering the sacred Apis bull died a month ago to the day. I decided to keep him. You never know when a cat like this might come in handy."

"He suits you well," said Zoser, smiling. Then he sighed. "It seems my people see gods in just about everything these days—cows, birds, cats, lions, jackals, frogs . . . you name it! Why, beyond the official gods, I think every town and village has at least one or two gods of their own."

"The more gods the merrier, we Egyptians always say," responded Imhotep.

Ptah thought about a world in which so many animals were considered to be gods. He rather liked this idea, especially since it included cats! He tried to imagine what that would be like in the modern world from which he came. It would certainly help to protect nature, he decided, if people worshipped the animals that lived there. He looked up to see that Zoser's expression had clouded.

"Imhotep, I called you here today because there is a serious matter I need to discuss with you. Nubian warriors are making raids on Egyptian villages in the south, stealing cattle and wheat. My people demand that I do something about it."

"I've heard that the shifting desert has all but turned the Nubian grasslands into sand," replied Imhotep. "The people there have little to eat. They're desperate."

"My people are desperate too!" Zoser shot back. "I care *nothing* for the Nubians, except for their gold! Which brings me to another matter, Imhotep, your so-called pyramid. It took ten years to build that thing. I was able to pay the workers in grain and beer, but the priests and scribes demanded gold. I have emptied the palace coffers to build it!"

"But Sire," protested Imhotep, "your people are celebrating the pyramid's completion even as we speak! It is proof of your greatness, your devotion to the gods. It is a monument by which people will remember you for all time!"

"Imhotep, you don't understand," said the king. "Egypt is broke! Do I need to tell you how I will be remembered if people find out? A king needs *gold* to raise an army to protect the land. A king needs *gold* to pay the priests, or the gods will punish us with drought and famine. A king needs *gold* to keep his dozens of wives happy! The way I see it, the problem is with those Nubians again. They have gold—a mountain of it. Oh, what I would *give* to control those gold mines!"

Imhotep looked thoughtful and then spoke. "Your Highness, forgive me, but the answer seems simple. The Nubians need food, which we have in surplus, and we need gold, which they have in abundance. Why don't we arrange for a trade?"

"I am smarter than a jackal, Imhotep. I tried that!" Zoser snapped. "I offered them a mountain of food in trade for an equal size portion of gold. My offer was rejected."

"Rejected? But that makes no sense at all. I've heard the Nubian people are starving! I can't believe they're not interested in a trade."

Zoser's dark eyes narrowed. "Oh, they're interested in a trade all right, but only on their terms. King Shabaka is a proud and greedy man. He responded by saying that any trade between us must be based on weight, not size. A deal like that is no good to me. Gold is heavy! I would be trading a mountain of food for a pittance of gold. Let them starve, I say!"

Ptah began to wonder just who was the proud and greedy man— King Shabaka or King Zoser.

"Then why not take the gold by force?" suggested Imhotep. "Might makes right, we Egyptians always say, and besides, we haven't always bothered to trade with the Nubians for some time now anyway."

"I thought of that, too," the king said with a sigh, "but Shabaka has put together an army that rivals the best. It is said that his archers can shoot a man between the eyes from across the Nile with their poison-tipped arrows. Besides, I have no gold with which to raise an army, thanks to your pyramid."

"I see. This is a grave situation, indeed," replied Imhotep, while idly stroking Ptah's fur.

"That is why I need your help," said Zoser. "You are a clever man, and my highest official. I want you to go to Nubia and meet with the king. Tell him to stop making raids on my villages. And get him to agree to my terms of the trade: food for gold, size for size."

"But Sire, you've already made that offer and it was rejected. I may be clever, but I am no magician!" protested Imhotep.

"Then come up with another plan. I don't care how you get the gold—just get it! I will pay you handsomely for your troubles. But beware: you must leave quickly. Your boat will be ready in three days. A royal caravan of barges loaded with food will be sent shortly after you. They'll meet you upriver on the Island of Elephantine."

The king rose from his chair and motioned for Imhotep to leave. Imhotep stood quickly and bowed, knocking Ptah from his lap.

"Oh, one final word of advice," added Zoser. "Don't deal directly with King Shabaka. Meet with his mother, Queen Kandake. I hear she is wise. You may go now, Imhotep."

6
Imhotep's Fishpond

On the road again, the donkey caravan headed north toward Imhotep's villa, about an hour's ride from Memphis. Ptah sat beside his urn on the rear of the donkey and watched the changing landscape as they plodded slowly along. Almost no sooner had the caravan left the city than they were in the country. Vast farmlands, still covered in places by the floodwaters, stretched ahead of them like a muddy brown sea. The air smelled pungent, earthy, and sweet.

The farmlands were alive with activity. Much work had to be done after the flooding went down: clearing out irrigation ditches, repairing dikes, reestablishing property boundaries, and plowing the fields. Although the work was hard, the farmers they passed were in a merry mood because the flood had been good this year. There was a feeling of hope and renewal in the air, and this reflected well upon the king.

The caravan arrived at Imhotep's villa, a sprawling complex built upon a low hill out of reach of the flood. Around the perimeter stood an orchard, where figs, dates, and pomegranates grew. Inside was a large vegetable garden and vineyard, behind which stood the servants' quarters, a tidy row of mud huts with thatched roofs. Near the center of the complex stood Imhotep's house, a large, two-story whitewashed building shaded by sycamores and palms. As the caravan drew near, several children burst forth to greet them.

"Papa!" they cried as they gathered around, tugging at Imhotep's kilt and hugging him as he stepped down from his donkey chair. Imhotep laughed and hugged them each in return, then went over to one of the donkeys and removed a large basket filled with honeycomb, which he gave to the children. Delighted, they ran back into the house to tell their mother that Father was home.

Imhotep's wife, Tiye, came out to greet them then. She was a tall, willowy woman with light brown skin and jet-black hair that fell down to her waist. She was elegantly dressed in a slender, long white shift and a gold necklace set with blue and green turquoise. Green eye paint accentuated her large brown eyes. "Imhotep, you're home at last! How we've missed you!" she exclaimed.

"I've missed you, too, and the children, but I will not be able to stay long," replied Imhotep, giving his wife a kiss. "King Zoser has ordered me to go to Nubia on urgent business."

"Nubia! But you will be gone for at least a moon cycle!" Tiye said sadly. "Wennefer's birthday is coming soon, and he was so looking forward to his very first donkey ride with his father."

Imhotep sighed. "That will have to wait, I'm afraid. Why is it that for every great thing I do, I'm simply assigned another task?"

"As Grand Vizier of Egypt, you are the eyes, ears, and heart of the king," Tiye replied. She gave him a consoling embrace. "Don't worry, we'll manage. We always do."

Ptah knew that in Egypt, women were often given positions of responsibility, which was unusual when compared to other countries of the ancient world, where women were treated as property, or as second-class citizens at best. It was Tiye's job to oversee the running of the household and farm while Imhotep was away, which was more often than not. She supervised the servants, decided what crops would be planted, and consulted the priests to determine the best times for sowing and harvesting.

To lighten the mood, Imhotep announced, "I've received final payment for the work I did on the pyramid. Why don't we tell the servants to bring things inside so we can have a look?" He swept his arm outward, taking in the caravan with its array of finely crafted objects. "Oh, and by the way, meet our new cat." Imhotep strode over and picked up Ptah, holding him high for Tiye to see.

"Dear Isis!" Tiye exclaimed. "That cat looks just like—"

"The great and powerful god Ptah!" Imhotep finished for her. "I know. You should have seen the looks on the faces of the priests and the workers at the pyramid when they saw him."

Imhotep, Tiye, and Ptah proceeded to the house, which was encircled by a shaded porch decorated with potted palms and flowering hibiscus. Typical of many homes of the well-to-do, Imhotep's house was divided into two levels. The ground floor was where the servants did their work—the men in charge of the brewing and the cooking, the women handling the weaving and the baking. The family lived on the second floor, which was reached by means of a wooden stairway situated next to the ground-floor entrance.

Upstairs, the linen-white walls of the spacious reception room had been adorned with a frieze of green leaves and blue lotus flowers. Columns made from palm tree trunks carved in the shape of papyrus bundles supported the ceiling, which was painted blue. The room had an open, airy feeling, due not only to the breeze that wafted through the windows, but also because the ceiling had been drilled with holes to let the sunlight in. *A ceiling like this would never do at home*, thought Ptah, but then he remembered that Egypt received virtually no rainfall south of the Delta. The furniture was sparse but elegant: a low ebony table surrounded by eight padded stools, a colorful carpet woven in patterns of blue and green, several potted plants, and a few wooden chests. Ptah noticed a hallway leading off to the bedrooms on the right.

The servants began bringing the things from the donkey caravan up to the room a few at a time. Tiye was delighted with what she saw, and quickly set about redecorating. "What a lovely alabaster vase!" she would exclaim, or, "Such a beautifully carved chest! Take it to the bedroom and transfer all of the linens to it at once!" She especially liked a set of four wooden chairs with legs carved in the shape of ducks' heads. Things were going wonderfully; however, when Ptah's urn was brought in, Tiye's expression changed completely.

"Ugh! What is that dreadful thing?" she blurted.

"It's an urn," replied Imhotep, rising from his stool and picking it up. Turning it around in his hands, he said, "I know it doesn't follow the Egyptian standards of beauty, but I'm quite drawn to it myself. Something about all of these little images—it's almost as if they're telling a story."

"Well, I think it's an eyesore!" said Tiye. "It's way too fat in the middle, and there's no rhyme nor reason to its pattern, other than it twists around like a snake."

"Do you think so? Well, the cat sure seems to like it," Imhotep replied.

"The cat can have it! I don't want that thing anywhere near this house!" Tiye swept back her long black hair, then folded her arms across her chest. "Why don't you take it with you on your journey into Nubia? You'll have plenty of time to look at it then." Having made her position clear, she turned her attention to a shining set of copper pots.

Alarmed by her statement, Ptah was trying to think of what he could do about it, when a loud hissing noise distracted him.

"Pssst! Hey, Ptah! Over here!" It was Narmer, hidden behind a potted plant near the door to the room.

Ptah scurried over to meet him. "What are you doing here?" he whispered.

Narmer flicked his ear for silence, then motioned for Ptah to follow. The two cats crept down the stairs and onto the porch.

"I figured you and Imhotep would be going to his villa," Narmer replied. "Never been here myself. I was curious so I followed. Nice place! Did you see all of those big fat geese running around? So anyway, what did King Zoser have to say?"

"He said the Nubians are making raids on Egyptian villages in the south. He also said he's run out of gold," Ptah answered.

"No gold!" gasped Narmer. "Oh, that's bad for any king, but especially for King Zoser. Did you know that shortly after he took the throne, Egypt went through seven years of poor floods? Let me tell you, it was awful! Crops failed and people went hungry. It's the king's job, you know, to make sure the flood rises high enough to cover the fields—but not too high, or the water will sweep away the dikes that protect the villages. So Zoser's name was mud—or should I say dust!—until we started having good floods again."

"That's one thing I don't understand about Egyptian people," said Ptah. "How can they possibly hold a king accountable for something as unpredictable as the weather?"

Narmer shrugged. "To understand that, you first have to understand that the Egyptians' worst fear is chaos. They want things to stay nice and orderly and predictable."

"But life's not like that!" protested Ptah.

"Well, it sure seems to work that way around here most times," responded Narmer. "I mean, have you ever seen a land more predictable than this? Every day the sun is shining, the river flows onward like it should, and each and every year the three seasons of flooding, planting, and harvesting follow one another likes ducks on a pond. From the time that people are very young, they're told that it's the king's job to keep it that way. Why do you think they're willing to pay such outrageous taxes?"

"It sure seems silly, but I guess I can understand," said Ptah. "It's much more comforting to believe someone is in control of things than to think you've been left to the whims of fate." Ptah reflected on his own situation, wondering if he had, indeed, been left to the whims of fate.

"What else did the king have to say?" Narmer asked.

"He said he wants Imhotep to go to Nubia and arrange for a trade—food for gold, size for size." Ptah frowned. "It looks like I have to go with him, since he's taking my urn along."

"Nubia, eh? Mysterious land of ivory, ebony, incense, and gold," Narmer said, using a spooky sounding voice. "How long until you leave?"

Ptah groaned. "Three days."

"Three days!" Narmer said brightly. "Then we have time to do some exploring! Hey, let's go find Imhotep's fishpond! It's legendary among cats. I can't believe that in all the times I've been to Memphis, I've never seen it for myself. Rumor has it it's filled with giant carp, and once a day one of Imhotep's servants catches a fish and gives it to whichever cats are hanging around. As you can imagine, they come for miles!"

The two cats hopped down from the porch, and then followed a cobblestone path to the back of the house. Crossing a wide brick patio, they entered a lush green garden. Overhead, a canopy of date palms and sycamores provided a welcoming shade, while down below, honeysuckle blossoms filled the air with a gentle, sweet fragrance. The cats continued through the garden until they came to a large rectangular pond dotted with blue lotus flowers. Looking about, Ptah saw a few cats lying here and there, but overall the place seemed deserted.

Narmer sauntered over to an old gray tabby relaxing in a patch of sun and asked, "Can you help us? We're looking for Imhotep's fishpond."

"You've found it," the cat replied, smiling.

"This is it?" Narmer exclaimed incredulously. "If this is it, then where *is* everybody? I've heard this place usually swarms with cats!"

"Oh, hardly anyone bothers to come here anymore," the tabby said. "See those three cats sitting over there on the far side of the pond? They've pretty much taken the place over. Each time a fish gets caught, they claim it for themselves. Any cat who tries to wheedle in and take his fair share gets beaten to within an inch of his life! Then, to top it all off, after the cats have had their fill, they throw the remains of the fish back in the pond, just for spite."

"I know that gang of cats," Narmer said dryly, "and they're not as tough as they seem. See the brown one in the middle? His name is Geb, and he's the leader of the gang. The black and gray one on his right is called Kha. He's the brains of the group, if you could call it that. And the big orange one on Geb's other side is simply known as 'Shredder.' Nobody knows what his real name is."

"Nobody has to!" exclaimed the tabby, licking a bald patch on her fur.

Ptah studied the three tough cats, who were eyeing the newcomers with suspicion. They certainly were big, and did they ever look mean!

Just then, one of Imhotep's servants came striding down the path. In one hand he carried a heavy wooden club, and in the other a long wooden pole with a copper gaff on the end of it. At the edge of the pond, the servant hopped across some stepping-stones until he reached the pond's middle. He set down his club and scattered some fish food on the top of the water. After that, he raised the hand that held the pole and stood very still.

The three tough cats started pacing excitedly, swishing their tails while eyeing the cats around them for signs of a challenge. Narmer and Ptah moved in a bit closer so they could watch, but kept their distance by sticking to their own side of the pond.

Ptah peered into the water. Swimming beneath its surface he could see dozens of carp, their huge orange and white bodies slowly gravitating toward the food at the pond's middle. Soon they were swarming around the base of the rock on which the servant stood poised with his pole. Suddenly and without warning, the servant thrust his pole down into the water and gaffed a fish, pulling it out onto the rock. Very quickly he grabbed his club, and in one fell swoop, he knocked the fish stone-cold dead.

"Bravo! Bravo!" cried Imhotep, who was coming down the path. "If I didn't know better, I'd say that your father was a falcon."

The servant blushed. "Why, thank you, sir."

"Say, I have a special request to make," said Imhotep. "See that black cat sitting over there, the one with the special markings? I'd like you to give the fish to him. He can share it with whomever he likes."

The servant looked in the direction Imhotep pointed and gasped. "Yes, sir! In the name of the great god Ptah, I shall do as you ask!" He quickly made his way across the stepping-stones and over to Ptah. Kneeling before him, he proceeded to gut and clean the fish, then cut the meat into large pink chunks, scattering them around on the ground.

"Come on, everybody, eat up!" cried Ptah. At once, all the cats hanging around the fishpond jumped to their feet and came running over, giddy with the thought of having a fine meal for a change. All, that is, except for the three tough cats, who merely narrowed their eyes and stalked away.

7
Memphis and the Temple of Hoot-Ka-Ptah

The following morning Narmer and Ptah decided to catch a ride back to Memphis with Imhotep so they could explore the town. Imhotep had business to attend to: he needed to inspect the provisions he would be taking on his journey and line up the crew that would go with him.

Arriving before noon, the cats wandered freely about, first checking out the busy marketplace with its rows and rows of vendors selling everything from linen cloth to copper pots. All that Ptah saw amazed him. There were people there from every walk of life—merchants, craftsmen, noblemen, officials, farmers, laborers, and scribes—all going about the noisy business of bartering and trading their wares. And the heavenly smells he smelled! Roast duck and savory spices wafted from one set of stalls, while cinnamon and perfumes drifted over from another.

Leaving the marketplace, the cats headed down to the riverfront and strolled along the shoreline until they reached the place where the fishermen gathered. Eager to see how many fish had been caught that morning, Narmer and Ptah headed straight for the nets, but as they were cats, they were quickly shooed away. Continuing on their way upriver, they stopped again when they reached the place where the brick makers were making their bricks. Having already mixed together mud with bits of chopped-up straw and gravel, the brick makers were now pouring the mixture into large wooden molds, which would be left to dry in the sun. From the riverfront, the cats ambled through the residential district, where cramped little houses lined the narrow winding streets.

As Ptah could see, the people of ancient Egypt lived noisy, communal lives. Their houses tended to be dusty, sparsely furnished places with a few small rooms on the main floor and a kitchen on the roof. This lack of attention to their homes was largely due to the fact that Egyptians spent most of their time out of doors—in the village square or at the marketplace, out in the fields or down by the river.

Ptah soon learned that the entire city of Memphis was dedicated to his namesake. Ptah was the god of craftsmen, and this was evident in the beautifully carved statues and charming designs painted on the city's buildings. King Zoser was an avid supporter of the arts, and a large portion of the taxes he collected each year went toward beautifying Egypt's towns and villages.

Toward mid-afternoon the two cats happened upon the god's main temple, known as Hoot-Ka-Ptah. Its beauty astounded Ptah. The lower part of the outer walls had been etched with wavy lines and painted a brilliant blue to look like water. Across the top of the walls floated scenes of artists performing their crafts. Ptah saw sculptors and metalsmiths, painters and wood carvers, carpenters, jewelers, and scribes. The gates leading into the temple were clad with shining copper inlaid with semi-precious stones.

"I didn't realize the god Ptah was so important!" exclaimed Ptah.

"You bet he is," said Narmer. "Egyptian folklore says that in the beginning of time, the only gods in existence were the creator gods Atum and Ptah. When Atum brought forth a mound of earth from the watery Sea of Nun, Ptah willed all the other gods into being with his heart. These new gods went on to create the sky and the land—including the mountains, rivers, and valleys—and also the plants and creatures that inhabit the earth. They also brought forth the wind and the rain, fire, darkness, and chaos."

Since only priests and the highest of officials were ever allowed inside, the two cats snooped around until they found a side gate down a narrow dead-end alley with just enough space beneath it for them to squeeze through one at a time. Entering a lush green garden, they strolled around a rectangular pond surrounded by sacred persea trees, then went up to the temple itself, a beautiful little building etched and painted the same brilliant blue as the walls outside, with jeweled patterns that sparkled around its doorways. Passing through one of these doorways, Narmer headed straight for the base of the statue to see whether the priests had left any food there. He was not disappointed.

Their bellies full, the cats returned to the gate and squeezed back through. "Oof," said Narmer. "It seemed easier going in." Turning to go, they were heading down the narrow alleyway when they were met with a big surprise. Stepping in from the street and blocking the exit were the three tough cats from Imhotep's fishpond.

"Well, well. Will you look who we have here," snarled the brown cat named Geb. On either side of him, Kha and Shredder were smacking their lips and twitching their tails the way cats do when they want to fight. Fixing their eyes on Ptah, all three of them stalked forward, coming to a halt less than six feet away.

Ptah looked quickly around. The only way out was to pass by those cats! He nudged Narmer. "We're trapped!" he hissed in alarm.

Narmer leaned over and whispered, "Tell me, buddy. What do you know about cat fights?"

"Well," stammered Ptah, "I suppose I know that we're about to get into a big one."

"Argh, a tenderfoot!" groaned Narmer under his breath. Then, more loudly, he said, "You just sit tight and let me handle this." Taking a giant step forward, he spoke in a calm, clear voice. "Excuse us, gentlemen, but I believe you are in our way. So if you'll kindly step aside, we'll be leaving now."

In response, the three tough cats growled a low, menacing growl and stalked a few steps closer.

"Not so fast!" snapped Geb, adding, "Listen, Narmer, we've got no quarrel with you. You're free to go. It's that tall, skinny black cat behind you we're after."

"Yeah," piped Shredder, his orange fur bristling. "We don't need no stray cats like him hanging round our fish pond. Them fish is ours!"

"That's right," chimed in Kha, "so we decided it's time we

taught him a little lesson." Kha lifted his right front paw and began expanding and retracting his claws.

Ptah started to quake. In front of him, Narmer's spotted fur had risen to a stiff peak between his shoulders, and his tail was twitching every so slightly, but otherwise he remained calm. "That tall, skinny black cat you're talking about is with *me*," he said. "And besides, I don't think you know who it is you're dealing with. This here's the great god Ptah!"

Ptah's jaw dropped open. "Narmer, what are you *saying?*" he whispered.

The three tough cats burst out laughing. "*Him?* You've got to be kidding!" they cried. "He looks more like a moth than a god with those stupid wings on his back!"

"Don't laugh," challenged Narmer. "Those wings are special. I'm telling you, this cat can fly!"

"*Narmer—*" Ptah hissed again, but he was cut short.

"Shhh! Just watch what I do and do as I say. Would you rather be turned into mincemeat?"

Ptah buttoned his lip. Being turned into mincemeat was definitely *not* on the list of things he wanted to do while visiting Egypt.

Geb stopped chuckling. "Okay, Narmer," he said. "You've got my curiosity going now. I know you're throwing me a line, but I'll bite. What do you say, guys? Shall we watch this crazy cat 'fly' and then get on with our lesson?"

"This I've *got* to see!" cackled Shredder.

"The curiosity is killing me!" jeered Kha.

"Okay, then stand back!" Narmer ordered. He marched over to stand directly in front of the three tough cats and then turned to face Ptah, who was left standing—and feeling—very much alone. Narmer gave him a big wink and continued.

"Drum roll, please!" he shouted. "And now . . . for your entertainment . . . I give you the great and powerful god Ptah! Today he will demonstrate his ability to fly . . . over the temple gate, through the streets of Memphis, and back to Imhotep's villa." Narmer paused to give Ptah another big wink.

"Hey, knock off the fancy stuff," snarled Geb.

"Yeah, no more pussy-footin' around," snapped Kha.

"We haven't got all day," added Shredder.

"Okay, on your mark . . . get set . . . fly!" yelled Narmer, who instantly began burrowing his hind legs into the sand, kicking it into the eyes of the three unsuspecting cats.

Ptah just sat there blinking.

Narmer looked up from his frenzied digging. "Don't you get it—run!" he shouted as he jumped into the furry fray of cats, who had just figured out it was all a trick and were now beginning to charge.

Ptah hesitated. He hated to leave Narmer in such a tight spot, but he knew he'd probably do more harm than good by joining in. Besides, he convinced himself, the wily Mau seemed to be holding his own. Tossing his guilt aside, he darted past the thrashing ball of cats, ran through the streets of Memphis and all the way back to Imhotep's villa without stopping or looking back once.

8

Journey to the Island of Elephantine

The morning of departure soon arrived. Ptah awoke feeling miserable, his insides a jumble of emotions. There had been no sign of Narmer since the catfight two days before, and he was worried. He was also nervous about his impending journey into Nubia. Every time he thought about poison-tipped arrows and cat-eaters he wanted to faint! And he was missing the professor. Worse still was his knowing how much the professor must be missing him. So when Imhotep came to get him, Ptah dove deep inside his urn and refused to get out.

Imhotep just laughed and gave orders. "Load the cat, urn and all, onto the donkey caravan. We'll be moving out." He kissed his wife and children, made a few last-minute adjustments to the knapsack he was carrying, then mounted his donkey chair for the ride back to Memphis.

By the time they arrived, the riverfront was a steady stream of activity. Workers were loading sacks of wheat and corn taken from the great granaries of the king onto huge cargo boats waiting offshore. Also being loaded were bags of dried fish, fruit, and nuts, along with earthenware jars filled with honey, beer, and lard for cooking. King Zoser could well afford to trade so much because the past few years had been bountiful, with good floods. His storehouses were positively brimming with reserves.

Ptah emerged from his urn and went to find an out-of-the-way place from which he could watch. The first to catch his eye were the cargo boats—broad flat-bottomed vessels built from dark acacia wood that curved slightly upwards at either end. Nearly the entire length of each boat was taken up by storage cabins, leaving little room for the rowers, who sat in cramped, uncomfortable places along the sides. Even the helmsmen had to stand on the back cabin roof.

Ptah then watched as Imhotep went over to check on the boat that he would be taking. It was a marvelous vessel! Built from light yellow pine, it was more slender than a cargo boat but still flat across the bottom, with ends that curved steeply upward, tapering nearly to points. Attached to the bow was a wooden ram's head symbolizing the god Khnum, who controlled the floods. Rising from the center of the boat was a tall mast from which hung a huge rectangular sail made of papyrus matting. Behind the mast stood an open-framed cabin, the sides of which were covered with sheer linen. There were nine oars on either side and two rudder oars in back, all of which had been placed into oarlocks and were fastened to the boat by short ropes.

Upon Imhotep's arrival, his crew immediately set about unloading the things from the donkey caravan and hauling them into the cabin area. Soon all was ready to go. Ptah was just about to board himself when he heard a loud hissing noise behind him.

"Pssst! Ptah, over here!" It was Narmer!

Ptah rushed to greet his friend, a flurry of questions streaming from his mouth. "Narmer, are you all right? Where have you *been*? And what happened to your ear?"

"Stop it, will you? I'm fine!" declared Narmer, who was clearly enjoying all of the attention.

"At least tell me this," said Ptah. "How did the catfight go?"

"Let's just say those three tough cats won't be hanging around Imhotep's fishpond anymore," Narmer said dryly. He flicked his spotted tail, then added brightly, "I'm glad I made it here in time. I wanted to see you off!"

"Yeah, I guess we're about ready to go," Ptah said glumly. "What about you—where will you go now?"

"Me? Oh, I'll be heading back to Saqarra," Narmer replied. "I think I'll try to find that nice soft pillow the priests gave you to sleep on and take a really long nap."

Ptah laughed. "That sounds great," he said. Then, feeling bit chagrined, he added, "Hey, I want to thank you for getting me out of that scrape at the temple the other day. I don't know what I would have done without you."

Narmer shrugged. "Say no more. Those cats had it coming to them anyway." Looking over Ptah's shoulder and seeing Imhotep heading their way, he said, "Well, I guess I'll see you when you get back. Remember what I told you about those Nubians—don't turn your back on them for a single moment! Good luck!" Narmer turned and scampered off through the crowd.

"Time to go!" called Imhotep. He scooped up Ptah and carried him across the broad wooden plank that connected his boat to shore. Soon the boat pilot began pushing the vessel away from the riverbank with a long wooden pole. Then the rowers sprang into action, taking the boat out into the current, where the helmsmen turned it upstream. Following that came a volley of shouts and the creaking of ropes and rigging as the sail was lowered. At once, a stiff northern breeze caught the sail and the boat began to move by itself. The rowers gave a cheer and waved good-bye to the people standing on shore.

The journey to the Island of Elephantine was estimated to take two weeks. With wind like this, the rowers could rest easy on their oars while the breeze moved them along, even against the current. Ptah couldn't help but feel a twinge of excitement as the town of Memphis became a dot in the distance. They were on their way to Nubia, mysterious land to the south.

By the end of the first week, the travelers had fallen into a comfortable pattern. Rising early, they made good progress up the Nile for the better part of the day. In the late afternoons they would stop somewhere along the river to hunt and make camp for the night. Sometimes they stayed at small villages where they traded news with the people who lived there. Other times they camped near the marshes, where the rustling of wind in the reeds lulled them to sleep at night.

Ptah spent most of his time sitting at the bow of the boat, watching the scenery go by. The view he took in was pleasant, if somewhat boring, since the entire length of the valley looked virtually the same. There were very few trees in Egypt—the only native ones being the sycamore, the acacia, and the tamarisk—and, except for the marshlands, where tall feathery papyrus rushes grew in thick stands, all of the land had been cleared for farming. Manmade canals divided the farmland into uniform sections. Bounding Ptah's view on either side were steep limestone cliffs, which in the mornings were tinted with yellows and ochers. By midday, the bright light would bleach away all color, turning the cliffs into tawny planes of beige. Evenings were Ptah's favorite. Then the pinks and purples of sunset would dramatize the cliffs as the sun god Re dropped over the western horizon in a brilliant ball of fire.

From the professor Ptah had learned that the ancient Egyptians believed the sun god Re was born anew each day. Rising in triumph from the darkness, he made a glorious journey across the sky before sinking back down and traveling on a perilous journey through the Underworld at night. To the Egyptians, it was a miracle that he survived to rise again each morning—a miracle that brought them life.

Day after day of sunny weather, of skimming across the sparkling waters on the tails of a fine breeze, helped Ptah to forget all his worries. He hadn't fallen off of the boat, and while each day brought him closer and closer to the mysterious land of Nubia, any threat of cat-eaters or poison-tipped arrows seemed part and parcel of a distant future. He was on an adventure—with Imhotep, no less!— and it was proving to be far greater than any he could ever have imagined.

Life is so peaceful here, so carefree, Ptah mused one evening while down by the river getting a drink. The crew had stopped near the marshes that day. Some of the men had gone out hunting while others were setting up camp. Dreamily, Ptah watched the water flow slowly by, intent on a nubby gray log that was floating toward him. *What an odd-shaped log,* he thought, *and how very strange that it's moving against the current.*

An insect buzzed by Ptah's feet, momentarily distracting him. He bent down to inspect it, and found that it was one of those tasty bugs with a crunchy outer shell. Snatching it up in his mouth, Ptah sat merrily munching away, reflecting again on how easy life was in Egypt, how there seemed to be food waiting to be eaten every which way he turned. He looked up to see if another of those tasty bugs was flying around, when out of the corner of his eye, he noticed the nubby gray log had moved closer still, and was now hovering directly off shore.

How weird, he thought. *Now that log has stopped moving, almost as if it could tread water.*

Suddenly, rising out of the water and heading straight for Ptah, came an enormous crocodile! *Yikes!* Ptah jolted from his reverie just in time to leap from the monster's jaws as they crashed together with a sickening smack. Scrambling to catch his balance, Ptah scooted sideways as the crocodile lunged again, this time catching the tip of his tail in its teeth!

A searing pain tore through Ptah's body. Yowling and wild-eyed with fear, he yanked his tail from the crocodile's mouth and raced away from the river. Stopping momentarily when he reached higher ground, he turned to gauge his attacker's movement. The hideous beast lurched forward a few paces, then stopped, as though trying to decide whether a land chase was worth the effort for such a scrawny cat. Ptah didn't stick around for the decision. He bolted back to camp, landing on Imhotep's lap like a ball shot straight from a cannon.

"Whoa!" cried Imhotep, falling back on his stool. "What's going on here? You'd think this cat had seen Anubis!"

Imhotep's men laughed nervously. On the whole, they didn't know what to think of Ptah. Having a god traveling along with them was not necessarily considered to be a good thing. After all, if something were to happen to him, they would surely be struck down dead. They also didn't consider it to be a very good sign that the little god was now shaking from head to tail—and with a disheveled-looking tail at that. Anxiously, they murmured amongst themselves, casting Ptah suspicious glances, but outwardly they said nothing.

9
Thebes

As if to confirm their fears, the very next day the crew's troubles began. Rising early as usual, the men were met with a day that promised to be a scorcher. To make matters worse, not a single breeze blew, rendering their sail useless. Grudgingly, the men began to row, everyone knowing that progress would be slow now that they were powered by muscle and oar.

The long, hot laborious day dragged on and on. Sweat dripped heavily from the men's bodies, causing the oars to become slippery and requiring them to double their efforts. They tried wrapping their hands with strips of linen, but nevertheless, by the end of day, painful blisters needed tending.

The following day turned out to be the same, and so was the one after that. Tempers began to flare over trivial things, such as who would get to ride near the stern of the boat where the slightest of breezes could be felt, or how often they would stop and break for a swim. Through all of this, Ptah stayed well out of the way, hidden within the cabin area where he could nurse his sore tail.

By the middle of the fourth day, the men were exhausted. Imhotep knew they needed to rest, so he scanned the shoreline for possible places to pull out. The area they were traveling through was marshy; thick papyrus stands lined the river on either side. However, through one of the stands he spied a low, dry hill with a watery trail leading up to it. He ordered his men to row in that direction.

Once in the marsh, the water turned too shallow for rowing. A group of men climbed out of the boat, grabbed the towline, and began to pull the boat toward shore. The dense papyrus plants limited their sightline, but the watery trail was well defined, and this is what they followed.

Suddenly a great thrashing noise reverberated throughout the marsh, followed by a painful cry and a volley of shouts. Ptah and Imhotep rushed to the bow, where they watched in horror as a raging hippo charged, trampling one man and leaving the rest in chaos. All men feared hippos—more men died from them each year than from either crocodiles or lions. Cursing, the men grabbed for their daggers and lunged at the hippo in attack, but the thigh-deep water hindered their movements, and the angry beast lumbered away.

The injured man was brought onboard and was laid out upon the deck. At once, the boat priest began praying to the gods to spare the man's life, while Imhotep, who doubled as the boat doctor, knelt by the man's side and began wrapping his broken bones with strips of linen. Although working as carefully as he could, the wounded man moaned in agony.

"Hurry! Get this man some willow-bark tea for his pain!" cried Imhotep. When he was finished he turned to the priest and said, "This man needs better medical attention than this boat can offer. I've bandaged up all I can see, but it's what I can't see that worries me."

"How far is it to Thebes?" called the priest to the boat pilot.

"Nearly a day further," the pilot called back.

Imhotep looked thoughtful, then stood. "Gather round, men!" he shouted. When everyone was quiet, he said, "I know you all are tired, but the sooner we get this man to a doctor the better. The moon will be full tonight. Who is willing to keep on going until we reach the town of Thebes? Those who come will be granted two days rest at the finest inn in town. Those who stay will be picked up by the cargo boats, no punishment for remaining. All in favor say, 'aye!'"

"Aye!" shouted the men in unison, each man knowing that the injured man could just as easily have been him. Without so much as a grumble, they pushed the boat back into the river and continued on their way.

By the time they reached the town of Thebes, daybreak was

dawning. The rising sun, positioned low in the eastern sky, created a shining back-drop to an otherwise dreary little town. Imhotep and a few of his men went immediately to find a doctor while the rest of the crew secured the boat to the launch.

Everyone was hopeful that the injured man would live. Luckily, Egypt had the most highly advanced medical system to be found anywhere in the world at the time. People from as far north as Babylonia and as far south as Punt came in search of Egyptian doctors, who were performing miracles of surgery even as they prescribed such bizarre remedies as the swallowing of a whole skinned mouse for certain childhood illnesses.

Once the injured man had been housed, Imhotep secured lodging at an inn for the rest of his crew. The best the town had to offer turned out to be little more than a hovel; even so, they were given a fine meal and a clean sleeping bench made soft with papyrus matting. Finally, Imhotep retired to his own room, where he collapsed onto the bed. Ptah joined him in a long nap that lasted the rest of the day and into the night, the excitement of the journey having left him also quite drained.

The following morning Ptah decided to explore the town. Thebes, he soon discovered, was little more than a backwater village visited mostly by traders on their way to and from the south. It was a rough sort of place, and the people who lived there were known to be a headstrong bunch. They worshipped the relatively unheard-of god named Amun, or "the hidden one." Amun was the god of invisible forces, like the power that lay in the wind. He was also a god of war.

Thebes was divided into two parts by the Nile. On the eastern side was situated the main part of town—a collection of mud-brick houses, several temples, a seedy marketplace, and a handful of inns that tended to serve more beer than food. Across the river, the western side consisted mostly of farmland laid out in grid patterns separated by dikes and symmetrical waterways, now under repair from the flood. At the edge of the farmland, on the fringes of the desert, Ptah could see a long row of beehive-shaped buildings—some of the great granaries of the king. Next to them stood the town's necropolis, or City of the Dead. Despite its ominous name, the necropolis wasn't a scary place—at least not during the daytime—but rather it was a place of beauty, where princes and noblemen built elegant temples to preserve their bodies and their belongings for use in the Underworld.

Around noon Ptah returned to the inn to find Imhotep in better spirits. Sleep can work wonders, all cats knew, and it was gratifying to see this great man back on his feet and raring to go again. After a hearty meal, the two of them spent the rest of the day walking around town in search of traders, whom Imhotep hoped could provide him with information about Nubia. He particularly wanted to find any traders who had actually seen or met with King Shabaka. However, by evening time, he had found not a one.

The next morning the crew continued upriver. Though the injured man had lived, the mood onboard the boat was somber as the men set out, and talk was limited to only what was necessary for rowing and for steering. Toward mid-afternoon the men's spirits received a boost when the wind picked up and they were able to rest easy on their oars again. Little by little each man emerged from his shell, and soon the old jokes and good-natured bantering returned, so that it wasn't long before everything seemed back to normal again.

Time slipped quickly by, and before Ptah knew it, they had arrived at the Island of Elephantine. A rocky outpost jutting up from the middle of the Nile, the island was the center of trade between Egypt and the lands to the south. Its key position for keeping watch over all that came and went on the river also made it useful as a military base. Some people claimed that the island was named for its traffic in ivory, while others argued that it was named for the smooth gray rocks that lined its shore, resembling a herd of elephants getting a drink. Either way, the name was quite fitting.

Imhotep ordered his crew to bring the supplies ashore, since the final trek into Nubia would be made by land. Rocky stretches of river south of the island, with waterfalls and swift rapids called cataracts, made traveling difficult by boat. Far from being disadvantageous, these "bad waters," as the Egyptians called them, were actually a blessing in disguise because they served as a barrier to slow down invaders who might otherwise have come swiftly from the south.

While Imhotep was busy, Ptah explored the island's pathways and lookout towers, and poked his head into the dark, windowless rooms where weapons were stored. His favorite discovery was something called a "nilometer"—a series of stone steps leading down to the river that was used for measuring the flood. A low reading was ominous, likely meaning a year of hunger for the Egyptian people. A reading that measured too high was equally disastrous because it signaled the potential flooding of villages. Luckily, this year's reading had been good—news King Zoser had been happy to hear.

Other news on the island was not so good. Talk turned quickly to the Nubian raiders, who were feared by all. The soldiers on the island, known as the Lords of the Door to the South, told daring tales of battles fought against them. These battles had ended poorly for the Egyptians, the Nubian arrows landing sure and true. Imhotep's men listened to these tales, growing more and more grim.

10

The Nubians

Imhotep's party left Elephantine for Nubia at daybreak, taking a boat across the river to the eastern shore, then proceeding by foot along the broad trail that followed the Nile deep into the south. Although the trail showed signs of being well traveled, they met few people along the way. Word had gotten out that the route was now dangerous. Travelers had to pay a steep price to get through, if they were allowed through at all.

In time the trail passed into a canyon. Craggy limestone cliffs pressed in on either side; the land above was rocky and dry. The few scraggly little bushes had thorns on them. To Ptah, it seemed like a hostile place to make a home, especially when compared to the fertile farmlands of the north. He had to remind himself that this land had not always been this way; it had fallen on hard times. The forces that had been turning the vast grasslands that once covered the continent of Africa into desert were still at work.

Only a handful of Imhotep's men had been taken on this final leg of the journey. The architect had told his crew that the Nubians wouldn't consider a small group to be a threat. What he hadn't told them was that he wanted to put as few lives at risk as possible. Ptah knew that a good leader only reveals the information he deems necessary, and Imhotep was no exception. In this case, however, the information he withheld wasn't anything the men didn't already know. The chosen few walked on in trepidation, while the rest of the crew remained back on the island, awaiting the arrival of the food and the delivery of the gold.

Ptah was amazed by how little the men brought with them, considering the dangerous territory they were heading into. Besides the knapsacks and waterskins they carried on their backs, the men wore only simple white kilts tied with a knot in front; their arms, chests, and legs were left bare. On their heads they wore short black wigs, which puzzled Ptah, for he could see no advantage to this except that it did make them appear more unified. He supposed the wigs protected their heads from the sun. For weapons, the men brought bows and arrows, daggers, and swords. Lastly, each man carried a broad leather shield that bore his unique mark. A soldier grew attached to his shield as a gambler might a lucky pair of dice, for a shield was the only thing that would come between his heart and a well-aimed arrow.

The travelers walked onward the entire day, stopping near dusk to make camp for the night. The stretch of river by which they camped was too rough for fishing, so for dinner they made do with what they had brought in their packs. A quick meal of dried venison and spiced corn cakes was hastily thrown together. What little beer they'd brought was carefully rationed, each man dreading the day when he would be reduced to drinking nothing but water. That night they slept out under the stars. Ptah felt somewhat lost without his urn, which had been left behind on the island, but he greatly enjoyed the dazzling beauty of the ancient sky before the time of city lights.

The following dawn the men broke camp, everyone eager to begin their trek while the temperature was still cool. It was dark in the depths of the canyon when they first set out, but soon the slender rays of dawn slipped over the rim of cliffs, lighting their way. The men hadn't gone very far when they began asking Imhotep how he expected to find King Shabaka's village when they didn't know where it was.

"I have a hunch the Nubians will find us first," Imhotep replied.

Ptah did not like the sound of this statement one bit. Both he and the men kept careful watch the entire day, but by nightfall, it had ended just as uneventfully as the first.

The next day, however, Imhotep was proved right. The Egyptians had barely set out when a low whistling noise sounded an alarm.

Plop! An arrow landed deep in the sand, directly at Imhotep's feet.

"Halt," he said quietly. "Form a circle and set up the shields. We wait here."

Soon Ptah could see Nubian warriors approaching from both front and rear. They easily outnumbered Imhotep's men five to one. With the river on one side and the cliffs on the other, the Egyptians were trapped. Behind the wall of shields, the men sweated and frowned, raising and lowering their weapons while mumbling prayers under their breath.

"The king has sent us all here to die!" cursed one man. Murmurs of agreement circled round.

"Relax," Imhotep said calmly. "We have the great god Ptah on our side. No harm can come to us now."

Terrific, thought Ptah, who by this time was so frightened himself, he was close to piddling in the sand.

Meanwhile, the advancing Nubians were nearly upon them, and they were a fearsome sight. Dressed solely in leopardskin hip-cloths, their lean dark bodies were painted with wild patterns of yellow and red. Triple scars ran down their cheeks and short feathers poked from their curly black hair. Most frightening of all, each man carried a bow and arrow, cocked and ready to shoot. The warriors stopped just short of the huddled Egyptians.

One of the Nubians stepped forward, a man of importance, Ptah realized. In addition to his leopardskin hip-cloth, the man had on a leopardskin sash, draped over one shoulder and clasped at the hip with a gold brooch. His feet were clad in thick leather sandals, and on his head he wore a sort of crown made from thick gold wires twisted around ostrich feathers. Gold armbands encircled each of his arms, and around his neck hung a heavy gold chain. The man stepped directly in front of the shielded Egyptians and raised his hand high in the air. Clearly this was not meant to be a greeting.

"Lower your weapons and stand slowly," said Imhotep.

The Egyptians all gawked at Imhotep as if he were crazy, but they did as they were told. Slowly they set down their swords, muttering more prayers under their breath. The air was tense, ready to spark. Ptah squeezed shut his eyes and waited for the rain of arrows to begin.

Imhotep stepped out from the circle of shields and bowed low, saying, "King Shabaka, I presume. I am Imhotep, Grand Vizier of Egypt. I have been sent here to discuss a trade."

King Shabaka, for that was indeed who the crowned warrior was, eyed Imhotep and his men warily before lowering his hand. The Nubians responded by lowering their bows. The tension eased up a bit.

"Imhotep, your name travels far. I am honored your king saw fit to send such an important person to meet with me. I take it he has finally realized that I am not a man to be argued with."

Nor a man to be bargained with, thought Ptah, though Imhotep merely responded, "That is true."

"So, King Zoser has finally agreed to my terms of a trade!" Shabaka threw back his head and laughed, a deep hearty laugh that Ptah might have found pleasant were it not aimed at the Egyptians.

Imhotep paused. "Actually, Great Shabaka, King Zoser has sent me here to discuss new terms. I am to meet with your mother, Queen Kandake."

King Shabaka's dark eyes flashed with anger. The laughter fell from his voice. "You dare to come into my land to bring me this message? I should kill you all at once!" His hand shot back into the air. The Nubian warriors resumed their menacing position.

Imhotep answered smoothly, "Surely, Shabaka, you must know that if you were to kill me now, the entire Egyptian army would be on you in a matter of days. Your warriors may be among the finest fighters in the land, but they are no match against the waves and waves of Egyptian soldiers who would willingly give their life if their king were to ask it of them. Besides," he went on, "one of your spies, caught near the Island of Elephantine, has already been sent on ahead to tell your mother we're coming. She will be more than a little upset, I think, if we do not show up."

Shabaka narrowed his eyes. "So, you've chosen to handle things that way, have you? Then tell me this: how do you propose to discuss new terms of a trade when you have brought so little with you?" He pointed to the group's meager knapsacks lying pitifully on the ground. "We Nubians have a mountain of gold! Why should we waste our time bargaining with roadside peddlers?"

Imhotep laughed. "Do not think we were foolish enough to bring the food with us when we have no agreement in place and no army to back us up! We brought only a mere sampling of what awaits on the Island of Elephantine—assuming our safe return, of course."

Shabaka sniffed haughtily but slowly lowered his hand. The warriors followed suit. "Very well then," he said, "I will take you to my mother. But beware! The queen has eyes that see through all! She will not be fooled by hollow offerings, nor by lies cloaked in the lion's hide of truth."

By late afternoon the Egyptians reached the Nubian village, located further upriver, where the canyon widened a bit. Most of the houses in the village were small, flat-roofed structures made of thick mud brick, arranged in circular groups among the scattered trees. A few of the larger houses were made of stone; Shabaka's warriors led Imhotep and his men to the largest.

The Nubian people stared curiously at the foreigners as they made their way through. Egyptians rarely came to the village, since most trade was conducted downriver on the Island of Elephantine. Returning their gaze, Ptah could see at once these people were in trouble. Their brightly colored clothing and beautiful gold jewelry did little to hide the fact that they were much too thin, and their handsome faces looked drawn and haggard.

Despite this obvious hunger, Ptah saw many animals in the village. Cattle, goats, donkeys, and geese roamed freely about. The cattle, pale creatures with long horns and big bony humps on their backs, were particularly strange. The Nubians had twisted their horns into all sorts of interesting shapes, which they apparently found beautiful. Among all these animals, Ptah did not see any cats. A shudder ran through him. Eaten, perhaps?

At Shabaka's house the Egyptians were made to leave their weapons at the door. They were then shown inside, to a large reception room hung with vivid tapestries in yellow, orange, blue, and black. Each of the room's four corners held a tall pedestal on which sat a carved ebony statue. Ptah found the Nubian style of art to be somewhat similar to that of the Egyptians, although it was more free-form in its use of shape and color. In the center of the room stood a huge mahogany table surrounded by ten chairs, all of which had been carved and inlaid with ivory and gold. On the wall opposite the doorway was a large picture window left open to the breeze, to the village, and to the river beyond.

"Be seated," said Shabaka, who proceeded to order that wine be served and a meal prepared. He then turned to Imhotep and asked, "By the way, will we be having your cat for dinner?"

Ptah's heart skipped a beat.

"Oh, yes," answered Imhotep. "I think you will find him to be a very good cat."

Shabaka smiled. Clapping his hands twice, he called for one of his servants. "See to the cat," he commanded.

The servant, a thin, dark man with a solemn face and hollow, hungry eyes bowed low and then left the room. He returned shortly carrying a large gold platter covered by a domed lid. He advanced toward Ptah, one hand pressed firmly to the base of the platter, the other grasping the lid, as though he intended to trap Ptah between.

Ptah shrunk back. *Narmer was right,* he thought. *This is it! How could Imhotep do this to me?* Realizing that he shouldn't just sit there and make this easy for them, he sprang from his position and dashed for the door. King Shabaka moved quickly to block his way. Whirling around, Ptah raced for the window. Just as he took a running leap, the servant removed the lid from the platter, and he chanced to see what was on it: a dish of milk and a hunk of cheese. *Wham!* Thrown off by surprise, Ptah crashed into the wall beside the window and crumpled in a heap on the floor.

"You say he's a good cat, do you?" mocked Shabaka. The king threw back his head and laughed.

Imhotep turned a deep shade of red. He rose from the table and went to collect Ptah, who was also feeling terribly embarrassed.

Shabaka left them then, returning a short while later dressed in a long pleated robe belted about the waist with a tasseled cord. The robe's colorful pattern stood in vivid contrast to the plain white clothing the Egyptians always wore. Shabaka had added even more jewelry, including a spectacular gold brooch in the shape of a frog, which clasped his robe where it crossed his chest. A gold mesh cap studded with lapis and carnelian served as his crown.

With Shabaka were two women—one young, one older—both quite large and dressed in equal finery. In Nubia, it was fashionable for women to be heavy, the more so the better, since great size indicated great wealth. Ptah thought he had never seen such beautiful women! Their black skin, oiled and silky smooth, shone like onyx. Around their wrists and ankles shimmered delicate gold chains, and from their necks hung intricate necklaces set with emeralds, turquoise, and lapis. Peacock feathers adorned their braided black hair, and in their hands they carried ostrich-feather fans, which they swished from side to side as they walked. Ptah assumed the younger woman to be Shabaka's wife and the older one to be his mother, Queen Kandake.

The Egyptians stood and bowed.

"Be seated," said the queen. Kandake's voice was deep and resonant—the kind of voice that one listened to and obeyed.

A meal was then served of beef kabobs and thick brown bread, along with plenty more wine. The Egyptians' mouths watered at the sight of the richly spiced hunks of meat grilled to perfection over flaming coals. Beef was a rarity in Egypt—it was reserved for the most important of occasions or for offerings to the gods. The meal was eaten in silence until the end, when the queen turned to Imhotep and said, "Imhotep, it is a pleasure to meet you at last. I hear you persuaded King Zoser to build a mountain of stone. Impressive! Tell me," she added coyly, "did he send you here to use your persuasive powers on me?"

Imhotep smiled. "Queen Kandake," he said, "I do not know what you have heard. But I believe that in matters such as these, no man—or no woman, for that matter—can be persuaded to do a thing which he or she does not truly wish to do."

"Very well," said the queen, "then explain yourself. Surely you did not *wish* to come all this way if there wasn't something in it for you."

Imhotep laughed. "Ah, Great Queen, surely you underestimate the loyalty of a humble servant to his master! I am only carrying out the duties assigned to me. My own prosperity is of no regard."

Kandake and Imhotep continued their conversation along these lines, with the queen firing off her loaded statements and Imhotep doing his best to dodge them like arrows. Ptah sat back and watched, thinking their exchange looked a little like a cat-and-mouse game. He wasn't sure who was the cat and who was the mouse!

At last the queen got to the point of their meeting. "Shabaka tells me that King Zoser has sent you here to discuss new terms of a trade. I thought we had made our position very clear. Any trade between us must be based on weight, not size."

"You have made your position clear," replied Imhotep. "It's just that . . . well, King Zoser is concerned about your people. He's heard that your grasslands have all but turned to sand. He sent me here to tell you about a land further south, called Kush, where the grass grows green."

"Mother, he lies!" blurted Shabaka. "Do not let this man fool you into believing that Zoser cares for anything but our gold!"

Kandake nodded at her son, then turned to Imhotep and smiled. "We have heard of that land," she said, "but we cannot leave this place. Here we are rich! We have spent *years* gathering together our mountain of gold, and that is not something we can easily pick up and carry along with us."

"King Zoser is aware of that . . ." Imhotep paused, then added rather sheepishly, "so he, uh . . . he thought he might be doing you a favor by taking all that heavy gold off your hands."

Shabaka leaped up. "Enough! I've already heard more than I can stand to hear!"

Kandake remained seated, but her dark eyes flashed with the same intensity as her son's. "I think it may not be such a coincidence," she said evenly, "that your king has suddenly developed a concern for my people at the very same time that we have put together an army that rivals the best!" She clapped her hands twice, whereupon two servants appeared, carrying a large copper scale. They placed it on the table before her. "Now, show me what you have brought," she demanded. "Then we can discuss new terms of a trade."

Imhotep sighed deeply and reached into his knapsack. He removed several large pieces of dried fish and one sack each of wheat and corn. He also withdrew two small jars of honey and lard. To this he added one bag each of figs, dates, and nuts. "This is a mere sampling of what awaits on the Island of Elephantine," he said. "The finest emmer wheat, the sweetest of corn, honey from the lotus flower, and sturgeon and bass caught in the freshest waters of the Nile."

The queen gathered together the pile of food and placed it on one side of the scale. On the other side she placed several small hunks of gold, adjusting the amount until the two sides were evenly balanced. When she was finished, Shabaka threw back his head and laughed, a gesture that was beginning to annoy Ptah.

"Maybe you shouldn't have dried the fish," he mocked. "They are so much lighter that way!"

Imhotep stiffened. "I didn't know the Nubians preferred to eat their fish rotten!" he shot back.

"Silence!" roared the queen. "What's fair is fair! This is our offering. On behalf of King Zoser, you must accept it!"

Ptah watched Imhotep as she said this. Beads of sweat had formed on his brow and his face was flushed with anger. He had played the only good card he'd come with—that of persuading the Nubians to release their gold based on Zoser's apparent sympathies—and it hadn't worked. It was obvious that Imhotep did not have a backup plan, nor did he have any idea how to handle these stubborn Nubians.

11

Visions of Gold

During negotiations with the Nubians, and all the time the food and gold were being weighed, Ptah could see that Imhotep's mind had been hard at work trying to think of a way he might tip the scale in his favor. Now the architect wiped his brow and stood. "Queen Kandake," he said carefully, "we have shown you what we have brought to trade. King Zoser has gone to great lengths to deliver a mountain of food to the Island of Elephantine. He will be more than a little disappointed, I think, if we do not reach an agreement. However, all you have shown me so far are a few pebbles on a plate. So before we continue with our dealings, I must see your gold."

"Mother, be wary. It may be a trick!" cautioned Shabaka.

The queen stood and picked up her ostrich-feather fan. "It's all right, Shabaka. The Egyptians are unarmed. Let us take them to our gold so they can see for themselves how rich we are."

Imhotep and his party followed the queen out of the room. She led them down a narrow corridor to the back of the house, where they stepped out into a dusty, barren courtyard surrounded by high stone walls. The courtyard was empty except for a windowless stone building protected by fierce-looking guards. The guards snapped to attention when they saw the king and queen approach, while eyeing the Egyptians with the utmost suspicion.

Proudly marching to the door of the building, Kandake produced a large gold key that was attached to the tasseled cord around her waist. She unlocked the door, then pushed with both of her hands until it creaked open wide. The room inside was dark. "Light the torch," she commanded. One of the guards promptly grabbed a wooden club that was covered on one end with pitch and placed it into a bed of hot coals until it caught flame. He handed the torch to the queen.

"Come," she said as she entered the building.

There was an audible gasp as the Egyptians stepped into the room. From floor to ceiling, set row upon row into horizontal racks, stretched long wooden poles from which hung the gold in huge, yellow rings. There must have been hundreds of them shimmering in the torchlight! The Egyptians appeared stunned, no doubt thinking of what all of this wealth would buy them back home.

Ptah was dumbfounded by their reaction to the gold. They were practically drooling, and over something they couldn't even eat! Thinking about food again, his belly began to rumble. The meal he'd been served had been a meager one—understandably so—but he decided to return to the reception room anyway to see if he could scrounge up anything else. He slipped through the doorway, then scampered across the courtyard.

Back in the reception room, Imhotep's knapsack turned up nothing but a few dried figs. Ptah scanned the room, his eyes finally coming to rest upon a particularly plump piece of fish sitting on top of Kandake's scale. *No one will notice if there's one small piece of fish missing,* he reasoned.

Ptah knew he'd better hurry. He could hear the Nubians and the Egyptians coming down the hallway, so he leaped onto Kandake's scale to claim his prize.

Crash! The scale tipped violently with his weight, sending the food, gold, and Ptah cascading onto the table. Dazed, he lay there sprawled amidst the scattered pieces as Imhotep rushed into the room.

"Ptah! What have you done?" he cried.

No use lying, thought Ptah, the fish clenched in his mouth.

Imhotep glanced quickly down the corridor. There must have been a delay, for the others were still clustered behind Shabaka's wife, who was scolding one of the servants. Hurriedly, Imhotep picked up the food and the gold and rearranged them onto the scale. When he was finished, he frowned at Ptah and said angrily, "Why, you . . . you—" but suddenly his words broke off and his eyes lit up, and he finished by saying, "Why, you've just given me a marvelous idea! There very well may be, if not a god, then perhaps a benevolent spirit inside of you after all!" He gave Ptah a pat on the head, then turned to face the Nubians as they reentered the room.

"Queen Kandake," he said abruptly, "if I may be so bold, let me tell you what it is that I see and what I know to be true. Then you may be the judge of what's fair."

"We will listen to all you have to say. Be seated," said the queen.

As everyone took their chairs, Imhotep began to pace the floor, talking as he went.

"Queen Kandake," he began, "King Zoser has sent me here to arrange for a trade. He would like it to be based on size, while you and Shabaka would like it to be based on weight. Now, I think we can agree that there is no easy way for those two to come together. That being said, you should know that I am willing to make a compromise—the deal can be based on weight. But hear me out, because you must be willing to compromise, too!"

Imhotep waited for the queen to nod. "We both know King Zoser cares little about what happens to your people," he continued. "All he wants is your gold. But he is willing to trade a mountain of food for it if only we can come to agreeable terms."

"Get to the point," growled Shabaka. "You've told us nothing we don't already know."

"Then at least we agree on the situation," replied Imhotep, bowing slightly to Shabaka. "Queen Kandake," he continued, "I can see with my own eyes that your people are starving. If they go without food for much longer, they will sicken and die. And if that happens, where does that leave you and your son? You can't be rulers if you have nobody left to rule! You must consider that if we can reach an agreement, not only will you be getting Zoser's food, but you will be getting back the life of your people. So the deal that I offer is this: it is the weight of our food *plus* the weight of your people that will be measured against the gold. Think about it," he added swiftly. "Your people don't weigh very much, and if you do not act quickly, there will be nothing left of them at all!"

Shabaka leaped up from his chair and shouted, "Mother, this is insane! You can't agree to that! Do you know what our people will say if they discover that we have practically given away our gold? They will say—"

"They will say," interrupted Imhotep, pounding his fist on the table to regain the queen's attention. "They will say," he repeated more boldly, "that their king and queen loved them so well, they traded a mountain of gold to save their very lives! I ask you, Great Queen, which is more precious: your rings of gold or the rings of curls on the heads of the children in the village? Which would you cry for more if they were gone?" Imhotep gazed earnestly and fell silent.

Queen Kandake rose from her chair and strolled to the window. The room was quiet. Shabaka, for once, was speechless. "How much food did you say you brought?" she asked.

"Enough, Kandake, to make your people strong, and then some," said Imhotep. "Consider this: without the heavy gold to carry, your people will be free to move south, where the grass grows green. There is plenty more gold to be found there. You could build a great kingdom in the land of Kush!"

The queen looked steadfastly at her son. "Shabaka, I believe that Imhotep speaks the truth. Our people will thank us."

"But with this deal, the Egyptians will have won!" Shabaka protested. "Mother, I ask you, how many times must they lie, cheat, and steal from us before we take a stand?"

"Maybe they will have won, but we will have won, too," Kandake replied. "Shabaka, you must always remember: at the heart of every answer to our problems lies the soul of our people. Without them, we are nothing!"

Shabaka frowned and stomped to the side of the room. Grabbing a tall staff that was leaning against the wall, he clenched it in his fist and pounded it on the floor. Raising it up, he pounded it again. The room fell silent; so silent, in fact, that Ptah could hear the sound of a fly buzzing on the ceiling and the river flowing in the distance. Nobody moved or spoke. Suddenly, Shabaka spun back around and pounded his staff once more. Then he threw back his head and laughed. "It's a deal!" he shouted.

Calling to his servants, he cried, "Go forth and gather the people throughout the land. Tell them to meet us across from the Island of Elephantine, where we shall feast for seven days and seven nights! Oh, and don't forget," he added quickly. "Tell them to make sure they are weighed *before* they eat!"

12

The Feast

Two days after Shabaka's pronouncement, the last of the Nubians had joined the steady stream of people heading north along the trail to the meeting place across from the Island of Elephantine. Kandake and Shabaka were in the lead, accompanied by Imhotep and his men, minus the runner who'd been sent back a day earlier to announce the deal and to let everyone on the island know to begin preparing the feast. Behind the royal entourage followed servants, guards, cooks, and attendants. Bringing up the rear of the procession were the people of Nubia, thin from hunger but proud.

Ptah stared in amazement at the amount of gold being transported north along the trail. Pairs of the strongest men bore onto their shoulders the long wooden poles from which hung the gold in huge, yellow rings. It sparkled in the sunlight as they walked, in a dazzling display of wealth and beauty. The line of gold seemed endless!

Early on the third day of travel they arrived at the meeting place, a clearing near the edge of the river, shaded by a few leafy trees. On one side of the clearing stood tables and baskets piled high with food. On the other side sat a dozen scribes, ready to record the weighing. Ptah found these men to be very official-looking, with their long papyrus scrolls and their writing instruments laid out in front of them as though there were important documents to be signed.

Organizing the event was a man Ptah recognized at once—the head priest from Saqarra. At present he was coordinating the flow of things, making sure the Nubians didn't rush the food tables and that they got into the weighing line. Ptah watched as the colorful ribbons received from weighing were gleefully snatched and presented in return for heaping platefuls of food.

And what food there was! Ptah saw baskets filled with figs, grapes, pomegranates, and melons. There were salads made from lettuces, cucumbers, chickpeas, and radishes. There was a huge assortment of cheeses, and almond and date bars sweetened with honey. He counted at least twenty different kinds of bread, some shaped like cones while others were flat and rounded, or triangle-shaped, or twisted into braids. Beside the bread table was the roasting pit, from which wafted the heavenly aromas of roast goose, wild duck, and tender gazelle.

As the weary travelers arrived, urns filled with beer and wine, kept cool in the river, began to flow freely. For a while Shabaka ran hither and thither, trying to herd his people into the weighing line, but after a while he gave up and proceeded to enjoy himself.

A merry time was soon had by all. The Nubians toasted their king and queen a hundred times over, and it was not long before the musicians brought out their clappers, shakers, flutes, and drums. People began to sing and to dance wild acrobatic dances. The children all played or joined the storytelling circles, the trill of their laughter creating music of its own. As for Ptah, he was having a marvelous time. The Nubian people fawned over him, feeding him choice morsels off their plates and dancing with him high on their shoulders.

Meanwhile, the Egyptians were hard at work. They kept busy cooking and serving and counting and weighing, and also unloading the food from the cargo boats and reloading them with gold. The food deemed not necessary for the feast was placed onto wood-and-canvas travois, which the Nubians would drag with them on their long journey south. Despite the hard work, the Egyptians were also in a merry mood. Ptah wondered just how happy they'd be if they knew, as he did, that the kingdom of Kush would one day grow so strong that Kushite kings would sit upon the throne of Egypt for nearly two hundred years.

Although the feast would continue for days, Imhotep's crew readied to leave the following morning. As Shabaka now told it, the idea for the trade had come from him. This was fine with Imhotep; he cared only that the situation had been handled agreeably and he was able to return home with the gold. As far as he was concerned, the sooner they left the better. Once the Nubians' bellies were full, their thoughts might yet turn again to their rings of gold.

Down by the river, Ptah was watching the men put the final touches on the packing when a familiar voice caught him by surprise. "Hey, buddy, I've been looking all over for you."

"Narmer! How wonderful to see you! You look great!" Ptah exclaimed, jumping up to greet his friend.

"I *am* great!" Narmer declared. "Do you remember when I left you and went back to Saqarra? Well, the head priest found me napping on that nice, soft pillow they gave you to sleep on the night you were there. Apparently he had seen us sitting together on the ledge in the courtyard and thought I might have been sent down to earth as your servant. Not wanting to anger the gods, he adopted me. Boy, did my life change after that! No more chasing skinny rats for me; now I'm served my meals on a golden plate!"

"My servant, eh?" said Ptah, a wry grin spreading over his face.

"Don't get any ideas!" Narmer said playfully. "Anyway, I suppose that it's you I have to thank for my stroke of good luck."

Ptah smiled. "I think we can both be thankful for all that has happened. After all, if it wasn't for you, I wouldn't have met Imhotep." Suddenly remembering something he'd been stewing about, Ptah's brow furrowed. "By the way, Narmer, I have a bone to pick with you," he said sternly.

"A bone!" exclaimed Narmer. "Oh really, I'm stuffed! You can have it all for yourself. But if you insist—"

"That's not what I meant!" snapped Ptah. "Where I come from that means I'm upset about something. You said the Nubians eat cats!"

"Oh, *that* . . ." Narmer chuckled. "I only said that to add a little excitement to your life, put a little zing in your wing, so to speak. You didn't believe me, did you?"

"Narmer—" Ptah began in a threatening voice.

"Say, look!" the husky cat interrupted. "I think the boats are ready to go. The Egyptians are boarding them now. I'll be staying here until the head priest leaves. But when you get back to Memphis, stop by Saqarra and see me sometime. Who knows? Maybe Imhotep will decide to enlarge the pyramid like he did twice before. You'd think he was actually worried that someone might try to build something bigger!" Laughing, Narmer scampered away.

Ptah watched Narmer's spotted tail disappear through the crowd. He thought about Imhotep and wondered whether the great man would be jealous or pleased if he knew about future pyramids, some of which would be nearly double his own in size. Probably a little of both, he decided.

Glancing toward the river, Ptah spied Imhotep searching for something. Guessing it to be him, he ran up the broad wooden plank that connected the boat to shore and joined Imhotep in the cabin area. Soon the boat pilot pushed the boat away from shore and the helmsman turned it downstream. The men threw up a cheer. All Egyptians hated to leave their villages for any length of time, and they were glad to be returning home.

The journey to Memphis began smoothly enough. Though the cargo boats were heavy, the current moved them along. This delighted the rowers, who relaxed and told jokes or exchanged stories as the boats swept steadily onward. Everyone onboard was in a cheerful mood, the trek into Nubia having ended with hardly a hitch.

Three afternoons later they arrived at the town of Thebes. Although still early to be quitting for the day, Imhotep ordered his men to stop and make camp. He wanted to check on the injured man, to see whether he was well enough to travel.

Imhotep felt sure there would be trouble if word got out that the entire Egyptian treasury lay hidden at the launch, so he ordered his men to take out the boats on the western shore, across river from the main part of town. Tying up near a marshy place, the crew hiked inland a little ways and set up camp on a low-lying hill where they could keep watch. Soon the hunting parties went out, returning a short while later with three gazelle. The animals were skinned and the meat cut into thick chunks, which were then skewered onto sticks and roasted over flaming coals.

During this time, Imhotep and Ptah took the ferry to town, where they located the doctor who'd been tending the injured man. News there was both good and bad. While the injured man had lived, the damage caused by the hippo had rendered his left arm useless, and the doctor predicted that he would never walk normally again. He was well enough to travel, however, so Imhotep paid the doctor, and together he and the crewman made their slow and somber journey back to camp. Boarding the ferry to cross the river, Ptah steered clear of the injured man. For reasons unknown to him, the man had been throwing him sidelong glances—glances that were filled with spite and malice.

Afternoon turned quickly to evening, and soon the crystalline blue sky was ablaze with stars. One by one the men retired to their tents until at last Imhotep and Ptah were left sitting alone by the fire. Finally, Imhotep yawned and said, "Well, Ptah, I'd better go check on the boats one last time before I turn in for the night." He stood, pulling his woolen cloak tighter to ward off the chill, then bent down low to stroke Ptah's fur. "King Zoser will be so pleased, and it's all because of you. When we get back to Memphis, I'll arrange for a grand procession to be held in your honor. Artists will be commissioned to paint your likeness on the temple of Hoot-Ka-Ptah. Good night, my friend."

Ptah watched Imhotep light a torch and proceed down to the river, the torchlight bobbing along beside him like a giant firefly dancing in the night. Leaving the warmth of the fire, Ptah crawled inside his urn. It was chilly in there, making it difficult for him to sleep, so he lay awake for a while, thinking. He realized he was feeling melancholy. Having people treat him like a god was nice in a way, but he longed for the days when he was treated like a regular cat. And while he'd grown quite fond of Imhotep, he was still missing the professor. He found himself clinging to the hope that one day he might return home, to his *real* home, far in the distant future. At long last, he drifted off to sleep.

Late that night, after the moon had set and the fiery stars burned bright holes in the blackened sky, the injured man rose from his tent. Hobbling over to where Ptah lay sleeping, he gazed pensively down on the little god, the bringer of his misfortune, the reason, he assumed, for his injuries.

"I curse the day you ever came down to earth," the man growled under his breath. Reaching down with his one good arm, he picked up Ptah's urn, and then slowly limped to the river's edge. "If it's the last thing I do," he hissed, "I will rid myself of the evil demon who has ruined my life!"

Swinging back his arm away from the river, the injured man prepared to pitch the urn in. At the very last moment, however, the man thought twice. Angry as he was, he dared not risk further wrath from the gods. It would be unwise, he decided, to drown the cat. So instead he hobbled over to where the marsh grew thick and dropped the urn into the reeds. There it settled, completely out of sight.

Ptah Dreams:
Anubis, Maat, and the Monster Named Ammit

Throughout his near-fatal encounter, Ptah slept soundly inside his urn, and in the wee hours of the morning, when the stars were beginning to fade, he had his second strange dream.

He dreamed he was floating downriver in a *felucca*—the type of small, narrow sailboat made from bunches of reeds used commonly throughout Egypt. The river he was traveling on ran through an underground tunnel, pitch black except for an eerie green light that bobbed along behind him, casting a putrid glow over the boat and its surrounding waters.

It wasn't long before Ptah realized that he was not alone in the boat. A strange, dark beast with the head of a jackal and the body of a man stood in the rear of the craft, a pole in his hands, steering. From the end of the pole swayed a lantern—the source of the sickly light. The jackal-man said not a word to Ptah; he just stared straight ahead, intent on where they were going.

Soon the tunnel narrowed, and to Ptah's surprise they approached a gate. The gate was made of thick slats of wood, and it spanned the width of the river, blocking their way. As they drew near, the jackal-man slowed the boat, then fixed his pole, upon which the lantern began to glow even brighter. Answering this summons, an immense serpent appeared, grayish-green in color and with shiny scales running down the length of it back. Terrified, Ptah peeked over the edge of the boat. In the gangrene light, he now became aware that the river was filled with things—ghastly things, like slithering snakes and bug-eyed crocodiles and dreadful, unspeakable creatures with gaping mouths and sharp teeth. Through this morbid menagerie the serpent swam, and when it reached the side of the boat, it began to speak.

"Baked by the sun, blown by the wind; innumerable, unavoidable, inescapable. What am I?" it hissed.

Ptah stared at the serpent in bewilderment. *It was a riddle,* he thought. He tried to think of the answer, but the jackal-man swiftly said, "Sand," and the gate flung open wide.

The two continued on their way, the jackal-man plying the inky waters with his pole while the creatures below hungered in their wake. Not far from the first gate, they came to second, this one made of shining copper. In front of it lurked another serpent, and it posed to them a different riddle.

"Born of the rain, fed by the land; winding, shifting, changing. What am I?" it hissed.

Again Ptah tried to think of the answer, but again the jackal-man said, "A river," and the gate flung open wide. Soon they had passed through a series of gates—one bronze, one iron, one shimmering glass. Twelve in all they passed before the river ran wide. Finally the boat came to a halt.

They had arrived at a small beach. The dark beast climbed out of the boat and motioned for Ptah to do the same. Waiting for them there, standing next to a large copper scale, was a beautiful woman with long black hair, ruby-red lips, and ivory skin so pale it looked nearly transparent. She was dressed in a slender golden gown, belted about the waist with a jeweled sash. On her head she wore a gold headband in which was tucked a snowy ostrich feather. A pair of translucent wings, the color of pure cerulean blue, draped down her back and were attached by their tips to a pair of jeweled wristbands. When the woman raised her arms to speak, her wings fanned out wide like a graceful swan's.

"Greetings, young cat. I am Maat, Goddess of Truth," she said. "You have passed through the Twelve Gates of the Twelve Hours of the Night to reach the door to the Underworld, and this is your time of reckoning." The woman lowered her arms and took a step forward, then held out her hand. "Give me your heart, young cat.

If you have been good, your heart will be light as a feather and you may pass through to the other side." She plucked the ostrich plume from her headband and placed it onto the copper scale.

"But if you have been bad," she continued, "your heart will be heavy and the scale will tip—not in your favor, I regret to say. In that case, Ammit will take care of you." Maat stepped aside to reveal a horrible monster lurking behind her. The monster had the head of a crocodile, and a body part hippopotamus and part lion. The creature was drooling and licking its chops, certain that this was one bad cat.

Desperately, Ptah looked all around. *Whose heart could possibly be lighter than a feather?* he thought. With the river behind him and the monster in front, there was nowhere to run. At once he realized who the jackal-man must be—Anubis, God of the Dead!

"I . . . I didn't mean to play all of those nasty tricks on the professor," Ptah stammered. "Or rather, I meant to, but not in the way it might seem!"

"Give me your heart!" demanded the woman again. She took another menacing step toward him and smiled, an icy smile, which Ptah decided was not beautiful in the least. Meanwhile, the monster behind her crept slowly forward, a trail of spittle left in its tracks.

Ptah's heart started pounding wildly in his chest. It pounded so wildly, in fact, that he felt it might leap from his body and into Maat's hand of its own accord. Suddenly, a voice that was not part of Ptah's dream broke through to his consciousness.

"What's this?" the voice asked.

Part 3
The Boy and the Scribe

Middle Kingdom
Thebes, 2060 BCE

13

The Egyptian Way

Ptah opened his eyes and looked up from the bottom of his urn to see the face of a boy staring back down at him. The boy looked to be about ten or twelve years of age, and he had dark brown skin, short black hair, and large green eyes. Hanging from a leather cord around his neck was a small stone amulet—a carved good-luck charm intended to give him strength and to protect him from evil. The boy was grinning from ear to ear.

"It's a cat!" he cried, and before Ptah knew it, the boy had reached inside and pulled him out.

Ptah gazed around them in shock. Where rows of tents had been pitched and guards posted the night before, he now saw nothing but a large dirt field. Everyone and everything was gone! Even the footprints had been wiped clean!

Ptah meowed miserably. *There must be some mistake,* he thought. *Imhotep never would have left me here on purpose!* Struggling free from the boy, he ran to the river's edge. Just as he feared, the boats were gone, too; but even more shocking to him than that was the view across the river to the town of Thebes. Overnight it had more than doubled in size. Ptah's head was still reeling as the boy caught up with him.

"Don't run, kitty. I won't hurt you. My name is Nebre," he said softly.

Dazed, Ptah turned to face the boy. Looking beyond him, he now noticed that the western side of the river had changed, too. More temples had sprung up, and more storehouses. Slowly it dawned on him what must have happened: Imhotep hadn't left him; he had left Imhotep. Somehow he had traveled forward in time. But to when?

Seeing the cat in the full light for the first time, Nebre gasped and dropped to his knees. "Ptah, forgive me! I did not know it was you!"

Ptah shook his head, trying to make sense of his situation. He looked at the boy, who lay sprawled out before him, arms outstretched and forehead nearly touching the ground. Nebre's eyes were slightly lifted, however, and he watched the cat with consuming interest. He had such a friendly looking face and such sparkling green eyes that Ptah couldn't help but to walk over and rub up against him. When he did, Nebre jumped to his feet and snatched him up off the ground.

"I can't believe you've come down to earth," he exclaimed. "And to me! I just *knew* something good was going to happen! I must take you home to my parents. Oh, but first I need to catch some fish for my mother."

Nebre gingerly set Ptah back on the ground, then picked up the bow and the quiver of arrows he'd left lying beside him. He waded into the marsh, returning a few minutes later with a fine, fat fish. Removing the arrow from the fish's side, he gutted it, then laid it down before Ptah, saying, "Here you go, kitty. This first fish is for you."

Suddenly realizing how hungry he was, Ptah dove right in. Meanwhile, Nebre went back into the marsh and caught five more fish. Stringing them together by their gills, he was now ready to return home. Gathering Ptah in his arms, he carried fish, cat, bow and all to the reeds where Ptah's urn lay hidden. He stared at it for some time, thinking.

"What to do about this urn?" he murmured. "I can't bring it home. My parents would trade it for the goods it would bring. And it's obvious to me that it belongs to you. Why, look—there are pictures of cats all over it." He shrugged. "I suppose it will be fine right here for a while," he concluded. "Let's go!"

The two set off walking down a long dirt road that headed due west toward the desert mountains. Nebre walked briskly to keep warm, his sole piece of clothing being a coarse linen hip-cloth. Ptah noticed that the soles of Nebre's feet were calloused and dirty; he doubted the boy had ever owned shoes.

They traversed the vast farmlands that covered the western side of the river. Much work had been done since Ptah had seen them last. Canals had been cleared and rock walls now divided the fields, which were plowed and ready for planting. The road ended at the edge of the floodplain, where Nebre turned north along a narrow trail.

Ptah found the contrast between the two sides of the trail startling. To his right, he marveled at the rich, black earth of the farmer's fields. On his left, the reddish-brown sand of the desert sloped gently upward before meeting the cliffs, which jutted skyward from their base. As they progressed down the trail, Ptah felt as though he was walking along a ribbon of hope, a dividing line between life and death.

Before long Nebre and Ptah arrived at a small farm with a tiny house set under a large sycamore tree. The house, really nothing more than a crude mud hut, was nevertheless quite cheery because the yard had been planted with scarlet-red poppies, and four colorful chairs carved in the shapes of a lion, a cheetah, a baboon, and a cow had been set out front. On one side of the house, Ptah spied a vegetable garden where onions, garlic, cucumbers, chickpeas, and melons had started to sprout. On the other side he saw an animal pen; in it were a sheep, two goats, and an ox.

Nebre set down the fish and his bow and quiver, then burst into the house. At once Ptah was amazed by what he saw; it was as though they had stepped into a lush, green garden. Painted on the walls of the tiny reception room were flowering trees and bushes. A leopard stalked across one wall while baboons and cheetahs peeked out from another. And the furniture! Although sparse, what furniture there was had been whimsically carved and painted in beautiful soft colors like the chairs sitting outside. On a shelf in the far corner of the room, Ptah saw what looked to be the household shrine: amidst bits and pieces of pottery and dried flowers he recognized statues of Hathor, the cow-shaped goddess of love; and Min, the dwarf god who brought babies; and Bes, the ferocious clown-headed god who protected children and women in childbirth. On the other side of the room rose a series of stairs leading up to the kitchen on the roof. At the base of these stairs, a doorway led to the bedroom, the only other room in the house.

"Mom! Dad! Look what I found!" Nebre shouted.

"Shhh, Nebre, the baby's still sleeping," scolded a woman's voice.

It was then that Ptah noticed Nebre's mother standing on a stool to the left of the doorway. In her hand was a small paintbrush, and with it she was adding a yellow bird to the garden on her walls. She had the same round face and bright green eyes as Nebre, the same dreamy expression, but her skin was much lighter. Her curly, brown hair was tied back in a long, loose braid, and she wore a coarse linen shift belted about the waist with a colorful sash. Around her neck was a copper chain from which hung a beautiful pendant shaped like a scarab beetle set with bright blue stones.

"That's my mother, Wia," Nebre whispered to Ptah.

Wia stepped down from her stool and went to check on the baby. She had a graceful, unhurried way of walking, a way that made her almost appear as if she were floating. Ptah noticed that her hands and feet had been stained reddish-brown with henna, a style he knew was common among the artistic crowd in ancient Egypt.

When Wia returned, her face fell when she saw what her son was carrying. Before she could utter a peep, however, Nebre's father walked into the room. A dark-skinned man of medium height and wiry build, his father had deep-set brown eyes and a serious-looking face. Wearing but a coarse linen hip-cloth knotted in the front, he carried with him a long length of rope. The rope, which was used for measuring, had small knots tied in it every cubit—about the length of a man's forearm—with larger knots tied every ten cubits.

Nebre's father caught sight of Ptah, then turned accusingly toward his wife.

"Hay, I was just about to tell him—" Wia began, but Hay cut her short.

"Nebre, you know what we've told you about owning a pet," he said abruptly. By the tone of Hay's voice, Ptah knew immediately that he was not welcome.

"I know what you've said before, but this is no ordinary cat," said Nebre. "This one's special. Look at his markings! It's the great god Ptah come down to earth!"

"Maybe it is, son," allowed Hay, "but it's still another mouth to feed. And now with your baby sister—"

"But don't you see?" exclaimed Nebre. "He's a sign! The great god Ptah is all about turning ideas into reality, and you know how I want to become a scribe, and—"

"Enough!" interrupted Hay. "I thought we had agreed that there would be no more talk about you becoming a scribe. You will be a farmer like me, and like my father before me, and like his father before that. It is the Egyptian way." Coiling the rope, he tossed it on the floor near the door.

"But I don't want to be a farmer," protested Nebre. "Besides, we don't even own our own land. The king claims a fifth of what we grow for taxes, and our landlord, Smendes, takes nearly half of what's left. We end up with practically nothing!"

"Silence!" ordered Hay. "Do you not respect the fact that you have food to eat and a roof over your head? I'll admit that farming is a hard life, but it is a good one. And we *will* own our own land some day, sooner than you think! I was able to fetch a good price for the crops we grew last year due to the war effort, and this year, with the good flood we've had, I should be able to more than double that. For once our family may be able to get ahead. And you, as my oldest son, will inherit it all someday."

"But I don't want it, Father. I want to be a scribe so I can learn to read and write," Nebre said, sulking.

"The only thing a farmer needs to learn to read is the land," answered Hay. "Look at your brother. As second son, Merisu will inherit nothing. And yet at half your age, he already shows a oneness with the land. Tell me." Hay pointed up. "What is the name of the star that appears on the horizon just before the flood begins?"

Nebre hung his head. "I don't know, sir," he replied.

"It's Sirius, the Dog Star!" his father exclaimed. "Even your brother knows the answer to that! Nebre, *these* are the things you must learn. They are things you can *use*. What good are a bunch of scribbles on a piece of papyrus?"

"Let my brother be the farmer then!" yelled Nebre, who immediately winced at his mistake. Children who talked back to their parents were dealt with harshly in Egypt. It was seen as a sign of coming chaos.

But Hay did not strike him. He merely looked sad and said, "Son, you may as well know the truth. Even if I wanted to let you go, they would never accept you. Training to be a scribe is reserved for the rich and for people who have friends in high places. But don't let that make you think you're not as good as them, do you hear?"

Nebre nodded quietly.

"Now, run along and finish your chores," Hay concluded. "And while you're at it, take that cat back to wherever you found him. Then cheer up! Tomorrow starts the weekend, and we will all go to the marshes for a day of fun." He patted his son affectionately on the head.

Nebre smiled weakly. Picnicking in the marshes was how most families spent their weekends, and it was always a good time. Even if one didn't catch any fish or game, one could at least catch up on the latest gossip.

With a heavy heart, Nebre carried Ptah all the way back to the marsh, to the place where the urn lay hidden. Setting Ptah on the ground, Nebre slumped down beside him and stroked his fur for a while. "I just know you came to me for a reason," he said with a sigh. "If only I could keep you." Nebre's voice trailed off, his gaze following the river as it flowed into the distance. Suddenly, he brightened.

"I know what I'll do!" he said. "There's a hidden valley in the mountains behind my father's farm. Hardly anyone ever goes there; it would make a great place to hide your urn! You could sleep there at night, and during the day I'll come find you when I'm done with my chores. I'll bring you food!"

Nebre hopped up, happy again. He scooped up Ptah, fetched the urn, and once again they headed down the long dirt road that led toward home. When they reached the desert's edge, Nebre continued past the narrow trail until he reached the base of the cliffs. From there he turned north, picking his way through the rocks, taking great care not to be seen.

Shortly he and Ptah came to a deep cleft in the cliffs with a little-worn trail winding its way upward. They took this trail, at one point passing through a crevice no more than two men wide. The trail then opened onto a desert valley—an ancient watercourse of v-shaped channels now partially choked with stones that had rolled down from above. A pyramid-shaped mountain stood sentinel in the distance.

The valley looked vaguely familiar to Ptah, although he could not imagine when he could possibly have seen it before. Nebre walked over to a large outcropping of rocks clustered beside the trail and tucked Ptah's urn behind it, then set the cat down in front. Turning quickly to go, he tripped on a rock and stubbed his toe.

"Ouch!" he cried. Nebre's voice echoed around the rim of cliffs, breaking the complete and utter silence of the valley. All sounds of life—the call of birds, the flowing of the river, the rustling of the wind in the reeds—were cut off in this strange and desolate place. "Ouch!" he cried again, this time just for fun. "Hoo-ha!" he shouted, the valley laughing back at him. Nebre called out several more times before finally waving goodbye.

"You stay here, Ptah," he said. "I'll be back when the light of Re hangs over these mountains."

Ptah then watched as Nebre skipped back down the trail, whistling a happy tune as he went.

14

The Chaos Years

Nebre returned to the valley in the early afternoon carrying a small linen-wrapped bundle. He gathered Ptah up in his arms and together they headed down from the hills, turning south and then continuing until they reached the Necropolis, a beautiful tree-lined street edged with temples and pillars. From there they headed east along the main dirt road that led to the riverfront, where the ferryboats landed. Once there, they found a shady place to sit, apart from the crowd.

The ferryboat landing was always a busy place with lots of interesting things to see—boats plying the rippling waters, people traveling to and fro, slaves being bought and sold. Across the river, the main part of Thebes was even busier, with its densely packed buildings and its bustling wharves.

Nebre unwrapped his bundle, revealing a thick piece of barley bread and a small slab of cheese. "Are you hungry?" he asked. He set Ptah down next to the cheese. Ptah sniffed at it for a moment, then turned away. He was still full from the fish he had eaten that morning.

Nebre sighed. "What to do with this then?" he said. "I'm too full to eat it myself, but I can't take it home to my mother after all the fuss she made about not wasting good food."

Looking up, Nebre noticed an old man sitting on the ground across from them, an empty bowl held high in his hand. The man was clean-shaven and as bald as a priest, and he was dressed like one, too, except that his long white robe was dusty and tattered. Lying next to him was a spotted old cat, a canvas sack, and a wooden cane.

Nebre got up and approached the man. Clearly he was blind. "Excuse me, sir," Nebre said. "I have some extra bread and cheese. Would you like it?"

Nodding, the man lifted his bowl a little higher. Nebre placed the food inside, then stood there, wondering what else he could do. The man ate some of the bread and broke off a few hunks of cheese to give to his cat.

"And who might I have the pleasure of thanking for this very fine meal?" the old man asked.

"My name is Nebre," Nebre replied. "My father farms the land northwest of here, near the entrance to the hidden valley."

"Ah, your father is a landowner then. How lucky!" the old man exclaimed.

"Oh, no, we don't own our own land. We farm part of the land owned by Smendes. But my father is trying to grow enough barley this year so that he can trade for his own land," Nebre explained.

"I see," said the man. He paused to break off some more of the cheese for his cat. "Well, I'm pleased to meet you. My name is Ipuwer, and this is my cat, Horus." Ipuwer held out his hand, which Nebre shook in greeting.

"I have a cat, too!" Nebre announced. "Well, I sort of have a cat," he corrected. "My parents won't let me keep him—we're much too poor for that. But I found him just this morning, and he seems to like me. His name is Ptah."

"What a powerful name for a cat!" exclaimed Ipuwer. "He must be a very special cat, indeed!"

"He is!" replied Nebre. "He has the markings of the great god Ptah himself! I believe that he came down to me for a reason."

"Is that right? What sort of reason might that be?" Ipuwer asked.

"Well, I wish to be trained as a scribe," Nebre began, "and considering how Ptah has the power to turn people's ideas into reality, I thought that maybe my dream could come true, even though—" Nebre broke off.

"Even though what?" asked the old man.

"Even though my father says it's not possible for me to become a scribe," Nebre finished glumly. "I am to be a farmer like him, and like his father before that."

"Ah, yes, the Egyptian way," Ipuwer said. Looking thoughtful, he then said, "Nebre, I know this system might not make sense to you right now, but you should know that it has its advantages. What do you think would happen if the coppersmith's son suddenly decided he didn't want to make pots, and then the tanner's son decided he didn't want to make leather, followed by the fisherman's son who no longer wanted to fish? It would lead to chaos! By having sons follow in their father's footsteps, Egyptians are assured that all the important jobs will be taken care of."

"Yes, that's what my father says," Nebre answered miserably.

"However," Ipuwer said more softly, "I also believe that people should be allowed to follow their dreams. Tell me, son, is it working for the palace as a scribe that you want, or is it simply learning to read and write?"

"Both!" declared Nebre, but then quickly countered, "On second thought, I guess I've no real interest in working for the palace. Those officials are rotten to the pit, every one! At least that's what my father says. What I really want is to learn how to read and write, but the only way to do that is to become a scribe."

"No it isn't. I could teach you," Ipuwer said plainly.

"You?" blurted Nebre. "Excuse me for being disrespectful, sir, but how could you possibly teach me to do that?"

Ipuwer sighed. "I was not always like this," he said, waving a hand over his eyes. "At one time I was a scribe. But not anymore. Years ago my eyesight failed me. I was told then by those in power that my services were no longer needed."

"The king told you that? I'm surprised! Even my father grudgingly admits that Mentuhotep is a kind and just ruler," said Nebre.

"Oh, what I'm talking about happened long ago, during the Chaos Years before Egypt was lucky enough to have a king again," said Ipuwer.

"Then why don't you go to the palace and speak to the king

now?" suggested Nebre. "I'm sure he would find a place for you in court."

"I tried that once," said Ipuwer. "I got as far as the palace gates before the guards turned me back. Who can blame them, really? An old beggar man like me asking to speak to the king."

Nebre understood. As a poor farm boy, he stood no more chance of being let into the palace than the old man sitting next to him.

"But let's not talk about me, let's talk about you!" Ipuwer said brightly. "When would you like to begin your lessons?"

"Right now! This very minute!" exclaimed Nebre, but then his face turned red. "I forgot," he said glumly. "I have nothing to pay you with."

"No matter," said Ipuwer, stiffly rising from the ground. "As you can see, I'm not exactly needed anywhere else right now. Why don't we go to the Necropolis and walk along the Avenue of Temples? Tell me when we reach the place where the row of carved pillars begins."

The two set off walking along the same dirt road that Nebre and Ptah had taken to get there. Ipuwer strode briskly, his step surprisingly spry for a blind man his age. Horus and Ptah followed closely behind.

Ptah peered at the old cat padding along beside him. He seemed positively ancient! Horus's fur was scraggly and matted, the black spots peppering his light tan coat long since streaked with gray. He may have been a strong cat once, but time had stripped him of his muscular form so that now he appeared to be made of just fur and bones. His coat hung loosely, as if two sizes too big, and the fur around his muzzle had gone pure white, but when he turned to face Ptah, his golden eyes shone as bright and as sharp as an eagle's.

"It seems we've both been named after gods," Horus said, musing. "What a heavy burden to be placed upon such fun-loving creatures as we cats!"

Ptah laughed. "So you're named after the god Horus, then, the son of Isis and Osiris? Or is he the son of Re? I'm sorry, but I can never seem to keep the Egyptian gods straight. There are so many of them."

"Quite understandable," replied Horus. "Egyptian gods are plentiful—to say the least!—and they have a tendency to evolve over time, taking on different powers or different shapes, or merging with other gods to form new ones. Also, the same god can be called by a different name depending upon which town you're in."

"Why is that?" asked Ptah.

"I'm not sure exactly, but it makes a certain amount of sense that people who have so little opportunity to make changes in their own lives would only worship gods unfettered by the same limitations," offered Horus.

Ptah thought about Horus's statement, contrasting it with the modern world from which he came. There, change was all around, and many people held fast to age-old traditions in hopes of bringing some semblance of certainty to their lives. "Well, I've never met a cat who was named after a bird before," he remarked.

"A falcon, to be precise. Yes, I found that a bit odd myself," replied Horus. "And I've never met a cat who was named after a bull, but then your markings say it all." Turning suddenly quite serious, Horus said, "Listen, Ptah, I think you should know that the reason Ipuwer was forced to quit being a scribe was not because he lost his eyesight. It was much more complicated than that."

"How so?" asked Ptah.

"It's a long story. Are you sure you want to hear it?"

"Sure," said Ptah. "We've a long way to go before we get to the Necropolis, don't we?"

Horus nodded. Ahead of them, Ipuwer and Nebre were chatting comfortably, with Ipuwer telling the boy about the time he and Horus had traveled to Punt and had been entertained by pygmies dancing in the sun. An oxcart trundled by, distracting Ptah's attention, and as he turned his gaze to follow its movement, he took in the rich, black earth of the farmers' fields and the clear blue Egyptian sky. He realized that he was feeling happy in this new time.

"It will be easiest if I start at the very beginning," Horus said at last. "Ipuwer was born during the Chaos Years that followed the collapse of the Old Kingdom. Those were the years when Egyptians battled against each other and the country split apart. It was a time of greed, when noblemen thought they were as good as kings, and peasants refused to do their work. People no longer knew their places!"

Horus twitched his nose in disgust before continuing. "Throughout those years, however, the Old Kingdom's glory was not forgotten, and Ipuwer grew up hearing stories about a nation of heroes, and about wealth and harmony throughout the land. Over time he came to believe that the only way Egypt could ever regain her glory was to have a king again. Not one of those puppet kings controlled by the priests up north, mind you, but a real king, a strong king. Ipuwer also came to believe that if the new king was ever to succeed, certain things would need to be different, and by that I'm mostly talking about pyramid building."

"Pyramid building!" exclaimed Ptah, puzzled. "But I thought King Zoser's Step Pyramid was a good thing. It kept young men working during times of the flood, solving of all sorts of social problems the Egyptians were having. 'Idle hands cause mischief,' Imhotep always said, and besides, the pyramids are *the* symbol of the Old Kingdom's glory! They stand for everything that people believed in!"

Horus smiled ruefully and shook his head. "What led to Egypt's glory may have also been what led to her demise," he replied. "What started out as a good thing under the mastermind of Imhotep later turned terribly wrong. As each new king tried to outdo the ones that came before him, the pyramids grew taller, smoother, more complex. Each new pyramid placed a heavier burden upon the people. Taxes were raised, and more and more sons were pulled from their homes to work on them. It was dangerous work, too. Even with the addition of slaves to handle the worst jobs, people sometimes died!

"I think the turning point happened after the Great Pyramids of Giza were built," Horus went on. "King Khufu commissioned the largest pyramid ever, followed by his younger brother, Khafre, who demanded that not one, but two pyramids be built in his name. Only one was a giant, of course, but upon his death, his son, Menkaure, ordered yet a third behemoth to be built. After that the Egyptian people said enough is enough. Unfortunately, however, this came at a time when the Memphis priests had reached their pinnacle of power, and they were not about to let it end. You see, the priests had grown very rich from all the gold and tribute they said had to be paid to the gods. As if the gods are ever swayed by such a thing as gold!" Horus scoffed. "At any rate, the priests threatened the kings, saying the gods would punish the country with famine and drought if the building were to end. They pointed to King Zoser, who managed to build his Step Pyramid and still have a mountain of gold to show for it when he was done. So on it went."

Ptah blushed beneath his fur, knowing how Zoser had come by his gold. Not wanting to detract from the story, he merely said, "Didn't the quality of the pyramids go downhill after the ones at Giza were built?"

"Oh, yes, it most certainly did," replied Horus. "In order to lighten the people's load, architects came up with a way to build the pyramids faster and cheaper. The ones that were built during those later years were shams—hollow shells that looked good on the outside but inside were filled with rubble. Needless to say, things didn't go quite the way the architects had planned. Rather than lowering taxes, the puppet kings kept them high, even through times of drought. As you can imagine, the whole thing soon came to a head."

"What happened?" asked Ptah.

"The people in the south rebelled. Led by a group of local chieftains, called nomarchs, the south succeeded in splitting away from the north. Unfortunately, though, when that fighting ended a new power struggle began, this time between the nomarchs themselves, who each vied to be king of the south. All in all, the warring went on for years, which we now call the Chaos Years."

Ptah furrowed his brow. "So what has all that got to do with Ipuwer?" he asked.

"You have to understand that at one time Ipuwer was an important person. People listened to him," said Horus. "Early on in his career he began using his position as a scribe to write about the unhappiness of the Chaos Years and to argue for a king. He even went so far as to suggest that the Memphis priests should willingly give up their power in the north in exchange for being able to choose a king from among the nomarchs in the south." Horus paused. "I'm sure you can guess what the reaction to *that* suggestion was. Ipuwer's blindness was simply the reason everyone was looking for to have him excused from court."

"But Egypt has a king now; I heard Nebre say so. Doesn't that change everything?" Ptah asked.

"Well, it does and it doesn't. Change like this takes time. But the tide is slowly turning. One of the first things Mentuhotep did as our new king was to strip away much of the wealth of the priests and nomarchs and reclaim it for the crown. Ipuwer is pleased by this turn of events, even though his own situation has not improved." Horus sighed deeply.

"If Ipuwer is pleased, then why do you look so glum?" asked Ptah.

Horus stopped walking for a moment and turned to face his new, young friend. "Ptah, I am old," he said. "The door to the next world opened up for me a long time ago. All I have to do is to step right through it. It's tempting, too, because I can see what's there. You'll be happy to know that the next world isn't at all like what the Egyptians believe. There are no dark tunnels, no monsters waiting to devour you at the gate. Instead, it's filled with light and with music so indescribably beautiful it makes your heart want to sing for joy!" Horus raised his eyes upward and smiled, then lowered them back down.

"It's tempting, all right," he said, "but I can't go through just yet, not while Ipuwer still needs me. Before I die I would like to see Ipuwer redeemed by the king."

"Redeemed by the king—what do you mean by that?" asked Ptah.

"To have him noticed, thanked, that sort of thing," said Horus. "That is my wish."

15

Sacred Symbols

"Here we are," announced Nebre at last. They had arrived at the Necropolis and were standing at the place on the Avenue of Temples where the row of carved pillars began. Looking around, Ptah had been hoping to see inside some of the temples, but they were surrounded by thick, high walls, and the gates leading into them were solid. Even so, the walls and the gates were something to look at. Colorful scenes, usually depicting the nobleman whose temple it was, paraded out front, and the gates were clad in shining copper or coated with glistening glazes. The temples were built so closely together that where one ended, another began.

Ipuwer reached out and touched the first pillar. "Let's begin here," he said. "As you can see, each of these pillars is carved with writing that tells a story." He paused for a moment while he ran his fingers gently over the stone. "This one tells the story of creation. Now, to begin our lesson, I'm going to read you the story, and you must listen very carefully. When I'm finished, I'll go over the story again, tracing the symbols with my finger while I speak. After that we'll start once more, going over each symbol one at a time."

"How can you tell what the writing says?" asked Nebre.

Ipuwer smiled, the crinkles around his eyes adding character to his kindly face. "I taught myself to read with my fingers. It was a long, slow process, but it helped that these are the very same stories I learned when I was training to be a scribe. I know them all by heart. When we are done, you will know them, too." Ipuwer paused, then said, "Before we begin, can you tell me if you know any of these sacred symbols at all?"

"Only the ones my mother was able to teach me," Nebre replied while fingering the amulet that hung from his neck. "About fifty altogether, which seems like a lot, but it's not. There are so many!"

"Over seven hundred in all, and the number keeps growing. New inventions bring about new words," Ipuwer said matter-of-factly. "But you've got a good start. It will help you to learn more quickly if you already know some of the more basic ones. Did your mother happen to explain to you how the Egyptian writing system works?"

"No, and I just don't get it!" declared Nebre. "Some of the symbols are obviously words in themselves, while others seem to need the symbols beside them to make up a word. Then there are still others tacked on here and there that don't appear to have any purpose to them at all!"

Ipuwer laughed. "You've done a pretty good job of figuring out the system for yourself, Nebre. You're absolutely right when you say that some of the symbols are words, while others represent sounds that are pieced together to form a word. Often, those two types of symbols are combined, so you might see a word symbol within a grouping of sound symbols. In those cases, you simply sound them all out together. The mysterious symbols you sometimes see tacked on at the ends of words are there to make up for the fact that the Egyptian writing system doesn't include any symbols for sounds like 'ee,' 'ah' or 'oh'. Since many words are identical except for those sounds, the symbols at the end help clarify which of the words the scribe meant. And in those cases, the symbol at the end is silent."

"That's a dumb way of doing things," said Nebre. "Why didn't they just invent symbols for the sounds they were missing?"

Ipuwer frowned. "Do not question the wisdom of your elders. Those seven sounds possess the secrets of the universe! They are much too sacred to be shown in writing. Nebre, to be a good scribe, you must accept the fact that some things are done for reasons we can't understand."

"Like the fact that sons must follow in their father's footsteps," Nebre grumbled.

"Precisely," replied Ipuwer. Returning his attention to the pillar, he began tracing over the symbols until he found the starting point. "Now for the story of creation," he said, and he went on to tell Nebre a variation of the same story that Ptah had heard before. It began in a similar manner, with the world being covered by the watery Sea of Nun, and the creator god Atum bringing forth a mound of earth. In this version, however, a giant lotus flower sprouted from the mound and bloomed, releasing into the sky the sun god Re, who warmed the earth and brought forth life.

Ptah watched Nebre's reading lesson very closely. He didn't know much about the Egyptian symbols used for writing, called hieroglyphics, except that at some point the system died out, and that over time people forgot how to read them. And so it was until the early 1800s when a French scholar named Jean-Francois Champollion finally succeeded in doing what hundreds of others before him had tried: using the Rosetta Stone as his guide, he discovered the key that unlocked the symbols' mystery, bringing them back to life.

After Ipuwer had read the story of creation twice, he began going over it again, one symbol at a time. The pace was agonizingly slow, and Nebre wiggled his fingers and tapped his toes, trying hard to sit still. Finally, he could take it no longer.

"This is boring!" he declared. "I'll never learn anything at this rate!" He threw up his hands and stomped over to a temple wall, where he began kicking at a loose piece of brick until it crumbled to dust.

Ipuwer folded his arms across his chest. "Do you know how the behavior you just showed me would be handled in the classroom of a scribe?" he asked harshly. "When I was a student, my teacher used to beat me on the back with a leather strap, he said, so the words would enter my ears." Ipuwer paused, waiting for the meaning of his statement to take effect.

Nebre's foot dropped to the ground. His face looked stung.

"Don't worry, I won't beat you," Ipuwer said flatly. "I've suffered enough blows for the two of us, I'd say. If you do not wish to learn, then I do not wish to teach." He gathered his cane and sack and turned to go.

"Oh, but I *do* wish to learn!" cried Nebre. "I wish to learn more than anything else on Geb's green earth! *Please,* give me another chance!"

Ipuwer spun around. "Then hold that desire in the front of your mind like a ripe, juicy melon," he said. "Hold it high for you to see with your mind's eye at all times! You must believe that with enough effort on your part, one day you'll be able to taste its gentle, sweet fruit!"

"I will, I promise! I'll be the best student ever!" Nebre wailed.

"Fine then," said Ipuwer. "How often would you like to have these lessons?"

"Every day!" said Nebre, then countered, "except on the weekends, I guess. My family goes to the marshes to hunt and fish then."

"Ah, yes, the favorite Egyptian pastime. Well then, it will be eight days on, two days off for your lessons. Tomorrow starts a weekend, so I'll see you in two days. Let's meet here at the Necropolis around the same time as we did today. Good day, young man."

"Goodbye!" called Nebre, gathering Ptah in his arms and skipping down the avenue. "And thank you!"

16

Scattered Seeds

In the weeks following the beginning of his lessons, Nebre's parents witnessed a dramatic change come over their son. No longer did he dawdle and drag out his chores for the day; rather, he jumped out of bed and raced through his chores as though there was a busy beehive attached to his behind. Hay and Wia shook their heads with wonder, but they were not inclined to ask questions. After all, the boy was being productive, said Hay, whenever the topic of Nebre's behavior came up. As for where he went in the afternoons, Hay simply declared, "He's a boy, let him be! He's probably off hunting or fishing or who knows what."

"Who knows what is right," mumbled Wia. For her part, she had been watching Nebre very closely and was curious. Her son was happy, everyone could see, but there was something mysterious going on, and she aimed to find out what.

So one day when Nebre came home from his morning chores and climbed to the rooftop kitchen with Ptah to pack Ipuwer some food, Wia was waiting for him. She had been keeping herself busy by making beer. She was presently adding crumbled barley bread to the large earthenware jars she had already cleaned and filled with water. Some of the jars had been sprinkled with dates for sweetening. When she was finished, she would tightly cover the jars and take them down to the small cellar dug beneath the kitchen stairs. There, the bread would be left to soak until it fermented. Ptah knew that Egyptian beer was unlike the beer brewed in modern times. It was a thick, brown, nutrient-rich liquid, and was one of the staples of the

Egyptian diet. He still didn't like the taste of it, though. Most cats didn't.

Ptah scooted behind a basket near the top of the stairs before Wia could catch sight of him. He hoped that Nebre would hurry. He was always nervous when Nebre brought him into the house, and he kept looking over his shoulder for signs of Hay. The last thing he needed was to be caught in the kitchen where he might have to jump from the roof!

Wia's kitchen was a simple affair. An open space encircled by four low walls, the area was furnished with a single low table and six padded stools. Baskets for gathering, bowls for mixing, and jars filled with honey, lard, and spices were stacked along the walls. In the far corner, near the cone-shaped oven, sat a few copper pots and a pile of earthenware dishes. With the view of the fields and the sycamore overhead, Ptah thought Wia's kitchen felt very much like a tree house.

Wia had been humming one of the many love songs so popular in Egypt, but she ceased when Nebre came up. Except for the singing of birds and the rustling of wind in the leaves of the sycamore tree, the kitchen was quiet. The baby was sleeping, Merisu was in the vegetable garden tending the plants, and Hay was down by the river doing the laundry with the other men. In Egypt, men always performed this task, their heavy clubs close by their sides. The constant threat of crocodiles made washing the linens a risky undertaking.

Nebre rubbed noses with his mother, then moved to the cutting board, where he grabbed a thick loaf of bread and a slab of cheese. He began hacking off a large slice of each.

"Nebre, you eat like a hippo, but you don't gain a bit of weight," Wia said casually. "I hope you're not letting all that good food go to waste!"

"No, Mother, of course not," replied Nebre, who was glad to be telling the truth, for while he had not told his parents about his reading lessons, he had not exactly lied. He'd simply neglected to mention them for fear of what his father might say.

"Tell me, then," said Wia. "Is all of that food for you?"

The knife in Nebre's hand froze in mid-air. His palm grew instantly sweaty and his face reddened. His mother's question hung like a void in the air that sucked at his quickening breath. It didn't help matters much that Wia did nothing to break the silence. She simply sat there, waiting patiently for an answer to her question.

Over by the stairway, Ptah winced. This day was not going well for Nebre at all. Earlier that morning, while out in the fields, the boy had accidentally spilled an entire sack of barley seeds! It wouldn't have been half as bad had the seeds fallen on the Black Land—the rich, black earth of his father's field—but they had fallen on the Red Land—the barren desert beyond the reaches of the flood.

Actually, it had been Ptah who had knocked over the sack of seeds, but still, Nebre berated himself as though it was his fault. He had been showing Ptah the new symbols he'd learned by drawing them in the sand with a stick. Ptah hadn't been paying any attention; he'd been merrily digging away in one of the irrigation canals, kicking mud all over the place. When Nebre had shouted for him to watch, Ptah had jumped in surprise and had landed on the sack of seeds, spilling its contents. To make matters worse, the sack going over had startled him and he'd jumped again, this time tipping the bucket of water that Nebre had been using to wet the seeds after planting.

Nebre's father would be furious if he knew! Not only had the boy wasted good seeds, but he had wasted precious water on the Red Land as well. Ptah had watched as Nebre tried to gather the seeds all up, but in the end it was useless. Finally he'd simply covered them with wet sand and the bits of mud Ptah had scattered, and then got serious about his planting.

And now here was Nebre's mother questioning him about the food he was taking! After a long pause, the boy answered, "No, mother, the food is not for me. It's for my teacher, Ipuwer."

Wia perked up. "Your teacher? Tell me, who is this Ipuwer and what is he teaching you to do?"

"He's teaching me how to read and write!" blurted Nebre. Now that things were out in the open, the boy's excitement gushed out of him like a flood that's burst its dike. He went on to tell Wia the entire story about how he'd met Ipuwer and how they had arranged for his lessons. He even went so far as to tell her that he still had

Ptah, although he left out any mention of the urn he had hidden. He concluded by saying, "Ipuwer's mostly been teaching me how to read for now. The writing part is difficult because I lack the tools with which to write, but I've been practicing in the sand with a stick."

Wia listened attentively to all her son had to say. When he was finished, she looked thoughtful, then asked, "But Nebre, how do you pay this man?"

"He charges me nothing, Mother, only the food I bring. And even that he accepts more as a gift than payment."

Wia's face grew stern and her body stiffened. "Nebre, I know you're excited, but have you thought this over carefully? Doesn't it seem odd to you that a stranger would offer to teach you something so special in return for so little?" Her voice sounded shaky, the way it always did before she was about to give a big lecture.

Nebre interceded. "He's old, Mother, and *blind*. Of *course* I considered that he might be a bad man, but he's not! We spend our days at the Necropolis, out in the open where there are lots of people. Ipuwer told me he enjoys teaching and that he has nothing better to do with his time. You really ought to meet him. He's smart and he's kind—the best teacher I could ever have imagined!"

Wia sighed. "All right, Nebre. If this food is going to feed your mind, then it is well used. And, yes, I would very much like to meet your teacher, but that will have to wait for another day. I'm very busy right now . . ." Her voice trailed off and her face took on a dreamy expression as she fingered the pendant on her necklace.

"By the way," she said after a long pause, "where is this cat you have grown so fond of?"

"He's here!" Nebre ran over and fetched Ptah, carrying him to the table where Wia was sitting. "He's a good cat, Mother. I have taught him to do some tricks. Would you like to see them?"

Wia laughed. "Of course! Let's go down to the front of the house and call Merisu so he can watch, too."

Several minutes later they had all gathered. Nebre set Ptah on the ground and went to fetch the small cloth ball Wia had made him as a toy. While Ptah waited, he basked in the comfort of Nebre's family— Merisu was stroking his fur while Wia was rubbing behind his ears.

He didn't really mind performing Nebre's tricks, even though he knew most cats would be appalled if they found out. The fact of the matter was, Ptah had never really known a boy before. He hadn't realized they could be so much fun! Whereas the professor and Imhotep had always fed him and given him love—all very nice—Nebre liked to play! He let Ptah attack his toes, and he dragged strings around and threw balls for him to chase. He threw one now.

The ball flew high into the air. Ptah bounded after it, allowing it to barely hit the ground before snatching it up in his teeth. Running back to Nebre, he dropped the ball at the boy's feet, whereupon Nebre picked it up and threw it again, this time in a different direction. Ptah watched as the ball began to soar, then took off after it. No sooner had he started, however, than he screeched to a halt. The ball landed directly at Hay's feet.

"What is that cat doing here?" shouted Hay, dropping his laundry basket. "Nebre, I thought I told you to get rid of that thing a long time ago! How many times do I have to tell you, the last thing we need around here is a useless creature eating us out of house and home!"

"I'm sorry, Father," mumbled Nebre.

Wia went over and pulled Hay aside. She began whispering something in his ear.

Meanwhile, a rapid jerky movement out in the field caught the corner of Ptah's eye. He turned his head, and to his horror he saw a large rat scuttling toward the house. The rat froze in its tracks when it realized a cat was watching him. It lifted its nose and twitched at the air. Then, seeing no signs of a chase from the cat, the rat took off scuttling again.

Ptah hesitated. He had never seen a live rat before. He found himself mesmerized by its sleek, humpbacked shape and by its long hairless tail. But then something inside of him arose that he was totally unprepared for. A deep loathing, an anger so intense he started to tremble, welled up in his chest. Before he knew it, he was dashing across the field with the all pent-up fury of an angry lion. In one fell swoop, he captured the rat and bit off its head.

Ptah gazed curiously at the headless fiend sprawled on the ground before him. Its tail was still twitching, even as blood had started to ooze from its severed neck. He was shocked by what he'd done, and was struggling to come to grips with the idea that deep down inside he was a bloodthirsty killer. Abashed, he looked over at Nebre's family, whose faces were frozen in a unified expression of awe and disgust. All except for Hay, who leaped into the air.

"Did you see that?" he whooped. "The cat can stay!"

17

Smendes

From the moment he killed the rat, there was no question about whether Ptah was welcome at Nebre's house. He practically moved right in, oft times arriving in the wee hours of the morning and then staying for the entire day. More than once Nebre woke to find Ptah standing on his chest, the cat's small black nose inches from his face. In the evenings, however, Ptah always returned to the hidden valley to sleep inside his urn. He couldn't rightly explain it, but beyond what Bastet had told him in his dream, he felt safe inside, as though an awesome power was watching over him.

Rat-killing quickly became a sport for Ptah, one he no longer thought much about. Every time he would slay a new prey, he would carry the body home and drop it at Hay's feet. Much to Hay's delight, Ptah also began accompanying him on his hunting forays into the marsh. Hay was an expert boomerang hunter, and it was not unusual for Egyptians to utilize cats to retrieve the birds they brought down.

One day Ptah and Nebre were up in the kitchen sharpening Nebre's flint knife when Wia approached with a surprise. "I have a present for you," she said, holding out a small, linen-wrapped bundle. Nebre accepted the gift and removed its wrapping, revealing a plain rectangular wooden box tied with a fiber cord.

"What is it?" he asked.

"It's a scribe's kit," said Wia, smiling.

"Wow! Wherever did you get this?" Nebre carried the box to the kitchen table and carefully untied the special knotting that held it together. With a look of awe, he opened the box and proceeded to lay the pieces out on the table. Ptah hopped up and sniffed them. Wia came over and sat by his side.

"I got it at the market the other day," she said. "The man at the shop explained everything to me. Look! This slot is for storing brushes, which is what all of these different-sized reeds are. See how carefully the ends have been chewed so they'll hold ink? Over here is where the cakes of pigment are stored. The small slates beside them are for mixing the pigments with their binders to make ink. And the round stones are for burnishing sheets of papyrus to make them smooth."

"Mother, it's wonderful! But however did you pay for it?" Nebre asked.

"Yes, how *did* you pay for it?" asked a stern voice behind them. The two looked up to see Hay standing at the top of the stairs.

Wia got up from her stool and said quietly, "It cost our family nothing, Hay. I traded the necklace my mother gave me." Ptah looked up sharply. Wia's beautiful blue pendant was missing.

"You traded away your mother's necklace?" Hay sputtered. "Oh, Wia, how could you have *done* such a thing? It was the only nice piece of jewelry you owned!" He strode across the kitchen and slumped on a stool, putting his head between his hands.

"Mother, I had no idea!" cried Nebre. "I feel horrible!"

"Do not feel badly, either of you," Wia said steadfastly. "The necklace wasn't made of real gems, only faience—ground-up quartz melted and colored to look like gems. It had no real value, other than the fact that it came from my mother. Still, I was able to make a good trade for it. I got the nicest scribe's kit they had! It's what my mother would have wanted," she added softly.

"Wia, why did you do this?" moaned Hay. "It's one thing for Nebre to take a few harmless reading lessons from that teacher you told me about, but owning a scribe's kit is a whole different matter. I don't know which pains me more, the fact that you've traded away your necklace, or that you have now given our son false hope when you know his only choice in life is to be a farmer."

"But it's not fair!" protested Wia. "Our son has talent! Why should his options be so limited?"

Just then, Merisu called up from the bottom of the stairs. "Father!"

"Not now, son!" said Hay. "We're right in the middle of something."

"But Father, Smendes is here! He wants to speak with you right away." Merisu's voice sounded edgy.

"Oh, of all times for the landlord to show up!" Hay threw up his hands, then stood. "Go ahead and show him in, son," he called.

Hay, Nebre, and Ptah headed downstairs while Wia rushed to the side of the kitchen and assembled a tray of honey cakes. Placing a pair of drinking bowls beside them, she hurried down to the cellar to fetch a pitcher of beer. After that she brought everything into the reception room and laid it out on the table. Then she straightened her dress and smoothed her hair.

Smendes walked into the room as if he owned the place, which in fact he did. He was a pompous man, tall, with a large potbelly and a bulbous red nose. His fleshy face, crowned by a ridiculous-looking braided black wig, was dotted with pockmarks and bore a pair of puffy red eyes. Were it not for the fine clothing he wore—a crisp, white tunic belted about the waist with a colorful sash and topped by a blue woolen cloak—Ptah thought he might just as easily have been mistaken for the town drunk. The fact that he wore wool clothing at all was a sign of his impudence: wool was forbidden in Thebes because its citizens worshipped the ram.

"Hay! Wia! So nice to see you again!" Smendes bellowed. "Congratulations on your new baby girl! Which reminds me, I meant to send over a fruit basket or something."

"Don't worry about it," said Hay. "Anyway, she's already three months old."

"Would you like to see her?" asked Wia. She hurried to the bedroom, returning quickly with the baby, holding her high for Smendes to see. Smendes, however, wasn't paying any attention. He was looking around the room instead.

"My, just look what you've done to the walls," he said dubiously. "It's a veritable jungle in here! And your furniture—quite nice, actually . . . for a peasant's home, that is."

"Wia made it," said Hay. "I carve, she paints. It's something we do during the times of the flood."

"Hmm, interesting use of color. A pity it looks so . . . different. Doesn't exactly follow the standards," said Smendes, clicking his tongue.

Hay shrugged. "Many people like it that way," he replied. "She's sold some of her pieces, you know."

"Really! I didn't know that. Some people will buy anything if it comes cheaply enough. As for me, I prefer—how shall I say?—more finely crafted furniture myself. But no matter, I didn't come here to buy, I came here to collect!"

Hay and Wia exchanged glances. "Collect what?" asked Hay.

"Why, taxes, of course!" boomed Smendes.

"Taxes . . . so soon? But we've barely finished planting! It's way too early to know how much the land will put forth," Hay objected.

"Now, Hay, you know very well that taxes are always collected well before the harvest," Smendes replied in a mock-fatherly voice. "The gods only *know* much grain would be traded behind my back if I waited 'til then. Besides, everyone knows that this year will bring forth a magnificent harvest due to the good flood we've had."

"But you've come even earlier than usual," said Hay. "There are still so many things that can go wrong."

"Precisely!" said Smendes. "Therefore, it's only fitting that the king and I should claim our fair share before the rats and insects eat into our profits. And anyway, I will be busy later. My son is getting married, and his new wife and her parents will be moving into my villa. An architect is working on designing another wing as we speak. Don'y worry, I'm only expecting to collect partial payment from you right now. Since you don't have any grain yet, you can pay me by helping to build my extension. Brick-making is scheduled to begin in two days."

"Build your extension!" cried Hay. "But I have my own work to do on my farm!"

"You mean *my* farm," corrected Smendes. He sniffed haughtily, then said, "I know you had enough barley left over last year to trade for an ox. Surely your workload has been cut in half. And you have your two strapping young sons to help you, as well. Peasants aren't meant to loll about all day, you know."

Hay's face flushed with anger. "They're *children*—" he began, but then held his tongue, being in no position to argue. Gritting his teeth, he merely grumbled, "Let's get this over with then." Ptah could tell that he was doing his best to control his temper.

Smendes withdrew a papyrus scroll from his sash. "Orders from the king," he said with a wink. He cleared his throat and then began to read out loud: "On behalf of King Mentuhotep, Ruler of Upper and of Lower Egypt, Lord of the Two Lands, Speaker of Truth and Son of Re, it is officially proclaimed that in this Year One of his reign, the crown shall be entitled to twenty-five percent of what each farmer grows. In addition, the percentage owed to landowners will be doubled this year to equal two-thirds of whatever is left."

"What? Taxes have gone up?" cried Hay. "This is an outrage! I was counting on the extra profits a good harvest would bring to put a down payment on my own land!"

Smendes shrugged and set the papyrus on the table, then walked the short distance to where the cakes and beer were laid. He began helping himself to a large portion of each. Ptah jumped onto the table and sniffed the papyrus. Nebre moved quickly to retrieve him. Once there, though, he lingered. He had never seen an official document before and was curious as to what they looked like.

"Don't blame me, I'm only the messenger," mumbled Smendes, his mouth stuffed with cake. "Besides," he continued, "don't think I couldn't use the extra profits myself. I have my son's wedding to pay for, and the extension on my villa. And soon I must begin construction on my temple at the Necropolis. So you see, Hay, I have just as many pressing issues on my platter as you have, if not more."

Hay narrowed his deep-set eyes. "It seems as though the rats have come early this year!" he snapped.

Smendes brushed the crumbs from his mouth, then retorted, "Don't get snippy with me just because you don't like the rules. Has it ever occurred to you that maybe you were simply meant to be a peasant? Do you not understand the Egyptian way? It's not natural for people like you to improve their lot in life. And with the good harvest we're likely to have, you shouldn't end up with too much less than you did last year."

Suddenly, Nebre snatched up the papyrus and cried, "Father! This document says *nothing* about taxes being raised! It says that in order to thank the farmers of Thebes for the part they played in the war effort, taxes will be lowered this year! The king will collect only ten percent of whatever is grown, and it goes on to say that landowners are only entitled to twenty percent!"

In three long strides, Smendes strode to where Nebre was standing and seized the papyrus from his hand. "Where did you learn to read, boy?" he growled. Then, realizing what he had just said, he blurted, "I mean, the boy lies!"

Hay stiffened. "I'll have you know, Smendes, that for all my son may or may not be, he is *not* a liar. Lying is considered to be the worst offense there is in my household, and I can assure you, it is severely punished!"

Wia hurried to embrace her son. Taking him by the shoulders, she said, "Nebre, are you absolutely certain what that document says?"

"I'm certain!" declared Nebre. "I can't read every word, of course, but that's the gist of it. Taxes will go *down* this year."

Hay turned to Smendes, whose fleshy face had turned pomegranate-red. "With all due respect, sir," he said in a calm, cool voice, "I suggest that we take this document over to the tax assessor's office in Thebes. Maybe lack of hard work has clouded your vision. Why don't we have him read it for us?"

"This is an insult!" yelled Smendes, stomping his foot. "I'll have you know, Hay, that the punishment for a peasant who revolts against his landowner is that he is thrown off his land, stripped of his rights! There are plenty of others who would welcome the chance to farm here!"

"I'll take that risk," challenged Hay.

The two stood in heated silence, neither backing down, until finally Smendes said, "Fine! I'll let you go this time, but I'm only doing this because I'm being gracious, what with your new baby and all." With that, he stormed out the door.

Hay ran over and hugged his son. "Nebre, is this the sort of thing that your teacher has been teaching you to do, to read these types of documents?"

"Yes, Father," replied Nebre.

Hay smiled, then said, "Son, run as fast as you can and warn all the other peasants who farm Smendes' land. Hurry! Take the back trail so you're not seen!"

18

The Red Land and the Black Land

The morning after Smendes' visit Ptah sensed a festive mood in the house. He didn't know what was going on, but Hay and Wia were acting very strangely. They kept smiling at Nebre, and at each other, and talking in hushed voices. At first he chalked it up to how happy they were over the incident with the landlord, but there seemed to be more to it than that. It was almost as if they were hiding something.

Then, just before Nebre left for his morning chores, his father approached him and said, "Your mother and I would like to meet this teacher of yours. After you're done with your chores, why don't you go fetch Ipuwer and bring him home for supper?"

So *that* was it. *Why all the secrecy?* Ptah wondered. He and Nebre set out for the fields, where the boy's job that day was to walk among the barley plants pulling weeds. It was a boring, albeit necessary task.

Midway through Nebre's labors, he and Ptah arrived at the sandy slope where the sack of seeds had been spilled. Nebre gasped, then fell to his knees, bending lower to inspect the desert sand. Barley plants had begun to sprout. "That's *impossible*," he murmured. "*Nothing* can grow on the Red Land!" He rubbed his eyes and looked again, then looked all around as if in search of an explanation. Seeing nothing, he shook his head with wonder and proceeded to weed and water the plants. "Why not?" he said to Ptah. "This day is turning out to be filled with mysteries."

When Nebre finished weeding, he scooped up Ptah, then dashed across the fields and down the trail that led to the Necropolis. He halted at the place where he and Ipuwer always met. No one was there.

"Where could he be?" Nebre asked impatiently. He set Ptah on the ground and searched the area, but still saw no sign of his teacher. Worriedly, he started running about, asking people if they had seen an old blind man dressed like a priest, but they all shook their heads no or turned away. He was nearly to the point of tears when finally he saw Ipuwer and Horus slowly making their way toward him.

"Where have you been?" cried Nebre, running up and throwing his arms around the startled old man. "You're late!"

"No, you're early," Ipuwer corrected. "I was down by the river taking my morning bath." Then he smiled and asked, "And to what may I attribute this very warm welcome?"

"My parents want to meet you," Nebre announced. "Come on; I'll tell you about what happened yesterday on the way home."

On the long walk home Nebre told Ipuwer the entire story about his new scribe's kit, and about how Smendes had tried to cheat his father out of undue taxes, and about how Nebre had caught him in the lie by reading the document. Several times he came back to the part where his father stood up for him.

"So the rat got caught in his own trap!" Ipuwer chuckled. Turning suddenly quite serious, he said, "Nebre, you and your family had better be careful. If what I know of Smendes is true, that's not the last you'll hear from him."

When they arrived home, Nebre burst through the door of the house, and then froze in his tracks, speechless. Coming in behind him, Ptah stared wide-eyed. If it weren't for Nebre's parents standing arm in arm in the middle of the room, smiling, he would have sworn that they'd entered the wrong house. The garden on Wia's walls had vanished. In its place was a field of pure white. The room seemed bigger somehow, but empty. To the right of the doorway, Ptah noticed a new sleeping bench on which lay a newly woven mat.

"What's going on?" Nebre demanded.

"Nebre, where are your manners?" Wia exclaimed. She rushed to help Ipuwer to a stool, then hung up his canvas sack, placed his cane by the door, and poured him a beer. Next she fetched Horus a dish of milk. After that she turned to Nebre and said, "Now, why don't you introduce us?"

Nebre just stood in the doorway and gawked.

"Allow me," Ipuwer responded for him, then proceeded to make the introductions.

"Would somebody please tell me what's going on?" Nebre insisted.

Hay heartily shook hands with Ipuwer, then turned to address his son. "Nebre, after what happened yesterday with Smendes, your mother and I decided that we needed to make some changes around here. Wia tells me you've made excellent progress on your reading, but your writing has been hindered by the fact that you've got nothing on which to write. As you know, papyrus is very expensive, and we couldn't possibly break enough pots for you to have pottery shards to write on, so we did *this!*" Hay threw up his arms and grinned.

Nebre just stood there blinking.

Wia smiled. "Son, what your father is trying to say is this: let the walls be your canvas. Fill them with your stories. We want you to write and write, and then write some more until your arm grows weak but your skill grows strong."

"And while you're at it," said Hay, "you can teach Merisu how to read because, as we all know now, every farmer should be able to do just that."

A smile crept slowly across Nebre's face, but then it slackened. "What about that new sleeping bench?" he asked. "Have I grown too old to sleep in the same room with the rest of the family?"

Wia laughed. "That sleeping bench is not for you, Nebre. It's for Ipuwer! That is, if he will honor us by coming to live here."

"What do you say, sir?" asked Hay. "We don't have much to offer, but we have a lot more now than we would have, had it not been for you."

"Your generosity is astounding," replied Ipuwer. "I can assure you, a hearty meal and a place to sleep when the nights are cold is far more than I have now. But I'm not so sure Nebre would like having his teacher living under the same roof. Most boys his age would not, I think."

"Are you joking? I'd love it!" Nebre ran over and gave Ipuwer a hug. "Say you will, please?"

Ipuwer smiled. "All right then, I would be honored to join your family, but on one condition: no more of this 'sir' stuff. Call me Ipuwer."

Later that afternoon Nebre and Ipuwer went back to the Necropolis to continue Nebre's reading lessons. Hay and Wia had decided it would be better if he practiced his writing during the evenings, when the entire family could be there.

Horus and Ptah went along as usual. Resting in the shade of a pillar, Ptah thought seriously about taking a nap. His belly was full from the meal of poached perch and roasted cattails that Wia had made, and he was feeling woozy.

The four of them hadn't been there very long when Ipuwer declared, "Nebre, you seem so distracted. Is it due to the changes at home?"

"What? Oh yes, it's that . . ." replied Nebre, his voice trailing off, "but there's something else, something that's been bothering me all morning. When I was out in the fields . . . well, you really won't believe this, but barley plants have begun to sprout on the Red Land!" He went on to tell Ipuwer how the sack of seeds had been spilled. "The plants are as real as . . . as this pillar here," he concluded, rapping his knuckles against the stone.

Ipuwer rubbed his chin. "This is truly amazing! Nebre, do you realize what this could mean?"

"I do!" exclaimed Nebre. "It means my father could grow even more barley and be able to get his own land that much sooner!"

"Nebre, this is far greater than that. Think of the big picture! The Red Land touches the Black Land all along the Great River. If every farmer on the fringes of the desert were able to add even a few cubits to their croplands, the combined result would be enormous!"

"Good Geb, you're right. We should go and tell my father at once!"

"Nebre, wait!" cautioned Ipuwer. "Your father would put your idea into practice immediately, upon which Smendes would catch wind of it and try to claim it for himself! No, Nebre, your idea is something you must take directly to the king."

"The king! Are you *crazy?*" gasped Nebre. "You yourself said that it was impossible to get past the palace gates!"

"I said it was difficult, maybe, but not impossible," corrected Ipuwer. "Son, I know your chances of getting through are slim, but you've got to try. I'll help you in any way that I can. Tell me, though, there's still one thing I don't understand. The Red Land is on higher ground than the Black Land, which is why the floodwaters don't reach it in the first place. How did you water the plants?"

"I hauled a bucket up there," Nebre replied.

"Oh, that's a problem," Ipuwer said gravely. "On the scale that I'm thinking, it would never do to have farmers lifting heavy buckets all day. I'm afraid that unless we can think of an easier way to do this, your idea will never work."

Nebre leaned his back against the pillar, and then slid to the ground. He and Ipuwer remained quiet for a while, thinking.

"I know," Nebre said at last. "All a farmer would need to do is to build some sort of contraption with a hinged base attached to a long wooden pole with a bucket on the end of it. The hinge would need to swivel, I guess, and there would have to be a rope . . . and also a weight so the farmer could operate the pole like a lever."

"Nebre," Ipuwer said urgently, "you must build that contraption yourself! It's what you need to prove to the king that your idea could work."

"Me?" cried Nebre. "But I've never done anything like that before in my life! I wouldn't even know where to begin. Besides, wood is scarce."

"Then build a small model out of scraps! It doesn't have to be full-size. As for where to begin," said Ipuwer, "use your mind's eye to envision what you've just described to me and then build that. Nebre, I know this is a huge and seemingly impossible task, but the chances of your father getting a farm of his own any time soon depend on it."

"Well, when you put it *that* way, I guess I'll try." By the tone of

Nebre's voice, he obviously was not nearly so certain as Ipuwer that this scheme was going to work.

Meanwhile, Horus's ears were on fire. "Ptah," he hissed. "Did you hear that?"

"Hmm?" Ptah murmured. He'd been dreamily watching a scarab beetle slowly push a ball of dung across the desert sand. The beetle had laid its eggs in the dung and was now searching for a safe place to harbor. Ptah knew that the ancient Egyptians considered the scarab beetle to be sacred, likening the way that it pushed its ball of dung across the sand to the way the sun god Re moved across the sky.

"Ptah, pay attention!" Horus hissed again. "Nebre is planning to go before the king. And when he does, Ipuwer is likely to go with him. This is exactly the sort of opportunity I've been waiting for!" Horus's golden eyes glittered with excitement. "Ptah, promise you'll help. It will be up to us to make sure everything goes smoothly."

19

Miracles Happen

Over the next few weeks Nebre toiled to build a model of his water-transport contraption that actually worked. He had many failures. For an idea that seemed so simple in his head, he could not imagine why it was so difficult to get the pole to be the right length, or to adjust the balance correctly, or to keep the hinge from sticking. Each time he failed, he would fix the source of the problem, only to have something else go wrong. On the good side of things, the barley plants growing on the Red Land were flourishing. Nebre and Ptah visited them daily, carefully watering and tending each little plant as though it was made of pure gold.

Hay and Wia had no idea what their son was up to, but that no longer mattered to either of them. Nebre was getting his chores done, and his tinkering seemed harmless enough. They were even beginning to get used to his strange new habits of getting up at the crack of dawn and of muttering to himself when he walked. With the business of farming in full swing, it was a busy time for all, so nobody paid much attention to what was happening around them.

Wia could hardly contain her excitement over having Ipuwer there. She found him to be a wealth of advice, a willing hand whenever she needed one. Each day when Hay and the boys came home from the fields, Wia would say things like, "Just wait until you taste the new recipe that Ipuwer taught me," or, "You should see the new technique I learned for mending the linens!"

As for Ipuwer, he could not have been happier. He thoroughly enjoyed sharing what tips he knew with Wia, who never failed to make a fuss over them. He adored rocking the baby to sleep, and he loved telling his stories to the boys—stories with names like *The Treasure Thief* or *The Shipwrecked Sailor*. But even more so than that, he relished the feeling of being appreciated again.

Finally one day it happened: Nebre succeeded. His model, about the size of a bread loaf, consisted of a tiny wooden bucket on the end of a long wooden pole, which was attached in the middle by a metal hinge to a wooden base. By use of a weight, the bucket was able to easily swing down, pivot around, and swing back up again. Nebre named his contraption a *shaduf*.

Secretly, he and Ipuwer made plans to go to the palace that very afternoon. To avoid arousing suspicion, they left at the same time they usually did for Nebre's reading lesson. Horus and Ptah went with them as always, and on the long walk to the ferryboat landing, the two cats devised their plan.

"Considering your markings, I think all that needs to happen is for you to show yourself," said Horus. "When the palace gates open, why don't you start winding yourself around Nebre's legs like we cats typically do when we fancy someone? The guards will take one look at you, fall down on their knees, and the rest will be easy."

Ptah could not think of a better plan, so he agreed to do his part.

Once across the river and through the main part of town, the boy and the scribe and the two cats made their way to the palace—a temporary one being used by the king while the new one was under construction. A nobleman's house that had been confiscated shortly after the war, the palace was built like a fortress, with towering walls and thick wooden gates plated with shining copper. After much prodding from Ipuwer, Nebre raised his fist to knock.

Before he made contact, however, Ipuwer exclaimed, "Nebre, wait! Your *cat*! If he looks the way you say he does, the guards will surely take him from you to give to the king! Here, put him in my canvas sack." Ipuwer held out his bag, and before Ptah knew it, he had been plopped inside.

Horus was on this in an instant. The old cat leaped up and down, yelling, "No! Stop! Pull him back out! You need Ptah to get through those gates!" Inside the sack, Ptah took up the cry, shouting, "Let me out! Let me out!" as loud as he could.

"Good heavens, will you listen to these cats!" exclaimed Ipuwer. "Nebre, did you remember to feed them before we left?"

"I did; they ate well," said Nebre. He shrugged, then cinched the strings on the sack and set Ptah on the ground. Horus immediately ran over and began working away at the strings with his claws, while inside, Ptah managed to chew a peephole in the fabric, but it was of no use. Their plan was ruined.

Nebre reached out and knocked, upon which the gates slowly parted and three soldiers emerged.

"What do you want?" growled the man in the middle. He was a stocky brute, as big as an ox, with scars covering most of his face. In his hand was a dagger, which he held out in front of him in a menacing position. The guards on either side of him looked equally mean.

Shrinking back, Nebre said weakly, "Excuse me, sir, but I wish to speak to the king. I have an idea I'd like to share with him."

The guards all looked at each other, then back at Nebre, and then back at each other before they burst out laughing. "Did you hear that?" they howled. "He says he has an *idea* he wants to share with the king!"

The guard on the right bent down low so his eyes were level with Nebre's. "Tell you what," he said grinning. "Why don't you tell your idea to me and I'll take it to the king for you? If he's interested, I'll come back."

"No," Ipuwer said firmly. "This is something the boy must deliver himself. It's important!"

"Quiet, old man!" barked the guard on the left, who then said, "Listen, kid. Let me give *you* an idea. Get lost! The king has no use for charlatans or beggars such as yourselves!" The guards abruptly turned on their heels and went back inside, slamming the gates behind them.

Nebre looked stung, but then his hurt turned to anger. "I *knew* it wouldn't work!" he said. "How could I *ever* have believed we'd get past those gates? I let myself get so caught up in making my model that I forgot about the really hard part: getting in to see the king. Why did I ever agree to do this?" He picked up the canvas bag that held Ptah and stomped off.

"Nebre, wait! I never said you would succeed the first time," Ipuwer called, trailing after him. "You can't give up now. You've only tried once!"

"Once is enough!" snapped Nebre. "I was a *fool* to think that Ptah could help me turn my ideas into reality. I'm just a poor farm boy; that's all I'll ever be!"

"There is no shame in being a poor farm boy," Ipuwer said firmly. "Most of the people who live in Egypt are poor farmers. It is a noble occupation. Without people like you, the rest of us would starve." Taking Nebre by the shoulders, he said, "I'll admit that you were wrong if you thought this would be easy just because you have a god on your side. Life's not like that; you still have to work hard."

"Ha! It would take a lot more than hard work to get in to see the king. It would take a miracle!" Nebre bent down and loosened the strings on the sack, setting Ptah free.

"Then I guess we'll just have to wait for that miracle to arrive," Ipuwer replied matter-of-factly.

What do you mean? I was only joking," said Nebre. "I don't believe in miracles, or . . . or in gods anymore either!" He slumped to the ground, crumpling the sack in his hands.

"Nebre, miracles happen all the time!" exclaimed Ipuwer. "You just have to open your eyes wide enough to see them."

"How can you say that?" Nebre shot back. "Look at you! Where's your miracle?"

"I'll have you know," Ipuwer said softly, "that I've experienced many miracles in my lifetime, not the least of which was you."

Nebre gave him a dubious look, though he knew Ipuwer couldn't see him.

"It's true," Ipuwer continued. "That morning we met I was on my way to the Necropolis, but for some strange reason I went to the ferry-boat landing instead. And there I met a boy who just happened to be searching for the exact same thing I had to offer. As a result, here I am today with a roof over my head, food to eat, people who care for me, and a way to be useful."

"That was just chance," scoffed Nebre. "Besides, how can you say that something so trivial as our meeting was a miracle? Miracles are big! Like when Atum brought forth the mound of earth from the Sea of Nun, or when Geb created the desert mountains, or when Nut brought forth the stars."

"That's not true at all!" exclaimed Ipuwer. "Miracles *can* be big, I'll grant you that, but ones like those are few and far between. Most miracles are small, but they can often set forth something into motion that becomes much bigger. For example, our little meeting completely changed my life . . . yours, too. So you mustn't give up now. You have *got* to keep trying!"

"But I *did* try," said Nebre, "and I don't see how I could possibly do anything different next time."

"Well, if we can't go to the king, then we'll just have to wait for the king to come to us," replied Ipuwer.

"Sure. Maybe when he comes over for supper next time, I'll leap out from the cellar and surprise him with my model," Nebre retorted.

"Don't be sarcastic," said Ipuwer. "There is a Heb-Sed festival coming up next week. You're too young to know what that is, since there hasn't been one for a very long time, but it's when the king comes out among the people and performs a series of athletic events to show off his strength. Usually it's held after the king has ruled for thirty years, but sometimes one is held in honor of a special occasion—like now, when we'll be celebrating the reuniting of the Two Lands. During the festival the king will be well guarded, but we must try to find a way to approach him. You'll just have to do your part to keep your eyes wide open so that if and when your miracle arrives, you are ready to make it work for you."

20

The Heb-Sed Festival

Boom! Boom! Boom! Clash! With the beating of drums and the clashing of cymbals, the palace gates parted and the festival parade began. Drummers, acrobats, dancing girls, and musicians burst forth in an amazing spectacle of color and motion, marching and leaping and cavorting down the wide avenue that ran through the center of town. Lining the street were throngs of people, clapping and cheering and having a good time.

From within the crowd, Ipuwer exclaimed, "Nebre, tell me what you see!"

"I can't see anything just yet," replied Nebre, hopping up and down. "The parade is still too far down the street. And anyway, there are way too many people in front of me!"

Nebre's family had arrived late, Hay having insisted they do some chores before going into town. By the time they got there, all the good places were taken. The family had to make do with an empty patch of dirt sitting unprotected from the sun.

"Tell me about the people, then," said Ipuwer. "What's everybody doing? What are they wearing?"

Nebre looked around. "Well, I've never seen so many people before in my life," he began. "They look to be from all over the country, what with the different styles of clothing they're wearing, and they're all dressed up. The men are wearing fine linen kilts and tunics, and the women have on embroidered dresses edged with tassels and fringes. Everyone's got on lots of jewelry, even the peasants, but you should see the nobles! Each and every one of them glitters with more gold and jewels than my father could earn in a lifetime! And they're wearing those thick dark brown and black wigs, some as wide as their shoulders."

"I can smell their perfumes," said Ipuwer, breathing deeply. "Mostly saffron, I think, but I detect a hint of frankincense and myrrh. What's everybody doing?"

"Most people are watching the parade," replied Nebre, hopping up and down again. "The nobles are all sitting up front on stools under colorful parasols, and they're swaying to the music and eating and drinking and talking. Behind them are the merchants and officials, and behind them are the peasants, like us. Back where the crowd thins out are street vendors selling shish kabobs, cinnamon rolls, and honey cakes."

"Ah, I can smell those, too!" declared Ipuwer.

Ipuwer had been to a Heb-Sed festival before. He'd told Nebre that there would be three events—in this case archery, running, and swimming—and that after each event the king would stop for a few minutes to rest. He decided that Nebre should try to make contact at the very first stop, and if that failed he could try again on the second stop, and so on. Ipuwer had somehow found out the course the king would be taking, and had already chosen three possible places where Nebre might gain access.

Nebre's family was also festively dressed. Wia had on a new linen shift, sewn from finer material than her usual one, and a beautiful necklace made from fresh flowers strung with tassels and beads. Hay and the boys had on new linen hip-cloths, and Ipuwer was wearing a new linen robe. Wia had also sewn Nebre a small canvas knapsack to hold his scribe's kit, which he carried with him always. Ptah and Horus had not been ignored, either. Both cats had been thoroughly brushed, the hairballs having been carefully removed from Horus's fur beforehand. Ptah was every bit as excited as everyone else, and was waiting just as impatiently for the parade to come near.

"Look! It's in front of us now!" cried Wia. By this time the music was playing so loudly she had to yell to be heard.

Nebre and Ptah could stand it no longer. They wormed their way forward until they reached a place where they could see. And what a sight it was! First to pass by were the flag bearers waving colorful banners of purple and gold. Next marched the musicians, who blared out a cheerful tune on their trumpets and horns. After that came the acrobats, performing handsprings and back flips, somersaults and cartwheels. Behind them strode the jugglers, some of whom were juggling balls of wood, but others juggled sticks of fire! Following them marched more musicians playing flutes and drums to accompany the dancing girls, who swished and swirled and leaped and twirled as they frolicked down the street.

After the dancers came people dressed up like gods. Ptah saw Isis and Osiris, and Nut and Geb, and the lordly Thoth, and many more besides. Two people filled most costumes—one sitting on the other's shoulders—so the gods looked larger than life. He even saw a few walking on stilts! Behind the gods strolled the priests, who were waving scepters of incense and looking far too serious for such a joyous occasion. Next came the war heroes, many of whom were deeply scarred or were missing an arm or a leg, but whose faces were etched with pride. The crowd clapped extra loudly as they passed by. And then last, but certainly not the least, Mentuhotep himself appeared.

The king was a solidly built, dark-skinned man with wide-set eyes and a powerful square jaw. He was dressed in a knee-length white kilt trimmed with gold, and a broad, jewel-encrusted belt. His muscular chest was bare except for a stunning gold necklace set with emeralds, turquoise, and lapis. Strapped to his chin was a rectangular wooden beard, painted black, and on his head he wore the crown of Egypt set firmly into place. Ptah knew that the crown was actually a combination of two crowns: a low red hat, once the crown of the northern Delta, merged with a high white peak, once the crown of the South. In his hands the king carried a crook and a flail. Attached to the back of his kilt was a black bull's tail, which swished from side to side as he marched nobly by.

Mentuhotep passed cubits away from where Ptah and Nebre were sitting. The boy jerked forward, then shrunk back, apparently remembering Ipuwer's warning that the parade was not a good time to make contact. So the king continued unhindered down the street, stopping when he reached a large public square where a target had been set up. Here he would show off his archery skills. Bit by bit the crowd gathered around; once again, the best places had been reserved for the nobles.

After giving a short speech, Mentuhotep picked up his bow, whereupon one of his guards handed him an arrow. Then, as a low drum roll sounded, the king took aim and fired. A hush fell over the crowd as the arrow soared through the air, landing dead-center in the middle of the target. Cymbals clashed upon impact and the crowd began to cheer. Taking another arrow, the king shot again, this one also landing sure and true. More cheers went up. After that the event got more interesting as the guards began tossing clay discs into the air so that the king had to strike moving targets. One after another, Mentuhotep hit his mark.

Nebre and Ptah rejoined Ipuwer and Horus, and together they worked their way through the crowd until they reached the place where the king's table had been set up. Using Ipuwer's blindness as a ploy, they managed to get real close: only a single row of guards remained between them and the table. From there they watched and they waited, their minds focused on the task at hand.

Finally, to the roar of the crowd, the king took his last shot and the event ended. The band struck up a boisterous tune as Mentuhotep turned and began walking toward the table. Flattening his ears against the noise, Ptah watched nervously as the king approached. Beside him, Nebre must have been nervous, too, for the king was still too far off when he pushed through the row of guards, shouting, "Sire, I have an idea!"

No sooner had he said these words than the guards were upon him. Snatching him up from behind, the scar-faced brute from the palace tossed Nebre over his shoulder and carried him to the far side of the crowd, where he unceremoniously dumped him onto the ground. "Get lost, boy," he ordered. "The king can't be bothered by pesky flies like you buzzing around!" The guard brandished his dagger and gave Nebre a menacing scowl before returning to the king.

As the crowd drifted apart for the next event, Nebre slunk back to Ipuwer. He was embarrassed by the way he'd been handled and by the way people were now looking at him. "I just made a fool of myself," he sulked. "And the king didn't even notice me."

"Nonsense!" declared Ipuwer. "Besides, why do you care what those people think? You don't even know them." Patting Nebre affectionately on the head, he added, "Come on, cheer up! We've still got two more tries to go." Undeterred, Ipuwer set off for the next table where the king would be taking his rest.

"That's easy for you to say," grumbled Nebre, trailing after him. He rubbed his sore shoulder where it had hit the ground and tried not to limp from the pain in his leg.

Horus and Ptah exchanged glances. "Ptah, we've got to *do* something!" said Horus. "There's too much at risk here to let Nebre try this by himself. We need to distract the guards. I say we use the same plan we were going to use at the palace, only this time I suggest that you wait until the very last moment to show yourself so you don't get popped in the sack again."

Ptah nodded, saying simply, "Right, I'm on it," before dashing off into the crowd.

The next event had already begun. Having stripped off his heavy jeweled belt and necklace, the king had set off running on a course that would take him back along the parade route to the palace gates, west to the river's edge, and then south along the shoreline to the ferryboat landing. The event was intended to show off his speed and endurance.

After Mentuhotep had disappeared from sight, the crowd dispersed, some people going to buy snacks from the street vendors, while others made their way to the ferryboat landing so they could watch the final leg of the run.

Weaving his way through the scattered crowd, Ptah could see Nebre and Ipuwer already in position near the second table. He stopped several yards short of where they were—close enough to see what was happening and to be ready for action, but not so close as to be seen himself. Waving a black paw, he signaled to Horus, receiving the same in return. Then he relaxed; the king would not be returning for many minutes.

Suddenly from behind, a canvas sack came swooping down over his head! It scooped him up so fast he barely had time to realize what was happening. Ptah felt confused—Nebre and Ipuwer were still standing by the table—but then he heard the most horrible sound he could possibly have heard right then.

"I gotcha!"

It was Smendes!

Tightly cinching the strings on the sack, Smendes said gruffly, "I'll teach *you* to go sniffing around in *my* affairs. You cost me a lot, you mangy fur ball, and I aim to make you pay!" Smendes swung the sack over his shoulder while Ptah wiggled and squirmed inside.

"Let's go down to the river," he continued. "I have a big surprise waiting for you there. I'd tell you what it is, but I wouldn't want to *let the cat out of the bag!*" Smendes chuckled a low, evil chuckle, which stopped Ptah's heart mid-beat. The hefty landlord then started walking briskly while roughly shifting the sack from side to side to avoid the claws that were now desperately trying to scratch him from within.

Ptah was frantic. He could hear the throngs of people clapping and cheering as Mentuhotep slowed to a triumphant jog. The noise they made was deafening! He strained his ears until at last he heard Nebre's faint voice, shouting, "Sire, I have an idea!" Then he heard a telltale *ooph!* as the boy was grabbed and hauled away.

As the cheering faded, Ptah could hear and smell the river. It was a rank smell compounded of fish, mud, rotting vegetation, and crocodiles. He could also smell the beer on Smendes, who now stood biding his time, waiting for the crowd to disperse.

"You know how the saying goes," the landlord said. "You can either sink or swim. Well, with a few rocks thrown into your sack for good measure, something tells me that you're going to sink!" He gave Ptah a whack through the fabric of the bag. "Now, for some rocks." Smendes set the sack on the ground and began searching about.

This was the moment Horus had been waiting for. Racing over to the squirming sack, he whispered, "Ptah, it's me! I saw what happened. Pull with your claws!" Then he began gnawing away at the strings with his teeth.

After a few minutes, the cats had managed to widen the opening enough for Ptah to stick his head through, and then his front legs, but that was as far as he got—the strings on the sack had become twisted and had tightened into a knot.

"Hurry, Ptah!" urged Horus.

Ptah struggled harder. He strained and he pulled, but his back legs were caught in the fabric and wouldn't budge.

"I'm stuck!" he wailed.

Suddenly a voice from behind them bellowed, "Hey! What do you think you're doing?" A rock whizzed by Horus's head, barely missing him by an inch.

"It's Smendes!" yelled Ptah.

"Scat, you old flea farm!" Smendes threw another rock, this time hitting Horus smack-dab on the rump.

Horus's golden eyes filled with fury. He whipped around and arched his back, making his speckled fur stand on end. Baring his teeth, he began to hiss. "Ptah, run with the sack if you have to," he shouted between hisses. Horus then leaped in front of Smendes, who was coming up on them fast.

Ptah started running. At once he tripped on the sack and fell, but he picked himself up and started running again, this time moving his front legs only while dragging the sack from behind. Smendes reached down and tried to grab him, but Horus was much too fast for that. He leaped onto Smendes' back, digging his claws in deeply, and then bit the back of the landlord's neck.

To the sound of the scream that followed, Ptah blundered his way forward, lurching and tripping and pulling himself back up. In the distance he could see the final event, already in full swing. The king had waded out into the Nile—milky green this time of year—and was swimming with broad, clean strokes to a barge anchored offshore. Among the crowd of spectators lined up along the shore, Ptah could see Nebre and Ipuwer standing near the king's table, ready to make their move. If only he could get there in time!

Ptah could tell that Nebre's spirits were low. The bruises on the boy's arms and legs had begun to welt, and he hung his head, pouting.

Were it not for the old man standing next to him, with an unwavering determination to see things through, he would surely have run away. As it was, however, Nebre remained rooted where he was, probably hoping and praying that this day would end quickly so they could all go home. Through bleak eyes, he watched as Mentuhotep reached the barge and then turned back around, swimming briskly toward shore.

The king emerged dripping from the water, whereupon two of his guards began toweling him off. Once dry, his attendants replaced his jeweled belt, necklace, and crown. Then, to the roar of the crowd, Mentuhotep began making his way up from the river toward the small clearing where his table had been set.

As Ptah staggered forward, Nebre steeled himself for his final attempt. Waiting until the king drew near, he was just about to leap out and try again, when all at once a mass of guards marched in from the rear and formed a ring around the king seven men deep. This time they were taking no chances that the ragamuffin who had troubled them earlier would do so again.

Nebre cringed. "There's no hope," he said. He went on to tell Ipuwer what had just happened, and described for him how the guards were now moving apart, expanding the circle outward, until Mentuhotep was left standing alone in the ring. Shortly, a few of his advisors and guards joined him. Nebre shuddered when he saw the scar-faced brute who had roughed him up earlier enter the ring.

With a final surge, Ptah came stumbling through the crowd and collapsed at Nebre's feet, his furry chest heaving from exertion.

"Ptah! What has happened to you?" cried Nebre. "How did you get all wrapped up in that canvas sack?" The boy knelt down and tried to untie the strings, but quickly gave up and pulled out his flint knife instead. A few moments later, Ptah flopped onto the ground.

Suddenly Ipuwer reached down and grabbed Nebre's shoulder. "Did you just say that Ptah brought you a canvas sack?"

Nebre shrugged. "Well, he didn't actually bring it to me—it's more like he was all wrapped up in it. But yes, he has one. Why?"

"Oh, why didn't I think of this before?" cried Ipuwer. "Nebre, don't you see? Your miracle has arrived! Hurry! You can use that sack to write down your message to the king!"

Nebre jumped on this plan in an instant. Spreading the sack before him, he opened his scribe's kit, then wetted the ends of a reed in his mouth. Next, in as large of symbols possible, he wrote, "Great King, I have an important idea!" Then he placed the sack on the end of Ipuwer's cane, lifted it skyward, and began slowly waving it about.

21

King Mentuhotep

Mentuhotep cleared his throat and prepared to deliver a short speech. Raising his powerful arms for silence, he turned in a wide arc, looking out among the people. Suddenly, something moving caught his sight. It was a flag or banner of some kind. To the scar-faced guard standing next to him, he said, "What's that?"

The guard looked to where the king was pointing. "It's nothing, Sire," he said scornfully. "Just a troublesome boy who's been following you around all day trying to get your attention. I'll see to him at once." The guard made a move in Nebre's direction.

"Hold on," said the king. "Can't you read his sign? It says he has an important idea! Bring the boy to me. I want to hear what he has to say."

The guard grumbled but did as he was told, and the next thing Nebre knew, he was kneeling before the king.

"You may rise," said Mentuhotep. "Now, what is it, son? What is this idea you have that is so important you would risk your family's honor by coming before me like this?"

Trembling with nervousness, Nebre mumbled, "Well, Sire, I—"

"Speak up, son, I can't hear you," interjected Mentuhotep.

"I've come up with a way to turn the Red Land into Black Land!" Nebre sputtered.

Instantly, whispers and guffaws began to ripple through the crowd. People started snickering and pointing their fingers at Nebre, whose face had turned reddish-brown, like henna. "What foolishness is this?" someone shouted. "The boy's been touched by the gods!"

cried another. Soon the crowd was roaring with laughter.

Watching from a distance, Ptah empathized with the boy. He wouldn't trade places with Nebre for anything! Suddenly, from within the crowd behind him, Ptah heard Wia cry, "Dear Isis, Hay, look! It's *Nebre* who's causing all the commotion! What does he think he's doing out there? People will scorn our family for *years* if he makes a fool of himself! You were right; I've encouraged the boy to go too far. We've got to stop him!" Ptah turned to see Wia surge forward, but Hay put out his arm and held her back.

"No, Wia, wait," he said. "I risked it all on the boy with Smendes, and I'm prepared to do it again. Nebre's *got* to know what's at stake here, so it must be important! He came through for us last time. We owe him this chance."

"Do you think Ipuwer's behind it?" asked Wia.

"If he is, then so much for the better," said Hay, adding, "Let's move forward in the crowd so we can be there for Nebre if he fails at whatever he is attempting to do."

Ptah smiled and returned his attention to the center ring. Mentuhotep had raised his heavy eyebrows in disbelief at what Nebre was saying, but he also raised his arms for silence. The crowd hushed immediately. Looking around, the king shouted, "Listen! I know what you all are thinking. You're thinking that a boy such as this couldn't possibly have an idea worth hearing, that he couldn't possibly be telling the truth. Well, as your new ruler I have this to say to you: let this kingdom be a place where *ideas* are judged, not the people from which they came! Let this kingdom be a place where *all* people—even poor peasants like this boy here—can share their thoughts freely without ridicule or punishment!"

Thinking Mentuhotep had finished, the crowd broke out in whispers. Once again, the king raised his mighty arms for silence. He was just warming up.

"People," he cried, "do not judge a person by the way that he looks! It matters *not* whether a man walks this earth dressed in worn and tattered clothing. If his words speak of kindness and his actions bring goodwill unto others, then *treat him with respect!* By the same token, do not be fooled by fancy clothing or other fine trappings of wealth. If a man's words speak of hatred and his actions bring sorrow, then *do not heed him!* Do not give him your time or encourage him in any way, because he is like the *rot* in a piece of *fruit* that needs to be *cut out!*"

Turning toward Nebre, he said, "Now, son, explain to me how you propose to turn the Red Land into Black Land. We *all* want to hear it." Mentuhotep's dark eyes shot the crowd a menacing glance.

Still trembling, Nebre knelt and made a mound in the dirt with his hands. Beside the mound he drew as straight a line as his shaky fingers would allow.

"Okay, pretend for a moment that this is the flood line," he began. Pointing to the mound beside it, he said, "On this side of the line is the Red Land, the desert sand beyond the reaches of the flood." Pointing to the other side, he said, "And over here is the Black Land, the fertile farmland of the farmers' fields. Are you with me so far?"

"Yes, keep going," replied Mentuhotep.

"Okay. I believe that the only thing the Red Land needs in order to grow food is water and some nutrients," Nebre went on. "I believe that farmers could increase their yields by sowing the Red Land that touches the Black Land all along the Great River. The farmers could irrigate this land by digging their retaining ponds closer to the desert, like this." Nebre dug a small hole next to the line in the lower half of the dirt. "To help the water flow freely, they could dig canals in the Red Land like this," he added, drawing several thin lines in the mound beside it.

Mentuhotep scratched his head. "I see all that," he said. "But the Red Land is on much higher ground than the Black Land, which is why the floodwaters don't reach it in the first place. How do you propose to fill those canals?"

"With this!" exclaimed Nebre, leaping up and running over to Ipuwer and Ptah. Retrieving his model from Ipuwer's sack, he carried it into the ring and placed it on the ground. Kneeling beside it, he said, "I call this a shaduf," and he went on to explain how it worked.

When he was finished, Mentuhotep looked kindly upon Nebre and said, "Son, I commend you for your innovative thinking. Your idea is very intriguing. However, everyone *knows* that even if water and nutrients were added to the Red Land, it would not grow food. It's impossible!" The crowd started snickering again.

Ipuwer stepped forward. "Who among you has tried it?" he cried. The snickering subsided as people began turning their heads, looking at others around them. Not a single person raised his hand. Even the king was silent.

"I have tried it, Sire, and it works!" declared Nebre, rising to his feet. "On my father's farm, I have seen for myself that the only thing the Red Land needs in order to grow food is water and some nutrients. If you like, you may come see it also."

"Do you mean to say that your father's farm has plants growing on the Red Land this very moment?" the king asked.

"Yes, Sire. Barley plants, Sire," replied Nebre, who was feeling much more confident now knowing he had the proof to back up his words.

The king turned to his advisors and asked, "What do you think of this plan?"

"I think it's truly amazing!" exclaimed one. "The boy's idea is so simple, and yet so elegant, I'm surprised no one thought to try it before."

"I agree," said another. "We'll need to test it, of course, but if his idea works as well as I think it will, do you realize what it could mean? All the new farmland brought under cultivation by this method could be claimed by the crown. The surplus crops could be used to trade for wood, gold, jewels. Sire, if his idea works, you could keep the taxes low and still become rich beyond your wildest dreams!"

"Then give this model to our engineers and have them start working on a full-size model at once!" commanded Mentuhotep, smiling.

Addressing Nebre again, he said, "Congratulations, son! As my advisors have said, your accomplishment is truly amazing, especially given your standing in life. Tell me, however did you come up with such an idea? And for that matter, wherever did you learn to read and write? It's highly unusual—to say the least—that in a country such as ours, where only one out of a hundred people knows how to read, a boy such as yourself is able do just that."

"I learned from Ipuwer, the best teacher there is on Geb's green earth," exclaimed Nebre. He went over and gently took the old man's hand, and then led him into the ring. The boy motioned for Ptah to come too, but Ptah refused. He didn't dare show himself for fear all of the attention would suddenly shift to him.

"Did I just hear you say the name Ipuwer?" Mentuhotep asked as Nebre rejoined him in the ring. Shaking the old man's hand, he said, "You couldn't possibly be the same Ipuwer who wrote so eloquently about the Chaos Years, could you?"

"Yes, Sire, the very same," replied Ipuwer, bowing low. "It is an honor to meet you at last."

"The honor is all mine!" exclaimed the king. "Why, it was your writings that inspired me to raise an army and reunite the kingdom in the first place! All this time I thought you were dead. What a joyous day this has turned out to be! You must come and live at the palace. You can have your own staff of servants, your very own quarters . . . you can even teach at the palace school if you like."

Ipuwer smiled. "Your offer is very gracious, Sire, but my place is with Nebre and his family." He placed his hand gently on Nebre's shoulder.

Mentuhotep looked from the boy to the scribe and then back again before saying, "Then you can *all* move into the palace! What do you say, son? Would you like to train to be a scribe?"

Nebre's face lit up like a lamp, but just as quickly the glow faded and he said, "I don't know, Sire. My father is a farmer with strong ties to the land. I doubt he'd be very happy living within the confines of a palace. And as for training to be a scribe, well, I . . . I am to be a farmer just like him, and like his father before that." Nebre lifted his chin and pulled back his shoulders, trying hard to look proud, but his lips were quivering as he spoke.

"A farmer . . . I see. Where is your father's land?" the king asked.

"Oh, he doesn't own his own land just yet," replied Nebre. "Right now we farm part of the land owned by Smendes. But my father works very hard! And he *will* have his own land someday soon, you will see!"

Mentuhotep folded his hands across his jeweled belt and nodded slowly. "I think I understand the situation quite clearly now, and I think I know *exactly* what your father would like."

"Well, you can ask him, because there he is now," Nebre exclaimed, suddenly spotting his parents standing in the crowd. Mentuhotep motioned for Hay and Wia to come forward; a few moments later, they were bowing before the king.

"You may rise," he said.

After introductions were made, Mentuhotep turned to Hay. "I have a proposition to make to you," he said. "Your son, here, has come up with an idea that could prove to be quite profitable for me. If his idea works as well as my advisors think it will, then your family will be granted a choice piece of farmland quite near to the palace."

Hay's mouth dropped open and his eyes grew wide.

"There is one condition, however," the king went on, "and that is that you must agree to let Nebre train to be a scribe, with Ipuwer as his primary teacher, of course. I will provide you with one of my servants to make up for the fact that you will have lost a pair of useful hands. So tell me, what do you think? You do not have to give me an answer today, of course. You may think about it and—"

"Agreed!" sputtered Hay.

"Does this mean that I'll have to shave my head and wear one of those silly braids on the side like the palace boys do?" Nebre asked.

"Are you referring to a sidelock? No, not if you don't want to," Mentuhotep replied, smiling.

Wia turned to Ipuwer. "Are you sure you don't want to move into the palace?" she asked. "You would be given your own staff of servants, and they could do everything for you. We certainly can't compete with that," she added wistfully.

"What?" exclaimed Ipuwer. "And miss being there when your baby takes her very first steps, or when Merisu brings down his first duck with that boomerang he's been practicing with? I still have *hundreds* of stories to tell! If your family will continue to have me, my place is in your home. Especially since it will soon be a nice, new home!"

The king laughed. "Fine then, it's settled! Tomorrow we shall visit Hay's farm to see for ourselves this miracle Nebre speaks of."

Suddenly, from down by the river, a horrified scream ripped through the crowd. "Cat killer! Murderer!" it cried. The crowd quickly parted to reveal Smendes. Horus lay dead at his feet.

"I didn't do it!" protested Smendes. "That cat just sort of up-and-died. I swear it!"

"Then why are you all covered with bites and scratches?" an angry man demanded.

"I . . . I—" faltered Smendes.

"Let's get him!" yelled the crowd.

Smendes took off running, a mob of angry Egyptians chasing after him. Meanwhile, Nebre turned to Ipuwer, his eyes brimming with tears. "Oh, Ipuwer, it's Horus! He's . . . he's dead!"

"Take me to him, son," Ipuwer said solemnly.

Nebre led Ipuwer to the place where Horus lay sprawled on the ground. With a heavy heart, Ptah followed. Ipuwer knelt beside his beloved old friend and stroked his fur while gently prodding the bones of his body. "He doesn't seem to have suffered any trauma. There are no broken bones," he said at last. "Nebre, look at his face and tell me what you see."

Ptah followed Nebre's gaze as he studied Ipuwer's cat. Horus looked peaceful, happy even. There was something about the way the corners of his mouth were turned up in a mischievous grin that made Ptah do a double-take. *I know I'm being silly,* he thought, *but Horus looks just like he's played a fine joke on someone and can't stop laughing.* Nebre must have seen the same thing, for that's what he told Ipuwer.

"Smendes didn't kill my cat," Ipuwer said, his dark eyes glistening. "It was simply Horus's time to go."

"Shouldn't we say something then? About Smendes, I mean?" asked Nebre. "Those people look angry enough to stone him."

"Egyptians have a way of taking the law into their own hands when it comes to cat killers," said Ipuwer. Pausing, he mused, "No,

I think we should let Smendes get whatever he's due. Something tells me that's what Horus would have wanted."

Later that evening Wia carefully prepared Horus for his final rest. Following Ipuwer's instructions, she sprinkled his body with natron salt and special oils scented with myrrh and cassia. Then she wrapped him from head to tail with strips of linen coated with adhesive resin until he was all done up like a little mummy. When she was finished, Wia painted a large pair of golden eyes and a mischievous grin over Horus's face. While she worked, Ipuwer sat next to her in a cross-legged position, chanting spells and incantations in a musical voice.

Ptah sat off to one side and watched the ritual with a mixture of emotions. He was happy for Horus, who had finally crossed over into the beautiful world of music and light, but he was sad for himself. He missed his dear old friend. Death, he decided, was not nearly so bad for the one to go as it was for those who were left behind.

Horus was to be laid to rest downriver on the Island of Bubastis. There he would be given a place of honor among the hundreds of cats already buried in the Temple of Bastet. The temple was known to be one of the loveliest in all of Egypt. Its pinkish stone building graced a serene setting of flowering gardens and manmade lakes surrounded by sacred persea trees. Mentuhotep had arranged for a boat to take Ipuwer, Nebre, and Ptah to the island the very next morning.

It had been a long day for everyone, so by the time the sun had set, Nebre's family was ready to go straight to bed. It was a cool, clear night as Ptah made his way up the pathway that led to the hidden valley. He was glad that Nebre had finally told his parents about the urn, and that they would be bringing it to the house upon their return.

Passing through the narrow crevice that marked the valley's entrance, Ptah stopped for a moment to look around. Despite the full moon that shone brightly that night, the valley seemed even more desolate than usual. The complete and utter silence felt as much a presence as it did a void, and the shadows that loomed near the base of the rocks looked like deep holes leading into the Underworld.

Forcing himself to go on, Ptah crept the rest of the way to his urn and crawled inside. For a while he just lay there thinking about Horus and wondering what the next world was like. His thoughts then turned to others he knew, like Imhotep, who had already passed into that world, and the professor, who had yet to be born in this one. But these thoughts were fleeting, and soon the soft hissing sound that hummed inside his urn lulled him to sleep.

Ptah Dreams:
Thoth

That night, when the radiant moon had reached its peak and a donkey brayed deep in the heart of the valley, Ptah had his third strange dream.

He dreamed he was standing in a storage room, much like the one he had found himself in when he first arrived in Egypt, except that it was filled with treasures even more wondrous than those Imhotep had received. Everything in it was fit for a king! He saw delicately carved tables and huge wooden chests, golden dishes and gleaming copper pots. He saw vases and jars made of alabaster and faience, and tools and papyrus scrolls that could be used for writing. There was a vast selection of wigs, and necklaces and armbands inlaid with semi-precious stones. There was even a small army of shabit—painted wooden servants that could be summoned to life in the Underworld to answer a king's every beck and call.

There were no windows in this room; however, an oil lamp shone brightly from a table in one corner. Sitting at the table, busily writing on a long papyrus scroll, was a strange creature with the head of an ibis and the body of a man. Ptah knew at once who this creature must be: Thoth, the divine scribe, god of knowledge and the written word.

Curious as to what the birdman was doing, Ptah walked closer and said, "Excuse me, sir, but what are you writing?"

Thoth glanced up and scowled at Ptah, then bent his head back down and continued writing.

Thinking the creature had not heard him, Ptah repeated, "Excuse me, sir, but—"

"Silence!" roared Thoth. "I must work quickly! They will be coming at any moment!"

"Who will be coming at any moment?" asked Ptah, taken aback by the anguish in the creature's voice.

"Desecrators—evil ones who would destroy the king!" Thoth boomed.

Ptah gasped. "What desecrators?" He had no idea what desecrators even were, although from the tone of Thoth's voice, he knew they must be bad.

Thoth stopped writing for a moment and glared at Ptah. "If you must keep talking, young cat, then at least make yourself useful. Start naming the objects in this room. I'm done listing all of the things along that wall, but I have everything else in here to go, plus two rooms after that. Begin there." He pointed a long, slender finger at a pile of treasure.

Ptah ran to the spot and named the very first object he came to. "A vase," he said.

"Be more descriptive!" ordered Thoth. "There's bound to be many more vases than that. What does it look like?"

Ptah studied the vase for a moment before saying, "An alabaster vase covered with amethyst jewels."

"Good, now keep going!" encouraged Thoth. "But hurry, we've no time to lose!" A muffled tapping noise, like the sound of a ticking clock, could now be heard coming from the wall behind where Thoth was sitting.

Ptah quickly began running from one object to another, describing them as best he could, while Thoth scribbled away on his long papyrus scroll. Faster and faster they went, Ptah not really knowing what all the fuss was about, but hurrying just the same. All the while the tapping noise behind the wall kept getting louder, and was beginning to sound more and more like the hammering of metal against stone.

Ptah felt exhausted when they finished. He collapsed in a dazed heap while Thoth gathered up his writing instruments. Rolling up his scroll, the god rose to go.

"Thank you, young cat. I have recorded everything," he said. "Now no matter what happens, the king will have his treasures during his next life in the Underworld." Thoth bowed deeply and then vanished.

Part 4

What Makes a Man Great

New Kingdom
Thebes, 1275 BCE

22

Tomb Robbers

Chink! Chink! Chink! Chink! Ptah was disturbed from his sleep by a steady pounding that sounded like the hammering of metal against stone. He opened his eyes and looked up from the base of his urn. The stars were shining brightly overhead; it was still night.

Chink! Chink! Chink! Chink! As Ptah lay there listening to the rhythmic hammering, he thought about the strange dream he'd been having. His dream had seemed so real!

Chink! Chink! Chink! Ptah was just beginning to drift back to sleep when the hammering stopped. Now he could hear voices—grunts and groans as if heavy work was being done, mixed with murmurs of excitement. *What could possibly be going on out there?* he wondered. Curiosity finally got the better of him so he decided to go see.

Although it was night, the full moon lit the valley like a stage, casting deep shadows amongst the rocks. In many ways, the valley looked just like the moon itself—a desolate landscape of rock and sand. Ptah stood there listening for a moment before he realized that the voices were coming from further on up the trail, around the bend that led deeper into the valley. Heading in that direction, he was surprised to see that the pathway had been widened and the rocks that normally littered the trail were gone. *When did that happen?* he wondered.

Rounding the bend, Ptah could see about half a dozen men busy working. Tipping the end of his ropy tail in greeting, he was just about to go up to them when he caught himself. The men he was seeing were strangers, and not very nice-looking ones at that. Their clothes were ragged and filthy, and their faces had been darkened with soot. Attached to their belts he saw razor-sharp daggers glinting in the moonlight.

Ptah crouched off to the side of the trail and watched what the men were doing. They appeared to be pulling things straight from the hillside—fabulous things, like delicately carved pieces of furniture and beautiful objects made of gold. The men were loading the treasures onto a donkey caravan standing nearby. Suddenly Ptah's stomach lurched, for there in the hands of one of the men was an alabaster vase covered with amethyst jewels, just like the one he had dreamed about!

Ptah was baffled. What he was seeing made no sense at all. The Middle Kingdom kings didn't dig their tombs in a valley. They dug them in the cliffs overlooking the town of Thebes. He was trying to sort this all out, when suddenly from behind, an arm reached around his neck and grabbed him by the throat! Something sharp was pointed at his face.

"Put up your paws and pull in your claws!" a voice hissed. It was a cat!

"Who . . . who are you?" Ptah stammered, struggling to break free.

The cat tightened his grip. "I was just about to ask *you* the same question," he hissed, "except that I *know* who you are. You're one of *them*—a tomb robber! Probably a scout keeping watch. Well, you're my prisoner now!"

"Let me go! I'm no thief!" Ptah shouted.

"Yes, you are!" yelled the cat, wrestling Ptah to the ground. The two cats started to fight—biting and clawing and kicking as they rolled round and round in the sand.

A man's voice cracked the night. "What's that racket?"

The two cats instantly froze.

"Sounds like a couple of cats fighting," bellowed another. "Hey, Baba, why don't you go check it out? See if you can find those cats and shut them up—for good!"

Ptah's attacker quickly let go of him, and both cats bounded to their feet. One of the thieves was heading their way.

"Now look what you've gone and done!" snapped the cat.

"Me? You started it," blurted Ptah, who quickly added, "I don't know about you, but I'm getting out of here!" He darted back down the trail and scrambled up the hillside, the other cat hot on his tail. They dove behind a large outcropping of rocks just as the thief named Baba came lumbering round the bend. He was brandishing his dagger, looking for a target.

"So," whispered the cat hoarsely, "if you're not with them, then who *are* you with?"

Ptah turned to face his attacker. Now that he wasn't wrapped in the other cat's clutches, he was able to get a good look at him. The cat was a little on the small side, but he looked lion-tough. He had a lean, muscular body covered with short brown fur that had black stripes running though it all the way down to his ringed tail. His face was fixed with a look of absolute determination, and his hazel-green eyes glared back at Ptah, waiting for an answer to his question.

"I *said*, who are you with?" repeated the cat more forcefully.

"I . . . I'm with Nebre and Ipuwer," Ptah began, becoming all flustered. "And before that I was with Imhotep, and before that—"

"Ipuwer, the sage?" interrupted the cat testily. "Now you listen to me, buster. Don't go thinking you can pull any of your tomfoolery onto this cat! I'm much too clever for that. Ipuwer's been dead for nearly eight hundred years, and Imhotep . . . why, he's been gone for nearly twice that long. In fact, Imhotep's been gone so long people now think of him as a god! What did they teach you in spy school, anyway?"

"*What?*"

"Shhh, keep your voice down," whispered the cat. He tipped his ear in the direction of the thief, who was now looking their way. The two cats ducked lower, blending with the shadows of the rocks.

Baba took several steps up the hillside toward them, and then stopped. Squinting around in the dark, his attention suddenly shifted elsewhere, and he headed back down. "I don't see any cats here now," he called. He strolled over to a large cluster of rocks sitting beside the trail. Reaching behind it, he yelled, "Hey, look what I just found!"

Ptah gasped. The thief had picked up his urn!

"This thing looks like an antique," Baba announced giddily as he held the urn up to the light of the moon. "Must be a thousand years old, maybe more. And in such good condition, too—it looks practically new! I'll bet it's worth its weight in gold. Hey, Pepy, you're the artist, take a look at this!" Baba turned and began striding down the trail toward the others.

"My urn!" Ptah cried. "I've got to get it back!" He lunged forward, but the other cat stretched out his paw and held him back.

"Wait!" he hissed. "You can't take on those thieves by yourself. There are way too many of them. Why don't you stay put until they're done loading the donkeys? Then we can follow them to their hideout. This has been my plan all along."

"Your plan? What do you mean? Who are you, anyway?" asked Ptah.

"I'm Khufu, Chief Warrior Cat of the Royal Egyptian Army," the striped cat announced, snapping to attention. "I belong to Souti, Chief of the Charioteers and Driver of his Majesty's Chariot. As you probably guessed, I'm named after the famous King Khufu, the pharaoh who built the largest pyramid of them all on the plains at Giza." Khufu lifted his chin even higher and puffed out his chest.

Ptah sniffed. By the airs this cat was putting on, he obviously thought his name was a sign of his own importance. Returning to the subject at hand, Ptah said, "You were saying something about a plan?"

"Oh, yes, my plan," Khufu responded, relaxing his guard. "You see, I'm on a mission here tonight to catch those thieves. It's been weeks since I first started watching them dig all over the Valley of the Kings, and now that they've hit pay dirt, so will I! Ramses will be sure to award me a medal of honor for this!"

Ptah gulped. *Ramses! Valley of the Kings!* All at once, panic gripped his chest and his ears became filled with a rushing sound. He struggled to stay focused while the cat beside him continued, ". . . and now that I know you're not with them, you may have the honor of joining my army to help me catch them. I'll make you my captain."

"Your captain!" Ptah exclaimed, regaining his senses. "I don't know about that. How many cats do you have in your army, anyway?"

"None yet," Khufu confessed. "Those dumb cats over in Thebes. All they want to do is eat and sleep all day. But not me; I've got big plans. And besides, who needs them now that I have you?"

"Well, count me out, too," said Ptah. "I'm a lover, not a fighter."

Khufu narrowed his hazel-green eyes. "Do you want to get your urn back?"

"I *must* get it back," said Ptah.

"Fine, then it's settled. You'll have to come with me." Before Ptah could object any further, Khufu set off running on a course that took him across the hillside and over to a new outcropping of rocks situated directly above the tomb robbers. Reluctantly, Ptah followed.

"Look!" Khufu whispered. "If I'm not mistaken, they're just about ready to go."

The tomb robbers were indeed ready to go. The donkeys, now laden with treasure, had begun a slow, single-file march down the trail that led deeper into the valley. Unnoticed by all, Khufu and Ptah scampered down from the hillside and crept closely behind.

"Where are they going?" whispered Ptah. "I thought the entrance to the valley was back that way." He tipped his ear in the direction he had always taken from Nebre's house.

"The main entrance is heavily guarded, even at night," replied Khufu. "They'll probably be taking the southern way out, although they'll have to pass right by the Medjay's fortress to do it. The thieves would never dare try this during the daytime, of course. The Medjay are master Nubian archers from the deserts east of the Nile—every one a crack shot! But at night the lookout tower is manned by only one guard, so the chances of getting through are better."

Soon, just as Khufu had predicted, the donkey caravan turned south onto a well-defined trail that zigzagged up the rim of cliffs. Eager to be moving along, the robbers whipped the poor beasts with leather straps, mumbling curses as they went. After a while they reached the top, where the Medjay's fortress stood sentinel over the valley. A solid-looking building made of thick mud brick, the fortress blended so well into the hillside that Ptah didn't even notice it until they had reached its base. Glancing about, he secretly hoped that Khufu would be wrong and there would be plenty of guards on hand; but overall the place looked deserted.

"Why don't we do something now?" he asked. He was anxious to recover his urn and put an end to this unfortunate situation.

"Shhh, this isn't the time," whispered Khufu. "I don't know about you, but I smell a rat! If you'll look directly above us, you'll see that the lookout tower is empty. And those robbers are sure making a lot of noise for men who should be more than a little concerned about waking up the guards."

Ptah hated to admit it, but Khufu seemed right. It did seem a bit fishy for robbers to be brazenly passing by the fortress, even at night, without so much as gagging the donkeys or slowing them down. Disheartened, he stuck by Khufu's side as the robbers skirted the side of the fortress and moved to the back. From there they continued south, high atop the rim of cliffs that paralleled the river valley. Looking to the east, Ptah could see the darkened hulks of the Necropolis and the broad expanse of fields stretching all the way out to the river. From the look of the many shadufs, rising like dinosaur skeletons near the edge of the desert, Nebre's invention had clearly worked. Beyond the fields, he could just make out the town of Thebes as it lay sleeping across the Nile.

The trail stuck to the ridge for a short while, then dropped down on the western side. The valley and its lush greenery fell from view as the robbers and the cats descended into the bleak terrain of the desert. The course that they followed was still well worn at this point, and Ptah was just beginning to wonder where they could possibly be going when he spied a small village nestled into the wall of cliffs.

23

The Village of Dier el-Medina

The robbers approached the village and waited outside the gates while the thief named Baba produced a set of keys and quietly opened them up. Goading the donkeys inside, the robbers closed the gates behind them, leaving Baba outside to keep watch.

Khufu and Ptah scampered to the place where the top of the village wall met the side of the cliff. From there they tiptoed along the wall, arriving at the gates just in time to see the robbers entering the first house on the right.

"Where are we now?" Ptah whispered.

"We're at the village of Deir el-Medina," replied Khufu. "It's where the artists who work on carving and painting the kings' tombs and temples live. You'd never know it," he added, flicking his ringed tail toward the village below. "This place could certainly use an artist's touch."

Ptah had to agree. The houses—maybe sixty of them in all— were little more than hovels. Some had roofs that were rife with holes, while others had walls that were crumbling to dust. Not one tree or bush grew in the village; it was as barren as the desert hills surrounding it. Looking down from above, Ptah thought that the layout of the village looked a little like a fish's skeleton—the narrow street running down its middle forming the fish's backbone, while the walls that separated the tightly packed houses resembling the fish's spines.

"Why would any artist want to live *here?*" he asked.

"To work in the Valley is every artist's dream," replied Khufu.

"Even with the rotten living conditions, there's no better place to practice one's craft. Few Egyptians besides the king can afford to buy the quality of materials these artists are given to work with. And it's not so bad, really. Food and water are brought in by donkey every day, and the artists are free to do side work on their days off, so many are able to purchase a nice villa in town when they retire."

"Why do you think the robbers came here?" asked Ptah.

Khufu shrugged. "My guess is that the house they went into belongs to an artist who believes he's not getting paid what he thinks he's worth. I'd also be willing to bet that at least one of the pharaoh's guards is in on the heist. Ramses' guards keep a pretty tight watch over the Valley; if they loosened up tonight it means that someone from the inside must be involved."

The thieves began unloading the treasures from the donkey caravan and taking them into the house. Although working as quietly as they could, they still made considerable noise.

"Aren't they worried they'll wake everyone up?" Ptah asked. The houses were scrunched so tightly together he wondered how anyone could do anything without the whole village noticing.

"If they're not, then they should be," said Khufu. "Tomb robbing is a capital offense! Those robbers aren't going to get off lightly if they're caught . . . I mean, *when* they're caught."

After a few minutes, Khufu said urgently, "Okay, we've sat here long enough. Here's the plan. I'm not going to ask you to put yourself into any kind of danger; I'll take care of that. What I want you to do is to stay up here on the top of this wall and watch for the guards. My owner, Souti, is heading up the patrol tonight, and he usually checks on the village shortly after sunrise. In the meantime, I'll go down to where the thieves are and lay in wait. When you see the patrol, all you have to do is to give me a signal, like this." Khufu swished his tail back and forth. "Once I see the signal, I'll start howling, the guards will come running, and before you know it, the honor and glory will be mine! Does that sound all right to you?"

Ptah thought it over. Khufu's plan seemed simple enough, and besides, what could possibly go wrong? He scanned the pathway they had taken from the ridge top, looking for signs of the patrol, while Khufu ran back along the village wall to the place where it met the cliff. From there he jumped down—this time inside the village— then he scampered into the shadows near the gates to wait for the signal. Meanwhile, the robbers had gotten serious about unloading and were moving at a fast pace.

As Ptah waited for the patrol to show up, the sky began to lighten in the east, heralding the break of dawn. Slowly the outline of the ridge top above him became backlit with hues of orange and yellow, while to the west, the depths of the desert remained cloaked in darkness. He was reveling in this exuberance of color when all at once he saw them! Marching along the rim of cliffs, silhouetted against the gingery backdrop of the sky, were six Nubian men dressed in the uniform of the crown. Ptah was surprised at first to see that these men weren't Egyptian, but then he remembered Khufu telling him that the Medjay guarded the Valley.

The patrol descended from the ridge and advanced toward the village. Nervously, Ptah glanced back over his shoulder to check on the robbers' progress. They were nearly finished! One of the thieves was already leading the donkeys quietly down the street while the others were carrying the last bits of treasure into the house. Peering down on the other side, Ptah noticed that the thief named Baba was still standing near the gates, apparently oblivious to the fact that the patrol was coming up on him fast.

By the light of dawn, Baba did not look nearly so menacing as he had in the Valley. A heavy-set man with coppery-colored skin and bushy black hair, Baba had the kind of jovial but vacant expression on his face that made Ptah wonder whether the lights were all on inside.

Suddenly, Ptah did a double-take. In shock he now realized that Baba had changed his clothing and was presently dressed in the uniform of a guard! Very quickly Ptah changed his opinion of this man, now knowing he must be one of those few Egyptians to be allowed to join the Medjay. *Khufu was right,* he thought. *Somebody from the inside was in on the heist!* Confused, Ptah was trying to sort this all this out, when Baba stepped away from the gates and headed down the path, greeting the patrol as they came walking up.

"Ho, Souti!" he called.

"Baba! What are you doing here? Isn't this your night to man the lookout?" The young man at the head of the patrol broke into a broad grin, made all the more vibrant by its contrast with his dark brown skin. Ptah couldn't help but notice that Khufu's owner was at most twenty years of age; his tall and wiry frame hadn't finished filling out yet. Despite the stately uniform he wore—a crisp pleated kilt topped by a bronze coat of mail—Souti looked to be the high-spirited sort, and he had a certain boyish charm.

"I heard rumors of a disturbance in the village so I came to check it out," replied Baba. "But I'm happy to report they were rumors, nothing more."

"So you've already checked on the village? Well then, I guess our work is done for the night," said Souti. He signaled his men to leave.

Up on the wall, Ptah panicked. In all of his confusion over Baba, he had forgotten to give the signal! Instantly he began swishing his tail from side to side while hoping and praying that Khufu was watching.

He was! Like a cat with its tail caught on fire, Khufu sprang from the shadows and began racing around in circles howling, "Guards! Guards!" at the top of his lungs.

Outside the gates, Souti whirled back around. "What's that?" he shouted. The patrol halted.

"It's nothing, only a cat," Baba replied nervously. "Seems as though the cats are out all over the place tonight. Must be the full moon. Forget it! Let's go back to the fortress. I could sure use a cup of hot tea. How about you?"

Baba took several steps down the path, but Souti remained standing where he was. "That cat sure is making a lot of noise," he said. "Maybe we should go see what we can do to help. The gods would look unkindly upon us if we left a poor creature in distress."

Baba was about to respond when, just as quickly as it started, the howling stopped. "See?" he said. "I told you it was nothing. Let's go!"

"I guess you were right," said Souti, frowning. "I know this sounds crazy, but for a moment there, I could have sworn that cat was yelling for the guards." He shook his head and laughed.

Baba eyed him suspiciously. "You'd better be careful, Souti. People are already gossiping about the way you whisper to the horses. I can only imagine what they'd think if they heard you say that!"

Souti blushed. Turning about face, he announced, "Okay, men, let's call it quits for the night." The patrol reversed direction and began walking down the path, apparently satisfied the disturbance had been taken care of.

Up on the wall, Ptah searched the shadows, wondering what could possibly have made Khufu stop howling. To his horror, he saw the reason why. Khufu had been caught! Directly beneath him a struggle was going on, with Khufu biting and clawing to save his life while one of the robbers was trying to get a stranglehold around his throat!

Clamping down on his fears, Ptah plunged off the wall, landing smack-dab onto the robber's back. He dug in his claws deeply, then took up the cry, yelling "Guards! Guards!" at the top of his lungs.

The robber shrieked. He spun round in circles, trying to swat Ptah off his back. Khufu took advantage of the situation and bit the man on the hand. The robber cursed and let go, whereupon Khufu fell to the ground and shouted, "Ptah! Follow me!"

Ptah leaped off the robber's back. He didn't know whether the patrol had heard his alarm, but one thing was certain—the robbers sure had! No sooner had he hit the ground than they burst forth from the house like a swarm of angry hornets.

"It's those same two cats we heard over in the Valley. Kill them!" they cried. Next thing Ptah knew, he and Khufu were running for their lives, dodging swords and daggers while screaming at the top of their lungs.

This time, Souti didn't hesitate for a moment. "Back to the village!" he cried.

The patrol rushed the gates, barreling through to the other side. "Drop your weapons and surrender!" they shouted, but the robbers weren't about to give up without a fight. They quickly switched their focus from the cats to the guards, and soon the narrow street became a battleground, with both sides determined to fight to the finish.

Awakened by the noise, the artists of the village began flinging their doors open wide. Ptah ran for safety, but Khufu stayed right in there, biting and kicking for all he was worth. Swords clashed, punches were thrown, and the fur was flying, but in the end the robbers were no match for the Nubian guards, who were among the finest fighters in the land. At last the robbers lay tied up in a heap.

At this point, Baba, who'd been cowering outside the village gates, ran inside shouting, "Gag them quickly! You never know what evil words might spew from the mouths of men such as these!"

As the guards responded to his order, Khufu ran triumphantly to his owner. "We got 'em, sir! What a fight! Did you see it when I scratched that robber on the arm and made him drop his sword? Or when I tripped the guy who was about to clobber you? Ramses will be sure to award me a medal of honor for this, won't he? Huh? Won't he?" Khufu danced around Souti's feet, causing him to stumble a bit.

"Khufu, what are *you* doing here? And what's all that meowing for?" asked Souti. Smiling, he said, "I know; you're probably hungry. Well, hang on for just one moment, kitty, while I go check things out." Striding to the robbers' house, he leaned inside the doorway and gasped. "Amun protect us! These treasures look like they came from Seti's tomb! The robbers will pay for this treachery with their lives!

"Baba," he called out, "take these things and return them to their rightful place in the Valley of the Kings. After that, destroy the entrance to the tomb so that others won't find it. Ramses must never know of this!"

"Aye, sir," replied Baba, whose face had taken on that same jovial expression Ptah had seen before.

Khufu was aghast. "What do you *mean* Ramses must never know of this? How will I be awarded a medal of honor if he doesn't find out?"

Hunkered in a doorway, Ptah was also aghast, but for a different reason. It was clear to him that Seti's treasures would never find their way back to his tomb. Souti had entrusted the cat with the mouse, so to speak. Running out into the street, he shouted, "No, stop that man! He's guilty! *Guilty,* I say!"

Everyone in the village gawked. Even the Medjay had been in Egypt long enough to know who it was they were looking at. "It's the great god Ptah!" they shouted and began dropping to their knees. Very quickly the street turned ghostly quiet except for the few grunts and groans that emanated from the robber's heap.

Khufu looked at Ptah in astonishment. "I guess you forgot to tell me that you were a god!" he said huffily.

"I'm not a god," Ptah said. "People just think I am because of these white spots on my fur."

"Humph," snorted Khufu. "Here it is, my moment of glory, and you have to go and ruin it all by stealing the show!"

Suddenly a voice called out from beyond the village gates. A runner soon appeared. "Souti!" the man cried. "We've received news that the Hittites are gathering in the east. Word has it that King Muwatallis will march upon the city of Kadesh. Hurry! The pharaoh wants to speak to you right away!"

Souti snapped to attention. "Khufu, come kitty! We must go to the palace at once. Oh, and bring your new friend. I feel sure that he is an omen—though an omen of what it is too soon to tell."

24

The Hyksos

The reception room outside Ramses' chambers was quiet. The usual stream of people who came to see the pharaoh each day—noblemen, priests, foreign ambassadors, and scribes—had not yet begun to arrive.

Souti sat rumpled and unshaven on the floor near the door to the king's chamber. His back against a pillar, he silently sipped a cup of mint tea. He sighed at the welcoming warmth that spread through his body, and the sweet taste of honey that helped to calm his nerves. It was to be expected that a man in his position might lose a night's sleep from time to time, although it never came easy. And now a foreboding shadow hung over his head. The Hittites were strong and well armed, and it was said that their king, Muwatallis, was determined to spread his empire west to the banks of the Nile.

In the corner of the room, Ptah sat huddled beside his urn. It had been a stroke of good luck that he had been able to keep it with him. At the village, when Souti had announced they would be going to the palace, Ptah had run inside the robber's house, had located his urn, and had jumped inside. Once there, he refused to budge. Any attempts to remove him were met with so many bites and scratches that Ptah quickly became known as "the Little Lion." Finally Souti had announced, "This urn doesn't look like it belongs with the other things anyway. It appears to be quite old and of a strange design. We may as well take it with us. Maybe it belongs to the great god Ptah."

The journey from Deir el-Medina to the palace in Thebes had

been an eye-opener for Ptah. Time, and the hard work of many men, had transformed the small, backwater village he once knew into a booming metropolis where the king himself lived.

As a capital, Thebes lacked the playful beauty and elegant splendor of Memphis. It was a sullen city of tightly packed houses, wide avenues, and dark-shaded temples. The favored artwork around town were "smiting scenes," in which oversized pharaohs clutching maces or swords annihilated hoards of their enemies with their mighty blows. Nevertheless, what Thebes may have found wanting in beauty, it more than made up for with its grandness of scale. Its temples and monuments were huge, and its sculptures massive, so that Ptah could not help but be impressed as they made their way through town.

Khufu sat on Ptah's other side, edgy with excitement. "We might get to go to *war,* Ptah, and if we do, there will be all *kinds* of chances to gain honor and glory then!"

"I'm not going to war," Ptah said flatly. "War is a horrible thing, Khufu. People get killed."

"Yes, that is an unpleasant but unavoidable byproduct, I'm afraid," allowed Khufu. "But you must admit, there is no more honorable way to go than to give your life in the service of your country."

Ptah shook his head. "Correct me if I'm wrong, but the city of Kadesh is far off in the land of Amurru near Syria, right? Why would anyone in Egypt care about what happens over there?"

"Kadesh *is* far away," Khufu conceded, "but the city is on the edge of what we Egyptians consider to be our buffer zone—the area between where we end and our enemy begins. And we can't afford to lose a whisker of it! Let me give you a little history lesson, Ptah."

Khufu settled in on his haunches. "Back in the old days," he began, "Egyptians didn't think too much about what was happening in the rest of the world. After all, we had everything we needed right here: plenty of food and water, and the resources necessary to make tools, clothing, and shelter. With the exception of a few important things like wood, we didn't even have to deal with anyone outside our borders. We felt protected by the deserts to the east and to the west, by the bad waters of the Great River to the south, and by the harborless shores of the Great Green Sea to the north. We were at ease because we knew that no army of any size could cross those barriers to come here. But after a while, come they did!"

"What happened?" asked Ptah.

"About four hundred years ago, people from the east—foreigners, or Hyksos, we called them—attacked the Delta region, taking Egypt by surprise. Within a matter of a few short weeks they had marched their army all the way upriver to the city of Memphis, conquering everything in their path. It was a dark time for Egypt, a time that's been burned into our nation's consciousness forever."

"How could that have happened?" asked Ptah. "I thought you just said Egypt was well protected."

"It *was* protected, but while Egyptians were busy living the good life, our neighbors were busy building better weapons," Khufu explained. "When the Hyksos arrived, they brought with them the horse and chariot, a war machine that turns men into whirlwinds of fire. They carried bronze swords, which ripped though our copper ones like papyrus, and they shot their arrows from bows made of wood, horn, and sinew, which cast arrows twice as far as ours. These things gave them such an advantage, they blew us away like the desert sand."

Ptah remembered the professor teaching him that the coming of the Hyksos ended the Middle Kingdom. "Were the Hyksos really that strong?" he asked. "I mean, it seems to me that even with better weapons, the sheer number of Egyptians fighting on their own turf would have been enough to turn them back."

Khufu spat. "Never underestimate technology, Ptah. He who wields the better weapons usually wins. Besides, there weren't many Egyptians living in the Delta at the time. It was wild country back then, difficult to farm because of its dense stands of papyrus. Add to that the fact that Egypt had no real standing army, just a bunch of loosely organized farmers, and I think you get the picture of how we allowed it to happen."

Khufu shook his head ruefully. "The sad thing," he continued, "is that we should have seen it coming all along. Hyksos had been trickling into the Delta for hundreds of years. Nobody thought twice about it at the time, of course, since Egypt has always been a melting pot of sorts. In truth, it's been one of our country's greatest strengths, that we've been able to attract the best the world has to offer. However, when the Hyksos attackers arrived, this strength turned into our folly, because those of them who already lived here quickly joined their side. As it turned out, the enemy was already among us."

"I don't understand," said Ptah. "If the Hyksos had been living in Egypt for hundreds of years, why would they suddenly turn on their neighbors like that? Weren't they well treated?"

"They were treated well enough . . . for foreigners, that is." Khufu snorted.

"Do you mean to say that Egypt opened its doors for these people, but then treated them as though they didn't belong?" Ptah asked. "That sounds like a recipe for disaster to me!"

"Hindsight can see in the dark," Khufu said dryly while lifting a striped foot and scratching his ear. "At any rate, the Hyksos built their capital at the city of Avaris in the eastern part of the Delta and ruled from there for over a hundred and fifty years. During this time, the Egyptians in the north came to accept these miserable foreigners and even paid tribute. Their willingness to capitulate is somewhat understandable, I guess, since the Hyksos at least had the decency to adopt our style of writing and to worship our gods, especially Set, who was a match for their god Sutech, the dark god of necessary violence. And they did bring with them some good things, like the horse and chariot, the lyre and the lute, and the apple and the olive.

"But the people in the south remained bitter. They despised the Hyksos because they had stolen our land and destroyed our temples; because they treated the Egyptian people poorly; and simply because they were foreigners, of course."

"So the people in the south revolted?" asked Ptah.

"You guessed it," said Khufu. "Led by a prince of Thebes named Kamose, who convinced the Medjay to join forces, the Egyptians drove the Hyksos out of Memphis, pushing them all the way north until they were walled up at Avaris. When Kamose died there in the battle to win the city, his younger brother, Ahmose, took up the fight. Ahmose succeeded in conquering Avaris and chasing the Hyksos all the way back to Canaan. Those who didn't flee were made slaves."

Khufu paused intently. "Now, here's where we come to the important part of the story, the part you need to understand," he said. "In order to make sure our enemies wouldn't come back to fight another day, Egyptian rulers began expanding our territory outward: to Syria in the east, to the Sudan in the south, and to the edge of the Libyan desert in the west. Under strong warrior kings like Thutmose III, Egyptians perfected the weapons brought in by the Hyksos and developed some new ones of our own. Boys were trained at an early age to become soldiers and a standing army was formed. As a result, Egypt became the most feared nation in all the land!"

Ptah nodded, wide-eyed.

"But do you think our work is done?" asked Khufu. "Oh, no! Ramses can't afford to relax for one moment. The Hittites are threatening to attack from the east; the Libyans are making raids on our villages in the west; the Sea People are making constant attempts to settle in the north; and the Kushites have built a powerful kingdom in the south!"

Khufu wagged a brown paw. "Egypt learned a hard lesson, Ptah. When a country becomes rich, it runs the risk of its people becoming lazy. They begin to pay more attention to their own little lives than they do on what's happening around them. Their children grow up spoiled, thinking they're entitled to the good life simply because they live there. Meanwhile, other countries are working hard to compete. And then one day, sure enough, the rich country wakes up to find the other countries beating down their door. All of a sudden, it seems, they've lost their place in the world, and worse than that, they've lost the know-how to get it back. That's what happened to Egypt, *and we cannot let it happen again!*"

Ptah jumped, startled at his friend's vehemence.

"So you see," concluded Khufu, "war is the greatest good there is for our country right now. You *have* to go. It's your duty!"

"Duty, my patooty. I'm staying here," said Ptah.

In the awkward silence that followed, two men walked into the room. "Paser! Setau! What took you so long?" Souti sounded both annoyed and relieved.

Ptah turned his attention to the newcomers. One of them was an older man—tall and thin, with medium-brown skin, close-cropped gray hair, and a narrow, angular face. He was dressed rather plainly for an official, in a simple white knee-length tunic cinched about the waist with a leather belt. Around his neck he wore a thin gold chain from which hung an *ankh*—a figure shaped like a cross but with a loop on the top, the Egyptian symbol of eternal life. The man wore no wig, which Ptah thought worked to his extreme disadvantage because his ears were huge, adding a hint of comedy to an otherwise serious demeanor.

The other man was middle-aged, black and muscular, with a strong square jaw and massive square shoulders. He reminded Ptah of a brick wall. Surprisingly, his clothing was ornate: a colorful pleated kilt, a broad leather belt studded with jasper and carnelian, and a leopardskin sash. Around his neck he wore a thick gold chain from which hung a cluster of golden flies—medals of honor that had been awarded to him for his bravery in battle. The man's powerful build, combined with his extravagant clothing and the traditional Nubian scars that etched his face, made him an imposing figure indeed. Compared to Souti, the two men looked well rested.

"Who are they?" Ptah whispered.

"Those are Ramses' closest advisors," Khufu replied. "The older man is Paser, Grand Vizier of southern Egypt. He served under Ramses' father, Seti, so he knows a lot about the Hittites. Did you happen to notice the size of his ears? Well, the joke around town is that he attained his coveted position by virtue of the fact that he can hear everything being said from here to the Delta!"

Khufu chuckled before continuing. "The other man is Setau, Viceroy to Kush. He's a seasoned warrior who has fought for Egypt on many occasions and is known for his brilliant military tactics. Did you see all of his golden flies? There must be a dozen of them." The striped cat sighed in admiration.

"Souti! What happened to you? You look like something the cat dragged in!" Setau exclaimed in his deep, commanding voice.

Souti scowled. "We had trouble in the Valley last night," he confided. "Robbers broke into Seti's tomb and nearly cleaned the place out. Speaking of cats, if it weren't for those two sitting over there, the robbers might never have been caught." He pointed at Khufu and Ptah.

"By the light of Re, will you look at that cat!" exclaimed Paser, while walking over and bending down to pick up Ptah.

"Be careful! If he jumps into that urn, leave him be," warned Souti, holding up his scratched and swollen wrists. Paser smiled as though Souti was joking, but all the same he backed away.

"I thought we'd let Ramses take a look at him," Souti continued. "A cat with his markings may be an omen, especially showing up now, when the miserable Hittites are breathing down our throats."

"The miserable Hittites are *always* breathing down our throats," growled Setau. Looking around, he then asked, "So where *is* the Redhead, anyway?"

"He's still in there going through his morning rituals—bathing, shaving, getting oiled, what have you. I don't think I could stand having a bunch of people fuss over me like that every morning," Souti replied.

Just then, the door to Ramses' chamber swung open and four beautiful young maidens walked out. They were carrying oil and perfume jars on their hips and talking in whispers as they passed through the reception room. Souti's jaw dropped open when he saw them.

"Don't think you could stand it, eh, Souti?" quipped Setau.

Souti blushed and then stood, grimacing with pain from the fight. "Come on, let's go in." Turning to the cats, he called, "Khufu, come kitty! Ptah, here god!"

25

Ramses II

The three men stopped inside the entrance to Ramses' chamber and bowed. Cowering behind them, Ptah stared at the larger-than-life figure seated before him. "Wow, Ramses the Great," he murmured.

"What's so great about Ramses?" Khufu whispered. "I mean, he's okay, I guess, but he's nothing like his father was."

Ramses stood to greet them. He was a tall, athletic-looking young man with light brown skin and curly, coppery-colored hair. He had a hawklike nose, piercing blue eyes, and an engaging smile. Possibly owing to his crisply pleated kilt, fancy embroidered shirt, and broad, gold-collar necklace, Ptah found him to be quite regal-looking for someone he guessed to be in his early twenties.

"Paser, Setau, Souti! Thank you for coming so quickly. Please join me for breakfast." Ramses motioned them to the table where he'd been sitting. Suddenly, his attention was riveted to the floor and his piercing blue gaze locked eyes with Ptah. "Amun protect us! What do we have here?" he asked.

"It's Ptah, Your Highness, or at the very least it's a cat who looks like Ptah," replied Souti. "I found him just this morning at the village of Deir el-Medina. Nobody's ever seen him before, and it would be highly unlikely for a cat with his markings to go by unnoticed for very long. Strange, don't you think, that he should turn up at a time like this? I believe he may be an omen."

"An omen of what?" asked Ramses.

Souti shook his head. "I don't know. 'Tis not the nature of omens to make themselves readily known. But I took no chances and brought him here. If he is the great god Ptah, then better he be with us than to fall into the hands of someone who has an *idea* to be king."

"Yes, good thinking as always, Souti," replied Ramses. "We'll ponder over the meaning of his arrival later. For now, though, let's eat!"

The four men sat down to a sumptuous breakfast of scrambled eggs, cinnamon rolls dripping with honey, sliced mandrake fruit, and piping hot tea. Souti served up two small dishfuls for the cats and set them on the floor behind him.

While they ate Ramses made small talk, asking Souti about the warhorses, and Paser and Setau about their families. Ptah noticed that Ramses looked each man directly in the eye when he spoke to him, making them feel as though they were the complete focus of his attention. After everyone finished eating, Ramses got down to business.

"King Muwatallis is on the march," he began. "Word has it his troops are heading south toward the city of Kadesh, with plans to keep on going if left unchecked. Now, I have no need to tell you the importance of this city to our nation's defense. Not only is it Egypt's last stronghold before the Hittite empire begins, but Kadesh is in a key position for guarding the main route that any southbound army would have to take to get here. I'm thinking about putting together an army to go meet Muwatallis in battle. Paser, you have the most experience with the Hittites. What do you think of my plan?"

"Sire, I advise caution," the older man replied. "We've had nothing but trouble in trying to hold onto Kadesh. That miserable king of Amurru seems to change loyalties at the drop of a feather! And while I fully realize the importance of the city to our nation's defense, there is such a thing as becoming overextended. Kadesh is far away. Maybe we should let it go. Pull back our forces to Megiddo, perhaps."

"Setau, what about you?" asked Ramses, noticeably dismayed by his grand vizier's answer.

"I agree with Paser," said Setau. "King Muwatallis is a crafty foe, and you, Sire, are young. This would be your first big battle."

"My first big battle?" Ramses' voice rose. "Why, I've been a captain in the royal Egyptian army since I was ten! Just last year we put down that uprising in Canaan, and the year before that we ran out those Sea People who were trying to settle in the Delta."

"I don't deny that you are a good fighter, but may I remind you that you didn't actually *lead* any of those battles," said Setau. "Your generals were already well in control of the situation before you arrived on the scene. Most of what you did was just for show."

"Just . . . for . . . show?" Ramses repeated slowly while shooting the viceroy a menacing glance.

"And a very good show you made of it, too!" Setau added quickly.

Ramses scowled. "All the more reason that I should lead the battle against Muwatallis this time," he said vehemently. "I'm *tired* of everyone always saying how great my father was. *I* want to be the one they call great, do you hear?" He pounded his fist on the table for emphasis. Turning toward Souti, he asked, "What is your opinion of all of this?"

"Begging the pardons of Paser and Setau, Sire, but I'm with you. I don't think we can afford to just sit around here and wait for King Muwatallis to come knocking on our door. Besides, if we let that miserable king of Amurru off the hook so easily, what does that tell the other kings who rule in the lands you control? Why would they bother to keep sending you riches if they didn't think the royal Egyptian army would pounce on them like lions if they stopped? And as for people calling you great, well, there would be no better proof of your greatness than to claim a victory over the likes of King Muwatallis!"

"My sentiments exactly," declared Ramses. "Gentlemen, tell me this. Who is it that people remember? Who do they call great? I'll tell you who: Ahmose, who drove out the Hyksos; Thutmose, who conquered the lands around us; and men like my father, Seti, who kept the battle alive!"

"Those weren't the only great kings," argued Paser. "Think of the Middle Kingdom, a relatively peaceful time of great prosperity. Never before had peasants and slaves been treated so well. Surely it takes a certain amount of greatness to accomplish that."

"Maybe it does," Ramses replied testily, "but you know as well as I do that times have changed. Egypt has no choice but to be a warrior state. 'Conquer or be conquered,' that's our motto now!"

"I'm aware of that," said Paser, "but for someone of your limited experience to go up against King Muwatallis—"

A knock interrupted the conference, and Ramses' secretary entered the room. "Sire, your first appointment has arrived," he announced.

Ramses looked up. "We're right in the middle of something. Can you ask whoever it is to come back?"

"The man says he will only be in town for one more day. Apparently, you've put him off twice already," the secretary replied.

Ramses blew out his breath. "Okay, show him in. Who is he, anyway?"

"He claims to be a master of makeover, a purveyor of perception—whatever that means." The secretary shrugged.

"Oh joy, another fruitcake." Ramses sighed, rising from his chair.

"This I've *got* to see," mumbled Setau, grinning.

The secretary left the room. While he was away, Ramses prepared to receive an audience. From a large wooden chest, he gathered the kings' cloth of blue and white stripes and wrapped it tightly around his head, letting the two ends hang down in front like a sphinx. On top of the cloth he placed a golden crown, carefully adjusting the snake and vulture heads so they reared upward from the center of his brow. Then he donned a stunning blue cape, encrusted with enough rubies, diamonds, and emeralds to finance a small nation. After that he ascended to his throne—a marvel of silk, gold, and jewels atop a lush carpeted platform.

The secretary returned a few minutes later, followed by a dapper-looking man with dark brown skin and a trim physique. In addition to his sleek, square-cut black wig, the man was wearing the clothes of a dandy: a fancy tasseled tunic, an embroidered cape, and a pair of snakeskin sandals polished to a gleaming shine. As he entered the room, his keen dark eyes darted around, taking in every detail. His perfume practically announced his arrival before the secretary did.

Paser, Setau, and Souti all exchanged glances.

"Good morning, sir," said Ramses. "What can I do for you?"

"Your Highness, the question is not what *you* can do for *me,* but what *I* can do for *you!*" the man exclaimed with a sweeping bow. "Allow me to introduce myself! My name is Sashai. I am a master of makeover, a purveyor of perception, a—"

"Enough already! Egypt has more than its fair share of vacuous titles," interrupted Ramses. "Just tell me, what exactly is it that you do?"

"Simply stated, I make people look good," replied Sashai, straightening up from his bow. He smiled broadly, revealing a side gold tooth.

"Are you saying that our pharaoh does not look good?" snarled Setau.

"Most certainly not!" declared Sashai. "It's just that . . . well, Ramses is suffering from what I call the *shadow syndrome.* In his case, it's his father who looms so large in the public eye that Ramses gets lost in his shadow."

"Argh! That's just what I was talking about," groaned Ramses.

Setau stiffened. "And what do you suggest that Ramses *do* about this . . . this shadow syndrome?" he snapped.

"I suggest that he employ a simple strategy of marketing," replied Sashai. "And you'll be happy to know that I'm just the person to show him how to do it."

Ptah noticed that neither Setau nor Paser was looking very happy at the moment. Paser's huge ears had turned a bright shade of red, and both men's faces were set into a scowl.

Ramses stared blankly at his visitor. "Marketing? As in going to the market?" he asked.

"Well, yes and no," said Sashai, pushing his cape aside. "Let me give you an example. Take Paneb, for instance. You know the guy—he sells the same quality of fruits and melons as the other vendors at the market, but he charges half again as much. And people buy them. Do you know why?"

Ramses shook his head.

"Marketing, that's why. He hangs up signs saying his fruits and melons are the juiciest, and he has beautiful young women walking around handing out free samples. His melons are no longer plain old melons; they are *Paneb's* melons. Do you see?"

"So you're going to teach me to sell melons?" asked Ramses.

"No, I'm going to teach you to sell yourself!" exclaimed Sashai.

At this point Souti spoke up. "Excuse me, sir, but what you just said about that Paneb fellow . . . well, what he's doing sounds a little dishonest, if you ask me."

"And so it is, so it is," declared Sashai, his sly smile revealing a flash of gold. "But here's the beauty of it: there's a sucker born every minute! If people choose to believe in Paneb's marketing schemes, that's their problem. Paneb makes no apologies, and neither should Ramses."

"I get it . . . I think," said Ramses. "So tell me, how do I do this marketing?"

Sashai cleared his throat. "Well, Sire, I would simply *love* to give you the answers for free, but my services don't come cheap. My fee is one hundred gold debens up front, with an ongoing rate of ten debens per visit, of which you'll need plenty for a while. Only the best for the best, you know."

"*What?* That's *outrageous!*" yelled Setau.

"Who do you think you are?" demanded Paser.

"Get out! Get out!" they cried together.

Unruffled, Sashai took another sweeping bow. "Very well, Sire. Just know that I shall be ready and at your service when you decide the time has come. Good day." And with that he left.

"When you decide the time has come, indeed!" snapped Paser.

"Good day and good riddance!" Setau growled, adding, "It's certainly a good thing there aren't more men like *him* running around, lining their pockets with gold by deceiving the masses with lies."

Souti ran a hand over the stubble on his chin. "I'm not so sure about that," he said thoughtfully. "Maybe we should have at least listened to what the man had to say. It's not as though Ramses can't afford his fee, and he might have had some good advice."

"For crying out loud, Souti!" exclaimed Setau. "*You're* the one who's nearly convinced Ramses to go traipsing off to war, and now you want him to listen to the advice of that . . . that *baboon!*"

Souti shook his head. "I don't know what's gotten into me," he said. "Maybe it has something to do with that cat. It's just that I feel there is something important about to happen, and we can't afford to sit around here and waste our time while trying to decide what to do."

"I agree," said Ramses. "Not to decide is to decide to do nothing, my father always said. Take your pick, gentlemen. It's either off to war to fight Muwatallis or call what's-his-name back in here. Ptah has arrived, and so the time has come for me to fulfill my destiny. One way or another, I will step out from the shadow of my father to become the great pharaoh I know I am meant to be!"

"What a choice!" groaned Setau. Grasping the hilt of the dagger that hung from his belt, he said, "Well, when you put it *that* way, I for one would choose fighting that dog Muwatallis over listening to what that snake-oil salesman has to say, any day."

Paser sighed. "I'd have to agree. A necessary choice between two evils, I'm afraid."

"It's decided then. We're going to war!" Ramses jumped up from his throne and began giving orders. "Paser, notify my generals in Memphis, Heliopolis, and Avaris. Tell them each to assemble an army of five thousand with plenty of horses and chariots.

"Setau, you'll be in charge of putting together the army that will represent Thebes. Send out the call for men. After that I'd like you to forward a message to the king of Kush. Tell him we want to carve his likeness on the temple I'm building at Abu Simbel or some such thing—anything to distract him. The last thing I need is for the Kushites to flex their muscle while I'm off fighting in the east.

"Souti, see to the warhorses and to the chariots. Oh, and make sure to bring that cat along with us when we go. I feel sure that his presence will assure us a stunning victory." Ramses waved a regal hand. "We'll gather the army in the main square at dawn tomorrow to distribute the weapons."

Setau's thick eyebrows rose in disbelief. "Dawn *tomorrow?* Sire, surely you must realize how difficult it will be to raise an army of that size on such short notice! You have your retainers, all right, but you'll need many more men than that to fight Muwatallis. Where will we get them all? Years of prosperity have returned the Egyptians to their peaceable nature. They are loath to travel, particularly to fight. Besides, it will be harvest time soon, and the farmers will be busy with their crops."

"Then hire mercenaries—men who fight for pay," retorted Ramses. "There are always plenty of men among the Libyans, Nubians, and the Shardana who would welcome a purse of gold and the chance for plunder once we reach Kadesh."

"Mercenaries . . . again?" questioned Paser. "Sire, I spoke repeatedly against this practice with your father, and I feel that I must bring it up again with you. It is unwise to have foreigners fight our fights. In times of crisis, leadership of a country often falls into the hands of the military. Mark my words, it will lead to Egypt's downfall one day."

"Amun almighty, Paser!" cried Ramses. "We both just heard Setau say that Egyptians are reluctant to fight, so we've no choice in the matter. *End* of discussion!" Ramses stepped down from the platform and motioned for the men to leave.

Down on the floor, Khufu jumped for joy. "Did you hear that, Ptah? We get to go to war! You'll see; it will be just like I told you. There will be *plenty* of chances to reap honor and glory then!" Khufu's eyes lit up like two little suns, but just as quickly a cloud passed over them and he turned on Ptah like a storm. "Let's get one thing straight before we go," he hissed. "Don't get in my way this time. I'll have you know that if push comes to shove, I'm going to make very sure that I'm the cat who ends up on top. Understood?"

Ptah nodded weakly. A deep feeling of dread had seeped into his bones. He vaguely recalled hearing about the Battle of Kadesh from the professor. He knew that there was something important—something terribly important!—about the battle he should know. But no matter how hard he tried, he simply could not remember what it was.

26
Ships that Sail on the Desert

"Whoa, easy now," whispered Souti as he slowly moved among the horses, calming their jangled nerves while the stablehands groomed and inspected them for the long journey ahead. Watching him from the loft above, Ptah marveled at how the horses responded to his voice, how they seemed to purr like cats in his hands. He had a way with them; that was for sure. It was no wonder he was chariot driver for the king.

Ptah glanced outside. It was nearly dawn on his second day in this ominous new time. He was currently housed in the palace stables, a sprawling labyrinth of stalls, storage rooms, and washrooms, with even a medical facility attached. Great care had gone into the construction of the stables. The warhorses lived far better than many a poor farmer, he reflected.

Ptah yawned. He was tired, so tired in fact that his eyelids felt as though they had bronze weights attached to them. All he wanted to do right now was sleep; however, beside him, Khufu was wide awake and was rambling on.

"Magnificent creatures, aren't they? Sure make you feel small, don't they? I tell you, no matter how many times I'm around the warhorses, they never cease to amaze me by their sheer strength, especially those two over there." He tipped a striped ear in the direction of two stallions—one chestnut brown with a white star on its forehead, the other pure black except for its feet, which were dipped in white.

"Mmm," mumbled Ptah, feigning interest while trying hard

to ignore Khufu's jabber and go back to sleep. He'd actually been thinking that the warhorses looked quite small, at least compared to modern horses. He doubted they were even big enough to carry a rider, although the people of ancient Egypt were small, too.

"Those are Ramses' horses, Victory-at-Thebes and Mut-is-Satisfied," Khufu prattled on. "Bar none, they are the finest pair of warhorses in the land. They fear nothing! You should see the way Souti handles them, but then again, you soon will."

Ptah winced. He wished that Khufu would just shut up, or better yet, go away. He'd been trying hard to forget about the situation he now found himself in, secretly hoping that if he slept long enough, he would magically awaken to a new time. But now Khufu's words brought it all back to him: his uneasy feeling that there was something about the Battle of Kadesh he ought to know; his sense of impending doom; his fear of dying on the battlefield, or worse, his fear of what sights he might live to remember should he happen to survive.

For the second time in as many days, Ptah weighed his options. He could bolt, but where would he go? He could try finding a nice, poor farm family to take him in, but what if someone like Smendes found him first? He tried to imagine what sort of advice Horus might give him if he were here. Bide his time and wait for the right moment, no doubt, which was probably good counsel, all things considered. In the end Ptah decided that his best course of action was to continue doing what he'd been doing, which was to sleep as much as he could in hopes of awaking to new time.

Khufu nudged him rudely. "Are you listening to me?" he asked. "Cat got your tongue? You've hardly said a word since we left Ramses' chamber yesterday. All you've done is sleep! What's with you?"

Ptah shrugged. "I just don't want to be here, okay?"

Khufu snorted. "No, it's *not* okay. You *are* here, so snap out of it. You're making me mad!"

Ptah's blood began to boil at this altogether annoying cat. "Listen, Khufu, you don't understand. I had it really great before I came here. I had a boy who loved me and a family—"

"So, where are they all now?" Khufu interrupted.

"They're *gone*. And I'll probably never see them again." Ptah quickly turned away; it was unthinkable for a cat to let anyone see him cry. Why couldn't Khufu just leave him alone? He needed time to grieve. He needed time to heal the ache in his chest where it felt as though Maat had ripped his heart out.

Mercilessly, Khufu kept rambling on. "Your first mistake was in becoming too attached," he said. "Cats should remain aloof. And I hate to be the one to fill you in on this little secret, but life is fleeting. Things come and go, so you'd better enjoy them while you can. There's no use in crying over spilt milk, my mama used to say. I tell you, if there's one thing I've learned in this world, it's that the only thing you can count on is yourself. Look out for number one; that's my motto."

Ptah buried his head between his paws. Was there even an ounce of pity in this cat? He found himself wishing that a miracle would happen—a lightning bolt or maybe a massive flood—and Khufu would instantly be erased from the face of the planet. Not only was he an insensitive brute, he was a selfish one as well. Unlike Narmer, who had traveled hundreds of miles to say thanks, Khufu had made no mention of the fact that Ptah had risked his life to save him at the village of Dier el-Medina. In fact, he even had the nerve to imply that Ptah had gotten in his way! What kind of a friend was that?

Ptah took a deep breath, letting the musty scent of dried grass and horse dung fill his lungs. These were strong smells, not altogether unpleasant, and he found them comforting, if only for the fact that they seemed so real.

Suddenly he heard a loud clamoring at the far end of the stables. Ptah looked up to see Ramses striding through the entrance, looking glorious in his full-dress uniform—a crisp pleated kilt topped by a bronze mail breastplate studded with bits of carnelian and lapis. Around his neck he wore a stunning gold necklace, and around his waist was a jeweled belt from which hung a bronze metal sword. Blue leather shin guards protected each lower leg, and on his feet he wore a pair of thick leather sandals. Draped over Ramses' shoulders was the same magnificent blue jeweled cape Ptah had seen before, and on his head he wore the war crown of the pharaoh: a gold hat fronted by a blue metal shield that extended about a cubit above his forehead. On the front of the shield were the golden heads of a snake and a vulture—symbols of the Two Lands.

Ramses strode across the room, coming to a halt directly below the loft where the two cats were sitting. "Good morning, Souti! You look well rested," he said.

"Thank you, Sire, I am," Souti replied. He bowed quickly, grimacing with pain from the fight, for while he'd certainly gotten enough sleep, the bruises on his body were hurting more now than they had been before.

"Harness up my warhorses, will you?" Ramses ordered. "We'll be taking the chariot into the square."

"You don't wish to be carried in on a litter?" Souti asked incredulously.

"You heard me," said Ramses. "I've been thinking about what it means to be great, and I've decided that, at the very least, it means standing on your own two feet."

Souti didn't argue. He fetched Ramses' two stallions and dressed them each in a shining gold cloth adorned with tasseled fringes. On their heads he placed headdresses made of ostrich feathers—the Egyptian symbol for victory. Ptah thought the horses looked rather silly in their fancy getups, especially with the ostrich plumes bobbing about their faces, but they didn't seem to mind. After the horses were dressed, Souti led them into the stableyard, where the chariots were stored. Khufu and Ptah scampered down from the loft and followed closely behind.

Ptah caught his breath as he exited the building. The morning sun, inching its way up over the eastern horizon, cast a golden glow upon the row upon row of gleaming chariots. The beauty of their simple but elegant design amazed him. Each chariot was made up of a low wooden platform surrounded on three sides by a lightweight wooden railing covered with thick leather. Wicker baskets, used for carrying weapons, hung from the sides. Extending from the front of the platform was a long metal pole, which ended with a crossbar to harness to the horses. Perpendicular to this pole was a shorter pole attached to two metal wheels that had six spokes apiece. These being royal chariots, their metal parts were gilded, and their wood and leather parts were painted with colorful patterns of purple, red, and blue.

"Wow!" was all Ptah managed to say.

"Never ridden in one, eh?" asked Khufu. "The Egyptians call chariots 'ships that sail on the desert.' As you can see, each chariot is drawn by two horses and is wide enough for two men to stand abreast. One man is the fighter, and the other man doubles as both driver and shield-bearer. Come on; let's hop inside!"

"Where will we ride?" Ptah asked. The chariots didn't look big enough to accommodate two cats without their being trampled on by the men's feet.

"We'll ride in the baskets . . . until they're needed for weapons, of course," Khufu replied. He marched over to Souti, who was busily harnessing the horses, and let out a loud meow. Dutifully, Souti stopped what he had been doing and went over to stuff some rags into two of the chariot baskets, upon which Khufu and Ptah jumped inside. When the horses were ready, he and Ramses also boarded. Souti gave the reins a shake, and they were on their way.

27

Mercenaries of War

By the time they arrived at the broad square in the center of town, the area was swarming with men. Just as Ramses had predicted, the promise of gold and the chance for plunder had resulted in a call that had been quickly answered.

Ptah had never seen so many rough-looking men gathered in one place before. Wearing coarse linen kilts with daggers and axes suspended from their belts, these were burly, muscular men who had teeth ground down to nubs from years on the road eating bread filled with sand. He noticed that the mercenaries seemed to be gathering in groups—the Nubians toward the front of the square; the pale-skinned Libyans in the center; and the Shardana of the Sea People spread out along the back. Sprinkled in here and there were other small clusters of men, the nationalities of whom Ptah was unable to distinguish, although he knew from Khufu that some of them must be Hyksos fighting in order to gain their freedom.

Waiting for Ramses at the entrance to the square were his retainers, the elite group of Egyptian soldiers whose membership was reserved for royal princes and the most valuable of men. These soldiers made up the chariot corps, and like Ramses, they were all dressed up in their finest, wearing braided wigs, pleated kilts, bronze breastplates, and plenty of jewelry. On the whole Ptah found the retainers to be quite dashing, although he couldn't help thinking that they looked as though they were going on some kind of golden adventure rather than off to war. He found the contrast between them and the mercenaries startling.

Souti halted the chariot at the head of their ranks, upon which Ramses leaned over to see where the shadow had fallen on the sun clock, a tall stone column set on a circular base carved with six straight marks. "Right on time," he observed. Then, lifting two fingers in a half salute, he signaled the herald, who blew three shrill blasts on his trumpet. The retainers fell quickly in line and began marching two by two across the square. "Make way for the pharaoh! Make way for the pharaoh!" they cried as they led the procession.

The crowd of mercenaries parted as Ramses and his entourage crossed to the other end of the square, where a platform had been set up holding Ramses' throne. In front of the platform stood a long row of tables, and behind these tables sat a small army of scribes. Marching right up to them, the double column of retainers split, one line going around to the left and the other to the right until they had filed in behind the scribes, forming a wall of soldiers two rows deep. Riding around behind them, Ramses and Souti dismounted from their chariot and then ascended the stairway that led to the top of platform. Khufu and Ptah hopped down from their baskets and followed.

Setau was waiting for them there. "Attention everyone! Take your places, men!" he shouted. Lifting a silver-and-copper war trumpet to his lips, he blew a long, low blast, signaling the ceremony to begin. Slowly the mercenaries quieted down, and after several minutes, Ramses began to speak.

"Oh, brave and loyal soldiers," he began. "I have called you here today because Egypt is being threatened from the east. Word has it the vile Asiatic King Muwatallis has plans to capture Kadesh, and will keep on going if left unchecked. His mission is no less than to spread his empire west to the banks of the Nile! Now, I have no need to warn you of the dire consequences of his actions should he succeed. Your freedom would dissipate like the dew on the morning grass! You would be forced to bow down before him like slaves, toiling from dawn until dusk. So I ask you this: will we let his miserable army defeat us? Will we let him win? I say *no! Not* while Egypt stands tall, *not* while Egypt stays strong, *not* while we have the greatest army in all the land, because *we . . . will . . . prevail!*"

Ramses paused to take a breath while a polite round of clapping issued from the retainers.

From his perch on stage, Ptah looked out over the square. He noticed that the words of Ramses' speech seemed lost on the masses of men who either could not understand the language or could not have cared less about what was being said. Turning to Khufu, he said, "What's going on? Those men don't seem to be paying the least bit of attention."

Khufu chuckled. "That's because they're not. Horse feathers and tasseled fringes are what mercenaries think of speeches. They're all waiting for the important part of the ceremony to begin: when the soldiers are picked, the teams formed, and the captains chosen from among them."

Considering their behavior to be rude, Ptah returned his attention to Ramses, who was indeed now droning on, listing past victories of the mighty Egyptian army while extolling the powers of Amun. He tried hard to listen to it all, but after a while, even he became bored. When it came to official business, Ptah had learned that the Egyptian language was overwrought with flowery phrases. Nobody but the priests really talked that way.

Thinking more about the way people talked, Ptah remembered something he'd wanted to ask. Nudging Khufu, he said, "I've noticed that people now call the king a pharaoh. When did they start doing that?" While he'd often heard the professor use the phrase before, he had not heard it in Egypt until he'd arrived in Ramses' time.

"Oh, that started after the Great War," Khufu replied. "You see, during the Middle Kingdom, the relations between the Egyptian kings and their people became a little too familiar, leading to a loss of respect. So when Ahmose took over, he issued a decree stating that no one except his highest officials could ever call him by name or even refer to him in person. Instead, people were told to refer to the 'pharaoh,' which means the 'palace.' Over time people got used to saying the 'palace' did this, or the 'palace' did that, and after a while, the two words sort of became one and the same."

"Speaking of the Great War," said Ptah, "I know you explained everything to me about the Hyksos and all, but I still don't understand why war has to happen in the first place. It seems senseless to me, people killing each other like that."

Khufu lifted a hind leg and scratched his shoulder, then shrugged. "Well, from what I've learned about people, wars are always started between the 'haves' and the 'have-nots'. Either somebody tries to take something away that someone else has, or somebody feels threatened that someone will try to take something away, so they strike first. It's as simple as that."

What Khufu said did not sound simple at all to Ptah. He was still trying to work out all the "somes" in his head when a loud cracking noise riveted his attention back to the stage. He looked up to see Ramses holding a broken bow in his hands, which he promptly threw down before being handed another. Taking the ends of that new bow in his hands, he lifted his knee and then in one sweeping motion, he broke that one in half as well.

"What's Ramses doing now?" Ptah asked.

"He's performing the ritual destruction of the enemy," Khufu replied. "That stack of bows you see is called the Nine Bows, each symbolizing one of Egypt's nine enemies. By breaking them in half, Ramses symbolically destroys his enemies. The ritual is thought to bring good luck."

After the last bow had been snapped, Setau stepped forward. "Form the lines, men!" he shouted. Immediately the mercenaries all rose to their feet and began pushing and shoving their way to the front of the square. Watching them in disgust, Setau turned to Ramses and grumbled, "This is the most ragtag bunch of men I've seen in a long while. Look at them all! That one over there may be strong as an ox, but I can tell he is totally untrained, and that one over there can barely walk!"

"Then it will be your job to winnow them out," Ramses replied brusquely. "Pick the best among the lot and tell the rest to go home. You'll have plenty of time to turn these men into soldiers on the way to Kadesh." Stepping to the front of the platform, the pharaoh called, "Bring forth the weapons!"

The scribes in charge of supplies swiftly moved to the sides of the square and began leading huge ox-drawn carts to the front of each line. The carts were filled with every sort of equipment needed to wage a battle: visored helmets, shirts made of thickly-wadded material, short-sleeved coats of bronze mail, leather shields, curved swords called scimitars, daggers, battle axes, javelins, and double-curved bows with bronze-tipped arrows. Ptah marveled at how much the weaponry had changed since the days when Imhotep and his men had marched into Nubia carrying little more than a dagger and a shield.

Fifty at a time the mercenaries stepped forward to be judged by Setau and to collect their gear. All the while, the scribes sitting at the tables recorded the name and rank of each soldier as well as the equipment he was being issued. With over five thousand men in all, the distribution was expected to last well into the evening.

After the first group of men had received their gear, they were escorted to the river, where huge flat-bottomed boats awaited to take them to Avaris. Once there the soldiers would disembark and then trek on foot to the meeting place at the town of Sile.

With the situation under control, Ramses, Souti, and the two cats returned to the palace. There, preparations were already well under way for the chariot corps, which would be traveling north by land and would meet up with the others in about two weeks. Ptah watched as the horses were harnessed and the oxcarts filled with food and supplies. His heart sank when he saw his urn being loaded in with them.

It didn't take long for the retainers to begin to arrive. Most brought with them oxcarts of their own, which they had filled with soft Persian rugs, golden goblets, and other fine luxuries they felt they needed for a comfortable journey. Much to the cats' dismay, they also brought with them hunting dogs, greyhounds for the most part.

Soon the chariot corps was ready to depart. It was late in the day when they finally set out, riding through the streets of town accompanied by flag bearers and musicians in a grand parade. Leading the way, Ramses cut a glorious figure in his full-dress uniform, his jeweled cape sparkling in the sun. The townspeople lined the streets and cheered as the procession passed them nobly by.

When they reached the edge of town, the flag bearers and musicians stopped, while the chariot corps forged on ahead, taking the wide dirt road that traveled north through the vast farmlands that hugged the Nile. It being springtime, the land before them was lush and green. Not a single cloud marred the clear blue sky.

Khufu rode inside one of Ramses' chariot baskets; however, Ptah chose to travel inside his urn. While not as comfortable as a basket, it was quite peaceful. Exhausted from the long, eventful day, Ptah curled himself into a ball and closed his eyes. Like it or not, he was on the road to Kadesh.

28

The Fortress of Taru

Ramses' chariot corps hadn't gone very far when they reached a point where the road split—one branch curving off to the left and following the river as it made a wide westward arc, the other branch veering off to the right and heading northeast into the desert. They took the latter of these two roads, continuing along its course until they reached the edge of the floodplain near the base of the Arabic Mountains. There the road intersected with one of the many patrol roads established by the royal Egyptian army. Turning onto this road, the chariot corps traveled north and slightly to the west, following along the mountains' craggy, barren ribs.

It was nearly dark when they arrived at a small fortress set into the mountain lowlands. Built out of thick mud brick and with towers all around, the fortress was a lonely outpost populated by a few dozen men. Due to a runner Ramses had dispatched earlier, the chariot corps had been expected, and the soldiers had prepared for them a simple but tasty meal of rabbit stew, grilled venison steaks, and crusty bread. During the meal, talk turned quickly to King Muwatallis, and chilling tales were told of battles fought against him.

The following morning the retainers rose before the break of dawn and continued on their way, reaching the next lonely outpost near dusk.

A traveling pattern soon emerged, which Ptah noticed was very similar to the sleeping patterns of a cat. The Egyptians would wake just prior to dawn and ride through the cool of the morning. Shortly before noon they would stop for a light meal and then nap through the hottest part of the day. When they awoke, hunting parties would go out. Deer and hares were hunted in the desert, while antelope, addax, and wild boar were hunted in the *wadi*—dry gullies along the edge of the floodplain that filled with water during the flood. The retainers were excellent marksmen, and therefore good hunters. They hunted mostly on foot, using bows and arrows or spears and lassos, with their greyhound dogs flushing the game before them. After a successful hunt a meal was prepared, and then they would set off again, riding until they reached the next outpost shortly before dark.

It was a grueling pace, although Ptah could not complain, because they were anything but roughing it. The men—the king, especially—knew how to travel in style! They ate gourmet meals prepared by cooks who had been brought along on the journey. They drank spiced wine from golden goblets and slept on soft Persian rugs. And while they traveled long hours during the day, in the evenings they relaxed and played senet, a game of rods and pieces similar to chess that mimicked the passage through the Underworld, or the serpent game, in which stone marbles raced to the center of a circular checkerboard by use of lion-shaped counters. They also took turns telling stories.

Storytelling was an art in ancient times, the success of which had as much to do with the story itself, as the way it was being told. As men will do, the retainers often embellished their stories many times over, so it could be difficult to separate the truth from lies. Ptah didn't care. The tall tales they spun were not only entertaining; they made him forget about his troubles for a while.

Ptah spent most of his time while on the road sleeping inside his urn. He still harbored some small hope that by fate or by luck he would be transported again to a different time. One day merged into the next, and soon Ptah noticed that the mountains had diminished and the land before them was becoming green again. Finally he realized that they had crossed into the Delta, the fan-shaped region at the northern end of the Nile where the river separated into many small branches before emptying into the sea. Ptah welcomed the moist, fresh change in the air after the dry desert heat.

The chariot corps was traversing the Delta when Ptah emerged from his urn one morning to see a great walled city ahead, unusual in that he had yet to see a city in Egypt that was surrounded by walls. As the corps drew near, the gates to the city parted, revealing a wide avenue flanked by two rows of identical stone statues, all of the same towering pharaoh. Passing between them, Ptah could see a city under construction. Everywhere he looked he saw hundreds—maybe thousands!—of curly-haired slaves toiling away in the blazing hot sun.

Although he hated to get Khufu's motor-mouth running, Ptah was curious to know his whereabouts. So when the chariot corps finally came to a halt near the center of town, he sprang from his urn and bounded to Khufu's chariot basket. Turning his blue eyes upward, he shouted, "Where are we now?"

"We've just entered the dual cities of Pithom and Ramses—better known as Pi-Ramses," Khufu replied. "This city is named after the pharaoh himself! Did you see all of those huge statues of him lining the street when we entered?"

"Those statues are supposed to be of Ramses?" Ptah asked incredulously. "But they don't look anything like him!"

"Of course not." Khufu chuckled. "Every pharaoh wishes to be remembered as having the classic Egyptian look: a slim, muscular body with a rounded face, a wide-set pair of eyes, and a benevolent smile. It would never do to show Ramses' unruly red hair or his hawklike nose! Haven't you noticed that all kings' statues look pretty much the same? Only a truly gifted artist can follow the Egyptian standards of proportion and beauty while still incorporating the slightest elements of the real person."

Ptah looked back to gaze upon the statues, but his eyes came to rest instead upon the hundreds of slaves toiling in the sun. "Are those the Hyksos you told me about?" he asked.

"Yes," said Khufu. "As you can see, Ramses has been putting them to good use. This city will soon be the new capital of Egypt."

"I had no idea Egypt had so many slaves! Has it always been this way?" Ptah wondered whether he had somehow missed seeing them in earlier times.

"Oh, no. It wasn't until Egypt conquered the Hyksos that we

began using slaves to this degree," Khufu replied. "To be sure, wealthy landowners and successful warriors have always owned slaves, typically prisoners of war, but those were usually set free after a while, or at least their children were. But when it came to the Hyksos, the Egyptians were so mad about the whole affair that their attitude toward slavery changed. It was even quite popular at first, because it really cut down on the number of 'duty days' people had to spend working for the king—hauling rocks, clearing canals, digging ditches, those types of things."

"But it's been hundreds of *years* since the invasion took place!" Ptah protested. "The original Hyksos are gone! How long do the Egyptians plan to keep these people enslaved?" Even with Khufu's explanation of how it all began, slavery was something he couldn't even begin to understand, much less justify.

"Now don't go getting all soft like the others," Khufu hissed. "More than one Egyptian has expressed dismay over the continued enslavement of the Hyksos. It's like you said—now that the original Hyksos are gone and it's the children of their children who are enslaved, people aren't feeling so good about it anymore. I've even heard Ramses say he would set them all free if it didn't make him look weak. He's waiting for a signal from the gods, I guess, something he can point to, to let them go."

"Why should Ramses care what other people think? After all, he's a god himself, isn't he?" asked Ptah.

Khufu rolled his eyes. "Nobody believes the king is a god anymore. They haven't thought that since the time of the Old Kingdom. There have been too many wars, and the throne has changed hands too many times, for people to believe in that. Besides, people only need see that Ramses has just as many bad hair days as everyone else to know he's not a god. Nowadays, the palace claims instead that the king is the *son* of a god. Supposedly, on his day of coronation the spirit of Horus enters his body, making him holy."

While the two cats were speaking, Ramses and Souti had been carrying on their own conversation. Now, having decided upon a course of action, Ramses headed off in one direction while Souti took off in another. Khufu leaped down from his chariot basket;

then together, he and Ptah accompanied Souti through the vast, gridlike streets of the city, watching as the young man haggled with street vendors over a new set of harnesses for his horses. They were on their way back, and were just coming around a corner, when they happened upon a familiar face.

"Baba! What are *you* doing here?" Souti exclaimed.

Baba whipped around. By the expression on his face, it was obvious that he was just as surprised to see Souti as Souti was to see him. Glancing nervously about, he whispered, "Not so loud, Souti. Do you have to announce to the entire Egyptian army that I'm here?"

Souti must not have heard him, for he continued on in a very loud voice. "Where have you *been?* We were looking all over for you. And wherever did you get that really fine horse? He's *huge!* He must be worth his weight in gold!"

"The horse is, uh . . . *not mine,*" Baba stammered, a little too forcefully. "I was hired by a nobleman in Thebes to, uh . . . to take his horse to Ashkelon."

Yeah, right, thought Ptah. Baba had obviously bought the horse with his profits from thievery.

"Good timing," said Souti. "We'll be going right by Ashkelon on our way to Kadesh. We're off to war to fight Muwatallis. Harness up and join the ranks!"

"Oh, not Muwatallis again!" groaned Baba. "That man is a crafty foe. We'd be far better off joining up with his side than to do battle against him."

Souti shrunk back. "Bite your tongue, man. Those are words of treason! If you're not careful, I *will* call the entire Egyptian army."

Baba's broad face turned red. "It's just that I . . . I don't think the nobleman who hired me would be very happy to have his horse going off to war."

"Nonsense!" declared Souti. "There isn't a nobleman alive who wouldn't willingly lend his horse to the king. You know as well as I that the palace owns everything there is in this land, and that anything anyone has is merely on loan from the pharaoh. Ramses gives it and can just as easily take it away. I'm on my way back to see him now. I'll tell him that you're here. He will be so pleased to know that he has one of his finest fighters on hand. We'll be leaving for Sile in the morning. You *will* be joining us, won't you?" Souti posed his last sentence as more of an order than a question.

Baba smiled and nodded, his face taking on the same jovial expression that Ptah had seen before. He shook hands with Souti, telling him he'd be there. But when Souti turned to go, Baba's dark eyes flashed with anger, and he glared at the cats with the same look of spite and malice that Ptah had also seen before.

The following morning the chariots corps continued on its way, heading east across the greenery of the Delta. Baba reported for duty as promised, his horse causing quite a stir among the retainers. Riding on its back, he was forced to field endless questions, such as how much the horse was worth, and where a man might get another just like him.

Late in the afternoon on the third day of travel they arrived at the border post of Sile, a mean little town of dusty, narrow streets and crumbling mud-brick houses located near the shores of what the Egyptians called the "Great Green Sea." Ptah was thrilled by his first sight of the aqua waters of the sea he knew as the Mediterranean. Spread out for miles on either side of the town was a vast sea of tents, where mercenaries could be seen milling about or practicing their drills. Behind them, eclipsing both town and tent city, loomed a massive square fortress with giant guard towers on each of its four corners and a central tower in front. Extending from both sides of the fortress, a great wall, strengthened by many small guard towers, traveled north and as far south as the eye could see.

Once again, Ptah's curiosity got the better of him, so he hopped out of his urn and went to find Khufu. By the time he caught up with him at the head of the ranks, he was panting and out of breath. "Wow! That's some fortress! And some wall! What *is* this place?" he asked.

"That is the Fortress of Taru, the starting point of every eastern military expedition," answered Khufu, waving a striped paw before him. "The endless wall that you see runs along Egypt's border from the Great Green Sea in the north to the Red Sea in the south. Directly behind that wall lies another tremendous feat, the canal dug by the Hyksos following their defeat. Together they provide a near-impenetrable barrier between us and our enemies."

"I guess!" exclaimed Ptah, who was just beginning to realize how seriously the Egyptians took the matter of their defense.

With a little help from the mercenaries, Ramses and Souti located the Amun division, which was camped on the north side of town. Setau snapped to attention when he saw the pharaoh approach. "Sire, we have assembled the troops and have finished counting. All told, we have two thousand charioteers, eight thousand archers, and ten thousand spearmen, all marching under the banners of Amun, Re, Set, and Ptah."

Ramses smiled. "Very good," he said. "We are twenty thousand strong."

29
Sekmet, Goddess of War

As the sun god Re crested the horizon to begin his journey across the eastern sky, Ptah was rudely awakened by screeching noise that erupted inside his urn. "On guard!" a voice shrieked. "On guard, I say!" He opened his eyes to find Khufu's tight-fisted paw an inch from his face.

"Go away," groaned Ptah. "Can't you see I'm still sleeping?"

"I will *not* go away," Khufu hissed. "It's high time you crawled out of that urn and started practicing your drills. You need to learn a thing or two about fighting before we reach Kadesh. And you'll be happy to know that I'm just the cat who can teach you." Khufu moved his paw sideways a bit and boxed Ptah's ear.

"Hey, knock it off!" Ptah ducked lower and scowled.

Khufu snorted. "Listen, Ptah, you've been nothing but a sour puss this entire journey. All you've done is sleep. What kind of a captain are you?"

"No kind!" Ptah snapped. "Look, it wasn't my choice to come here, okay?"

The striped cat rolled his hazel-green eyes. "Ptah, when are you going to realize that there are some situations in life where you *have* no choice. Or rather, I should say, where your only choice is how you *choose* to react. Now, you can stay put inside that urn and keep on whining about how you don't want to go to war, but the fact of the matter is, you *are* going to war. On the other hand, you can get out here and try to make yourself ready, because if you don't, you won't know a pounce from a bounce! Now get up!"

Ptah sighed. Khufu was right; he knew it. He'd been acting as though this ghastly war situation would simply go away by itself, which of course, it wouldn't. He'd been refusing to accept the reality he now faced, pinning his hopes instead on escape by means of magic, which he knew was never wise. In one clear moment Ptah realized that it was time he looked to himself for answers, and that maybe, just maybe, if he found a way to live through this thing, there might yet be something good waiting for him to happen down the road ahead.

Ptah crawled out of his urn and followed Khufu onto the sand. *Whack!* Before he knew it was coming, Khufu's hind leg hit him upside the head. "See? I knew you weren't ready," Khufu gloated.

Ptah let out a deep growl. He rubbed the place where he'd been hit with his paw and glared at Khufu, who was sitting back on his haunches, paws held high in some sort of attack position.

Suddenly a commotion arose near Ramses' tent. A runner had approached with important news. "Sire, your quarry has been spotted at a desert oasis southeast of here in the land of Canaan. It's time for the hunt!"

Ramses leaped to his feet. "Souti, man the chariot! Setau, alert the generals! We'll be moving out!" Furious activity instantly swirled through the camp as orders were given and runners dispersed. A small band of retainers was chosen to accompany the king. Plans were made for them to meet up with the others at the end of the day.

Khufu dropped down from his fighting position and raced for the chariot.

"What's all the excitement about?" Ptah cried, chasing after him. "Men go on a hunt every single day!"

"This is not *a* hunt, Ptah, it's *the* hunt," said Khufu, reaching the chariot and jumping inside. "It's tradition for the king to make an offering to the gods before any important battle. Frankly, this is one scene I'd rather miss, but it's all part and parcel of war. Come on; hop in! You don't want to be left behind."

Ptah had no clue what Khufu was talking about, but he did as he was told. Giving up on his urn for the moment, he jumped inside an empty chariot basket while Souti busily filled the others with arrows.

The band of hunters quickly made their way to the central tower of the fortress, where the guards above heralded them. The heavy gates slowly parted. Passing through, Ptah gaped in amazement: the fortress walls were at least ten feet thick!

Once inside the fortress, Ptah was surprised to see another fortress built within, this one made up of many small guard towers built solidly side by side. The gates to this fortress were open, and inside Ptah could see racks and racks of weaponry, as well as the barracks for the soldiers who lived there. Skirting around the inner fortress, Ramses and his retainers exited the outer one via a second set of heavy wooden gates at the back. The gates opened onto a massive bridge, which extended about three quarters of the way across the canal. On the other side of the canal was yet a third fortress, this one with a drawbridge that was just now being lowered into place.

As they waited for the drawbridge, Ptah looked out over the bridge wall. Down below he saw the great canal Khufu had told him about, impressive in its width and depth. He pictured in his mind the Hyksos digging the trenches that connected the natural lakes on the narrow strip of land between the two seas, digging the beginnings of what would one day become the Suez Canal.

Once over the bridge and through the far fortress, the hunters headed southeast into the barren sweeps of the Sinai Desert. A minimalist landscape of sand and sky, the desert looked hauntingly beautiful to Ptah. They rode until they reached an oasis surrounded by scattered palms and tall clumps of grass. Geese and ducks floated on its shallow waters, while herds of antelope and gazelle grazed peacefully. The hunters drove their chariots in a wide arc around the oasis until they reached a position downwind from the animals. Once there, they came to a halt. The cats jumped down from their baskets and went to sit in the shade of a palm while Ramses and the rest of his men watched and waited.

After a while, Ptah became impatient. "What are they waiting for?" he asked. "There must be a hundred gazelle out there!"

"They're not hunting gazelle, Ptah, or antelope or ducks or even geese," Khufu replied.

"Then what—" Ptah started to ask, but he was cut short.

"Shhh! I see one now!" Khufu pointed.

Ptah peered across to a clump of grass about a third of the way around the watering hole from where they were sitting. He saw nothing unusual at first, only the animals and birds that had been dismissed, but then he spotted it. Crouched low, her golden fur blending discreetly with the grass was the most powerful and at once magnificent creature he had ever seen. It was a lion!

"Sekmet, goddess of war," Khufu whispered in awe.

Ptah drew in his breath. He felt humbled by the lion's sleek, muscular body, and by the intensity of her gaze, which was focused entirely upon the animal that she was stalking. "Wow, I wish I were a lion," Ptah murmured.

"There isn't a cat alive who doesn't wish that very same thing," Khufu replied knowingly.

Suddenly remembering why they were there, Ptah blurted, "Ramses isn't going to shoot her, is he?"

"He will if he can . . . he will if he can," said Khufu. "But don't feel too badly about it. That one there is a miserable *foreign* lion. Lions are never hunted at home. They bring a country great strength. To kill your own would be senseless."

Ramses' stallions seemed to sense the lion's presence before they even saw it. They fidgeted about, tossing their heads and straining at the harness. "Whoa, steady boys," whispered Souti. He nudged Ramses on the arm. "Sire, are you ready?"

Ramses pulled an arrow from a basket and tightened his grip on his bow. He nodded.

Souti grasped the reins on the horses and gave them a hard shake, whereupon the horses took off in a gallop. As if on cue, the oasis came alive. Ducks and geese rose honking into the air while antelope and gazelle bounded out across the desert plain. At that very same instant, the lion sprang from her position and chased after them.

"Faster!" yelled Ramses.

Souti shook the reins harder, and the horses picked up speed. From beneath the palm, Ptah watched transfixed as Ramses' chariot pulled parallel with the lion. Running in tandem, they were beauty in motion. One of the retainers, an artist by trade, quickly sketched the image of the king riding along in his chariot with his bow cocked and ready, while the lion thundered along by his side. It was a common artistic scene, one that represented the goddess Sekmet accompanying the king to war.

Despite the horses' obvious fears, Souti rallied them onward. They kept pace with the lion as she swerved to her left, having singled out a particular gazelle slower than the rest. Ramses steadied himself, and as the lion closed in on her target, he took aim and fired. Ptah's heart skipped a beat as the arrow flew, and he had the strangest sensation that it moved in slow motion, so clearly could he see the wind in its feathers and the sunlight glinting off its deadly bronze tip.

The lion seemed not to have even registered this menace, so intent was she on pursuing the animal that she was chasing. But at the very last moment, the split second before it hit, the lion jerked to her right and the arrow missed, landing deep in the sand. Very quickly, Ramses fitted another arrow in his bow as Souti wheeled the chariot around to follow. The horses performed brilliantly, but by the time they renewed their chase, the lion had thundered away.

No one said a word about the hunt on their way toward meeting the others. It was considered bad luck for a king to fail, but even worse for the men to talk about it afterwards. Ptah was secretly elated that the lion had lived, but Khufu was worried. He sat in his chariot basket and glowered.

30
A Tale of Two Spies

The entire Egyptian army was soon marching toward Kadesh. The Amun and Re divisions were in the lead, with the Ptah and Set divisions traveling some ways behind.

Each division was comprised of three units of soldiers: the chariotry, the archers, and the spearmen, with the latter two units collectively known as the foot soldiers. The units were further divided into squadrons, with two hundred and fifty men apiece for the foot soldiers, and fifty men with twenty-five chariots apiece for the chariotry. In addition, the army had generals and chiefs of war, advisors, heralds, runners, and scouts, the latter of whom belonged to no particular unit.

Leading each squadron were the captains, who carried special painted wooden ensigns. The ensigns bore the mark of each division and served as rallying points in battle. The Re division's ensign was pale blue with a bright yellow disk. The Set division's ensign featured a large black boar upon a field of red, while the Ptah division's was green with a black bull on its surface. Ptah and Khufu were traveling with the Amun division. Their ensign was more elaborate, featuring a golden crown with two ostrich feathers, flanked by a ram and a goose on a field of white.

When marching into battle, the chariotry usually led the units. However, when traveling across country, the units were led by the archers, who marched in columns eight ranks deep. Following the archers strode the heralds carrying their polished silver-and-copper war trumpets. After that marched a portion of the spearmen. At the core of each division rode the generals and chiefs of war, followed by the remainder of the spearmen. Next came the chariotry. Bringing up the rear of the army was the supply train, a miles-long column of ox-drawn wagons and heavily laden donkeys accompanied by cooks, servants, and the ever-present scribes, whose job it was to obtain the supplies the army needed en route to battle. Also traveling with the supply train were hundreds of boys, ranging in age from ten to their mid-teens, whose job it was to act as runners and "go-fors," and who were training to be soldiers themselves one day.

Ptah was overwhelmed by how it felt to be marching with an army of twenty thousand men. There was an energy in the air, impossible to see but equally impossible for him not to feel. As Khufu explained it, this was the invisible force of Amun spurring them on to victory. The air was thick with the smell of dust and dung, and of sweat from the men's bodies as they trudged along under the searing sun.

Ptah soon learned that traveling with the mercenaries was far different from traveling with the retainers. For one thing, having so many men on foot forced them to move more slowly. For another, the preparation of meals had become a huge production. Also, the evening entertainment had turned a little rough for Ptah's taste, the mercenaries' favored pastimes being stick fighting and wrestling, with plenty of gambling on hand for each. Lastly, now that they had left the safety of Egypt, the men traveled more cautiously, carrying their weapons with them always and pitching their tents behind a great wall of shields at night.

Across the burning hills of the Sinai Desert there were no villages to speak of, so the only people they passed were occasional bands of roving nomads. Despite the sandstorms that plagued this region, the Egyptians had little trouble in finding their way. Had they not known the location of every oasis in this desert, a journey such as this, with so many men, would have been impossible.

After eight days of marching over endless hills of windblown sand, the army reached the desert's edge, where tall grasses grew. Following the grass line, the men picked up on a wide dirt road, which was the main caravan route between Egypt and the lands to the north. The road led them west to the coast, where yellow sea daffodils flourished in wild bunches. From there it continued north through a fertile land in which wheat and barley grew. Ptah found this land to be particularly beautiful, though he knew he was seeing it at its loveliest time, before the hot dry days of summer withered everything to brown.

Soon they arrived at the wealthy city of Gaza. Built upon a hill overlooking the sea, Gaza was known for its citrus fruits, and the lush groves of citron trees surrounding it attested to that. Through many recent times of strife, Gaza had remained loyal to Egypt, and in honor of that loyalty the Egyptian army had built a beautiful plaza inside its walls, known as the Square of the Unknown Soldier.

As Ramses would do at all the cities he passed, he made his way to the city gates and demanded that food, wine, and water be provided for his men, as well as tribute paid in the form of precious metals, gems, or other expensive "gifts." No minor king would dare refuse him. By now, most lesser kings had succumbed to their fate. As far as they were concerned, better it be the Egyptians than the Hittites.

The army stayed but one night at Gaza before moving on, arriving late the next day at Ashkelon, a great walled city surrounded by fields of wild onions, or scallions, from which the city got its name. Located on the shores of the Great Green Sea, Ashkelon was an important trading center and was blessed with a lovely sandy beach and by rolling groves of olive trees and vineyards.

Ramses, Souti, Setau, and Paser dismounted from their chariots and approached the city gates, where a large pair of bronze-and-silver calves stood waiting to greet them. The guards in the towers above heralded them, and as the gates slowly parted, a man stepped out. To their surprise, it was someone they knew.

"Sashai, what are *you* doing here?" Souti exclaimed.

Setau was more to the point. "Have you been following us?" he demanded.

Sashai, who was equally surprised to see them, swept his cape aside and exclaimed indignantly, "Most certainly not! I came to Ashkelon of my own accord, arriving before you did, I believe. If you must know, I had an appointment to meet with the king."

"*You* had an appointment to meet with the king?" snarled

Setau.

"Indeed I did," retorted Sashai. "It seems the king has been distressed of late. His people don't believe he is a true son of god. They claim to be waiting for their real king to come along—someone who can bring them salvation from people like you."

Suddenly an Egyptian runner approached. "Pharaoh, the mercenaries anxiously await your order to begin sacking the city," he announced.

Sashai raised his eyebrows. "What's this?" he asked. "I was under the impression the mighty Egyptian army never stooped so low as to plunder faithful cities."

Ramses looked chagrined. "Normally we don't, although these mercenaries seem to have a mind of their own. I promised them booty, and it's booty they're after."

Sashai stiffened. "Sire, I would advise you to control your men. It would take a month to lay siege to this fair city. Its walls are as thick as a fortress, and its people have an endless supply of fresh water from an underground spring, not to mention they have ready access to the sea."

"We've conquered this city before," scoffed Ramses.

"I'm not saying you couldn't do it, I'm only saying that it would take you some time. And you have bigger fish to fry. While you dally here, Muwatallis will be conquering Kadesh, and if I'm not mistaken, he will then start heading this way."

"How did you know that?" demanded Setau.

"It is my *job* to know such things," Sashai stated.

"Well," snarled Setau, "the pharaoh takes orders from no man, especially not *you*."

Sashai shrugged. "Do what you will then. No skin off my sandals. And anyway, you will save me a trip. I'm on my way to meet Muwatallis now."

"You have an appointment to meet with him, too?" exclaimed Souti.

"Yes. From what I hear, his reputation as a murderous, raw-flesh-eating barbarian isn't doing much in the way toward helping his relations with the ladies, if you know what I mean," Sashai said with a wink. "I thought I'd show him how to present a more sensitive side. You know, have him bounce a few babies on his knee, eat some apple pie, that sort of thing."

Ramses was not amused. "Consorting with the enemy? That sounds like treason to me!"

"Not at all, not at all," Sashai said hastily. "I do not supply Muwatallis with weapons, only knowledge, although I suppose one could argue that knowledge is the strongest form of weapon there is. At any rate, you can't blame a guy for making a living. My services are still available to you, you know."

Souti nudged Ramses on the arm. "What do you say, Sire? You're certainly entitled to anything and everything those other kings have. Since we're heading the same way, why don't we take him with us?"

Ramses nodded. "Good thinking as always, Souti." Turning to Sashai he said, "You *will* come with us." By the tone of his voice, this was not a request.

"As you wish, Sire. I shall remain by your side." Sashai performed another of his sweeping bows.

Setau's dark eyes narrowed. "Not so fast, mister. If you must come with us, then you'll be riding with the Ptah division, where I can keep an eye on you. If Ramses needs you, I'll know where to find you."

Much to the disappointment of the mercenaries, the army stayed but one night at Ashkelon before resuming its journey. Continuing north along the caravan route, they followed the coastline through a gentle terrain dotted with small towns and villages. Groves of palm trees laden with heavy clusters of brownish-red dates intrigued Ptah. After six days the road turned inland, and for two more days the army trudged upward through a steep mountain pass before arriving at the gates of Megiddo, a wealthy city of lavish temples and palaces surrounded by mighty fortifications. Situated atop a hill, Megiddo boasted a picturesque view of mountains and valleys, and was known for its remarkable water system.

Even more than Kadesh, Megiddo was a city the Egyptians felt had to be kept under their control at any cost. As Khufu so aptly put it, to capture Megiddo was to capture a thousand cities, because it controlled the mountain passage that linked Egypt with the lands to the north. Due to its strategic location, Megiddo was the site of some of the bloodiest battles in ancient history, the most recent of which had been fought by the legendary Egyptian warrior king, Thutmose III, who defeated the combined Canaanite forces by convincing his army to take a narrow, difficult route through the mountains so they could surprise the enemy from behind. From the professor Ptah had learned that Megiddo also carried another, more ominous, name: it was the city of Armageddon later referred to in the Bible.

Resting but one day again, the army continued on its way, traveling down the other side of the mountain pass and then marching westward until they reached the sea again. There they were met by a gentle spring rain, which the Egyptians in the army found freakish. Coming from a land with virtually no rainfall, they referred to places like this as having a "Nile in the sky." Traveling north along the coast, the army passed through many small towns, such as Tyre and Sidon. At each of these towns, Ramses continued to collect tribute, so by the time they reached the seaport city of Byblos, the Egyptian army had amassed a huge fortune.

Byblos was the largest trading center on the eastern Mediterranean Sea. Great wealth flowed through its harbor as ships came and went, both in search of and bringing goods from distant lands. In Byblos one could find silk from the Orient; pottery from Greece; rope, linen, and alabaster statues from Egypt; olives, wine, and citrus fruits from Canaan; ebony, ivory, and rare jewels from Nubia; perfume and exotic animals from Punt; and silver and copper mined in the Far East. Byblos itself was known for its trade in papyrus and wood, especially cedarwood logged from the forests nearby. Ptah knew from his studies that Byblos was the city in which the ancestor of all modern alphabets was invented.

The Egyptian army stayed two days before leaving the coast and heading inland along an ancient riverbed, now dry. The land they passed through was wild and hunting was good. After three days they came upon the Orontes River, wide and swiftly flowing from spring run-off. Following its course, they climbed their way through steep terrain as the river carved its way into a canyon.

It was late in the day when, two days later, they found themselves standing on the edge of a rocky plateau looking north across the grassy plain of Kadesh. From the heights they could see the walls of the city, still ten miles off in the distance. Below and to their right, the Orontes River flowed out from the canyon, cutting a silvery path across the plain. Further east, a second branch of the same river also wound its way northward, the two merging just past the city, so that Kadesh was protected by water on three sides. The Egyptians scanned the horizon. Nowhere was there any sign of the Hittite troops.

"Send the scouts on ahead!" ordered Ramses.

"Sire, my horse is still fresh. I will go," Baba offered.

Ramses nodded, and Baba galloped off. The army proceeded to set up camp. Supplies were unloaded, tents were pitched, and hunting parties went out. Things had just started to settle down, and Ramses, Souti, Setau, and Paser had just sat down for their evening meal, when Baba returned. With him were two men, nomads by the look of them. Their long, loose robes were thin and pale, and they wore head cloths that hung down their backs. The men appeared to be Baba's prisoners, for their wrists were bound and he was pulling them along with a rope.

"Make way! Make way!" Baba shouted as he strong-armed the men toward the pharaoh. Pushing them to their knees, he reported, "Sire, I've captured two spies!" Baba then turned to the men. "Now, tell us! Where are Muwatallis and his Hittite army?"

Although visibly shaken, the bearded captives remained silent.

"Leave this to me," growled Setau. Rising from his stool, he loomed momentarily over the kneeling men, then yanked off one of the men's head cloths. Grabbing the man by the hair, he pulled back on his head to expose his throat. Next he whipped his dagger from its sheath and pressed it firmly against the man's skin. "Speak!" he demanded.

"Have mercy on me!" the man cried. "We are not spies! We are merely Bedouin nomads passing through on our way north!"

"Tell us what you know about the Hittites," snarled Setau, his dagger sliding sideways a little and drawing a trickle of blood.

"Muwatallis was here a few days ago, but . . . but he's gone now," sputtered the man. "His troops fled north to Aleppo upon hearing that your mighty pharaoh was coming."

Ramses smiled. "Perfect," he said. "This will be an easy victory. We will regain Kadesh with hardly a fight! Souti, go tell the general of the Set army to turn back around. It shouldn't take twenty thousand men to capture one tiny, unarmed city."

"Sire, I advise caution," warned Paser. "Things are not always as simple as they seem. I've said it before, Muwatallis is a crafty foe—"

"Who has run like a goose with his head cut off!" Ramses finished for him. "That miserable king of Amurru should be more careful about whom he places his loyalties with. Now, let's eat and then get some sleep. Kadesh will be ours in the morning!"

Overhearing their conversation, Ptah was thrilled. After all of his fears, after all of his worries, it now appeared that no battle would be fought at all. Even Baba's slight wink and a nod at the huddled captives could not dispel his newfound feeling of calm.

31
The Trap

Gazing across the plain in the morning light, Ramses was anxious to get going. To appease him, the generals and chiefs of war agreed to let him lead the Amun division down from the heights on the condition that he stop after crossing the western branch of the Orontes and wait for the Re division, which would soon follow. Much to Setau's objection, the Ptah division was made to remain on the heights, while the Set division was ordered to return home.

Setau wasn't the only one disgruntled by the arrangements. Khufu was furious he was made to ride with the Re division, rather than in the basket of Souti's chariot, where he felt he rightfully belonged. With the baskets now full of weapons, Ramses had determined that there was room for only one cat, and he had decided it would be Ptah. As for Ptah, he didn't much care for this decision either, preferring instead to remain on the heights with Setau. Nevertheless, it seemed that once again he no choice in the matter, and it only made things worse to have Khufu's hazel-green eyes glaring holes in the back of his head as he climbed inside.

"Victory is in the air, Souti. I can feel it!" Ramses bellowed as they descended the rocky hillside to the grassy plain below. Reaching up, he adjusted his jeweled cape, then straightened his blue war crown so it extended high over his head. Following that, he instructed Souti to begin searching the river for a good place to cross.

After they had gone a few miles, the Amun division forded the western branch of the Orontes, then continued north for several more miles before coming to a halt about a mile south of the city. Here

Ramses decided to set up camp and wait for the Re division, which could be seen approaching the river in the distance. With plenty of time to spare, Ramses ordered the scribes to bring forth the cartloads of tribute so they could begin the long, slow process of divvying up the booty. The scribes had already prepared lists itemizing and categorizing each object, which they presented to the pharaoh. Ptah jumped onto the oxcart that held his urn as Ramses removed his crown, loosened his cape, and sat on a stool beside Souti to review them. No sooner had he unfurled the papyrus sheets, however, than a runner approached.

"Sire!" the young man panted. "I have . . . *terrible* news!"

"What is it?" Ramses asked casually, thumbing through the pages.

"*Spies* . . . captured on the plain . . . Muwatallis—" The runner's chest heaved with the effort of saying these few words.

"Rest easy, soldier," Ramses interrupted. "We already caught some spies last night. They told us that Muwatallis fled north to Aleppo upon hearing we were coming."

"But, Sire . . . these men tell a different story," the runner said in gasps. "Muwatallis has been hiding behind the eastern wall of the city this entire time! His army crossed the river just north of here this morning. It's a *trap!*"

As if a massive flood gate had been flung open wide, the sound of a thousand horses' hooves could suddenly be heard thundering in the distance. Ramses looked up to see the Hittite army charging south across the plain, bearing down upon the unsuspecting Re division, which was just now crossing the river.

The pharaoh leaped from his stool, his heavy jeweled cape falling to the ground behind him. "What are they *doing?*" he cried. "There are *rules* to war! Muwatallis was supposed to make an *appointment* to fight! Ambushes are *not* allowed!"

"Apparently Muwatallis forgot to read the rulebook," yelled Souti. Shielding his eyes from the sun, he scanned the oncoming tide before shouting, "Sire, look! The Hittites are riding *three*-man chariots!"

Ptah looked up from the oxcart to see that Souti was right. Far superior to the chariots the Egyptians were driving, the Hittite chariots sported three men: a driver, a shooter, and a shield-bearer whose only job was to protect the other two. Suddenly he remembered what it was about the Battle of Kadesh that the professor had told him: the Egyptian army had fallen prey to a vicious trap!

Ramses' face turned ashen. He stood there immobilized, mumbling something to himself about fair play, while the Hittite troops stormed ever onward, a plume of dust rising in their wake. Souti shook him on the shoulder and cried, "Sire, I suggest that you *do* something!"

Ramses snapped to attention. Striding over and snatching a silver-and-copper war trumpet from an oxcart, he blew the signal to charge, then yelled, "Man the chariots! Form the lines! Prepare to fight!" Next he thrust on his blue war crown, grabbed his bow, and took off running after Souti, who was already racing toward their chariot.

At the sound of the trumpet, Ptah had expected to see the Amun division spring into action. But instead they just stood there, paralyzed with fear, while staring transfixed at the grisly scene unfolding before them. Across the plain, the men of the Re division had been caught off guard. Panicking at the sight of the oncoming terror, they had broken their ranks and were now running in all directions—some southwest toward the rocky heights, others due south toward the narrow river canyon. Those who had already crossed the river ran northeast, straight for the Amun division's camp. Meanwhile, the enemy chariots were pursuing them mercilessly, cutting them down as they ran.

Ptah couldn't bear to watch. He leaped to the rim of his urn, and then dove inside. Scrunching into a ball, he was determined to remain hidden there, when a horrible thought struck him. Khufu had been riding with the Re division! At once he jumped back up and poked his head outside, searching the plain for his beleaguered friend.

Minutes later, Ptah's whole world turned upside down as the first of the terrified Re division came stumbling through camp. "Run for your lives!" they shouted and then kept on running, heading east toward the opposite branch of the Orontes River.

Hearing their cry, the Amun division jolted into action. The foot soldiers ran for the supply wagons and began arming themselves with anything they could quickly lay hands on. The retainers raced for their chariots. Things looked to Ptah as though they were moving toward a counterattack, when all of a sudden the soldiers turned on their heels and began chasing after the others. Seeing their flight, the retainers took off also, riding east as fast as their horses would go.

Aghast, Ramses tried to rally his troops. "Turn and fight!" he yelled, but it was of no use. To a man, the Amun division beat a hasty retreat. Ramses and Souti rapidly found themselves alone in their chariot on the open plain.

Meanwhile, the Hittite army had crossed the river and was heading for them fast. "Sire, what would you like me to do?" yelled Souti. He turned to face Ramses, but the pharaoh stared after his men, mumbling, "They've deserted me," over and over and over again. Souti had no choice but to decide for himself what action to take. Knowing that first and foremost, his job was to protect the king, he shook the reins on his horses and bolted after the rest.

Ptah's heart plunged to his stomach as he watched them go. They were doomed; he knew it. The odds against Ramses and Souti surviving were the same as what they were outnumbered: about five thousand to one. Sadly he realized that it would take one of Ipuwer's miracles to save them now. He wracked his brain, trying hard to remember what it was that Ipuwer had told Nebre—something about keeping his eyes wide open so he could see the miracle when it arrived. All Ptah knew was that if a miracle was going to happen, it had to happen fast. The Hittites were already storming past the Amun camp, hot on the heels of Ramses and Souti.

In a last ditch effort, Ptah forced his eyes wide open and looked all around, searching for something—anything!—that might save them. He looked to the sky—no storm. He looked to the sea—no hurricane. He looked toward the heights—no sandstorm. He tried to stay focused, but the thundering of hooves and the sunlight reflecting off the jewels on Ramses' cape, getting into his eyes, was making it difficult for him to think.

Then it hit him. *The cape!* Without wasting another moment,

Ptah leaped from his urn and raced to where Ramses' blue cape lay fallen on the ground. Snatching it up in his teeth, he started to run, or rather he tried to, but the cape was too heavy.

Ptah was devastated. As fast as he had come up with a plan, it had been ruined. Giving up all hope, he was just beginning to wonder whether it would be better to be run through with a sword or trampled to pieces by horse's hooves, when a brown and black blur came streaking across the plain and screeched to a halt beside him. Khufu!

"What's the plan?" the striped cat hollered.

"A . . . distraction," Ptah grunted, the cape still gripped in his teeth.

"Good thinking, captain!" cried Khufu. "Quick, you take that end and I'll take this one. Now, let's go!"

Like a lightning bolt, the two cats zipped out onto the plain and began running in a wide arc around the Amun camp. Behind them, Ramses' cape billowed in the breeze, its mass of glittering jewels catching the sunlight and reflecting it in an undulation of shimmering sparkles. Back and forth, and back and forth the two cats ran, while waving the beacon they hoped would lure the Hittites away from the king.

It worked! Like a river that redirects its flow when a new channel is cut, the Hittite army began swerving in the direction of the glittering cape. All eyes were upon it, all hearts beating fast at the thought of owning such treasure. Closer and closer they came, and as they drew near, for the first time they noticed the rich booty of the Amun camp, now deserted of men.

Ptah and Khufu were thrilled when they saw that their plan was working, until suddenly they realized they had ten thousand men bearing down on them fast. "Drop the cape and run for it!" yelled Khufu as he released his corner and bolted into camp. Out of breath and out of his mind with fear, Ptah dropped his corner and ran for his life, diving under an oxcart on the tail of Khufu just as the Hittite army descended.

32
The Battle of Kadesh

The first man to arrive on the scene jumped down from his chariot and snatched Ramses' cape, holding it high for everyone to see. "I'm rich!" he shouted. No sooner had he said this, however, than another man dismounted, socked him in the gut, and grabbed the cape for himself. All chaos broke loose then, as more and more Hittites poured into camp and began fighting over the treasure the Egyptians left behind.

Khufu and Ptah quickly found themselves in the middle of it all when the oxcart they were hiding under was overturned and its contents dashed to the ground. They swiftly darted under another cart, only to have that topple over as well. Soon they found themselves racing from cart to cart, dodging hooves and falling equipment while bodies thrashed all around.

Suddenly Khufu let out a screech that bristled Ptah's fur. "My leg!" he cried.

Ptah whirled around to see Khufu lying on his side, his back leg hanging at an odd angle to the rest of his body.

"Hang on, Khufu, I'm coming!" Ptah shouted. Running over and grabbing Khufu by the scruff, he struggled to drag him to safety.

"Don't be a fool! Save yourself! Remember what I told you: look out for number one!" screeched Khufu as Ptah barely missed being knocked stone-cold senseless by a flailing horse's hoof.

That may be your creed, but it's not mine, thought Ptah, while vowing to himself never again to leave a friend in distress. Spying a nearby overturned oxcart, he doubled his efforts, finally managing to drag Khufu the rest of the way to safety.

"Now go!" yelled Khufu. "Find Setau! Get help!"

Ptah looked at Khufu as though his leg wasn't the only thing he had broken. "Are you crazy?" he cried. By now the fighting had reached its peak and the clashing of Hittite swords could be heard all around.

"You must! Do it for duty! Do it for honor!" Khufu yelped.

Honor, I'm a goner, thought Ptah as he plunged back into the fray. Dashing through the Amun camp, he shot out on the other side and started running across the grassy plain as fast as his furry legs would carry him. Reaching the river, he stopped momentarily to catch his breath and to check on the pharaoh's progress.

To his surprise, Ramses and Souti's chariot had stopped. The two men were studying the Hittites, who they noted had ditched the pharaoh in pursuit of an even bigger prize. Above the din, Ptah could hear Souti's faint cry, "Sire, look! They've forgotten all about us! What would you like me to do?" Souti swiveled to look at Ramses, who in turn looked back at him, both men seeing the same glint in each other's eyes.

"Attack!" they cried in unison.

Ptah's eyes bugged out in horror as he watched Souti wheel the chariot around and the two men hurtle back across the plain. Soon they were circling the Amun camp, targeting the mass of Hittites who were swarming over the mounds of Egyptian booty like ants upon an anthill.

"Hold her steady, man!" Ramses shouted as he let loose a volley of arrows. One after another the Hittites fell, so intent they were on their looting that they didn't even realize they were being attacked from behind. Round and round, and round and round Souti's chariot flew, while Ramses shot them down by the score.

Suddenly they were spotted! A cry of alarm rose up as a dozen or more Hittites raced for their chariots. Souti reversed direction and began barreling across the plain, moments before the enemy arrows started raining down, landing with a sickening plop in the grass. Shaking the reins on his horses, he shouted, "Sire, remove your crown!"

"What?" yelled Ramses. The shouts and cries and the pounding of hooves made it difficult to hear.

"I said, for Amun's sake, remove the pharaoh's crown! You may as well be wearing a bull's-eye on the top of your head!"

Ramses reached for his crown, but could not bring himself to remove it. "I can't!" he shouted.

"Okay, then hang on!" yelled Souti as he began jerking the reins from side to side, sending the chariot on an erratic flight across the plain. The Hittites doggedly pursued them, but it didn't take long for the enemy to begin falling behind. Minutes later, Souti glanced back and shouted, "Sire, look! Our chariot is lighter than theirs, so we're faster! What do you say, shall we turn and fight?"

"On my father's good name, yes! We turn and fight!" Ramses braced himself against the chariot railing and grabbed for an arrow as Souti wheeled the chariot around. Taking the reins in one hand, Souti picked up his shield with his other hand and held it aloft. They charged.

Ramses was ready. His arrows, sure and true, found their mark as one after another of the enemy soldiers fell. Wild-eyed with fear, the Hittite horses began careening sideways, smashing the enemy chariots into each other and throwing the drivers onto the ground. Through it all, Souti stayed well in control, moving his shield up, down, left, and right, deflecting the Hittite arrows while weaving a course in and around and through them. In a matter of minutes, the last of their attackers had fallen.

"Yow!" whooped Souti, but their victory was short-lived. Hundreds more Hittites had seen what was happening, had mounted their chariots, and were now storming their way.

Watching this, Ptah jolted to attention as a wave of panic rushed through him. *Yikes! I'd better move fast!* he thought. He gulped as he turned toward the river—cats hate to swim!—but then he steeled himself and jumped right in, doing the best imitation dog paddle he could. Crawling out on the other side, and feeling refreshed for it, he took off running for the heights.

Meanwhile, on the other side of the plain, the Amun division and what was left of the Re had crossed the eastern branch of the

Orontes and had stopped to look back around.

"Set!" cried one man. "We left Ramses alone on the battlefield!"

"Forget about Ramses," bellowed another. "The Hittites are stealing our booty!"

"Argh!" the men shouted as they plunged back into the river on their way to reclaim their treasure.

Ptah ran on and on. His lungs were searing with pain and the dust was blinding his senses, but he couldn't stop now—he had reached the base of the heights! Half running, half clawing, he scrambled his way to the top of the hill and then dove into the Ptah division's camp, collapsing at Setau's feet.

Setau took one look at him and knew that something had gone wrong. Leaping from his stool, he shouted, "To your chariots, men. Now! Move, move, move!"

What happened next was all a blur to Ptah. He felt himself being lifted up and plopped into a chariot basket. Then he heard a volley of shouts and suddenly, with a lurch, he felt the chariot take off. Next he was aware of being tossed around inside the basket, and of being too tired to care. After that he heard the splashing of water as the horses barreled through the river and out across the grassy plain. At this point, he mustered the energy to lift his head over the rim.

Straining his eyes against the dust, Ptah could just make out Ramses' blue war crown bobbing along in the distance. Very quickly he realized that Ramses and Souti were in trouble. An angry band of Hittites was chasing after them and was gaining on them fast! The situation looked grim, and Ptah was just about to shrink down into his chariot basket so he wouldn't have to watch, when all at once his heart leaped for joy because there, storming across the plain from the east, was the Amun division and what was left of the Re, returning to the rescue!

The situation looked hopeful until the very next moment, when a great commotion arose to the north. Ptah turned his head to see the gates of Kadesh burst open as thousands of Hittite reinforcements came streaming forth. Leading the way in a golden chariot led by two pure white horses was King Muwatallis himself, his frizzy black beard flapping in the breeze and his red and gold uniform blazing in the sun.

Setau spotted the reinforcements as soon as Ptah did. "Onward, men!" he shouted. The Ptah division thundered even faster, the speed of their horses' hooves matched only by the speed of Ptah's heart pounding in his chest. Meanwhile, the Amun division and what was left of the Re closed in as well, until with a flash of swords and a cry of fury, the Egyptian army coming from both directions descended upon the Amun camp and began cutting their way into enemy lines. No sooner had they arrived, however, than so did the Hittite reinforcements. The true battle had just begun.

Riding high on the basket of Setau's chariot, Ptah refused to let his mind take in what his eyes were now seeing. Everywhere he looked, men were being beaten and bludgeoned and hacked to death with daggers and swords. Arrows were raining all around, spouting forth a river of blood. The plain echoed with the din of shrieks and shouts, and with the clashing of metal against metal, but above it all Ptah could hear the most dreadful sound of all: the sound of horses screaming.

Both armies were going at it so fiercely that Ptah could hardly tell which side was winning. The Hittites were making deep strides; however, the mercenaries were proving to be far tougher on the battlefield than he'd imagined they'd be, so it appeared to be anybody's battle.

It didn't take long for Ptah to decide he'd seen enough. He dove down deep in his basket, covering his ears with his paws. This move was risky, he knew, but if the basket he was riding in was run through with a sword, then so be it. There wasn't anything he could do about it now, and besides, there was no place he'd rather be in this battle than riding with Setau, who was every bit living up to his reputation as a seasoned warrior. In a word, the man was awesome: one minute organizing the lines of defense, the next minute leading the attacks. All this and still managing to keep his head—literally!—in the midst of chaos.

The battle raged on and on, lasting the entire day and into the evening. As nightfall approached and the sky grew dark, both armies blew on their trumpets, signaling retreat. The Hittites fled to the safety of the city walls, leaving the Egyptians behind to lick their wounds for the night.

Utterly exhausted, the Egyptian army staggered back to the heights. Few men spoke as they walked, for it was a sorrowful journey. The plain was littered with corpses, and the air was filled with the moans of men who had survived the battle but would not live to see morning. Ptah was grateful for the veil of darkness that had begun to fall. As hard as he tried, he could not quit shaking.

Setau located Ramses and Souti, and together they made their way through the Amun camp, now in ruins. Suddenly remembering Khufu, Ptah leaped from Setau's chariot and raced to the oxcart where he'd seen him last. Steeling himself for what he might find, he slowly peeked underneath. Khufu was alive! Barely breathing and delirious with pain, but still alive! Ptah instantly began yowling at the top of his lungs, upon which the men came to investigate. Soon Souti had retrieved his cat and had carefully placed him in an empty chariot basket. Then he thoughtfully retrieved Ptah's urn.

The men continued on their way, at one point coming upon Baba lying face down on the ground. In his hand was clutched Ramses' cape, and in his back was thrust a Hittite dagger.

Souti stopped the chariot and got out. Shaking his head sadly, he said, "Poor Baba, a soldier to the end. He even tried to rescue Ramses' cape."

Ha! thought Ptah, rolling his eyes. *A thief to the end is more like it.*

33
Where Greatness Lies

The morning after the battle Ramses called together all of his generals and chiefs of war for a war council inside his tent. It was a somber gathering, made all the more painful by the fact that the general and most of the chiefs of the Re division were noticeably absent. Khufu and Ptah took their places in a corner while the men filtered in. Near the center of the tent, Ramses sat slumped on a stool, rubbing his temples. He looked as though he'd aged ten years in one night. Paser stood off to his left; Setau and Souti to his right. When all who were coming had arrived, Ramses began to speak.

"Good morning, men, although I'd say this morning is anything but good. As you all know, we faced a terrible foe yesterday—one who chose to remain hidden, one who fought a different sort of battle than any we have fought before. That being said, is there anyone here who can tell me the situation as it stands right now?"

One of the chiefs of the Ptah division rose from his stool and bowed. "Sire, the Hittites are cowering like dogs behind the city walls. They shake at the mere mention of your name! They cringe—"

"Enough!" barked Ramses, holding up his palm. "This is no time for false indulgence. I wish to know the *real* situation."

The chief winced. Letting out a deep sigh, he said, "The Hittites have inflicted serious losses upon us. They are presently sitting safely behind the city walls. Muwatallis has sent for fresh backup troops; they should be here within a few days."

"I see," Ramses said quietly. "That is not the situation I had hoped to hear."

"On a good note, Sire," the chief added, "we weren't the only ones to suffer heavy losses. Our estimates show that the Hittites lost an equal number of men."

Unimpressed, Ramses rose from his stool and began pacing the floor. "How could this have happened?" he lamented. "My army was filled with cowards who deserted me at the first sign of danger!"

"Pardon my bluntness, Sire," said Paser, "but what did you expect? Your army was made up of mercenaries! They came here for the profit, not because of any loyalty to you or to Egypt."

"And if you don't mind my asking," said Setau, "just what did you think you were doing out there, fighting all those Hittites by yourself? You could have been killed! And then what? Paser's too old to succeed you, and you've no sons yet. There would have been a fight for the throne. It would have led to chaos!"

"He was only trying to be great," mumbled Souti, who instantly wished he'd remained silent. Setau turned on him like an angry lion.

"And *you!*" he roared. "How *dare* you endanger the life of our king? What were you thinking, racing around the enemy lines like that? Why didn't you flee like the others?"

"I . . . we . . . *did* flee at first," Souti stammered, "but then the Hittites caught sight of Ramses' cape, and they turned their backs on us, and . . . and . . ." Turning quickly toward Ramses, he said, "Let me be the first to tell you, Sire. You really *were* great out there!"

"And so were you, Souti, so were you," Ramses said grinning. The two men stood there beaming at each while the tent remained silent.

Finally, Setau cleared his throat. "Excuse me, Sire. Your heroism is in no doubt, but we're in a bit of a tight spot."

Ramses sighed. "All right, Viceroy, maybe you can tell me what our options are."

"I regret to inform you that our options are limited," replied Setau. "We can either try to storm the city, in which case we'd lose a lot more men, or we can surround the city and try to starve the Hittites out, in which case Muwatallis's fresh back-up troops would arrive and we'd have twice the army to deal with."

"Those are our only options?" exclaimed Ramses.

Setau's expression turned sour. "We could always go home in defeat," he added.

"Go home in defeat—that is *not* an option!" bellowed Ramses. "I *cannot* not win! I want to be known as *great*, do you hear? There must be *something* we can do!"

"Sire, do I need to say it any more bluntly?" asked Setau. "We've no chance of winning this battle. The best you can hope for is a draw."

Ramses looked desperate. "Paser, surely you must have some advice!"

"My advice is to tally this one up to experience. A great man knows when to cut his losses and move on," the old vizier replied evenly, tugging at one of his ears.

"Humph! You two are a lot of help," Ramses snorted. Scanning the tent, he then asked, "How about the rest of you? Surely there must be some way out of the mess we're in. Doesn't anyone have any ideas? Any of you?" A silence, as utterly complete as the Valley of the Kings, descended upon the tent while the generals and chiefs of war all looked at their feet and twiddled their thumbs.

Finally Souti spoke up. "What about calling what's-his-name in here? You know, the guy with the snakeskin sandals? He seemed full of ideas."

"You mean Sashai?" asked Setau. "He seemed full of himself! That man's oilier than an olive. He should not be trusted."

"Well, it couldn't hurt to at least hear what he has to say," suggested Souti.

"I agree," said Ramses, shooting the viceroy a nasty scowl. "His ideas can't be any worse than yours. Somebody go get him. I think he's camped with the Ptah division. In the meantime, let's take a break."

Twenty minutes later the council had reconvened. Entering the tent, Sashai strode confidently over to the pharaoh and performed a sweeping bow. "Sire, you called?" he asked. Then, looking around the tent at the solemn faces surrounding him, he exclaimed, "What's going on in here? Everyone looks like the guest of honor at his own funeral! Didn't you call me in here to help plan a victory celebration?"

"We didn't win, you idiot!" Setau snapped. "Muwatallis tricked us! If it weren't for those two cats sitting over there, who just happened to distract the Hittites by playing with Ramses' cape, we would all be dead! If we fight again today, we're finished!"

"Whoa, back up!" exclaimed Sashai. "Explain the whole situation to me again, but more slowly this time."

"Okay, have a seat," said Souti, who proceeded to recount the Battle of Kadesh, beginning with the first two spies and ending with the retreat.

In the corner of the tent, Khufu was fuming. "Did you hear that?" he huffed to Ptah. "Setau said we were *playing* with Ramses' cape!"

"Don't go getting your tail all twisted up in a knot, Khufu. Forget it," said Ptah, who hoped his friend wouldn't push it any further. Ever since his leg had been set in a splint, Khufu had been in a bad mood. Choosing to ignore the grumbles and grunts that emanated from the cat beside him, Ptah stretched, then cleaned himself before settling back down on his haunches and returning his attention to Souti, who was just finishing up.

"And so," concluded Souti, "while we certainly didn't win the battle, we didn't exactly lose it either. Our estimates show that the Hittites lost an equal number of men. Our options now are to either storm Kadesh, squandering more men in the process, or we can surround the city and try to starve the Hittites out, in which case Muwatallis' fresh backup troops would arrive and we'd have twice the army to deal with."

"Whew, those are some options," murmured Sashai. "Storming is out, starving is out." Stroking his chin, he asked, "Couldn't we arrange some sort of a peace treaty?"

"Based on what?" asked Ramses.

"I don't know. There's got to be *something* Muwatallis wants," Sashai replied. Suddenly, he brightened. "Say, doesn't he have a daughter he's been trying to get rid of . . . uh, to marry off for a long time now? You could offer to take her hand in marriage in exchange for peace."

"Marry his daughter!" exclaimed Ramses. "That old thing? I've heard she is missing half her teeth!"

"Half her teeth, I didn't know she had that many," mumbled Paser under his breath.

"At least you'd know she wouldn't bite you," quipped Setau.

Ramses shot his advisors a menacing glance before turning to Sashai and saying, "Listen, I know you're trying to help, but a marriage such as this—"

"Please, Sire, before you reject this plan too quickly, we should at least discuss it," Sashai said. "A peace treaty would allow you to return home with your head held high. And Muwatallis would be sure to accept. What father does not dream for his daughter to become an Egyptian princess? And as for her missing a few teeth, well, you could always fit her with a lovely set of golden choppers just like mine!" Sashai smiled broadly, his golden tooth gleaming in the light.

"The man does have a point," allowed Setau.

Ramses groaned. "Oh, how did it ever come down to this? What will Nefertari say?"

"Don't worry about Nefertari," replied Paser. "Your wife knows she is safe in her position as first queen, and that it will be her son who will become pharaoh after you. You're allowed to have a favorite among the queens, you know."

"He's quite right," added Setau. "Accept this marriage and then set up Muwatallis's daughter in a corner of the palace somewhere and visit her once a month. How hard can that be? You know the Egyptian saying: If you can't beat 'em, marry 'em!"

Ramses sulked. "A peace treaty is all very fine and good, but it doesn't go very far toward making me look great. Who remembers any of Egypt's peaceful kings, like Amunhotep III or that woman-who-would-be-king, Hatshepsut? Any of you? Of course not!"

"What would you say if we could solve that problem? Would you agree to the marriage then?" asked Sashai.

"I suppose so." Ramses sighed. He slumped to his stool, then ordered half-heartedly, "Send a runner to speak with Muwatallis."

Sashai clapped his hands together. "Okay, men, the challenge is on! In order for Ramses to agree to this marriage, we need to come up with a way to make him look great. So I ask you: what makes a man great?"

Setau drew up his massive frame, pulled back his muscled shoulders, and puffed out his chest. "That's easy," he replied. "A great man is a brave warrior who wins many battles."

Ramses slouched forward, putting his head between his hands. "See, I told you," he murmured.

Sashai winced. Turning to Setau, he said coldly, "Why don't you go outside and polish your sword for a while, will you?" Then, addressing the other men, he said, "Let's forget about battles for the moment, shall we? I ask you again, what makes a man great?"

This time Souti spoke up. "A great man is one who is honest, loyal, hard-working, and fair—all the things that truly count."

Sashai nodded his head. "There's truth to that statement," he said slowly. "But . . . *boring!* How am I supposed to market that? I need something with spark, something with pizzazz. I need something that people can sink their teeth into! Come on, men. Help me out a little here. Give me something I can *work* with."

"Being great is different for every man," Paser replied. "Whether he be farmer, official, merchant, or scribe, the key to any man's greatness is for him to understand where his own greatness lies." Turning toward Ramses, he said, "You, Sire, are a diplomat. Your greatness will come, not through the slash of a sword, but through the stroke of a reed, not through the death of your foes, but through the birth of diplomacy."

"A diplomat," muttered Ramses. "That sounds like something you wipe your feet on."

"Not at all," replied Paser. "A diplomat is someone who possesses great skill in dealing with others. He is the type of man who—"

"Greatness lies . . . greatness lies," Sashai interrupted loudly before suddenly exclaiming, "*That's it!* I think we can all come up with a few 'greatness lies,' don't you, men? All we need to do is remold the meaning a bit. Now tell me, what's the first thing you think of when you think of a man who is great?"

"I know . . . he's rich!" shouted one chief.

"And famous!" cried another.

"He has many wives!" spouted a third.

"And many children!" hollered a fourth.

"But most of all, he builds, builds, builds!" yelled several in unison.

Sashai clapped his hands excitedly. "Now you're talking!" he exclaimed. "These are things I can work with! These are things I can *use!*"

Paser angrily grabbed hold of his ankh. "That's not what I meant!" he snapped. "Those statements *are* lies, myths about what it means to be great. They have no basis in fact!"

"Who cares?" Sashai asked giddily. "They *sound* good, and people tend to believe in them whether they're true or not." Turning toward Ramses, he said, "Let's go through these one at a time, shall we? Riches you've got. Wives? Those should be easy considering you've got the rich part. And children? Well, they just sort of come along with the territory. Sire, when you get home you need to get serious about increasing the size of your harem. A hundred or so wives should do it, and you should have a goal of, say, a hundred and fifty children!"

Ramses' face flushed crimson while the generals and chiefs of war all winked and smiled at each other.

"But how do we get past the fact that Ramses didn't win this battle?" asked one man. "The news is bound to get back to Egypt at some point."

Sashai stroked his chin slowly before a sly smile spread across his face. "Who's to say he didn't win?" he quipped. "It will be our story against theirs. And our version of the story—the *official* version— will get there first! Sire, who is your official palace scribe?"

"Uh, Pentaur here," Ramses answered, motioning toward a slender young man seated nearby.

Addressing the young man, Sashai announced, "Pentaur, as head of the palace scribes, it will be your job to record the Battle of Kadesh. Not the way it *really* happened, mind you, but the way we want people to *think* that it happened. Scratch the part about the

Egyptians falling into Muwatallis's trap, and the part about the two cats saving Ramses' life, but keep the part about the army deserting him. Write it so that Ramses faced hundreds—no thousands!—of Hittites all on his own. Spice it up a bit. You know, flaming arrows, merciless foes, so on and so forth. When you're done I want you to arrange for the story to be copied and read aloud in every town and village from here to Elephantine. I want it to become the bedtime story that children grow up with. I want Ramses to become famous!"

Turning toward the pharaoh, Sashai then said, "So let's see, we've covered rich, famous, wives, children . . . ah yes, we missed the building part. Sire, when you get home you need to ramp up your building spree. Your construction at Pi-Ramses and Abu Simbel are fine starts, but you should plan on building at least a hundred monuments."

"A hundred monuments! But there are only so many years in a lifetime," protested Ramses, running a hand through his auburn hair. "I know of many kings who had building projects underway their entire reign and still barely dotted the landscape!"

Sashai nodded his head in amusement. "Well, who's to say which monuments were built by whom? I say we go on a victory tour up the river Nile. Everywhere we stop, we'll chisel the names off monuments the other kings have built and put your name on there instead. You know the adage, 'Time erases all memory except that which is written in stone.'"

Paser could stand it no longer. "Now, hold on a minute!" he barked. "With that you have *definitely* gone too far! Everyone knows that the dead kings' spirits will come back and get Ramses for that."

Sashai shrugged. "Then we'll chop the noses off their statues so they can't come back." He paused, then said, "What do you say, Sire? I think a victory tour is a grand idea. We can throw a big party in every town—food, wine, beer, dancing girls, the works! And to top it all off, we'll hold an awards ceremony at the Pyramids of Giza. Our theme could be something like, 'Come and see something great!'"

Ramses was about to respond when the runner he'd sent to his rival burst into the tent. "Pharaoh! King Muwatallis has agreed to the marriage of his daughter in exchange for peace! He is presenting you with this special gift in order to seal the deal." The runner approached, holding forth a spectacular sword made of dark gray metal with a jewel-encrusted hilt.

The chiefs' eyes grew wide.

"The blade is made of iron," one gasped.

"I've heard of this strange, new metal but I've never seen it for myself," a second one murmured.

"Harder than bronze, they say, and twice as lethal," proclaimed a third.

Brandishing the sword, Ramses stood. "Do you think this plan will work?" he asked.

"I know it will," declared Sashai. "Mark my words: before long, people will be calling you Ramses the Great! Think about it, Sire. It's a small price to pay for eternal fame."

Ramses ran his hand hesitantly over the flat part of the blade, admiring its craftsmanship, then asked, "Souti, what do you think?"

"I think you should go for it," replied Souti. "Remember what the men were just saying—many wives, many children? Well, there's no better time to start being great than right now."

Ramses swept the air with his new sword. "Okay then, I'll do it! I'll marry the toothless hag if it means fulfilling my destiny! Send the word to Muwatallis and then gather the troops. We head back to Egypt tomorrow!"

34

Victory Tour

Three and a half weeks later the Egyptian army arrived at Avaris, the city founded by the Hyksos on the eastern side of the Delta some four hundred years before. The timing was favorable for their return. Sirius, the Dog Star, had recently been spotted on the evening horizon and the waters of the Nile were just beginning to rise, marking the start of the Egyptian New Year. This occasion always called for a weeklong celebration of its own, and Sashai planned to tie into it with the kick-off party for Ramses' victory tour.

While everyone was busy making the arrangements, Khufu and Ptah decided to explore the town. Khufu's leg had healed nicely while on the road to Egypt, which both pleased and annoyed Ptah, who rather preferred the hobbled and humbled Khufu to the boastful and bragging one he had come to know so well. Beginning at the old Hyksos palace, the two cats wound their way through the narrow streets, passing by houses and temples until they reached the outskirts of town.

The fields surrounding the city were a bustle of activity. With the river on the rise, people were working hard to complete the harvest. The first sign the cats saw of this were some farmers harvesting wheat. Men using long sickle-shaped knives were cutting away the golden stalks and throwing them onto threshing floors, where cattle were led across to break them down with their hooves. After the spent stalks were forked aside, the women took over, tossing the grain into the air with winnowing fans to remove the chaff. Finally the grain was gathered into baskets, which were then counted and recorded by scribes sitting nearby.

The cats moved on, stopping again when they reached some farmers who were harvesting flax. Using similar sickle-shaped knives, men were hacking away the tough brown stalks at their base and laying them into parallel piles. The flax being harvested now would be used to make ropes and matting. Earlier, when the stalks were still yellow, some of it would have been used to make canvas and the good strong cloth needed for ordinary clothes. Earlier than that, some of the young green stalks would have been harvested for the fine threads needed to make sheer linen.

Weaving their way through town, the cats happened upon a priest making paper out of papyrus plants. Having already placed a row of stems that had been soaked in water upon a broad stone, the priest was pounding them flat. Next he added a second, crosswise layer and pounded that too, the sticky juice from the stems gluing the two layers together. As the cats looked on, the priest carefully removed the delicate sheet of papyrus and laid it out in the sun to dry. Nearby, also drying in the sun, Ptah spied an assortment of linens that had been pressed into grooved boards to produce the pleated fabric so popular in Egypt.

By the time the cats returned to the palace, a magnificent party was in session. People were reveling in the streets, and there was wine, music, and food galore. Ramses was parading around in his war uniform, exhibiting his fine new sword, while Sashai was making the most out of the show. Being carried around on a litter, the Hittite princess was on display, wearing a red and gold dress and a colorful veil, which conveniently covered her mouth.

The party continued for several more days until at last they boarded the ceremonial barge that would take them upriver on their victory tour. Built from the finest cedarwood available from Byblos, the barge was a huge flat-bottomed vessel nearly three hundred feet long and fifty feet wide. It was equipped with both sails and oars. Where it was not gilded, it had been carved and painted with colorful patterns. On the bow of the barge was carved the head of a ram, the sacred animal of Amun. With its elegant banquet rooms, bedchambers, and temples, Ptah found the boat to be much like a floating palace. All in all, nearly a hundred ships accompanied them as they started their voyage up the Nile.

Truly a master of ceremonies, Sashai had orchestrated the tour down to the very last detail. He had arranged for a convoy of boats to travel ahead of the barge to alert the priests that Ramses was coming. He provided the priests with a written schedule of events, a copy of Pentaur's *Battle of Kadesh,* a few speaking points, and even a suggested menu for the feast. The tour was scheduled to last the entire month, with the city of Thebes slated as its last stop. There the party would coincide with the Feast of Opet, which celebrated the flood at its peak and was one of the biggest holidays of the year.

The victory tour began smoothly enough, and as the days passed by, Ptah found that he was having a marvelous time. All Egyptians loved a good party, and the priests were more than happy to oblige, especially since a large part of any celebration included donations to the temples.

Over the course of the week, Ptah monitored the river as it rose higher and higher. It was exciting in a way, and disturbing in another, to see the land get swallowed up by water. No one ever knew when the flooding would stop, although typically when it reached its full height only the hills remained above water, looking rather like the islands of the Great Green Sea.

One morning Ptah emerged from his urn to see a large city ahead, the center of which featured a majestic temple painted a pale shade of yellow. Flanking the gates to this temple stood a spectacular pair of granite pillars, called obelisks. Each obelisk was cut from a single piece of stone and rose more than a hundred feet into the air.

Spying Khufu sitting at the bow, Ptah scampered over to him and said, "Wow! What city is that?"

"That'll be the town of Heliopolis," Khufu replied. "It's one of the oldest, and certainly the holiest, of all Egyptian cities."

"It's beautiful!" exclaimed Ptah. "Everything looks so quaint and peaceful, what with those lovely old buildings and those tree-lined walkways. And you don't see the color yellow used elsewhere on buildings like you do here."

"Heliopolis is known as the City of the Sun," said Khufu. "As you probably guessed, the sun god Re is worshipped here above all others. Knowledge is revered as well. The priests of Heliopolis are known to be among the wisest in the land. It was they who did the mathematical and astronomical calculations necessary to build and align the Great Pyramids, and it was they who developed the Egyptian calendar based on twelve months of thirty days each, with five days left over at the end to celebrate the birthdays of the gods."

While Khufu and Ptah were chatting, Ramses' barge pulled alongside the quay. Awaiting him was a small group of priests wearing long white robes. Out of respect for the many men of the Re division who had died in the Battle of Kadesh, there was to be no party held in this town. It was considered a tragedy of the very worst kind to die outside of Egypt, because it was only through Egypt that a dead man's spirit could find its way to the Underworld and to eternal life. Instead, Ramses planned on spending the entire day at the temple, praying to the gods that the dead men's spirits might somehow find their way home.

The very next day the tour continued. The royal fleet hadn't gone very far when a wave of excitement began to ripple through the boats. Two tiny glimmering white triangles had been spotted on the horizon, and soon they were joined by a third. Then, with each passing hour, the triangles grew larger and larger until at last they loomed like three breathtaking white mountains above the groves of palms that clustered around the harbor at the town of Giza. The pyramids!

Giza was a quiet little town. A thousand years earlier it had been a busy place, populated by priests, pyramid workers, and scribes, plus there had been all of the farmers and merchants necessary to feed, clothe, and house all those people. After the pyramid building had stopped, the town continued to flourish for a while, but now the old kings' cults were long forgotten and the town had dwindled, being visited mostly by tourists on holiday. Ptah was amazed to realize that even in Ramses' day, the pyramids were considered ancient.

Once the barge was secured to the quay, Ramses and a select group of his men climbed into a series of smaller boats operated by rowers whose job it was to ferry visitors back and forth to the pyramids. Although the awards ceremony would not be held until the following evening, they were going to the pyramids now so that Sashai could choose the best backdrop for the ceremony, and also work out some of the logistics. Souti, having become well trained by now, placed Ptah's urn into one of the boats, after which Khufu and Ptah hopped inside. When all was ready to go, the rowers took off.

The boats headed due west across a wide manmade canal, which linked the Nile to the rocky plateau at the edge of the desert. When they reached the desert's edge, Ramses and his men disembarked and proceeded up a wide ramp that led to a small temple. There they stopped to cleanse themselves before continuing down the long, stone causeway that led to the pyramid complex. At the end of the causeway, Ptah could see a gigantic stone statue with the head of a man and the body of a lion towering above the swirling sands of the desert.

"It's the Great Sphinx!" he murmured in awe. From the professor he had learned that it was the Sphinx's job to guard the gates to the Underworld, protecting the dead kings from evil spirits. No one knew quite when it was built, although Khufu claimed that it had been there since the dawn of time.

Beyond the Great Sphinx, the pyramids rose in magnificent splendor, practically filling the sky. From a distance they had seemed impressive, but up close their grandeur was overpowering. King Khufu's pyramid alone covered an area of almost thirteen acres and rose more than four hundred and fifty feet into the air. It contained over two million stone blocks, each weighing an average of two and a half tons. It was said that it took twenty thousand men twenty years to build it. Standing beside it, Ptah felt small and insignificant, like a tiny grain of sand beside a vast desert. He was sure this was the intended reaction.

Seeing the pyramids up close, Ptah could now understand why, in modern times, some people claimed they must have been built by space aliens, so complete was the knowledge necessary to build them. Ptah knew this was bunk. The professor had told him many times just how the Egyptians—using simple tools, such as saws, chisels, ropes, and wooden wedges—had performed such a feat, and it was not as mysterious as it might seem.

Although the techniques used to build and align the Great Pyramids were easily explained, Ptah knew that other things about them were not. For example, how the Egyptians were apparently able to base their unit of measurement, called the "sacred" cubit, on an accurate knowledge of the circumference of the earth remained a mystery. Another great mystery was how they were able to design King Khufu's pyramid so that its height, when multiplied by the proportion of its height to its width, resulted in a number that was equal to the distance from the earth to the sun. This was especially puzzling because, while the Egyptians knew advanced principles of geometry, they did not know how to multiply or divide. They simply added or subtracted as many times as it took them to reach the desired end product. Interestingly enough, when the number of sacred cubits that made up the perimeter of King Khufu's pyramid was divided by one thousand, the resulting number was 365.25, the exact number of days in a year. The priests of Heliopolis must have been very wise indeed!

Sashai strolled around the pyramid complex in search of the perfect backdrop while a crew of men got busy hacking away the nose on the Sphinx. When they were finished, they planned on carving a new plaque dedicated to Ramses between its front paws. These activities took quite a while, so by the time they climbed into the boats for the return to Giza, the sun was setting. Lit from behind, the golden capstones on the peaks of the pyramids radiated outward, looking as though they had pierced the base of heaven and been touched by the hand of a god.

Back at town, the men ate their supper down by the quay—stewed beef and kidneys for Ramses, grilled catfish and corn for the rest. Ptah and Khufu sat on Souti's either side, receiving tidbits from his plate. When supper was done, Souti stroked their fur, saying, "Well, guys, tomorrow will be a very big day so I think I'll turn in for the night. Imagine . . . I'll be receiving my first golden fly. You should know that Ramses is planning on awarding a golden fly to you, too, in honor of your bravery in battle." Souti yawned and stretched, then gave each cat one last stroke on his fur before sauntering away.

Khufu's face filled with horror as he watched him go. "Did Souti say that Ramses is planning on awarding us *a* medal of honor, as in *one?*" he asked Ptah.

"I'm sure he meant there will be medals for each of us," replied Ptah, "but even if he didn't, don't worry. You can have it. Medals don't mean that much to me."

"Oh, but they should!" exclaimed Khufu. "Medals are proof of your glory. How will it look to the cats in Thebes if I return from the battle without one?"

Ptah attempted to respond, but Khufu kept muttering, "And then there's the ceremony to think about. If we both step forward to claim the same prize, people will secretly be wondering which one of us earned it. *No!* Because of your markings, they'll assume that it's *you!*" Khufu's mouth was starting to froth and the hair between his shoulders was standing on end.

"Khufu, I'm telling you, you're getting all worked up for nothing!" exclaimed Ptah, who, even as he said this, could tell that his words weren't making a lick of difference.

For the rest of the evening Khufu seemed distracted. He looked as though there was a private conversation going on in his head, and from the way he acted—lips curled, eyes twitching—he appeared to be having one heck of an argument.

Ptah kept his distance. Now that the ghastly business of war was over, he no longer depended on Khufu so much for guidance. And, while he was begrudgingly grateful for being taken under the the striped cat's wing, he couldn't help but have the sneaking suspicion that Khufu was not really his friend, at least not in the true sense of the word.

Sleepily, Ptah wandered down the quay and located the small boat that still held his urn. Crawling inside, he lay there staring up at the stars, letting his thoughts turn where they may. Time had become a strange thing to Ptah. Its movement felt fluid, like the flow of a river, and like a river, he now knew that it was possible to travel upstream.

Suddenly a shooting star streaked across the night sky in a flash of brilliance, then was instantly gone. Immediately, Ptah began to make a wish, but then he wondered what it was he wanted to wish for. As it was, he felt lucky enough just to be alive, so in the end he wished that Khufu would somehow find the glory he so rightly deserved.

Late that night, long after everyone else was sound asleep, a stealthy midnight visitor made his way down to the quay and crept up to the boat where Ptah lay sleeping. Finding the rope that held the boat secure, the uninvited guest began to wrestle the knot, while inside his head, he wrestled the demons that lived in his mind. Words like "double-cross" and "betrayal" kept rearing their ugly heads, but doggedly he pushed them back down, replacing them instead with words like "honor" and "glory" and "looking out for number one."

Deep down inside, Khufu hated the feelings of jealousy and resentment that swept over him at times, that drove him to act in ways he knew were deceitful. Even so, he didn't know how else to deal with these feelings except to remove their cause. Besides, the way he saw it, his quest for honor and glory was a lone struggle, and he'd just as soon keep it that way. And while he knew that Ptah was probably telling the truth when he said the medal could be his, why take the chance? Cats were known to be fickle.

Finally the rope came free. Quietly, Khufu dropped it into the water, then waited anxiously for something to happen. Nothing seemed to at first, but then the boat started slowly drifting away from the quay. It floated toward the harbor exit before being snatched by the current and carried out into the main part of the river, where it began heading swiftly downstream.

Khufu watched until Ptah's urn was swallowed by the darkness. Turning to go, he whispered, "Now all the honor and all the glory will be mine."

Ptah Dreams:
Isis and Osiris

Throughout the night the boat sailed steadily onward. Blissfully unaware, Ptah slept soundly inside his urn, and toward morning, just before the darkness turned to dawn, he had his fourth strange dream.

He dreamed he was walking down a narrow marsh trail. Tall papyrus reeds arching overhead created the illusion of a lush green tunnel through which dappled rays of sunlight filtered, landing in tiny splotches on the ground. The earth was soft and damp, spongy beneath his paws. He sniffed at the air; the marsh smelled heavily of sweetness and decay.

Suddenly, Ptah heard a strange noise. It began as a low moan and then rose in pitch until it had reached a mournful cry. It was the sound of a woman wailing in anguish. Ptah crept cautiously forward. There was an unearthly quality about the woman's voice; it floated upon the breeze as though made of the breeze itself.

He spied her in a clearing, huddled over a large linen-wrapped bundle. Despite her disheveled appearance, the woman had a queenly bearing, dressed as she was in a colorful gown woven with patterns of fruits and flowers, over which she wore a shiny black sash embroidered with silvery stars and a golden moon. On her head was a wreath made from flowers twisted around two golden snakes, which held between them a mirrored disc in the shape of the sun. The woman's lovely face, gentle and wise, was streaked with tears.

Ptah crouched at the edge of the clearing and watched as the woman began pulling something greenish out of the tangle of reeds beside her. Her wailing ceased at this point, only to be replaced by a series of low muffled sobs. When at last she removed the object she sought, the woman slowly unwrapped her bundle.

Ptah nearly retched when he saw what was inside: the pieces of a man! There were six of them in all, and to these she added a seventh, the leg she had just pulled from the marsh. Ptah stared transfixed as the woman spread out her linen and began rearranging the greenish pieces into their proper order, like she would a gruesome puzzle. When she was finished, she looked directly over to where Ptah was sitting and said, "You have come. I knew you would."

Ptah's sapphire blue eyes grew wide. He looked to either side of him and then behind. She was speaking to him! "Uh . . . excuse me, ma'am, but you must be mistaken," he stammered as he stepped into the clearing. "I have no idea why I'm here, or even how I got to this place."

"You are here because you're going to help me bring the life back into my dead husband," the woman replied matter-of-factly. "As for how you got here, I do not know. I only know that I prayed you would come."

"Who . . . who are you? And whatever happened to *him?*" Ptah stammered, tipping his ear toward the greenish pieces, fearful for a moment that the woman before him was the one who had done the man in. Behind her, coiled at her feet, Ptah now noticed an immense cobra, brownish-green in color, and with pale yellow crossbands running down the length of its back; and around her, nearly hidden in the grass, he was able to count seven deadly scorpions, each and every one of them eyeing his every move.

"I am Isis, Mistress of Magic," the woman replied. "And this is, or was, my husband, Osiris. Together we ruled as king and queen of Egypt. It was we who taught the people to till the soil, and it was we who gave them their laws to control chaos. We did this, that is, until Osiris's evil brother Set put an end to it all." As Isis spoke, she reached into the pocket of her gown and removed a golden needle and a skein of gossamerlike thread. Carefully threading the needle, she began to sew the pieces of her dead husband together, beginning with his head.

"Set was jealous of my husband," Isis continued. "He craved Osiris's wealth and power, and the respect he received from the people. Believing he could have these things for himself, Set murdered my husband and chopped his body into seven pieces, which he scattered throughout the land. Believe me, I cried a river of tears while I searched for them all, but now my search is complete. For here, in this marsh, I have found the last piece."

Isis's fingers moved deftly as she spoke, her stitches small and even. One by one the pieces of Osiris came together. When she was finished, she drew out a copper knife and sliced the linen from her bundle into thin strips. With these she wrapped Osiris's body from neck to toe like a mummy. Finally, with a look of satisfaction on her face, she said, "Now my husband's body is complete and so his *ba*—or mind—will be able to return to him. Next I must attend to his *ka*—or spirit."

Isis beckoned to Ptah. He dared not refuse her, even though the deadly creatures surrounding her terrified him. Reluctantly, he padded across the clearing to Osiris's side.

"Place your paw over his heart," the queen instructed. Ptah did as he was told and then stared with morbid fascination as Isis gently parted her dead husband's lips. Bending down low, she put her face very near to his and blew her breath into his mouth. As she did, for the first time Ptah noticed she had wings! Rising up from behind, they shimmered with opalescent colors as they pulsated back and forth. After Isis had expelled her first breath, she lifted up and drew in another, then repeated the process again and again.

Ptah watched Isis's movements with a sorry sense of detachment. It was sad, really, and hopeless. Nobody could bring a dead man back to life. Why couldn't she see that?

And then the most terrifying and amazing thing happened. Osiris moved! Beginning with a twitch of his finger, followed by a jerk of his leg, his whole body soon shuddered. Finally, with a great heave of his chest, Osiris sat up and opened his eyes. He seemed not to know where he was at first, nor even to recognize his own wife smiling sweetly beside him.

Ptah jumped back. Osiris still looked more dead than alive to him, the greenish tinge still disfiguring his face. Color aside, however, Ptah could see that he had once been a handsome man. Dark, curly hair topped his strong chiseled features, and his eyes were a brilliant shade of blue. It was through these eyes that the first glimmer of recognition passed. Reaching over, he took Isis's hands in his.

"My lady, you have brought me back," he said. "No man has ever had a finer, more devoted wife than I."

Isis blushed, saying hurriedly, "I'm sorry it took me so long to find you, and I'm sorry for—"

"Hush!" Osiris said softly, putting his finger to her lips. "There is no reason for you to be sorry, my dear. It is I who am sorry, for I cannot stay."

"What?" cried Isis, the agony evident in her voice. "But why? Where will you go?"

"I do not leave you by choice," said Osiris. "I must go because I am no longer a part of this world. When Set carried out his heinous crime, my *ka* was set free. It has already traveled on to the next world, so even though you have brought back my body and with it my *ba*, it is in the next world that I belong.

"Then I shall go with you," Isis declared firmly, "even if it means I must take my own life!"

"No! There is a different place set aside for people who do that, and believe me, you do not want to go there." Osiris shuddered.

"Then what is there left for me here to do?" asked Isis. Fat tears began to roll down her face, and the wings on her back went limp.

Osiris gently tipped up her chin. "You shall remain and rule in this world as queen of kings, a mother to all, while I shall rule in the Underworld," he replied.

At this point, Ptah noticed that something was happening to Osiris. He was turning more pale. No, he was fading away!

"Fear not, my lady," said Osiris, fading fast, "for ours is a love that can span both worlds. It is a love everlasting, the story of which will be told for all time." Osiris's final words echoed upon the breeze, and in the very next moment he was gone.

Her face numb with grief, Isis gathered Ptah in her arms. She began rocking him gently back and forth while humming a mournful tune. Behind her, the cobra slowly uncoiled itself and slithered away in the grass.

Part 5
Where East Meets West

Kingdom of the Greeks
Alexandria, 31 BCE

35

Marc Antony

Ptah awoke to a gentle rocking motion. For a while he just lay there listening to the sound of the waves lapping softly against the sides of the boat. Suddenly he remembered what day it was—the day that he and Khufu would be receiving their first golden fly. Although he hated to admit it, Ptah was excited, and he secretly hoped that there would indeed be two.

Stretching up and poking his head over the rim, Ptah was about to leap out and find Khufu when his stomach lurched. The Pyramids of Giza were gone! In their place was a magnificent stone city and a harbor of ships bearing flags from many lands.

Bewildered, Ptah looked up and down the small stretch of beach where his boat had landed. In the early morning light he could see three men walking toward him, none of whom appeared to be Egyptian. One of them was older, and was obviously a servant because he trailed behind the others at a constant but respectful distance. Of the other two, one was tall and muscular, a noble-looking man with bright blue eyes, bronzed skin, and a ruggedly handsome face topped by a full head of dark, curly hair. He wore his tunic loose, belted low about the hips, and a coarse brown outer robe left open to the breeze. A broadsword hung conspicuously by his side. The other man was equally tall but he was thin and pale, with a narrow, shrewd face capped by a long hooked nose. This man wore a toga—a long piece of cloth wrapped many times around him—and he carried no weapon at all, at least none that Ptah could see.

The two men were locked deep in conversation, their heads bent slightly downward. They hadn't yet noticed Ptah, although by now they had come so close that he could hear every word they were saying.

"Antony, the time is ripe for you to make your move," the hook-nosed man was saying. "With the death of Lepidus, there are only two men left in this world who wield enough power to take control, and you are one! The one in the best position to win, I might add. Why, look at you! You command the mightiest army on the face of the planet and you've won the love of the richest woman—correct that, the richest *person*—to have ever lived! You have the strength and the finances behind you to claim what is rightfully yours. What are you waiting for?"

"Titus, you know that I am waiting until I have succeeded in conquering the Parthians before I move to consolidate my holdings with the lands in the West," the man named Antony replied. "I may control most of the East right now, but Octavian still controls Rome, and that is where the Senate is."

"Octavian is nothing but a fool!" spat Titus. "He may be Julius Caesar's nephew, but few men in the Senate respect him. *You're* the one they like. And as for conquering the Parthians, well, once you've consolidated the Roman republic you can be sure that the king of Parthia will come crawling."

Julius Caesar! Ptah gasped. *I've jumped forward in time again.*

Antony ran a hand through his curly hair and frowned. "I don't know. Considering the suspicious circumstances surrounding Lepidus's death, I think it's too soon for me to make such a move." He walked thoughtfully, gazing at his feet.

"Nonsense—the time is *now*," replied Titus. "Ambassadors from all over the region are already gathering here for the weeklong celebration the queen has planned in honor of her son. You must make your declaration then, perhaps during the ceremony that marks the end of the festivities. The donations will come as a surprise, no doubt; but I'm certain that people will be pleased by their boldness." Titus smiled an evil smile that Ptah thought was not to be trusted. He ducked inside his urn as the men approached.

Antony raised his head just in time to avoid tripping over the boat in which Ptah lay hidden. "Great Zeus! Where did *this* come from?" he exclaimed. Rummaging around inside, he said, "The supplies seem harmless enough: a few ropes, some old-fashioned tools, some—whew!—some rotten food." Then he whistled. "Hey, look! This thing must be a thousand years old!"

Ptah felt the urn being lifted into the air.

"Ugh! It's heavier than it looks!" Antony grunted.

"Perhaps there's something in it," suggested Titus.

Antony set the urn down in the sand and peered into its dark interior. "Why, it's a cat!" He chuckled, and before Ptah could escape his grasp, he reached inside and pulled him out.

"This little fellow looks friendly enough," Antony continued, petting Ptah's fur. "I think I'll take him with me when I return to the palace to give this urn to my lady as a gift. In the meantime, why don't you and Eros go and alert the guards. Have them confiscate this boat and then search the premises. By the look of things, there could not have been more than six men on board. We can't be too careful, you know, with all of the foreign ambassadors coming to visit."

"As you wish, General, but before I go, tell me. Have you considered at all what I've said?" asked Titus.

"Yes, I have, and I agree with your advice," replied Antony. "However, I'd like to take the matter up before the general council so that I may hear others' opinions. I'll call for a meeting this afternoon in the Great Hall to discuss it." Antony waved his hand in dismissal, then gently placed Ptah back inside the urn. Hoisting it onto his hip, he began walking down the small stretch of beach toward a narrow stairway that breached a massive stone bulkhead. Titus and the elderly servant named Eros headed off in the opposite direction.

Ptah stretched up and peered over the rim, hoping to catch a glimpse of something that might tell him where he was. At the top of the stairs, Antony continued walking along a winding, tree-lined path that led him through a lovely terraced garden filled with fountains and statues and beautiful blooming flowers in pink and blue. At the edge of the garden he crossed a courtyard before entering a majestic stone building, which Ptah decided could only be a palace. The building was immense, having more wings than a flock of geese, and it was surrounded by gleaming marble columns and statues of people wearing long flowing robes. Inside the building, brilliantly colored tapestries adorned the creamy stone walls, and thick Persian rugs graced the elaborately patterned mosaic-tiled floor.

Without stopping for even a moment to take in all this luxury, Antony strode across the entrance hall and proceeded up a wide marble stairway complete with carved ivory hand railings. He continued down a series of long, carpeted hallways before coming to a halt in front of a particular door, where stood half a dozen armed guards.

"Theo!" Antony exclaimed, slapping one of the men on the back.

"Antony, you're up early for a change," the man named Theo replied. "Or should I ask if you've even been to bed yet?" Theo was much shorter than Antony but every bit as muscular, with sandy brown hair, twinkling brown eyes, and a quick smile.

"Hey, I'm on my best behavior—queen's orders, you know." Antony grinned, then said, "Say, I'm glad I found you here. Titus, Eros, and I were just out walking on the beach and we discovered an abandoned skiff, quite old and filled with relics. It's probably nothing to be concerned about, but I'd like you and your men take a look around. While you're at it, spread the word that there will be a general council meeting this afternoon in the Great Hall. I have something important I'd like to discuss with everyone."

"Aye, General," Theo replied. He motioned for two of the men to follow, leaving three behind to guard the door, upon which Antony now knocked.

The knock was answered by a pretty, young Egyptian woman with large brown eyes and long black hair. Ptah assumed she was a handmaiden of some sort because she was wearing a pale blue dress with an apron on top, and her hair was bound into a practical braid, which hung down her back. She curtsied when she saw who it was.

"Good morning, Charmian. Has my lady awakened?" Antony asked.

"Yes, General, she's been up for some time now," Charmian

replied, smiling sweetly and batting her eyelashes shamelessly. "She told me to tell you whenever you stumbled out of bed that you could find her in the kitchen going over the menu for the week with the chef. She's quite harried, you know, over the thought of all of these guests! It's so unlike her!"

"Well, Caesarion's thirteenth birthday is an important occasion, and I'm sure she wants everything to go smoothly," Antony replied. "By the way, how *is* everything going? Have any more of the guests arrived?"

"Oh, yes," said Charmian. "The ambassadors from Macedonia, Italy, and Greece arrived yesterday morning, and I believe the kings from Thrace, Cappadocia, Babylonia, and Cilicia arrived late in the afternoon. Several more are expected today, and I hear King Herod himself will be arriving early tomorrow morning. As you can imagine, everyone's quite busy setting up rooms for all these people, not to mention the hordes of servants they bring with them. Why, the King of Babylonia alone brought over a hundred people!"

Antony chuckled. "It's a good thing my lady's palace is the size of a small city." Pausing, he added, "If things are so busy, why are you up here?"

Charmian blushed. "I only came up from the kitchen a moment ago to fetch these notes for the queen. I must return quickly."

"I'll come with you," said Antony. Bending down, he set Ptah's urn on the floor inside the room. "By the way, Charmian, I've brought my lady a gift. Will you see that she gets this when she returns to her chambers?"

"You never tire of giving gifts, do you, General? A woman should be so lucky." Charmian sighed.

Ptah did not hear Antony's response because the door to the room closed and a key turned in the lock.

36

Nefertiti

Alone at last, Ptah jumped out of his urn. The room he was in was breathtaking! It seemed to function as a living room, bedroom, and office combined. It had a fanciful wooden desk, a few sofas and chairs, a dressing table, and a bed that looked so soft Ptah thought he might settle down into it and never get back up. The decor was positively dripping with elegance. From the beautiful tapestries spun with silver and gold threads, to the richly patterned carpets that floated like islands upon the mosaic floor, to the vases of fresh flowers and the scores of large mirrors reflecting their brilliant light around the room—everything he saw proclaimed royal taste.

Ptah decided to poke around, still hopeful he might find a clue that could tell him where he was. Leaping onto the dressing table, he was astounded by the beautiful array of objects he found lying there: a silver mirror in the shape of a swan; combs made of ivory; hairpins fashioned from silver and bone; bottles of delicately blown glass; and jars made of alabaster and faience. There was even a razor carved in the shape of a dancing girl playing the tambourine. Each and every little thing on its own would have been considered precious, but when put all together it added up to a display of opulence the likes of which Ptah had never seen.

From the dressing table Ptah spotted a giant picture window, left open to the breeze. Crossing the floor and jumping onto its sill, he was awarded with a glorious view of the harbor, on the far side of which was a small island that was connected to the mainland by a narrow stretch of land. On the island towered a stunning lighthouse, and beyond that he saw the rolling waters of a great green sea.

Well, that's something, Ptah thought. He now felt certain he was in a city located somewhere along the Mediterranean coast. But whether that city was in Egypt remained a mystery because things looked so much different from what he'd seen before. And yet, mixed in here and there were definite traces of Egypt—from the colors of stone used on the buildings, to the shapes of some of the statues, to the details on some of the columns. Either the Egyptians had borrowed heavily from another culture when they had built this city, or the people who lived here had borrowed heavily from them.

Confused, Ptah turned to face the room again. Looking to his right, he spotted a narrow alcove leading off to the side he hadn't noticed before. Jumping down from the sill, he went to investigate.

The alcove turned out to be a short hallway, at the end of which was a darkened room protected by a heavy iron gate. Inside the room were stacks and stacks of wooden chests—a hundred of them, maybe more. As his eyes adjusted to the dim light, Ptah squeezed through the metal bars and trotted to one of the chests that had its lid cracked slightly ajar. To his astonishment, he saw that the chest was filled with emeralds, some as big as his paw! Excitedly, Ptah began poking his nose into other chests. These turned out to be filled with more jewels, or with gold and silver coins, or with pearls and precious objects made of ivory and ebony. The contents of the room made the Nubians' mountain of gold look like pocket change!

Dumbstruck, Ptah returned to the main room. Suddenly he noticed another cat! She was sitting on top of a plush stack of pillows, and she must have been watching him for some time, because her face bore a mixture of curiosity and amusement. She looked to be about the same age as Ptah, and she had to be the prettiest cat he'd ever seen. Her eyes were that startling shade of turquoise-green found only in glacier-fed lakes, and her snowy white fur looked to be as sleek and as soft as a baby seal's. It shimmered, too, when she moved, as though it had been dusted with gold. Around her neck was a purple silk cord from which hung a small gold medallion etched with the profile of a woman's face.

Ptah stopped where he was and said, "Hello. My name is Ptah.

I came here . . . what I mean is, I was *brought* here by that man, Antony. He just sort of dropped me off and left." Ptah broke off, feeling a bit awkward.

"I can see that," the snowy cat replied curtly.

So much for a friendly greeting, thought Ptah. He decided to ignore this beautiful but flippant cat and go back to exploring. He hopped onto the desk and began nosing around its contents; but, now that he knew the other cat was watching, he felt extremely self-conscious. He could practically feel her turquoise eyes drilling into the back of his head! Finally, he could take it no longer.

"What are you looking at?" he snapped.

"Why, *you*, of course," she replied. "Your markings, they're so . . . unusual. I suppose they are how you came by your name."

"Uh, yes, they are," said Ptah, feeling his face flush.

"I'm named after an Egyptian icon of sorts myself," the snowy cat said. "I am Nefertiti, named after the most beautiful Egyptian queen to have ever lived. Pity she was married to that lunatic Akhenaten, though. Did you know that he single-handedly tried to overturn the entire Egyptian religious system by claiming there was only one god, the sun god Aten? He even went so far as to build a new capital named Akhetaten, just so he could ditch the priests in Thebes. Scandalous!"

Ptah had heard about Akhenaten before. He knew that the pharaoh had lived a few hundred years before Ramses, and that because of his unconventional beliefs he was probably the most hated pharaoh of all time. So, to impress this lovely cat with his knowledge, he said, "Wasn't Akhenaten the father of King Tut?"

"Who?" Nefertiti asked, and then said, "Oh, you mean that poor boy Tutankhamun. Yes, he was the son of Akhenaten, although not by Nefertiti. She had only daughters. Tut was born of a lesser wife. A sad story, that one. Turned into a puppet king at the tender age of nine after his father was killed, only to be murdered himself a mere ten years later. Scandalous!"

"Murdered?" sputtered Ptah. This was something he didn't know.

Nefertiti shrugged, the golden flecks on her fur shimmering in the light. "Or so the story goes. The way I've always heard it, as soon as Tut grew old enough to defy the priests who controlled him, he began taking steps toward bringing back his father's legacy. So as far as the Theban priests were concerned, he had to be removed, if you know what I mean. There was a sudden death, hasty funeral—you know how it goes. I don't even know where they buried him, it all happened so fast."

"Speaking of where things are," Ptah said, "do you mind my asking where we are now? I've just arrived by boat, you see."

"Why, you're in the city of Alexandria, in Cleopatra's palace, of course. Where else do you think you'd see such luxury?" Nefertiti swept her paw outward, taking in both room and alcove with its chests of treasure.

Ptah gasped. "Cleopatra's palace! Do you mean *the* Cleopatra?"

Nefertiti laughed. "Well, m'lady is Cleopatra the seventh, to be exact, but by your tone of voice, I'm sure you're referring to my mistress. After all, she *is* the most famous of the bunch."

"Wow! This is incredible!" exclaimed Ptah. "Where I come from Cleopatra is considered to be one of the most mysterious women of all time!"

"I certainly don't see where the mystery is," Nefertiti said flatly. "M'lady is simply a woman who does—and has always done—whatever she must to survive. Like we all do, I suppose, except that Cleopatra's odds of survival have always been far outweighed by her chances of—how shall I say?—being done in."

"That's all you have to say about her?" asked Ptah. "Surely there is more to Cleopatra than that!"

Nefertiti shrugged. "Well, of course there's more, but it's a long and complicated story, one I'm sure you've no patience to listen to."

"Oh yeah? Try me!" Ptah marched over to the foot of her pillow stack and settled in on the carpet. He turned his blue eyes eagerly upward.

Nefertiti sighed. "Very well then," she said. "But in order for you to understand Cleopatra, we must go all the way back to her childhood, just as to understand the strength of a ship you must know the wood from which she was fashioned and the number of storms she has weathered."

"I'm all ears," said Ptah, wiggling them for emphasis.

37
Cleopatra

Nefertiti got up off her pillow and stretched, then took a deep breath before settling back down and beginning her story.

"Cleopatra was born the third child of Cleopatra VI and Ptolemy X. Her father was a direct descendant of the first Ptolemy, the army general who took control of Egypt shortly after the Greeks conquered it, some three hundred years ago."

"I thought it was Alexander the Great who conquered Egypt," said Ptah.

"Hush!" snapped Nefertiti, her turquoise-green eyes flaring. "It's *rude* to interrupt a storyteller. Yes, it *was* Alexander the Great who conquered Egypt, and who founded the city of Alexandria on its northern shore, but he went on to conquer more kingdoms shortly thereafter and died. Now, where was I?" She fluffed her fur, obviously miffed.

"Ah, yes. Cleopatra's mother died soon after her last child was born, leaving Ptolemy with six young children to raise on his own," Nefertiti continued. "The king did remarry, but his new wife had no interest in raising another woman's children, so each child was appointed his or her own staff of servants, tutors, and advisors. As a result, the children were basically raised apart. This is important to know, because in a royal family, distance can be deadly, as you soon shall see."

Ptah's eyes grew wide but he dared not speak.

"Now, in some cases tutors and advisors can be good," Nefertiti went on. "But at other times they can be greedy, self-serving individuals who use their position of power and trust to further their own gains. I'm afraid to say that the latter was more often the case than not with those chosen to oversee Cleopatra and her siblings. In other words, the children were often swayed by people who had something other than their best interests in mind. Add to this the fact that the children were spoiled, being given every toy, book, piece of jewelry, article of clothing—you name it!—they ever wanted, and I think you can get the picture of what life was like in the palace where Cleopatra grew up." Nefertiti paused, and then said, "Are you sure you're not bored?"

"Not at all! Go on," begged Ptah.

Nefertiti shifted on her pillow, sending another shimmer of gold rippling through her soft white fur. She took a dramatic breath before continuing. "Now, had their father been a strong king, all of this might have played itself out differently. But Ptolemy was not strong; in fact, the opposite was true. He was considered somewhat of a laughing stock around Alexandria, being given to heavy drinking and frolicking with his flute. 'The Piper,' people called him. And while Cleopatra loved her father dearly, the advisors for her two older sisters made much of the fact that he was a buffoon and an embarrassment to the family. And so it was that Ptolemy himself nearly fell prey to the first of his family's murderous schemes."

Ptah gasped, but before he could utter a peep, Nefertiti put up her paw, indicating silence.

"I'll get to that," she said, "but before I do, there's just one more thing in terms of background you need to know, and that is what was happening in Egypt at the time. When Cleopatra's father took the throne, the country was weak. Although it was extremely wealthy, Egypt had virtually no army of her own. The Greeks who lived here were busy living the good life, and the native Egyptians were not about to lift a finger to protect the foreigners who had usurped their land. The only thing that kept the country from being overrun by its neighbors was a deal Ptolemy made with Julius Caesar—who was the commander of the powerful Roman army at the time—in which he agreed to trade huge amounts of grain in return for protection from his enemies.

"This deal is the only thing that saved Ptolemy's life! When first one, then the other of Cleopatra's older sisters tried to seize the throne, Ptolemy was able to overpower their backers by use of the Roman army. After that, he had no choice but to repay his daughters' treachery in kind. Scandalous!"

"You mean he killed them?" blurted Ptah. "Sheesh, I'm glad I wasn't born into *that* family!"

"Oh, it gets worse," Nefertiti said with a sigh. "As it turned out, Ptolemy died soon after that anyway, which placed Cleopatra first in line for the throne. However, according to Ptolemy's wishes and Egyptian tradition, Cleopatra was told she must rule jointly with her younger brother, also named Ptolemy. Now, this situation did not suit her in the least. She was eighteen at the time and her brother only eleven, so she decided to ignore this royal decree and carry on as though she were the only ruler. You see, Cleopatra had a dream—one that her brother did not share—and that dream was to right the wrongs done to the Egyptian people by her greedy forefathers, and to lead her people in recapturing Egypt's long-lost glory.

"Naturally, her brother's advisors were furious. They immediately set out to destroy Cleopatra by publicly blaming her for the poor floods Egypt had been having and drumming up support for her younger sister, Arsinoe, to replace her. When that didn't work, they attempted to have her killed. She barely escaped with her life!"

"So Cleopatra fled the country?" asked Ptah.

"Yes, but only for a short while. You see, Julius Caesar had caught wind of all this royal bickering, and since he was worried it might disrupt the flow of grain still owed him under the deal he'd made with Ptolemy, he decided to go to Egypt himself to see what he could do about it. This was just the sort of opportunity Cleopatra needed to make her return."

"What happened?" asked Ptah.

Nefertiti's turquoise-green eyes twinkled. "She sailed back from Sicily on a cargo ship that made its port on the north coast of Africa, quite near to Alexandria. When she received word that Caesar had arrived in the city, she had one of her faithful servants, a Sicilian rug merchant, row her into the harbor in middle of the night. Come morning, she hid herself in a rolled-up carpet, which the servant then carried into the palace as a gift for Caesar, right under the noses of young Ptolemy's unsuspecting guards! The carpet was brought to Caesar's room, and when he was alone, Cleopatra unfurled herself in all her beauty and made her plea for justice."

"Wow!" said Ptah.

"Cleopatra's meeting with Julius Caesar is legendary," Nefertiti said proudly. "He was impressed by her bravery, and he instantly fell for her charms. He agreed to back her claim to the throne, promising that the Roman army would protect her. Imagine young Ptolemy's surprise when he emerged that morning to find Cleopatra back on the throne with Julius Caesar by her side!"

"What did he do?" Ptah asked.

"Well, to make a long story short, Ptolemy and Arsinoe raised an army to fight, but the Romans swiftly put it down. Both of them were eventually killed. Funny thing was, it later came to light that Arsinoe had been plotting to kill Ptolemy once Cleopatra had been taken care of. Scandalous!"

Nefertiti paused for a moment to groom her paws. "Now, I'd like to be able to tell you that through all of this, my mistress was innocent of causing any bloodshed, being given no choice but to defend herself, as you have seen. But if you've been doing your math while I've told this tale, you'll realize that Cleopatra had one sibling left. Her youngest brother died suddenly of mysterious causes soon after the others, and I can only imagine that Cleopatra had a hand in it, since it's been rumored he died of a scorpion sting. At any rate, when all was said and done, she was the last living heir to the throne."

"Whew! That's *awful!*" exclaimed Ptah. "What the Ptolemys did to each other is inexcusable."

"Oh, behavior like that is nothing new," Nefertiti said flatly. "Royal family members have been doing each other in since the dawn of time. Even the gods are no better—think of Set who killed his only brother, Osiris, just so he could be king."

Ptah thought instead about the hundred and fifty or so children Ramses ended up having. He shuddered to think of the palace intrigues that must have gone on then.

"Anyway," Nefertiti concluded, "what followed were some of the happiest years of m'lady's life. Caesar's intended short stay in Egypt turned into months, which then extended into years. The two of them were married in the Egyptian style and had a son together, whom they named Ptolemy Caesar, but who quickly became known as Caesarion, or 'Little Caesar.' So for a while, everything was looking rosy for Cleopatra. With Julius Caesar by her side, she had the love of the most powerful man on earth, and more importantly she had his son, whom she was certain was destined to inherit both the Egyptian and Roman lands combined. At long last, Egypt was poised to regain her long-lost glory, and Cleopatra was only a whisker away from making her dream come true."

Ptah felt confused. "I don't understand. If Cleopatra is married to Julius Caesar, then who is that Antony fellow?"

"Cleopatra *was* married to Julius Caesar; not anymore. M'lady's life has had more twists and turns in it than the river Nile. Unfortunately, living in Egypt got Caesar used to the idea of being a king. You see, in Rome they had rid themselves of kings long ago in favor of something they called democracy, which means that people are given the freedom to elect their officials. So, while Caesar had been elected to be the ruler of the Roman republic for life, this was not a title he could pass on to his children, as a king can do. Once he had a son, he wanted to change all that.

"To that end," Nefertiti went on, "Caesar made the fateful mistake of returning to Rome so he could declare himself a king of sorts, an 'emperor,' he called it. But news of his plan traveled faster than his sails, and by the time he and Cleopatra landed on Roman soil, a plot had been hatched to kill him. As he was entering the assembly room to make his pronouncement, some of his most trusted allies fell on him with daggers. Caesar died right then and there, his wounds so many and so deep that not even the goddess Isis could bring him back."

"Ah, yes, now I remember—beware the Ides of March," mumbled Ptah.

"Why, yes, it was the middle of March when he died!" Nefertiti exclaimed. "At any rate, once again Cleopatra had to flee for her life. She sailed back to Egypt on the winds of Roman chaos, aiming to rule her country as best she could and to concentrate on raising her son. She was met with some resistance by the Alexandrians at first—she was, after all, the daughter of the despicable Ptolemy, the frolicking flutist who had earlier been drummed out of town—but she made her case to be queen by going straight to the Egyptian people. Sailing up the river Nile dressed as the goddess Isis and using only the native Egyptian tongue, Cleopatra presented herself as having the near-mystical power to protect her people. At the same time, she declared null and void many of the restrictions laid down by her greedy forefathers. As a result of this clever move, she was unanimously hailed as queen—the 'New Isis' people called her—and her popularity soared. Alexandria had no choice but to take her back." Nefertiti broke off, took a long, deep breath, and then closed her eyes.

Ptah waited for her to continue, but she appeared to be drifting off to sleep. "Don't stop now!" he cried. "You haven't yet told me how Cleopatra met Marc Antony!"

"That will have to wait for another time," said Nefertiti. "I am tired and I need my beauty rest."

"But you haven't even told me what Cleopatra looks like!" Ptah protested. "I've heard that she was, uh, *is* one of the most beautiful women alive, that she's even more beautiful than the queen you're named after."

Nefertiti smiled and opened her eyes. "There are many forms of beauty, Ptah. Cleopatra is captivating, all right, but she is not fair in the face the way Nefertiti was. However, I dare you to find me the man who has been with her but five minutes, and who will not claim her to be, as you say, one of the most beautiful women alive. But why don't you see for yourself? Here she comes now!"

Ptah whipped his head around in time to see the door to the room swing open and Antony and Cleopatra walk in. As Nefertiti had said, Cleopatra was not what he had expected. While certainly attractive, her nose and chin were a bit too large, and her eyes set too closely together for her to be called a beauty in the classic sense. Still, she did have lovely, dark olive skin, thick black hair that curled pleasingly about her face, sparkling brown eyes, and a petite, curvy figure, which her elegant clothes did their best to enhance. She also had a wonderfully full mouth that turned slightly upwards at the corners in a natural smile. What really caught Ptah's attention, though, was when Cleopatra opened her mouth to speak. Her voice was like the sound of music, like a beautiful instrument with many strings.

"All right, Antony," she was saying in her melodious voice, "where is this mysterious gift you have brought me?"

"It is here," Antony said, picking up Ptah's urn and holding it high for her to see.

Cleopatra opened and closed her mouth several times before saying, "My, it's, uh . . . interesting. Wherever did you find such an urn? It looks positively ancient!"

Antony proudly displayed the urn while explaining about the boat.

When he was finished Cleopatra said teasingly, "Antony, darling, your only taste is in your mouth! This urn is—how shall I say?— horrendous! It's way too fat in the middle, and its images are drawn all out of proportion to one another. It ignores all standards of traditional Egyptian design! Here, give it to me. I'll have it tossed into the rubbish heap."

"No!" screeched Ptah, jumping up and running across the room.

Cleopatra gasped. "Good heavens! Where did that cat come from?"

"He was inside the urn when I found it," said Antony. "Kind of a cute little fellow, what with those funny little wings on his back. I thought I might keep him."

"Antony, do you not *recognize* who this is? Do you know *nothing* about Egyptian gods?" Cleopatra sputtered.

"Well, I know that you and I dress up like Isis and Osiris and go parading around town," said Antony.

"Oh, do be serious!" scolded Cleopatra.

"I *am* being serious!" insisted Antony. "You know, I rather preferred it when people compared me to the Greek god Hercules instead of that dead green guy."

Cleopatra blew out her breath. "Honestly, Antony, Hercules may have suited you well while you were in Rome, but you're in Egypt now. You must learn, as I have, that you can go a lot farther with people if you adapt to their ways. Besides, I thought you were happy now that people liken you to Dionysus, the Greek equivalent of the god Osiris."

Antony smiled. "Ah, yes, Dionysus. The god of wine and merrymaking—that's much more like it!"

"Don't forget that Dionysus is also the god of music, dance, and drama, and a savior god, like Isis," Cleopatra added. Turning her attention back to Ptah, she said, "As for that cat, do you see the white diamond on his forehead and those wings on his back? Those are the markings of Ptah, the Egyptian god of creation. His coming here must be a sign that something important is going to happen."

"Well, good timing on his part, because something important *is* going to happen!" exclaimed Antony. "Just this morning, Titus and I were discussing the possibility of my making an announcement during the celebration this week—an announcement that I'm sure will please you, my dear. We'll be discussing it further at the general council meeting this afternoon. You're welcome to attend, if you like—that is, if you're not too busy."

"I am busy, but I will *make* the time," Cleopatra replied. "Until then, though, do give me that urn. I'll have Charmian take it to the museum. They're always looking for old things to study." She grasped the urn, turned for the door, and took two steps.

"No!" screeched Ptah. "You can't do that!"

"Good gracious!" Cleopatra exclaimed, turning back. "What's gotten into that cat?"

"It's the urn, I tell you," said Antony. "I think it belongs to him. There *are* little cats all over it."

Cleopatra rolled her eyes. "There you go being silly again, Antony. That cat can no more understand what we're saying than most Egyptians can understand Greek! The poor thing's probably hungry. Why don't you take him down to the kitchen and find him some food?"

Turning again to go, Cleopatra glanced back over her shoulder at

Ptah, whose blue eyes had grown wide with fear. Hesitating briefly, she said, "On second thought, I think I'll leave this urn here. If it does belong to the great god Ptah, well . . . everyone knows that it's never wise to anger the gods." She set the urn on the floor at the very same moment that Antony picked up Ptah. Stroking his new cat, Antony accompanied Cleopatra out the door.

38

Sphinx

From Cleopatra's chambers, Ptah rode in Antony's arms down countless stairs and through bustling corridors before they arrived at the palace kitchen, where he gaped in awe. The kitchen was far bigger than most people's houses, and it was filled with thick wooden tables, enormous brick ovens, and copper pots and pans that hung from hooks along the walls. It was noisy, too, as orders were barked, pots were banged, and food was chopped upon the chopping blocks.

Antony approached one of the cooks, who agreeably cut off a large pheasant drumstick and laid it out on the floor. Antony set Ptah down and then left, having business to attend to. Ptah didn't mind. The sight and smell of the juicy drumstick, roasted to perfection, quickly erased any worries he might have had over being left alone in a strange place again.

Ptah was about to enjoy his very first bite when suddenly a tan and black blur came streaking across the room, snatched up his drumstick, and then took off running. It was a cat! Immediately, Ptah took off after him, chasing him through the kitchen and out the door, down a long hallway and up a short flight of stairs, around a corner, and then through a doorway, which led them outside. From there, he chased the cat around to the side of the building, into an alley surrounded by high stone walls. At the end of the alley, Ptah could see a narrow gap in one wall, and this is where the other cat was heading, fast. Ptah was losing ground, and he was just about to give up his drumstick for lost, when—*wham!*—the cat was knocked to the ground by the force of his speed as the drumstick he was carrying got wedged in the gap before he could go through it.

Ptah caught up with him, thoroughly out of breath. "That's . . . my . . . drumstick!" he panted.

The other cat glowered at him, then stood, shaking the dust off his fur. *What an unusual-looking cat,* thought Ptah. He was a large Siamese, tan with black fur on the tips of his ears, tail, and feet. His left eye was blue and his right eye was green. Wisps of hair sticking up from his ears curved inward like little horns, giving Ptah the overall impression of a sorcerer's cat. The two cats stood there for a moment, sizing each other up, before the other cat spoke.

"Take it then!" he spat. "Take it all, take *everything*, like the rest of your thieving bunch!"

"*What?* You're calling *me* a thief?" Ptah bristled indignantly. "Look, pal, *you're* the one who—"

"You know what I mean," hissed the cat. "I saw you in the kitchen with Marc Antony. You're in cahoots with those Romans and Greeks! You're a traitor, a disgrace to your kind."

"What are you talking about? I'm in cahoots with no one!" protested Ptah. "I'll have you know that I just arrived this morning. I was in a boat that washed up on the shore."

The other cat stared at Ptah for a moment before softening his stance. "My apologies then," he said, looking a bit chagrined. "It's just that my gang and I have been fighting so hard to get rid of the whole bloody bunch of them that we get carried away sometimes. Anyway, I'm pleased to meet you. My name is Sfeneneferaten. Don't worry, nobody can pronounce it; my friends just call me Sphinx."

Ptah smiled. "Apology accepted. I'm pleased to meet you, too, Sphinx. My name is Ptah." Stepping forward, he tipped the end of his ropy tail in greeting.

"Ah, a good strong Egyptian name!" declared Sphinx. "Say, listen, since you've just arrived at the palace, you've no allegiance to anyone yet. Accepting one measly drumstick does not constitute signing a pact. Come; join my gang! Help us fight!"

"I, uh . . . I can't do that," Ptah answered slowly. "There's something in the palace that belongs to me."

Sphinx chuckled. "Oh, you must be talking about Nefertiti," he said, winking his one green eye.

"No, it's *not* her," Ptah stammered a little too forcefully. "It's, uh . . . well, it's all very complicated."

"It always is," replied Sphinx. "Listen, Ptah, Nefertiti's a looker all right, but she's kind of naive. She thinks that the Greeks and the Romans being in Egypt is a *good* thing. She thinks that Marc Antony is going to help Cleopatra fulfill her dream by bringing Roman lands under Egyptian control. Ha! Wouldn't *that* be grand, but it will never happen! The problem with Nefertiti is that she's fallen in with those Greeks. Here in the palace, they live in a fantasy world."

"Well, from what I've seen, Marc Antony *is* very fond of Cleopatra," said Ptah.

"Oh, there's no question about that," replied Sphinx. "It's more a matter of whether he can do it. On the surface it may seem so. Cleopatra has the finances to back an army of thousands for ten years or more, and Antony has the men who can fight. But I think they're both underestimating the one man who can stand in their way: Octavian."

"I've heard mention of Octavian," said Ptah. "I've heard that he and Marc Antony now share control of the Roman republic. But I've also heard that he's a fool; that Antony is the one in the best position to win."

Sphinx shook his head. "Would that were so," he said. "Then my gang and I would have less to worry about. But although few take him seriously, Octavian is bad news! He was handpicked by Julius Caesar to succeed him, you know, and Caesar was no dummy. Everyone thinks that it was just because Octavian was his grandnephew, but I believe that Caesar knew *exactly* what he was doing. Octavian is smart and well spoken; he is shrewd and he can be merciless. He is willing to do whatever it takes to make Rome the most powerful capital on earth . . . with him as its sole leader, of course.

"The worst of it all," continued Sphinx, waving a black-tipped paw, "is that we were just beginning to make headway with those Greeks! Cleopatra is the first of their kind who speaks Egyptian and includes our people in court. She's lowered taxes for the Egyptian farmers and buys their surpluses. She even accepts the Egyptian gods. And now this!"

"So you think Octavian is a threat to Marc Antony and Cleopatra's dream?" Ptah asked.

"He is a threat to their very lives!" exclaimed Sphinx. "And to the life of Cleopatra's first son. Did I neglect to mention that Antony was married to Octavian's sister before he ran off and dumped her for Cleopatra? Or that Cleopatra's son by Julius Caesar is the only living person who can challenge Octavian's position as Caesar's heir? If you know anything about the Ptolemys' murderous ways, then you know what *that* means! At any rate," concluded Sphinx, "I think it's Octavian who's been dealt the upper hand. I think he's just biding his time, waiting for the right moment to make his move. Now maybe if Marc Antony were to act swiftly, before Octavian has the chance to garner support—"

"Oh, but I think that he will!" interjected Ptah. "This morning while on the beach, I overheard him agree that the time is ripe for him to make his move. Apparently he's going to make some sort of announcement during the celebration this week. They're planning on discussing it at the general council meeting this afternoon in the Great Hall."

"Now that *is* news worth hearing," said Sphinx. "Hey, I've got an idea. How about if, instead of joining my gang, you were to stay inside the palace and become our spy? You could tell me first-hand what's going on inside."

"I'd be willing to do that," said Ptah.

"That's the spirit!" declared Sphinx. "For starters, I think you and I need to be at that meeting this afternoon. Why don't you go scope the place out ahead of time? I'll meet you there." Sphinx winked his one blue eye, flicked his black-tipped tail, slipped through the gap, and was gone.

39
Where There's a Will, There's a Way

Ptah and Sphinx crouched discreetly under a long wooden table surrounded by dozens of chairs that had seats made of soft, red leather. Had any of the men filtering into the Great Hall cared to look beneath the table, the two cats would have easily been seen. While not a very good hiding place, it was the best that Ptah could do given the layout of the room: a large rectangular space hung with colorful tapestries, but lacking statues, curtains, or other adornments behind which to hide.

Antony had been the first to arrive, and while he waited for the others he began entertaining the men who were there by telling jokes. Sphinx had warned Ptah that Antony's humor could be crude at times; it was one of the traits that made him popular with his men.

"Have you heard the one about the drunken man who mistook his he-goat for a she-goat and tried to milk it?" Antony began. "As the man lay there pummeled on the ground, the goat turns to him and says, 'Get your kicks elsewhere next time!'"

The room erupted with laughter. "Tell us another!" the men shouted.

"Okay, okay," chortled Antony. "There once was a king who had three wives. The first wanted gold, the second wanted silver, the third wanted jewels, and *none* of them wanted to have *anything* to do with the king! So—" Antony suddenly broke off, seeing Cleopatra standing in the doorway.

"So what happened?" a man hollered.

"So he, uh . . . he treated them all like queens and gave them everything they wanted," Antony finished quickly, rising to greet her.

"Ah, that's not how it goes," someone chided.

Cleopatra rolled her eyes, swallowed hard, and then entered the room. She was the only woman there. "Antony, darling," she said, "have I missed anything? Anything of importance, that is?"

"Oh, no. The guys and I were just shooting the breeze," Antony replied. Then, noticing that a large group of men had entered the room behind her, he said, "Let's see; is everyone here? Theo?"

"Aye, General!" responded a voice, which Ptah assumed belonged to the round-faced, sandy-haired man he had seen earlier that day.

"Darius!" Antony called out.

"Here, General," a voice answered.

Ptah peered out from under the table, curious to see the owner of this voice because he shared the same name as the famous Persian King Darius, a man who had repeatedly battled against the Greeks until his final defeat by Alexander the Great. Standing away from the others with his back to the wall, Darius was a dark-haired, ruddy-skinned man of tall and muscular build. His chiseled face bore a pair of intense brown eyes, and a thin red scar that looked very much like a cat scratch etched the left side of his cheek. He wore his Roman soldier attire—a short pleated kilt and a bronze chest of mail.

"Titus!" Antony bellowed.

Ptah's attention was jolted away from Darius as the voice of another man he'd seen earlier that day responded, "At your service, General." Titus was seated at the table, so the most Ptah could see of him was the bottom of his toga and his sandal-clad feet.

Antony went on to call out other names, after which each man responded, "Aye!" in turn. When roll call was finished, Antony stood and drew up his powerful frame. Turning serious, he said, "Now that everyone is here, let's get down to business. As you all know, the untimely death of Lepidus has left the region teetering on the brink of chaos. The Roman republic is like a three-legged stool that has lost one leg—there is no longer any balance!"

"Untimely death, my foot!" Theo blurted. "You mean to say that Lepidus was *murdered* . . . by Octavian, most likely!"

"You've no proof of that," Titus interjected quickly.

"Oh, come on, Titus," scoffed Theo. "There's no need for anyone to catch Octavian red-handed to know that it was he who drew blood."

"Yes, and even a blind man could see that Antony is next on his list," someone added.

Titus shoved back his chair from the table, its wooden legs scraping harshly against the stone floor. "'Tis never wise to base judgment on mere speculation," he said. "It's been proven that Octavian was in Rome at the time."

"So what?" asked Theo. "To order a killing is the same thing as thrusting the knife! Besides, why do you defend the man? He is scrawny and sickly. His skin is sallow and his teeth are covered with scum. He rarely bathes! His only claim to fame is in being Caesar's grandnephew."

"*And* heir, as set forth in Caesar's will," said Titus.

"Caesar's so-called will was a sham! Everyone knows there was a new will in which Caesarion was named rightful heir," retorted Theo.

"Once again, mere speculation," said Titus. "That will was never found."

Theo snorted, and might have said more, but Darius burst forth in anger. "I don't give a camel's hump about either blasted will! The point is: how dare Octavian think he can lead us? He is *half* the man that Antony is!"

"Half the man, I'm *ten times* the man Octavian is," Antony boasted, tightening his fists and thrusting out his chest to accentuate his bulging muscles. Swaggering across the room, he huffed, "Why, Octavian isn't really a man at all. He surrounds himself with burly thugs who do his dirty work for him."

"Yeah, they do his dirty work for him!" chimed the men, whose fervor quickly escalated out of control, with curses and slurs being hurled Octavian's way.

"Order! Order!" cried Antony. "As I was saying," he continued when the room grew quiet, "The Roman republic is on the brink of chaos. No longer is it possible for Octavian and me to share control;

it can be one or the other of us, but not both. So it looks as if we're heading for a showdown, boys."

The men murmured their agreement while Antony went on, "Now, Titus here claims that I should make the first move. He says that Octavian's hold on Rome is tenuous and that I should take advantage of the situation by staking my claim on the republic in the form of land donations to Cleopatra's and my children. He argues that this would be a way to settle matters peaceably without a fight. See here," he said, unfurling a papyrus scroll and laying it onto the table.

More chair legs scraped against the floor as the men got up to take a look.

"Whew," whistled Theo, glancing over the list.

Darius was more direct. "Have you gone mad?" he exclaimed. "A move like this would most *definitely* lead to war. You would be giving Octavian the ammunition he needs to convince the Senate to back him. It would—"

"It would not lead to war," Titus interrupted. "Octavian would never dare to declare war on another Roman. The Senate would view it as an act of civil war. They wouldn't support it, especially since it would be aimed at a military hero like Antony."

"Why should we trust your opinion?" asked Theo. "Just a moment ago you were defending that sniveling, mealy-mouthed excuse for a—"

"Enough!" barked Antony. "Titus has been my loyal servant for many years. He deserves the right to express his opinion freely and without contempt."

"Be that as it may," said Darius, "what Titus is suggesting is risky. We've no way of knowing for certain whether what he says is true. When was the last time you were in Rome? Five years ago, maybe?"

"Yes, and wasn't that the time you went back and unceremoniously divorced Octavian's sister?" asked Theo.

Antony looked indignant. "Everyone knows that the marriage between me and Octavia was arranged for political purposes, not because I truly loved her," he said. "Besides, she proved to be of no use to me, acting as her brother's pawn, albeit unknowingly."

"Political or not, I'm sure you left a good impression on the Roman people *that* time, what with Octavia being considered the ideal Roman woman and all," replied Darius.

"Listen," said Titus, "I know that I am asking you to take a leap of faith when I tell you to believe what I say, but I have been to Rome recently and all is forgotten where Octavia is concerned. And, Antony's recent military debacle with the Parthians aside, he is still considered to be a war hero of the best and foremost kind. The Roman people revere him! They will welcome these donations as a way to usher in the Golden Age of peace foretold by the prophecies."

"Needless to say, we must accept the possibility that this action could lead to war. What then?" asked Darius.

"Then so much the better, I say," declared Theo. "As long as Antony moves swiftly, we can defeat Octavian, I know it! Antony has over five hundred ships spread throughout the Mediterranean, with nearly three hundred thousand soldiers on land and sea, whereas Octavian has only four hundred smaller ships and half that many men, most of whom are ill-equipped. Octavian has no money with which to finance a war, while thanks to Cleopatra, Antony is rich! We could crush him! In fact, let's not wait. Let's declare war ourselves!"

"That would be unwise," cautioned Titus. "What holds true for Octavian holds true for Antony. Any military move on his part would be viewed by the Senate as civil war. The whole country of Italy would rise up against him."

Theo sighed. Turning toward Antony, he said, "General, given the risks involved, what would you like to do?"

Instead of answering for himself, Antony turned to Cleopatra and said, "You've been awfully quiet during this entire discussion, my dear. Since you would be the one to finance our efforts if it came to war, I feel it is only fair for me to ask your opinion."

Cleopatra was resolute in her answer. She had seen the papyrus listing the donations and was quick to understand their meaning, both for her and her children. "I agree with Titus," she said firmly. "While the donations can be seen as risky, they will most certainly force things to a head. I'm *tired* of Octavian double-crossing you at every turn; I'm *tired* of his evil henchmen prowling around the region murdering whomever they please; but most of all I'm *tired* of tiptoeing on the brink of real power. We've known this day would come eventually and have been preparing for it for a long while. Let us stake our claim and be done with it!"

"My thoughts exactly," said Antony. "We'll move forward as planned."

"But, General—" protested Darius.

"No buts," said Antony, holding up his hand. "Darius, you know that I have valued your opinion ever since you and I were boys romping the hills of Macedonia with Theo. This time, however, the decision stands firm. Meeting adjourned!" Antony turned and headed for the door.

"Oh, one more thing, General," called Titus, motioning him back. "Can I get you to sign your name on this papyrus?"

"Whatever for?" asked Antony.

"It's just a formality," said Titus. "No one will see it except for the costume makers. We can't have little Ptolemy dressed as a Persian or Caesarion dressed as a Greek for the big event, now can we?" Titus handed Antony a quill, which he readily accepted and then scrawled his name at the bottom. After that, both men joined the stream of people who were filing out the door.

Meanwhile, beneath the table, Sphinx whispered, "Is *that* the announcement you were talking about? Donations of land? Whose hairballs-for-brains idea was that? I assumed that when you said Antony was going to make his move, you meant he would be declaring war!"

"I didn't know what sort of announcement he was going to make," Ptah said defensively. "All I said was that I heard Titus telling him the time was ripe!"

"Titus! I should have known," spat Sphinx. "My gang and I have been suspecting him of treason for a long time."

"Treason!" Ptah gasped.

"I wonder what's he up to," murmured Sphinx.

"Well, this could be your chance to find out, because there he goes now!" blurted Ptah, seeing Titus's tall, toga-clad body head in the opposite direction from the other men.

Sphinx jumped up. "What do you say, Ptah? I think it's time we played a little game of cat and mouse. Let's go!"

The two cats scurried after Titus, who quickly exited the building, then strode across the palace grounds before turning right onto a busy street. After several blocks he turned right again, this time heading across the narrow strip of land that connected the mainland to the island of Pharos. Once there, he made straight for the lighthouse, with both cats hot on his heels.

As they approached the lighthouse, Ptah's gaze soared skyward. The building was colossal! It reminded him of a giant birthday cake built in three layers of creamy white stone. The bottom layer was square; the middle octagonal; and the top was round. All of these layers had been frosted with a multitude of windows so that visitors climbing the interior roadway could look out at the views as they spiraled their way up. The 'candle' on the top of this 'cake' was really a room full of mirrors, which during the day made use of the sun, and during the night reflected the light from a huge fire built within.

Titus skirted around the lighthouse, passing by crowds of tourists and vendors selling souvenir trinkets and food. Waiting for him at the back was an old man dressed in a white woolen toga. The man had the same lanky frame as Titus, the same long hooked nose and small dark eyes, but his shoulders were hunched. Ptah and Sphinx crept up on them just as Titus began to speak.

"Uncle, everything has gone as planned," he announced.

"Good. Did you bring me the document?" The old man's voice was gravelly and thick with an accent.

"Yes. I had Antony sign it when the meeting had adjourned and his mind had turned to other things. Stupid man, to be so trusting!" Titus sneered, handing over the papyrus.

"And Cleopatra? How did she react? Was she suspicious at all?" the uncle asked, tucking the scroll in his sash.

"How could she be? She was blinded by the fact that the donations represent everything she's always wanted: for her children to be recognized as the future kings and queen of the Mediterranean region. But tell me," Titus said, "how do you intend to present this document to the Senate? Surely it will be questioned, turning up so quickly after Lepidus' death."

"Where there's a will, there's a way." The uncle chuckled.

"What do you mean by that?" asked Titus.

"Why, Antony's will, of course. If this document were to be presented as his last will and testament—"

"*Surely* you can't be thinking of marching into the Senate and presenting this document as Antony's will!" interrupted Titus. "That would most certainly arouse suspicion! There are those who still claim foul play was involved with Caesar's will."

"I've already taken that into account," said the uncle, "and I've arranged to have his 'will' hidden and then 'discovered' in a monastery of nuns. There will be few questions asked, if any. And once his will is 'found,' Octavian will have all the proof he needs to convince the Senate of Antony's treachery. I will set sail for Rome with this at once! Your job will be to stay here and enact part two of our plan, and then follow me as soon as you can." The uncle reached into his toga and removed a small leather pouch. Handing it to his nephew, he said, "See that these coins are distributed in places where they will reach the palace shortly after the donations are read. Octavian has assured me that you will be handsomely rewarded for your troubles." The old man nodded, then turned and began ambling away.

"Farewell, Uncle. May Poseidon speed your journey," called Titus.

Over near the lighthouse, Ptah turned to Sphinx. "What was *that* all about?" he asked.

"I'm not sure," replied Sphinx. "But there's one thing I am sure about: my enemies are shifting faster than the desert dunes. Who would have ever thought that I'd find myself fighting on the same side as Antony and Cleopatra?"

40

Carts Full of Cats

"It's lovely, isn't it?" Nefertiti sighed blissfully at the sight of the moonlit harbor, then drew in a deep breath of salty sea air.

It was late at night, hours since Ptah had bid his friend Sphinx a temporary farewell at the lighthouse and had returned to the palace. Nefertiti and Ptah were sitting on the windowsill of Cleopatra's chambers, gazing out at the scenery below. The sea this time of night was black, and the ships that floated upon its waters looked like great dark hulks lit eerily from behind by the lighthouse glow. The stars were shimmering overhead, a gentle breeze was blowing, and the sound of the waves could just be heard lapping against the sea wall.

Ptah drew in a deep breath, also. "I used to have a window like this," he said. "It looked out onto city of lights and a harbor of ships, and beyond that there were islands and snow-capped mountains beckoning in the distance."

"Oh, really, where was that?" asked Nefertiti.

"That was long ago and far away. Seems like another lifetime now," Ptah replied wistfully. "It doesn't really matter, but I miss it sometimes."

The two cats sat quietly for a while, each absorbed in their own thoughts, until finally Nefertiti said, "You know, it was a night very much like this when Antony and Cleopatra first met."

Ptah's ears perked up. "I would really like to hear that story," he said, "but could you please begin from the place where you left off before? I think Cleopatra had just fled back to Egypt after Julius

Caesar was murdered."

"Ah, yes, that was when her dream of a glorified Egypt was ripped to shreds like the robe that Caesar was wearing when he died." Nefertiti shook her head sadly. "Well, Caesar's death brought about a power struggle in Rome between those who vied to replace him. Many men tried and many were killed. During this time, Cleopatra was careful not to support any of the contenders for fear of backing the loser. She had no choice but to wait and see what the outcome would be.

"Eventually," Nefertiti went on, "three men emerged in triumph. I say three because the Roman Senate decided that having one man in control was too risky, considering how close they had come with Caesar to having a king again. So the republic was divided into three parts. Marc Antony, who was general of the Roman army and a good friend of Caesar's, was given control over the East, including Asia Minor, Syria, and Judea. Octavian, who was Caesar's grandnephew and adopted son, was given control over most of the West, including Italy, Macedonia, and Greece. A third man named Lepidus was allotted a smaller portion of the West, but he is gone now."

Ptah pictured in his head Antony's three-legged stool, and wondered what had happened to poor Lepidus, but he didn't want to detract from the story so he listened.

"One of the first things Marc Antony did upon receiving his portion was to journey east to survey his new lands," said Nefertiti. "While there, he also planned on meeting with the wealthy queen of Egypt, to ask for her financial support in his war against the Parthians. You see, although Marc Antony was extremely powerful, he was not a wealthy man. He could not afford to launch such a difficult campaign without the aid of a backer.

"Now, as you may recall," Nefertiti continued, "Egypt was in a precarious position at the time. Nearly all the lands surrounding her had been conquered, and although the Romans continued to allow self-rule, they nevertheless considered the country to be somewhat of a vassal state, due to the huge amounts of grain still owed them under the deal made by Ptolemy. As for Cleopatra, she did not share their opinion, but rather considered Egypt to be on equal footing with Rome. So when Antony ordered her to set sail for Asia Minor to meet with him, she ignored his command. Three times, I might add. But the fourth time he called, she went. This was all part of her plan to pick the timing and location of their meeting."

Nefertiti paused to groom her paw. "I'll be honest with you, Ptah. It was Cleopatra's every intent to woo Marc Antony, much the same as she had wooed Julius Caesar. She knew she needed his army to fulfill her dream. She also knew quite a bit about him—his zest for life, his passion for wealth and fame, his weakness for women and pleasure—and so she prepared herself accordingly.

"Cleopatra's arrival is still being talked about in the town of Tarsus, where Antony was staying at the time," Nefertiti said proudly. "She sailed up the river Cydnus on a golden barge with purple silk sails billowing in the breeze. The oars of her boat were silver, and her servants dipped them in time to the music of flutes, fifes, and harps played by handmaidens dressed as sea nymphs. Young boys dressed as cupids fanned peacock feathers around the center of the boat, where Cleopatra lay on a purple silk couch. Exotic perfumes wafted through the air, reaching as far as the river shore, where the people of Tarsus flocked, lining up three rows deep in places to watch her boat drift slowly by.

"When she reached the town of Tarsus, Cleopatra refused to go to Marc Antony. Instead, she invited him to dine with her on her boat. This he willingly accepted, but when he arrived at the appointed hour, her boat was dark. Angry at first, Antony was about to turn back when Cleopatra's servants, who were hidden in the trees and on the boat beams overhead, lit scores of lanterns all at once so that the boat instantly became ablaze with light. And in that soft light, Antony was met with the sight of a magnificent table laid with golden dishes and silverware, and with specially prepared foods from every land. Seated at the table under a canopy of gold cloth was Cleopatra herself, dressed in the silvery sheer robes of Aphrodite, the Greek goddess of love. On her head she wore a gold-leafed crown, and around her neck, wrists, and ankles sparkled an amazing array of exotic jewels. As she rose to greet him, Cleopatra was simply the most enchanting vision he had ever seen." Nefertiti paused and then sighed. "Never has m'lady looked lovelier than she did that night."

Ptah, too, sighed with enchantment as he imagined the scene.

"Of course," Nefertiti went on, "Antony was immediately taken by her charms, but it wasn't only her beauty that captivated him. Cleopatra quickly fell into his manner of speaking and humor, so that the allure of her conversation was irresistible!"

Nefertiti laughed lightly. "Now, as for Cleopatra, while she hadn't planned on it, she, too, became enamored of the powerful figure of Marc Antony, dressed as he was in the manly garb of a Roman soldier. And while he was a bit of a rogue when compared to Caesar—what with his drinking and bragging and his bawdy jokes—he was extremely charming and exceptionally good looking, and also very brave, if a little on the reckless side. How lucky for her that the leader of the most powerful army on earth should turn out to be handsome and charming as well! As the two sat down to a sumptuous feast, they were both quick to see the advantages of an alliance. Each of them had what the other one lacked. On their own they were like copper and bronze, but when forged together, they would be strong as steel.

"The greater the need, the greater the love," Nefertiti concluded, "and in a way, that is the story of Antony and Cleopatra. From Tarsus they sailed to Alexandria, and soon they were married in the Egyptian style, eventually having three children together. And, well, here we are today."

"What motivates Cleopatra?" asked Ptah. "Does she desire to make Egypt strong for her people or is it simply a matter of greed?"

"Hmm, what motivates her," murmured Nefertiti, thinking out loud. "Well, preserving her country's independence . . . and setting things right for her children, but beyond that, who knows? I doubt anyone will ever know what motivates Cleopatra. It is entirely possible that she does not know herself. What I *do* know is that she is a proud and determined woman. 'Where there's a will, there's a way'—that's her motto."

"Huh, that's the second time I've heard that saying today," Ptah said.

"Oh, really? Where else did you hear it?" asked Nefertiti.

"I, uh . . . I met a cat named Sphinx," Ptah answered, hesitant to say more because he didn't want Nefertiti to know he'd been spying on Titus.

"Ah, yes, poor Sphinx," Nefertiti replied. "Nothing but doom and gloom ever comes out of *that* one's mouth. He's quite disillusioned, you know. He thinks it was all our fault Egypt was taken over by foreigners in the first place."

"Whose fault?" asked Ptah.

"Why, we cats! *Surely* you know the story of Cambyssus, don't you?"

Ptah stared at her blankly.

"Honestly, Ptah, sometimes I think you dropped down from the stars!" Nefertiti stretched, and then looked at the moon. "Well, I guess I have time for one more story tonight, although it seems like all you've done all day is listen to me talk. There's really not much to tell, except that several hundred years before the Greeks arrived, a Persian king named Cambyssus discovered an Egyptian traitor who was willing to sell Egypt's secrets. The scoundrel told him where all of the oases were hidden between the two countries, and he told him how much Egyptians loved cats.

"Using this new knowledge, Cambyssus marched his army westward across the desert. When he reached the border, the Egyptians were ready, having already been alerted by scouts that the enemy was coming. What they weren't ready for, though, was what Cambyssus had hidden in his supply carts. As the two armies engaged in battle, the carts were overturned, and from them spilled hundreds of animals—dogs, ibises, but mostly cats! The Egyptians were instantly paralyzed, unable to shoot for fear of killing any of these sacred creatures. As a result, they were quickly and soundly defeated. The vile Persians then went on to use this method again and again, until they had conquered the entire country!"

"Wow, I had no idea!" exclaimed Ptah. "So the Persians took over just like that?"

"Well, yes and no," replied Nefertiti. "What Sphinx always seems to forget is that long before the Persians came, Egypt had already fallen into the hands of the mercenaries, first the Libyans and then the Nubians. It was the country's constant attempts to ward off the invasions of the Sea People that weakened it so. The mercenaries did set up a kingdom of sorts, called the Late Kingdom. But in any event, when the Persians came, they were just one more link in a long chain of foreign rulers."

"So where are all the Persians now?" asked Ptah.

"Oh, you still see them around—there are many Persians living in Alexandria. But their rulers were conquered some three hundred years ago by a man known as Alexander the Great."

"I knew it!" Ptah exclaimed. "Didn't he conquer more land than any other single person in history?"

Nefertiti laughed. "Alexander the Great earned his nickname, all right. Using speed, a bravery that bordered on lunacy, and the ever-effective element of surprise, he conquered the entire Mediterranean region from Italy to Egypt, and beyond. He is best known for perfecting the military formation known as the *phalanx*, in which a solid mass of heavily armed soldiers marches shoulder-to-shoulder into battle. Under Alexander, the front line of soldiers carried a great wall of shields, while the rows of soldiers behind them carried long poles of pointed steel, each man's weapon resting on the shoulder of the man in front. The enemy was met with this formidable force of steel before they could even get close enough to draw their weapons!"

Ptah shuddered at the thought of facing such weaponry.

"When Alexander conquered Egypt," Nefertiti went on, "he was hailed by the Egyptians as their savior. The Persians had been ruthless rulers, you see, worse even than the mercenaries or the Hyksos who had come before them. And for a while life did improve. Alexander was a generous ruler who kept little of the plunder from his conquests for himself. But sadly, he left the country soon afterward and died—some say by poison; others say it was fever brought on by a mosquito bite. In the aftermath, one of his generals—the first Ptolemy, it was—seized control, and the Egyptians soon learned they were no better off under the Greeks than they had been under the Persians. The jackals had replaced the hyenas, so to speak.

"Now, I really have to say that I've done a poor job in telling you about Alexander the Great. His is a story in and of itself! But that will have to wait for another time. I'm tired, and tomorrow will be a very big day." Nefertiti yawned and stretched, the golden flecks on her fur shimmering in the moonlight. She glanced over at Ptah, who was eyeing the soft bed in which Cleopatra slept soundly.

"M'lady looks so peaceful," she said wistfully, adding, "You may sleep anywhere you wish, Ptah, but I would recommend you do not jump up on Cleopatra's bed. M'lady sleeps the same way as Alexander the Great did: beneath her pillow, next to her copy of the *Iliad*, lies a dagger, which I can assure you will spring into action at the slightest hint of danger."

41

Alexandria

"Wake up, Ptah! Wake up!" Nefertiti reached her paw inside Ptah's urn and nudged him on the shoulder. "Wake up," she said again. "King Herod has arrived. Come see!"

"Okay, I'm coming," Ptah murmured sleepily. He yawned and stretched, then yawned again, finding it difficult to awaken. This time travel business was exhausting! No sooner did he start to get comfortable in a place when—*wham!*—on to the next. It took a lot out of a cat just to make these adjustments.

"Hurry up, Ptah. I'm *waiting!*" Nefertiti sounded impatient.

Ptah hopped out of his urn, and then followed Nefertiti to the window of Cleopatra's chambers. One by one they stepped out onto the ledge, which skirted the outside of the building and was the perfect width for a cat. Padding along, they peered into other windows until they found a room with an open door. Passing through, they scurried down several hallways and long flights of stairs before exiting the palace and entering a grand courtyard.

The courtyard was abuzz with activity. A new contingent of foreigners had arrived, and, as Ptah could see, these people did not travel lightly. Not only were there carriages and wagons for the royal family and all of their belongings, but there were carriages and wagons for their hordes of servants, horsemen, advisors, and guards. Among all these people, King Herod was hard to miss. Wearing a long blue robe and a brilliant jeweled crown, he was a young man with light brown skin, curly black hair, and a short black beard. Were it not for the dour expression engraved on his face, Ptah might have considered him handsome.

"It will be interesting to see if King Herod controls his temper," whispered Nefertiti, after they had settled on a bench from which they could watch. "When Julius Caesar died, Antony was given control over the land of Judea, and while he awarded young Herod the title of king, he also gave Cleopatra the choicest parts of Herod's territory as a wedding gift: the balsam-producing plantations and date-palm groves of Jericho. Cleopatra now leases the land back to Herod—for a hefty fee, of course—but he has remained mad at her ever since."

"Where exactly is Judea?" Ptah asked. He could not remember having passed through there on his way to Kadesh.

"You may know it better by the old names of Canaan or Phoenicia," Nefertiti replied. "That land has changed hands more times than a rod in a game of senet! As you can imagine, the hatred there runs deep. Perhaps that is the reason King Herod is so foul tempered."

As the servants began unpacking their things, Cleopatra emerged from the palace. She looked dazzling in a cream-colored gown adorned with layers of patterned beadwork in copper and red carnelian. On her feet she wore a delicate pair of red papyrus sandals. For the occasion her hair had been braided in rows with interwoven beads, red carnelian to match her dress. Following Egyptian tradition, Cleopatra welcomed each guest by presenting him or her with a glass of sweet wine and a necklace made of flowers. Her hairdresser, Iras, a plump, cherub-faced young Greek woman with wavy brown hair, assisted her.

"I can't get over the number of people they brought!" exclaimed Ptah. "Where will Cleopatra put them all?"

Nefertiti's turquoise-green eyes widened with surprise. "She'll put them up in the palace, of course. It would be scandalous if she didn't, and there's plenty of room. Cleopatra's palace covers nearly a third of the city, you know."

"No, I didn't know that. I've never been to Alexandria before," said Ptah.

"Oh dear, where are my manners?" Nefertiti scolded herself.

"Say, how would you like a tour of the city with me as your guide? We've plenty of time before the party begins."

"I'd like that!" exclaimed Ptah, who'd been dying to have a look around ever since he arrived.

The two cats immediately set out. It was a beautiful summer morning, bright and sunny, which might have been too hot but for the constant gentle breeze that blew out of the north.

"As you can see," Nefertiti began after they had exited the palace grounds, "Alexandria is a thriving center of trade and commerce. Within a hundred years of her birth, this city was grander than all others, surpassing even Rome in size, elegance, and luxury. As the famous historian Herodotus so aptly put it, 'Everything that is or can be found anywhere is here!'"

"Herodotus?" Ptah asked. He vaguely recalled hearing that name.

"Yes, he visited Egypt some four hundred years ago," explained Nefertiti. "Curious as a cat, that man. He traveled the region far and wide, gathering information and writing it all down. He devoted an entire book to Egypt alone, although that isn't surprising. He claimed that Egypt held one of the world's Seven Wonders: the Pyramids of Giza. Since then, one of Alexandria's own, the Pharos Lighthouse, has been added to the list, replacing the Walls of Babylon. Why the listmakers felt they had to remove one thing before they could add another is a wonder to me, although seven *is* a mystical number. At any rate, the lighthouse is not far ahead. Shall we go to the top?"

The cats made their way across the same stretch of land Ptah had traversed the day before. When they reached the lighthouse, they hopped aboard an oxcart that was headed to the top, filled with wood for the lighthouse fire. Round and round, and round and round the spiral roadway they climbed, until at last they reached the room full of mirrors. There the cats jumped down from the cart and began circling the perimeter of the room while gazing out at the scenery below.

"Alexandria is situated next to one of the finest natural harbors on the Mediterranean Sea," Nefertiti said, sweeping her snowy paw outward. "It is far enough away from the Delta to avoid being filled in by silt deposits from the yearly flood, but close enough to the Nile to be connected by a manmade canal. Alexander the Great chose this site, not only for its harbor but also because of its strategic location. Lake Mareotis lies just to the south, so there are only two narrow approaches to the city, both of which are easily defended."

Nefertiti led Ptah around to view the lake, which supplied the city's drinking water. She then pointed out the various quarters where the people lived. Nefertiti was very knowledgeable about her city, and she told Ptah many interesting facts, but no matter how fascinating she made these all seem, his eyes kept returning to the harbor with its magnificent bevy of boats.

There must have been twenty or more different kinds of ships floating upon its waters. He saw cargo ships, including the big Egyptian *barides* and the Syrian tubs called *gauloi.* He saw fast cutters used for dispatching messages, called *celoces,* and smaller crafts called *camarae.* There were war galleys, including the swift Adriatic ships called *lembi,* and the ones from Corfu, called *cercuri.* Of all these ships, Ptah's favorites were the *speculatoriae*—light, fast vessels used for scouting and spying. These boats and everything on them were colored blue-green to match the sea.

Cleopatra's sixty warships were there as well, and they were an awesome sight. Nearly all of her galleys were *biremes,* heavily-timbered ships propelled by two banks of oars on either side. If the wind was right, square-rigged sails could be hoisted for traveling long distances when out at sea. Decks covered both ends of her ships, while the centers were left open and were used for carrying cargo. Built upon the decks were wooden towers known as "fighting castles," from which men could shoot arrows or hurl iron missiles down upon their enemies. The decks were also equipped with huge catapults able to launch boulders, and grappling hooks, which could be used to pull enemy warships alongside so they could be boarded and captured. On the prow of each galley was a long underwater battering ram, used for punching holes in the enemy ships' sides. Several of Cleopatra's warships were *triremes,* propelled by three banks of oars, and Ptah spotted at least one *quadreme,* propelled by four. As would be expected of a royal fleet, her warships were beautifully carved and painted, and her flagship was gilded and had purple sails.

The cats eventually came down from the lighthouse and wandered back through the palace grounds. Ptah marveled at the clusters of beautiful columned buildings, the small lakes filled with fountains and statues, and the lush green gardens planted with flowering trees and shrubs.

At the edge of the grounds the cats happened upon a stately stone building graced with tall glass windows and a pair of elaborately carved doors. Pointing to the building with pride, Nefertiti said, "Over here we have the Alexandrian Library, famous the world over for its hundreds of thousands of rare manuscripts, books, and scrolls, many of which are the only known copy in existence! To name but a few, the library holds hundreds of ancient Egyptian texts, the original Hebrew scriptures, writings of the Persian prophet Zoroaster, and thousands of historical works sent to the Greek philosopher Aristotle by his most famous student, Alexander the Great. One of Cleopatra's ancestors, the second Ptolemy, I believe, was known to borrow rare works from other kings so he could make copies, but then send back the copies and keep the originals instead. Scandalous!"

Ptah was at once amazed and aghast. "Those writings must be priceless! What if this building were to burn down?"

"Nonsense!" scoffed Nefertiti. "The entire city of Alexandria is built of stone, even the door- and window-casings! Only the doors themselves are made of wood. Someone would have to purposely carry a lighted torch inside to burn its contents, and who is barbaric enough to do that? Besides," she continued, "the library is much more than a place to house books. It is a mecca of learning! Doctors, philosophers, scientists, and mathematicians from the region wide come here to learn and teach. There are guestrooms, and theaters for lectures, and outside there is a botanical garden with a collection of rare plants and animals. It is a library and university combined. No one would ever dare *think* of harming it."

Ptah remembered otherwise from his lessons with the professor, and was about to respond when several humped-backed creatures caught his eye. "You have camels!" he blurted.

Nefertiti shriveled her nose in disgust. "What's so special about them? Nasty, repulsive beasts, if you ask me. They're stubborn and they spit! It's a wonder that people put up with them. Did you know that camels were rare in Egypt until the Persians brought them in? 'Tis a shame, really. Elephants are much more friendly; but I'm afraid those poor creatures have been relegated to warfare. Scandalous!"

By the time Nefertiti and Ptah had finished exploring the library it was early evening. The sun sat low in the sky as they returned to the palace, drenching the pale stone buildings with an amber glow so that the entire city seemed to be made of gold. The red-tiled roofs appeared ablaze with fire. To Ptah, it was like a vision from *Aladdin*.

That night Cleopatra held a feast to end all feasts. The queen spared no expense to impress her guests. Her cooks roasted eight sides of beef upon the hour so that whenever people decided to eat, the meat would be done perfectly. The wine flowed as freely as water. There were delicacies served from every land: grilled tunny fish from Chalcedon, stuffed grouse from Phrygia, peacocks from Samos topped with acorns from Spain. There were oysters and mussels, sea hedgehogs and scallops, roast duck and grilled hare. There were dozens of salads made from cucumbers and chickpeas or tender lettuces mixed with radishes and onions. There were beautifully shaped breads, and pastries that tasted like heaven.

And the entertainment! Staged at different parts of the torch-lit gardens, various types of musicians played, so guests could relax to the soothing sound of flutes and harps or dance like crazy to the beat of clappers and drums. Everyone ate and drank and mingled and danced until the wee hours of the morning, when they staggered off to their soft feather beds.

When they awoke the next morning, Cleopatra's guests were greeted with trays full of fresh fruit, piping hot tea, and cinnamon rolls dripping with honey. They were also showered with gifts, it being a long-standing tradition for kings and queens to vie with one another in this arena. After breakfast, the guests were free to spend the day as they pleased—sightseeing or shopping, perusing the library, or strolling around the palace grounds. That night there was another party, equally stupendous as the last, and the following morning the guests awoke to do it all again—the food, the gifts, and the party at night.

Over the course of the week, Ptah studied Cleopatra as she moved among her guests. He noticed she had an uncanny ability to adapt her speech and manner to whatever the situation called for. She could speak a dozen languages, her musical voice passing from one to another with no more effort than it would take to begin a new song. She was funny and witty and charming. She even managed to make King Herod smile, though only briefly.

Ptah also accompanied Nefertiti as they continued on their grand tour of the town. First they traveled the width of the city along the Street of Soma. Next they traveled the length of the city, beginning at the Sun Gate in the east and ending at the Moon Gate in the west. Both of these streets were incredible! Wide enough for eight chariots to ride abreast, they were lined with palm trees and beautiful houses and endless rows of marble statues. At the point where they intersected stood a lavish tomb, in which lay the body of Alexander the Great.

Ptah occasionally checked in with Sphinx, bringing him bits of food and gossip, although there was really not much to tell. Everyone knew that the main event was scheduled for the final day of the celebration, and soon that day arrived.

42

The Day of Donations

"This is so exciting!" exclaimed Nefertiti. "I've never been in a parade before. Have you?"

Ptah shook his head. He was equally excited, although a bit nervous sitting atop the hump of a camel that looked as though it might turn its head and spit on him at any moment. The height was a bit nerve-wracking, too, although it afforded him a terrific view of the spectacle of the parade.

And what a spectacle it was! Lined up and ready to go were scores of musicians, acrobats, dancers, and clowns. There were horses dressed in tasseled capes, and monkeys wearing little red vests and hats. There were trick dogs and elephants, ostriches pulling carts, a zebra, a gnu, and a giraffe. There were pale oxen with multicolored Indian parrots tethered to their curlicue horns. There was even an enormous white bear and a huge male lion, both in wheeled cages that would be dragged along by slaves.

As usual when she went out in public, Cleopatra was dressed as the goddess Isis in a colorful gown patterned with fruits and flowers, over which she wore a shiny black sash embroidered with silvery stars and a golden moon. In her hair was a wreath made from flowers twisted around two golden snakes, which held between them a mirrored disc in the shape of the sun. Antony was dressed as the god Dionysus in a short white tunic, white Attic sandals, and a crown made of ivy. To enhance the theme of the day's celebration, "Many Lands, One Region," their brown-eyed, curly-haired children were dressed in the costumes of various lands. Little Ptolemy Phildelphius, age two and barely able to walk, was dressed in Macedonian style, with high red boots, a purple cloak, and a red cap encircled by a thin gold crown. Alexander Helios, age six, was dressed as a Persian, in turban and trousers and a long-sleeved tunic, over which he wore a flowing white cloak. His twin, Cleopatra Selene, was dressed as the goddess Athena, in a pale blue dress embroidered with silver stars. Caesarion, age thirteen and the very image of his father—tall, fair-skinned, with straight black hair and keen black eyes—was dressed as a Roman, in a white woolen toga and a purple cloak edged with gold stars. His head, recently shorn of its long hair of youth, was left bare.

Soon everyone was ready to go and a drum roll sounded. Ptah dug in his claws as the gates of the palace were flung open wide and the camel surged forth. Leading the parade were seven young girls carrying baskets of flower petals, which they sprinkled on the ground before them. It was a splendid parade, although the fact that a Roman military general would allow himself to be seen dressed as a Greek raised some eyebrows among the westerners in the crowd.

The parade traveled down Canopic Way, past the Hill of Pan and the Temple of Poseidon, before reaching the Gymnasium, a large outdoor sports stadium where athletic events were held. There, in the center of the ring, rose a silver stage upon which rested a pair of golden thrones. In front of the stage sat four smaller thrones, one for each of the children. Purple silk awnings protected the stage, as well as the terraced seats surrounding the ring, from the sun.

As people began taking their places, Ptah gazed all around. Not only were Cleopatra's guests in attendance, but a large crowd of Alexandrians had gathered as well. Moving through the crowd, servants offered wine, tea, and pastries.

When everyone was seated, Cleopatra stood and said a few words of welcome, which took quite a while because she repeated the message in twelve different languages. After her speech a drumbeat sounded, prompting a wave of Egyptian dancing girls to burst onto the scene. Dressed in colorful scarves and wearing plenty of bangles, they performed the belly dance. When they were finished, the Greeks took to the ring, enacting a three-act play. Following that, Babylonian jugglers dazzled the crowd with their torches, balls, and wands. A troop of Nubian dancers came next, followed by the Assyrians, who competed in a race between chariots drawn by lions. After that the Romans, who normally weren't fond of frivolity, presented a gladiator fight, in which two condemned criminals fought to the death. If that weren't bad enough, they followed it up with wild beast show, in which hunters hurled spears at bewildered elephants and giraffes as they ran helplessly around the ring. The Egyptians in the crowd were shocked by these acts of cruelty, which only served to confirm their opinion of Romans as boorish, uneducated upstarts interested only in gratuitous acts of violence.

Sensing the crowd's mood had slipped following these final acts, Antony stood quickly to make a toast. Raising his glass of wine, he shouted, "Honored guests, we are gathered here today to celebrate Caesarion. He is on the brink of becoming a man!" Cheering erupted as Caesarion rose to take a bow.

Downing his wine in one gulp, Antony continued. "I would also like to make an important announcement. Our region has been in chaos for far too long! Strong leadership is needed from rightful heirs who have descended directly from the gods! Therefore, it is with the greater good of this region in mind that I make the following donations."

Turning toward Cleopatra, he said, "To my wife, Cleopatra, I bequeath the lands of Cyprus and Judea. These shall be yours, in addition to the glorious land of Egypt you already own. You shall reign as queen of kings, the goddess Isis, a mother to all."

Stepping down from the stage and walking over to where his children were sitting, he said, "To my youngest son, Ptolemy Philadelphus, I hereby give you the land of Syria and the vast empire of Asia Minor west of the Euphrates." Moving to the middle thrones, he said, "To my son, Alexander Helios, I donate Armenia, Media, and Parthia, and to my daughter, Cleopatra Selene, I bequeath Cyrene and Crete." Antony strode to the fourth throne. "And lastly, to Caesarion, I hereby formally recognize you to be the *rightful* and *true heir* of Julius Caesar, and I appoint you ruler of Egypt, along with your mother."

"Hear! Hear!" shouted the eastern kings, who applauded Antony and Cleopatra's vision of a peacefully united Mediterranean world in which every country was free to rule itself. The greedy exploitation of Roman rule had left them resentful and bitter.

The reaction was quite different from the westerners in the crowd, who sat in stunned silence. It was Antony's last statement that caused their greatest alarm. Not only was it a direct insult to Octavian, but also a challenge to his rule. And while Caesarion's share of the donations included no more than the land of Egypt, not a one of them missed the significance of his being dressed as a Roman and wearing the purple color reserved for kings.

Finally, one of them stood up and shouted, "How *dare* you! The extent of these gifts is unheard of! Some of those lands belong to Rome; they are *not* yours to give!" In a unified display of protest, the western representatives all rose from their seats. "The Senate will hear of this!" they shouted as they stormed out of the stadium.

And hear of it they did, much sooner than anyone had expected.

43

Rome Declares War

Barely three weeks after the donations were announced Charmian rushed into the dining hall where Antony and Cleopatra were enjoying their noontime meal. "Oh, mistress!" she wailed. "They're spreading horrible rumors about you! They say you are a wicked sorceress, a monster who worships beasts instead of gods! And there's a dreadful new story going around about a garden, in which women and snakes are cast as evil in an effort to defile the goddess Isis, and by association, *you!*"

Cleopatra rose quickly from her chair, displacing Ptah, who had been sitting on her lap. "Slow down, Charmian. Who's saying this?" she asked.

"The Alexandrians, the Romans . . . *everybody!*"

Cleopatra looked thoughtful. "What is the source of these rumors, do you know?"

"Apparently they originated in Rome—one doesn't have to be Euripides to know who started them—but the gossip has now spread. The whole city is talking!" Charmian burst into tears.

Antony waved her off. "Ignore them!" he said brusquely. "Alexandrians are a vain and spiteful lot. You've seen how they badmouth their rulers. And talk about their penchant for gossip! If Zeus threw a lightning bolt, the people around here would be blabbing about it before it landed! Don't worry, it will all blow over soon."

"There are rumors about you, too, General," Charmian said softly. "They say you are a drunken and depraved man, and that you have fallen under the spell of the wicked and conniving queen.

They also say that you plan on making Cleopatra the queen of Rome and on moving the capital to Alexandria."

Antony raised his eyebrows and then smiled. "Well, there's a bit of truth to all of those rumors," he said. "Except for the wicked and conniving part," he added swiftly, seeing the astonishment on Cleopatra's face. "But I ask you, where's the harm in that? Am I the only one to see the merits of our queen, or to recognize that Alexandria is far better situated than Rome? It is but a few days sail from the eastern ports, and the East is where the true wealth of this region lies." Getting up from his chair, he said, "Don't worry, Charmian. Eventually people will come round to my way of thinking. So for now, let them say what they will."

"Speaking of wills, General," said Charmian, "they have found yours."

"Found my what?" asked Antony.

"Your will," she repeated.

"What are you talking about? I have no will."

"According to the rumors you do. It was discovered in a Roman nunnery about a week ago," Charmian replied.

Antony was about to respond when a loud knock thundered against the door. "General, are you there?" someone shouted.

"Come in!" Antony bellowed.

Ptah looked up from his perch on a chair to see the door of the room burst open and Theo and Darius enter. "General, we apologize for the intrusion, but there is an urgent matter we need to discuss with you," said Theo.

"You may proceed." Antony folded his arms across his chest.

Theo hesitated, tilting his head toward Charmian and Cleopatra. "The women—" he began.

I *said* you may proceed," repeated Antony.

Theo shrugged and gave Darius a slight nod, upon which Darius announced, "It has happened. Rome has declared war."

Antony stared at him for a moment before sitting back down in his chair. "So, it is as we feared," he said.

"Actually, General, it is worse than we feared. Here, read this." Darius handed Antony a papyrus scroll, which he quickly unfurled and silently read. His expression grew clouded, then turned grim.

"What is it?" asked Cleopatra. "What does the document say about you?"

"Nothing, my dear," Antony replied vaguely. "My name is nowhere mentioned."

"But Darius just said that Rome has declared war," Cleopatra insisted.

"They have," said Antony. "Apparently, though, this war is against . . . you."

Charmian instantly began wailing, "Oh, mistress, there were rumors as such, but—"

"Quiet down, woman!" Antony barked. Rising from his chair, he tossed the scroll onto the table and began pacing the floor. "On what grounds does Octavian base this action?" he asked.

"On the grounds of the donations, General," Theo replied. "He states they are a clear sign that Cleopatra intends to take over the region."

"The donations were *my* doing," said Antony. "And besides, I don't understand how Octavian could have convinced the Senate to back him. He has no evidence! Even if the Romans were to have returned from the celebration bearing news of the donations, they brought with them only rumors from a distant land. Words are only hearsay until they can be proven with facts."

"Well, General, apparently your will was found containing a list of the donations, and—"

"There's that talk about a will again!" interrupted Antony. "I have no will, I tell you!"

"—your signature was on it," Theo finished.

Antony stomped to the window. "I don't know what sort of underhanded scheme Octavian is trying to pull this time. Whatever was found is a fake! I've signed *nothing* in regards to the donations, only—" He paused for a moment, then bellowed, "Where's Titus?"

"Gone, General," Darius replied. "He was last seen at the lighthouse with his uncle, Mutinus Plancus, who has disappeared as well."

"Mutinus! I might have known!" spat Antony. "Deceit is in his very name." Sighing deeply, he said, "If that is the case, then Octavian has all the evidence he needs." He told them about the list he had signed, ostensibly for the costume makers, then rubbed his temples. "What is the reaction in Rome to all of this?"

"Our reports indicate that Rome is in chaos," Theo replied. "Octavian has doubled the taxes to pay for this war, and he is forcing the Romans to swear an oath of allegiance. Those who refuse are accused of treachery and their property is seized. In addition, a propaganda campaign has been started that casts you as a debauched man and the queen as an evil siren who lures men to their doom. As part of this campaign, Octavian has minted these silver coins, which are being distributed throughout the region." Theo set two denari on the table.

Charmian leaned over and inspected the coins, then gasped. "Oh, mistress, these coins have your name on it, next to the face of a . . . *a hideous crone!*"

Cleopatra gingerly picked up a coin. She peered at it silently for a moment before asking, "These coins are being distributed throughout the region?"

"We assume that is so," Theo replied.

Seeing the disappointment on Cleopatra's face, Antony strode over and snatched the coin from her hand. Giving it a quick glance, he tossed it back on the table. "The woman on that coin looks nothing like you, my dear. She looks more like . . . like that vulture Titus, with that huge beak on her face."

Cleopatra only sighed and turned away, whereupon Antony exclaimed, "Fire in Hades! There must be *something* we can do!"

"What's done is done," said Theo. "The donations, the rumors, this coin . . . all these things are out there, and we can't get them back. The important thing for us to do now is to act swiftly. We only have a short window of opportunity before the foul weather of fall makes the sea perilous for travel."

"The *sea!*" sputtered Antony. "Who said anything about traveling by sea? If we go anywhere it will be by land. The sea, why, she's as unpredictable as . . . as a woman! I've said it before and I'll say it again: service on land is an honorable duty; service at sea, a necessary evil."

"I think all Romans share your opinion," said Theo, "but we've no choice in the matter. Traveling by land will take too long and will give Octavian the time he needs to raise funds and get organized. Besides," he added, "he will be expecting you to come from that direction and will put most of his forces there."

"For what it's worth, General, I disagree," said Darius. "I think that swift and reckless action is *precisely* what Octavian wants. Though Theo may argue that traveling by land will allow him more time, you need only look at the situation in Rome and ask yourself how long it can last. The people there are near to revolt! Octavian's ability to sustain this effort will surely grow weaker by the day. His money will run out, his men will defect, his power will crumble before—"

"Waiting will only give Octavian free reign to spread his propaganda," argued Theo. "And while Antony remains in Alexandria, he can do nothing to stop it. He will lose support without Octavian ever having to lift up his sword. Let us gather our forces and go!"

Darius sighed while running a finger along the scar on his cheek. "You seem to forget, my friend, that this war is against Cleopatra, and while Antony's men may be willing to die for him, I dare say not a one of them would be willing to die for the queen. Also, if Antony were to strike first, it would be political suicide. The Roman republic would rise up against him."

"Curses!" swore Antony. "Either choice is bad! I may as well flip a coin to decide!" He picked up one of the silver denari left lying on the table and tossed it into the air. It landed face up, the ugly caricature of Cleopatra staring him in the face. Cleopatra frowned.

Antony slammed his fist on the table. "The coin decides it then! My lady's beauty has a value worth defending! If we can't attack Octavian in Rome, then we'll begin by attacking his dastardly propaganda campaign. I'll agree to travel by sea, but we'll stop at ports along the way. People only need see my lady's lovely face to know that this coin is a sham! And if Octavian should choose to crawl out from his hole and fight in a location that suits us, then so be it!"

"A delay like that may cost us," objected Theo.

"A delay like that may save us," countered Darius.

"Enough!" barked Antony. "There is never an easy solution to life's difficult problems. *Never!* Bring me the map!"

Theo left the room, returning shortly with a large sheet of papyrus, which he spread out on the table.

"See here," said Antony, pointing. "Our strategy will be to sail to Ephesus, where most of my fleet is stationed. From there we'll continue to Greece and gather our forces in Patras on the Gulf of Corinth. If Octavian's forces are still hunkered in Rome, we'll sail west to Italy and attack him by land. I am confident that we can crush him. Spread the word! Send out the dispatch vessels! We set sail in one week."

"Aye, General!" Theo and Darius took their orders and left the room.

Still tense with anger, Antony strode to the chair where Ptah was sitting. Attempting to calm himself, he gently picked up Ptah and began stroking his fur.

Cleopatra walked up beside him. "Will you be taking the cat along with you?" she asked, adding, "The Egyptians consider Ptah to be a bringer of good fortune—a god who helps people turn their ideas into reality."

Antony looked down at Ptah, whose blue eyes were closed, but whose ears were cranked open wide. "He may come if he chooses," Antony replied, "but I will not force him to go. My men follow me willingly; I would ask no more from my cat."

Ptah breathed a sigh of relief. He wouldn't be going to war! No more long and boring marches; no more cries of fury or screams of terror on a bloody battlefield; no more sad and horrible endings. This news of war, while chilling, was not going to affect him at all. And so it was that after Antony and Cleopatra had left, Ptah pranced away with a wonderful sense of detachment as he went to find Nefertiti and Sphinx to fill them in on the news.

44

A Matter of Honor

"It's not fair!" declared Nefertiti upon hearing what Ptah had to say. "Why did the Romans single her out? Why do they hate her so? They're spreading lies, all lies! Cleopatra didn't use sorcery to get Marc Antony or Julius Caesar to fall in love with her. M'lady's charms stand on their own! It's . . . it's *scandalous!*" Nefertiti ruffled her fur in anger, sending a cascade of golden flecks falling to the graveled path of the garden in which the three cats were gathered.

Sphinx eyed her impassively, the curly wisps of hair on the tips of his ears bent over in the breeze. "They hate her because she is rich and ambitious, and bold and outspoken. But mostly they hate her because she is a woman who seeks to rule in what the Romans view as a man's world."

"A man's world, huh!" huffed Nefertiti. "I'm here to tell you that it won't be long before the gods turn their backs on those Romans." Nefertiti's turquoise-green eyes flashed, challenging anyone who might try to contradict her.

Sphinx shrugged. "Be that as it may, right now they are strong. And declaring war on Cleopatra was a brilliant move on Octavian's part. What did I tell you about him? He's shrewd and he's smart. He knew that if he declared war on Marc Antony, all loyal to Rome would rise up against him. But if he declared war on Cleopatra . . . well, let's face it. She's an easy one to hate."

Ptah swatted a honeybee that was hovering near his face. "Even so," he said, "there must be *some* way they can prevent this war. What if Antony were to go to Rome and plead his case before the

Senate? He could tell them the truth: that the will they found was a fake and this is all just a silly misunderstanding. Romans are champions of democracy. Surely they would listen to what he has to say."

"Is that what you think this is? A silly misunderstanding?" asked Sphinx. "It's been my impression that Antony and Cleopatra have known war was coming for a very long time. And as for the Romans being champions of democracy, well, you haven't been to Rome lately, have you? Democracy is still a fledgling idea that has yet to find wings. A Roman senator who refuses a bribe is considered a freak! The senators are much more concerned about preserving their own wealth and privileges than they are in practicing good government. Not that I would call Antony and Cleopatra's form of ruling good government either, but—"

"How can you say that?" snapped Nefertiti, ruffling her fur again. "The Egyptians should be thankful for Cleopatra! They certainly aren't able to rule themselves. Why, look at them! They are like children, and to them m'lady is Isis, a mother to all. And frankly, dear Sphinx, while the rest of the world may envy Egypt's wealth, they have always considered the people who live here to be rather strange, what with their animal worship and their obsession with death. Even their choice of gods is a bit odd! Compare them for a moment to the Greeks. We have Dionysus, the god of wine and merrymaking; the Egyptians have Osiris, the god of the dead. We have Zeus, who carries a trident and throws lightning bolts; the Egyptians have a one-eyed bird named Horus and a mummy-man named Ptah. We have Aphrodite, the beautiful goddess of love; the Egyptians' goddess of love, Hathor, is a big fat cow! Now I ask you, where is the drama? Where is the romance? Where is the fun?"

"All you ever think about is having fun!" yelled Sphinx. "Let me tell you, Nefertiti, my people are *not* having fun. They're barely surviving. Thanks to you foreigners, Egyptians' lives are taken up by putting the next meal on the table. Up until the time of Cleopatra, they weren't even allowed to leave their villages without a pass! This kingdom of the Greeks is for the birds!" Sphinx's black-tipped tail flicked rapidly, displaying his rage and resentment.

"Then why don't they *do* something about it?" Nefertiti shot back. "Honestly, Sphinx, Egyptians are so fatalistic!"

"Just what do you mean by that?" demanded Sphinx. "You're always throwing big words around. Nobody knows what you're talking about."

"Words are a form of wealth, my dear Sphinx," Nefertiti replied haughtily. "The more you know and use, the richer you are. To say that people are fatalistic means that they believe events are fixed in advance and they can do nothing about it."

"Horse poop!" snapped Sphinx, narrowing his bicolored eyes. "They *would* do something about it if they weren't locked in the binding chains of poverty! The only reason the Egyptians were defeated in the first place is because they were being attacked from all sides for so long. That, and the unfortunate incident with us cats."

"Oh, will you stop it with the cats?" cried Nefertiti.

"Hey, break it up you two," Ptah shouted, stepping between them. "The *last* thing we should be doing right now is arguing amongst ourselves! We need to concentrate on solving this stupid war business! I tell you, it's a good thing Antony's not making me go along."

"What are you saying?" asked Sphinx. "Do you mean that Marc Antony is willing to take you with him and you're not going to go? I'd give my *right paw* to be on that ship, doing whatever I could do to help."

"Is that true, Ptah?" Nefertiti asked, her turquoise-green eyes gazing into his blue ones and melting his heart like stones of faience.

Ptah took a step backward, startled. Why were his friends looking at him like that? It wasn't up to *him* to save their world. Besides, did they have any idea what they were asking? Ptah had been to war, had seen its horrors, and had come away determined never again to go back. But now, how could he stay here and face them day after day if they knew he'd been given the chance to fight and had turned it down? What would they be saying about him behind his back? That he was a coward? A *chicken*? All of a sudden, Khufu's words rang true. It was a matter of honor. So, even though Ptah did not want to go to war, he knew it was the right thing to do. He wondered if this was how most young men felt when they volunteered for war.

Of course, all of these thoughts went through Ptah's mind in the flash of an instant, and he quickly said, "What makes you think that I'm *not* going to go? I only said they're not *making* me. Of *course* I plan to go!"

45

Mediterranean Wonders

One week after he'd volunteered for war, Ptah found himself down by the docks wishing he could take back his words. Feelings of fear and doubt now coursed through his veins, and thoughts of disaster flooded his mind. Looking across the way, he decided he must be alone in these sentiments, because Antony's men seemed positively filled with confidence. They laughed and they joked and they bantered about as they waited for their noble leader to arrive.

When at last Marc Antony came walking down the path, he gave reason for Ptah to draw hope. Dressed in his Roman general's uniform—a pleated kilt fringed with red leather, a bronze breastplate, and a purple cloak edged with gold stars—he was the very picture of strength. His steel helmet, trimmed with a white horsehair crest, shone bright as silver. Steel shin guards protected each lower leg, and on his feet he wore a pair of marching boots held in place with red leather straps. A sword and a dagger hung fiercely by his side. His face was proud, and his eyes blazed a bright, vivid blue.

Beside Marc Antony walked Cleopatra, wearing a long red dress embroidered with gold, a jeweled crown, and a purple cloak. She looked as lovely and graceful as usual, but the sight of her drew immediate outbursts from the men.

"What is *she* doing here?" one man shouted.

"Leave the women at home, where they can cook and clean and care for the children!" yelled another.

"Fighting is a man's job!" hollered a third.

"Aye!" agreed the rest.

Antony held up his hand for silence. "Listen, men, Cleopatra is financing our efforts and therefore has every right to oversee her investment. Besides, it would be unfair for us to prevent her from sharing in the glory of a victory just because she is a woman."

"Well, I'll take orders from *no* lass, be she queen or no!" exclaimed one man.

"Nor I!" chimed in the others.

"The orders will come from me!" shouted Antony. "And I'm going to start by giving you this one: load Cleopatra's treasure onto her flagship. We'll be moving out!"

The men grumbled amongst themselves but they did as they were told, and soon the ships were ready to go. Ptah stood at the prow of Cleopatra's flagship and watched as Antony blew the trumpet signal to weigh anchor, upon which the lighthouse bell rang three times. On cue, the steersmen started beating their drums—a heavy, steady beat intended to keep the rowers in sync. Ptah nearly jumped out of his skin when that happened. The rowers then sprang into action. Soon there were hundreds of oars going all at once, powered mostly by Greek mercenaries with shaven heads and clipped beards, whose faces were darkened by the sun.

Once the ships had cleared the harbor, the sailors hoisted the sails. A stiff southern breeze soon gusted, filling the sails with as much wind as the men onboard were filled with confidence, and heading them in the right direction for circling counterclockwise around the sea. While not the speediest route, it was by far the surest, since navigation was done by familiar landform sightings or by following the stars at night. Out on the open sea, it was very easy to get turned around.

Cleopatra's sixty war galleys cruised in columns four abreast. Ever wary of pirates who prowled these waters, the men stood guard at every moment. Should the immense treasure onboard her flagship be downed or captured, with it would go all hope of a victory.

As the ships cruised along, Ptah found himself a sunny spot on top of a weapons box from which he could view the sea. Sometimes emerald, sometimes turquoise, sometimes deep olive green—the shades of blue and green seemed endless. No wonder the Egyptians call the Mediterranean the Great Green Sea, he thought. At first Ptah wasn't quite sure of what use he might be on this journey, but he soon found one way to help. Moving from ship to ship, he made sport out of killing the rats that infested the holds. As a result, he became very popular among the men and became affectionately known as "the Rat Slayer."

Rounding the coast of Judea, the fleet made its first stop on the island of Cyprus. This island was a favorite of Cleopatra's due to its golden sandy beaches and the picturesque mountains that formed their backdrop. At the town of Kyrenia, near its horseshoe shaped harbor, Cleopatra threw a magnificent party, showering the people there with gifts, all at her expense.

Continuing west along the coast of Asia Minor, the fleet made its next stop on the island of Rhodes, known by the locals as Butterfly Island. Rhodes was a lush, green island covered by flowering hibiscus, jasmine, and bougainvillea. With its powerful trade fleet, the city of Rhodes was extremely wealthy and was home to one of the Seven Wonders of the World: the gigantic bronze statue of the Greek god Helios. Rising over one hundred feet into the air, the statue's massive legs framed the entrance to the harbor, so that ships coming and going passed between them. In Rhodes, Cleopatra threw another lavish party, complete with gifts, near the Temple of Zeus.

Moving on, they made their third stop at the city of Ephesus, where most of Antony's fleet was stationed. Like Rhodes, Ephesus was a wealthy city and boasted another of Herodotus's Seven Wonders: the majestic Temple of Artemis, goddess of the hunt. This temple was a marvel of the mythical: staring down from the red-tiled roof was a statue of the snake-haired Medusa, and griffins perched on each of its four corners. Painted on the walls and pillars paraded goat-legged satyrs, fire-breathing dragons, and warriorlike centaurs, while monsters embellishing the temple included one-eyed Cyclopes, the three-headed dog Cerberus, and the Minotaur, a creature half-man, half-bull that ate nothing but human flesh. Painted over the main doorway strutted the legendary warrior women called Amazons, and on either side of the door stood statues of Artemis, holding her silver bow, and Orion, holding his jeweled sword.

As incredible as the temple was, Antony's fleet equally impressed Ptah. Stationed at this port were over two hundred heavily armed warships. Built from great squared pieces of timber fastened together with iron bolts, nearly all of Antony's ships were polyremes, huge galleys with anywhere from four to ten banks of oars apiece. These ships had full-length decks and were equipped with wooden fighting castles, catapults, grappling hooks, and battering rams. Their sides were reinforced with iron to resist ramming by others. Although fitted with all the equipment necessary to wage a battle, to a large extent these ships were designed more for transporting huge numbers of men than for effectively fighting at sea. Their speed and maneuverability were deemed less important than their carrying capacity.

At Ephesus, Antony switched from Cleopatra's flagship to his own, a grand polyreme with six banks of oars and a gilded statue of Athena, the Greek goddess of war, jutting from its prow. The ship was one of the newest to have been added to the fleet. Its polished decks and metal parts still gleamed, and its sparkling clean cabins smelled of cedarwood and fresh paint. Ptah accompanied Antony onto his flagship, and soon descended into the lower levels to explore his temporary new home.

Below the main deck, Ptah found masses of sleeping bunks arranged in rows down the middle, and benches for rowing along the sides. He counted about thirty benches per side, with anywhere from two to five men stationed at each oar. To Ptah's horror, he realized that slaves captured in previous battles powered the oars of Antony's ships. Chained to their benches, they were considered little more than engines for these lumbering behemoths.

While Antony was busy organizing his fleet, Cleopatra made arrangements for another party to be held near the Temple of Serapis. Her popularity soared as she enriched the local merchants by purchasing from them the makings for the feast, as well as the costumes and the entertainment. To all outward appearances, Antony and Cleopatra's anti-propaganda campaign seemed to be working. Everywhere they went, they were hailed as the New Isis and the New Dionysus, and were pledged an oath of loyalty from the people who lived there.

Sailing on from Ephesus, Antony and Cleopatra's combined fleet of two hundred and sixty warships headed south to the island of Samos, where it was decided that they would stop and rest for a bit while attempting to persuade Octavian to come forth and do battle. All reports indicated that he was still in Rome, and while there, Antony could do little but try to ferret him out. Notes were sent back and forth between the two sides, each suggesting a battleground that would be beneficial to their own. At one point, Antony challenged Octavian to a direct duel, but of course this was rejected.

During their time on Samos, Antony and Cleopatra determined that a pre-victory celebration was in order. They sent out dispatch vessels inviting their friends from all over, and they gathered entertainers from throughout the land. It took nearly two weeks for everyone to arrive, but once they did, dancers and musicians reveled in the streets and the theaters were packed with people. To Ptah, this whole adventure was beginning to feel more like a moving party than an army going off to war. With each passing day, he grew increasingly anxious, as did many of Antony's men, especially Theo.

"We need to be moving along," Theo kept saying. "Foul weather may prove to be our Achilles heel."

Ptah joined with Theo in trying to persuade Antony to get going. He meowed and meowed until his throat grew hoarse, until Antony finally threw him into a closet in disgust.

More than four weeks passed by before Antony and Cleopatra finally left the island of Samos and sailed west across the Aegean. By now it was mid-August, and the summer sun had reached its peak. So, too, had the confidence of Antony's men. Reports from Rome revealed the situation had grown critical. Octavian had been confiscating all food to give to his troops, and as a result the people there were starving. Angry and desperate, the Romans had finally banded together and had forced Octavian to set sail. Now, with barely any weapons onboard, his fleet was headed their way.

Much to Ptah's dismay, Antony and Cleopatra stopped again when they reached the city of Athens. A serene city with four mountains rising in a semicircle around it, Athens was the home of many poets and philosophers who preferred its quiet, peaceful setting to the hustle and bustle of Alexandria. It was also the home of a magnificent sports stadium where, upon their arrival, athletes from all over Greece were invited to come and entertain the distinguished guests. The festivities that followed lasted for more that a week before being capped by a grand celebration held at the Acropolis. There, in honor of Cleopatra, a statue of Isis was erected next to the statue of Dionysus.

Finally leaving Athens, the fleet rounded the southern coast of Greece and then headed north to Patras. Antony was looking forward to yet another celebration to be held at the temple of his favorite Greek warrior hero, Hercules; however, he had barely set foot from his flagship when he was met with some terrible news.

"General! Octavian's forces have attacked your legions stationed north of here on the Dalmation Coast! Your men are surrounded!"

"We must go to them at once!" Antony ordered.

Darius was quick to object. "But, General, we just got here. We need time to restock our supplies."

"The wind is picking up. A storm may be brewing," cautioned Theo.

"I'll not leave my men to die!" boomed Antony. "I'll take a third of the fleet now and the rest can follow as soon as they're able!"

Despite further objections, and despite the dark wall of clouds that was building up in the north, Antony and nearly ninety of his ships set sail immediately, leaving Cleopatra behind. They set their course for the Dalmation Coast, where Antony assumed he would find Octavian and be able to settle matters quickly, once and for all. His ships, filled to the brim with weapons and men, sailed swiftly before the cool southern breeze, which hastened them onward.

At first Ptah welcomed the change in the weather as a pleasant respite from the sizzling summer heat. But after a while the breeze turned cold and then it started to rain. The sea grew rough. Soon, thunder began rumbling downward and lightning lit up the sky. As a mighty wind gusted, the crews let down their sails and began searching the shore for a safe place to harbor.

This proved to be a challenge. Even those familiar with the surroundings found it difficult to know where they were. The rain shrouded the shoreline with a mist of gray, so the landforms were no longer distinct. Unable to see where they were going, the crews ran the risk of being run aground, or worse, of being swept out to sea.

Although the situation looked grim, Antony refused to turn back. To leave his men stranded meant assuring their death. As a general, Antony was known for his bravery and for his willingness to come to the aid of others, no matter the risk. He was also known for his willingness to share in the same hardships as his men. For these reasons he was granted their utmost respect and unwavering loyalty. His decisions were rarely questioned.

The storm rapidly grew worse. The wind started howling and the rain sliced down in sheets. Vicious waves began thrashing the sides of the ships as they pitched and rolled over the mounting swells. Inside the vessels, the rowers boarded up their windows, but still the water poured in through the cracks, seeping down into the holds where the men who were chained to their benches sat in cold water up to their knees.

Up on the deck, Ptah's stomach churned and his legs jittered. Drowning was every cat's nightmare, but the thought of being eaten alive by sea creatures was even worse! Unable to lash himself to a tower like the rest of the men, he scurried to safety inside a weapons box. Once there, he closed his eyes and tried to shut out the storm. Unfortunately, this only served to make his hearing more keen. Above the wind he could now hear the creaking and groaning of wood as it strained to hold together, and the terrible cracking when it didn't. He longed for the safety he felt inside his urn, which Antony had left behind in Alexandria.

Suddenly there was a cry of hope. "Look there!" someone shouted. "It's the promontory of Actium! Behind there lies a small bay. Sanctuary ahead!"

Ptah opened his eyes, and in the flash of a lightning bolt he was able to see a high point of land jutting into the sea. He heaved a sigh of relief as the men unboarded the windows and let out the oars. Soon the steersmen joined with nature's cacophony as they attempted to beat back the storm with their drums.

Ptah wasn't quite sure when they'd entered the bay, but he knew they must have because the waves died down and the wind ceased its howl. The driving rain continued, however, so for the rest of the day and into the night the crews sat huddled beneath the decks, riding out the storm in the safety of the bay.

The following morning dawned cold and gray, but with little wind. Thick clouds hung low to the water, enveloping the bay in a heavy mist. By noon it started to rain again.

Cleopatra and the rest of the fleet caught up with them late in the afternoon. These ships were miraculously unharmed, having left Patras a day later and thereby having missed the storm.

The rain continued for three more days, but on fourth the men's spirits were raised when they awoke to a clear blue sky. Their spirits were soon dashed, however, when they made their way to the top of the decks and looked all around. While they had expected to see some damage to their ships, what they saw was far worse. Blocking the narrow entrance to the bay were over two hundred Roman warboats, armed and ready for battle.

A cry from the lookout tower confirmed what the men already feared. "Octavian's troops have taken the town of Actium and are camped all over the hills. We're completely surrounded!"

46

Omens of Disaster

By the end of the first week, the reality of their situation had begun to sink in. Antony and Cleopatra were trapped, cut off from their lifeline of food and supplies from Egypt. The area they were in was swampy, with little food to forage. A fourth of their fleet was in ruins, and the crew lacked the necessary materials to make any but the smallest of repairs. Octavian had sent word demanding their complete and unconditional surrender. And to make matters worse, mosquitoes had hatched in the stagnant pools of water left over from the storm rains. Already, the men had begun to fall ill with fever and die.

Though their situation looked bleak, Antony and Cleopatra refused to give in. To surrender now meant certain death, or worse, being dragged in chains through the streets of Rome to be spit on and hurled insults at *before* being put to death. And so they waited while the men argued daily amongst themselves over what action to take, with roughly half of them saying they should fight their way out by sea, while the others insisted they do battle on land.

Paralyzed by indecision, the days dragged into weeks, the weeks into a month. Onboard the ships, food rations dwindled, and Ptah began to get the scary feeling that he was now being viewed as a potential food source. The summer heat had returned with a vengeance, the only relief coming in the afternoons when the wind picked up. Talk of mutiny circled round. Desertion was rampant, and so was disease: those who hadn't already fallen to mosquito-borne malaria were being ravaged by scurvy and dysentery. To top it all off, wood-eating worms began attacking their ships. The situation had truly grown desperate. Something had to be done.

And so one morning Antony summoned together all of his captains for a war council onboard Cleopatra's flagship. Standing at the head of the prow, he looked to be a shadow of the man he had been before. His powerful frame had shrunken, and dark crescents drooped from his hollow blue eyes. When he spoke, his voice was strained.

"Men," he shouted, "there is division among the ranks. Some of you would like to do battle on land, while others insist we do battle at sea. I am open to either plan, but whatever we decide, we must do it quickly. Time is working against us! Let us discuss our options civilly. The floor is now open to anyone who would like to speak."

"General," Theo called out while stepping forward. "I speak for the men who would opt for a sea battle. We see no point in continuing to press Octavian to do battle on land when he has repeatedly denied our requests to be allowed safe passage to shore. Already we've lost a third of our crew to disease and starvation. We've no choice but to do battle at sea!"

"Aye!" shouted the men gathered around him.

"With all due respect, General, we disagree," said Darius, also stepping forward. "Antony, I ask you, how can you expect us to have faith in these miserable buckets of wood instead of our swords? We are *Romans!* Let the Phoenicians fight upon the sea, but give us land, where we know how to stand and fight, and either conquer or die!"

"Aye!" shouted the men gathered around him.

"There is no way we can do battle on land," protested Theo. "We'll be picked off one by one as we row ashore!"

"We'll be picked off one by one as we exit this miserable bay!" countered Darius.

"It would take men with nerves of steel to rush in and ram our ships!"

"Our ships are damaged—"

"The damaged ships are no longer an issue!" yelled Theo. "There aren't enough soldiers alive to man them all anyway. I say we burn the older, slower ships in favor of the fastest and best equipped. We'll take only as many ships as we have the men to arm them!"

Suddenly, from the other end of the flagship, Cleopatra burst from her cabin and came running across the deck. Her appearance alarmed Ptah because her hair was a mass of disheveled curls, and her eyes looked crazed, like those of a wild animal that's just realized it's been caged.

"Antony! We've got to get out of here! We must leave this place at once!" she cried.

"Cleopatra, we were just discussing—"

"There can be no discussion! We must leave now, today, this very instant! I implore you! I've received omens of disaster! Look there," she cried, pointing to her cabin. "Swallows have built their nest above my doorway, and I . . . I've just awakened from a terrible dream in which lightning bolts struck down our statues at the Acropolis!"

"My dear, there is nothing ominous about swallows. They're just birds," soothed Antony. "And as for your dream, well, it was only just that."

"Antony, you must take me seriously. Let us flee!" Cleopatra pleaded. "I have survived to this day by listening to my instincts, and I am not about to stop now. If we stay here, we are all doomed to die! And what sort of honorable death is that? To lay writhing away with fever or to wither away from starvation like a corpse that dries in the sand!"

"How just like a woman to propose we flee," grumbled Theo. "I say we destroy Octavian's fleet and then head for Rome!"

"Aye!" shouted the men in unison.

Cleopatra ignored their comments and continued. "Antony, there can be no talk about doing battle right now. Your men are too weak to fight. All that is left for us now is to escape with our lives. Once we are free from this miserable bay the afternoon breeze will speed us toward home. We can return to Egypt and gather strength. We can come back again to fight another day."

Seeing how distraught she was, Antony spoke slowly and evenly. "Cleopatra, an armada of warboats awaits us outside this bay. The hillsides are swarming with Octavian's troops. It is not possible for us to break free without a fight. There *will* be one. The only question now is whether it will be on land or at sea."

Cleopatra opened and closed her mouth several times before speaking. "Antony, there can be no question about whether we go by sea. Even if we were able to make it over the mountains and into Greece, where would we go from there? It would mean abandoning my treasure and all hope of rebuilding another army."

Ptah saw Antony stiffen. It was the last part of her statement that truly struck home. "She's right," he said firmly. "We cannot give up the treasure ship. We must do as she suggests."

"Romans do *not* flee!" protested Theo, whereupon another man shouted, "We've landed in Hades! The gods have sent us all here to die!"

"Silence!" roared Antony. "My hands are tied! Octavian refuses to grant us safe passage to shore, and we can no longer stay in this hellhole of misery. Curse these rotten ships!" Pacing the deck, he announced, "I've decided that we will enact all plans. Those of you who so wish may go overland with Darius. The rest will come with me. We'll do as Theo suggests and fight our way out by sea, but we'll take along the sails and rigging so we can flee if the tide should turn against us."

"The sails and rigging will slow us down," cautioned Theo.

"Enough!" barked Antony. "We'll leave as soon as we're ready."

The men spent the next few days organizing and consolidating the ships. Weapons and ammunition were removed from the damaged ships and loaded onto good ones. Men were reassigned as need be, which was often a disheartening task. Many were too sick to walk and had to be carried out on stretchers.

During this time, Ptah accompanied Antony as he went from ship to ship comforting the sick and dying, often breaking into tears at what he saw. And on every ship Ptah listened to him deliver a variation of this same speech:

"Men, in choosing to take action we have chosen to become the masters of our own destiny. No longer will we wallow and die in this cursed swamp, but rather, we'll go forth and claim the victory that is rightfully ours!

"That being said, I'm sure I've no need to tell you that there is danger in our taking this action, for we all know that the outcome of the greater war could depend entirely upon this battle. But do not fear! Do not be afraid of the battering rams you see on their boats! The strength of our iron and the thickness of our timbers will surely resist them, even if they should manage to come close. But how *could* they come close when shot at by the slingers and archers, who man our towers on high! How could they fail to be sunk by our catapulters, whose aim is sure and true? Our ships are *huge,* while Octavian's are small. We possess *many* arms, while his troops have few, and as you know, he who wields the better weapons usually wins."

Antony drew up his frame and paused for emphasis. "You should know by now that you are the best of soldiers, the kind who can win even without a good leader. And, while I hesitate to boast, you should also know that I am the best of leaders, the kind who can win even without good men. I am at my peak, both in body and in mind. I have the experience that lacks with youth and the courage found wanting in old age. I have known fear and I have known confidence! I have known victory and I have known defeat! I have learned to not venture too quickly, nor hold back too readily!

"Which brings me to our enemy, Octavian. He is young and inexperienced, a veritable weakling in body and mind. He has never by himself been a victor in any important battle. His funds are scanty and have been raised by force from the backs of men who ache under the heavy burden of his taxes. So great is the difference between us that any attempt at comparison would be futile!

"Nevertheless," Antony went on, "it would be unfair for me not to mention that Octavian does indeed posses one strength, and that is in his naval commander, Agrippa. Agrippa is a capable strategist, a Roman that any Roman could be proud of. Do not think, however, that just because he recently won a difficult battle off the coast of Sicily due merely to good luck, that he can defeat us. Because while we remain *fearless,* while we act together in *everything* we do, *he cannot gain the upper hand!*"

Antony finished each speech by circulating among the men

shaking hands, patting backs, and generally working to bolster their confidence. Though by and large the message he delivered was received as good news, Ptah noticed there was no cheering at the end, only the grim realization of the task that lay at hand.

The night after the council meeting, Darius and a small group of men rowed quietly to shore to begin their trek on land. Each night thereafter more men followed, although their numbers remained few. To avoid arousing suspicion, they disguised themselves as farmers and peddlers, wearing long woolen robes over their tunics and kilts; but beneath these robes they remained well armed.

Four days later the fleet was ready to go. That night, a great fire lit up the bay as the damaged ships were burned—sixty-five in all. Ptah stood beside Antony on the deck of his flagship and watched as the flames rose into the warm summer night, illuminating the ghostlike faces of the men standing nearby. Like them, he supposed, he was both relieved to be leaving and anxious about what the next day would bring. Long after the others had retired to their bunks, Ptah stayed on the deck and watched as the last of the fiery timbers fell crackling and sizzling into the sea.

47

The Battle of Actium

The morning of departure dawned bright and clear, the sea as smooth as glass. Ptah rose early and went to find himself an out-of-the-way place from which he could observe the day's events. Excited and tense, he settled in between the beams at the base of a tower and watched as the men prepared themselves for battle. They took their time, putting on their tunics and bronze breastplates, stepping into their war kilts and fastening their sword belts. Lastly, each man donned a bronze metal helmet, carefully adjusting the broad leather strap until it fit snugly beneath his chin. The mood was businesslike and solemn. Hardly anyone spoke.

As the sun rose high in the sky, the men began taking their places. The slingers and archers climbed into the towers and the catapulters manned the catapults. The soldiers whose job it was to board and capture the enemy vessels lined themselves up four rows deep along the sides of the upper decks. Down below, the rowers sat ready at the oars. A final check was done to the weapons stores. Then, after each crew had determined itself ready to go, Antony blew the trumpet signal to weigh anchor.

The ships began to advance toward the narrow mouth of the bay. They moved in an upside-down 'v' shape, with Antony's flagship positioned at the tip of the 'v' and the strongest warships positioned along the sides, or wings. The weaker boats sailed in the middle, and Cleopatra's sixty warships were clustered near the back. Despite the gentle breeze that blew, sweat dripped heavily from the men's brows as they raised and dipped their oars to the heavy beat of the steersmen's drums.

A few at a time, Antony's ships exited the bay, then rowed out about a quarter mile further and held their position. Directly ahead of them, hovering a mile off shore, Octavian's entire fleet of warboats was ranged in fighting formation. No one onboard any of Antony's ships was surprised to see them there. The fire the night beforehand would have been enough to alert anyone in the surrounding hillsides that something was afoot.

Ptah scanned the horizon, sizing up the enemy. Although Octavian's warboats were smaller than Antony's, he estimated there to be twice as many. The fleet was entirely made up of biremes, similar to Cleopatra's in that they had open hulls, exposing their rowers to attack, but different in that they were of a slender new design created by Agrippa himself, called a Liburnian. To protect themselves, the rowers wore bronze breastplates and helmets that covered their ears and most of their faces.

Once Antony and Cleopatra's fleet had made it outside the bay, the ships moved closer together until they formed a tight wedge. Then again they held their position, while across the water Octavian's warboats did the same, both sides now resting on their oars as if wondering whether they should begin this bloody battle or not.

Finally, one of Octavian's warboats advanced. Its rowers brought it to within shouting distance of Antony's flagship, then stopped. Standing in the bow were two men, one slight of build and wearing the purple cloak of a general, the other heavily muscled and with a swarthy face crisscrossed by scars. Ptah knew immediately who each man must be: Octavian, Antony's mortal enemy, and his military commander, the man known as Agrippa.

Antony saluted Octavian respectfully and received the same in return, for no matter what their personal views of each other, this was a battle to be waged between Romans, and was therefore a battle of the most serious kind.

"Fellow Romans!" Octavian suddenly cried out. "I give you fair warning. Defeat is upon you! Lay down your arms and surrender at once! I will still grant you mercy if you do as I say and hand over the queen! You are free men and can choose your own fate. Come, join my side!"

Antony let him finish before responding, "Ho there, Octavian! Your words speak of mercy, but your actions say differently! Why should we believe you would spare the life of any of the men onboard these ships when you've spared the life of no one so far? You had Lepidus put to death even though he was guilty of no wrong. A deal coming from you is no deal at all! The queen stays with us! Right men?"

"Aye!" shouted Antony's men fiercely, although to Ptah, not a one of them looked half as staunch in their loyalty to Cleopatra as did Antony.

Octavian turned and whispered something to Agrippa. Then he bent down and picked up his war helmet, bronze with a black feather rising from its crest, and placed it firmly on his head. After that he reached for his spear, the end of which had been dipped in fresh sheep's blood. Brandishing his spear high over his head, he let out a war whoop—weak though it was—then hurled the spear toward Antony's ship, where the men onboard watched in amusement as the spear came whizzing toward them, then quickly splashed into the sea, missing their ship by a long shot.

In response, Antony picked up his war trumpet and blew three shrill blasts, upon which his left wing of ships began to advance. Immediately, a trumpet rang out from Octavian's side as Agrippa ordered his opposing wing to try to outflank them. Another shrill blast from Antony's side caused his right wing to move forward, both wings now fanning out wide and curving around to form a crescent shape. Again Agrippa blew on his trumpet, and his left wing rushed forth to meet them.

Octavian's boat, meanwhile, had turned back around and was making a hasty retreat. Antony's ship surged forward, the men onboard hoping to capture the boat before it reached the relative safety of enemy lines. Their catapults loaded and ready, they were just beginning to close in on their target when suddenly another boat sped out to confront them. It advanced full speed, the soldiers onboard seemingly undaunted by the prospect of taking on a heavily armed warship more than twice their own size.

Antony's men readied themselves. The archers drew up their bows and the slingers pulled back their slings, but before either of them got close enough to pull off a shot, the catapulters aligned their deadly weapons, took aim, and fired.

Boom! Direct hit! One of the boulders landed dead-square in the center of the boat, ripping a gaping hole in its bottom. Water poured in as the enemy soldiers leaped from their benches and floundered about, trying in vain to staunch the flow. Antony's ship moved closer and fired again, scoring another direct hit. Soon the enemy soldiers were plunging into the sea to avoid the rain of arrows that was now showering down upon their useless craft.

Sensing their first small victory, Antony's men threw up a cheer. "One down!" they shouted. But their cheering was instantly cut short because, not far from them, another of Antony's ships had come under attack and was not being nearly so lucky. Three of Octavian's warboats had it surrounded and were attacking the ship at once, their metal battering rams wreaking havoc by shattering the blades of its oars and hacking away at its rudder. From up on high, the men onboard fought back as best they could, but the ship's sheer weight and size made it difficult for the rowers to position it properly for battle. As a result, by the time the ship had been turned around, the attackers had already backed away and were approaching again from different directions.

"To their defense!" yelled Antony.

From within the beams at the base of the tower, Ptah trembled with anticipation as both Antony's and Theo's ships converged onto the scene. Trapping two of the enemy warboats between them, the men began pummeling the boats with iron missiles, punching great holes in their bottoms. The archers then drew up their bows and began shooting the enemy like sitting ducks. Unable to escape their deadly trap, the soldiers bailed, only to have their heavy armor drag them down to the depths of the sea.

Meanwhile, the beleaguered ship was having a hard go of it. Two more warboats had replaced the ones that were trapped, and along with the third, they were now launching a series of attacks, using what seemed to Ptah to be a carefully thought-out, albeit dangerous maneuver. First, one of the warboats would advance and distract Antony's men by taking on the brunt of the counterattack. Then the other two boats would zip in, seeking out the ship's vulnerable places while doing as much damage as they could with their rams. When the first boat had had enough, a signal would be given, and they would all pull back, swiftly changing roles and places so that Antony's men never knew from which direction they would be coming next.

Suddenly, a horrific cracking noise shattered Ptah's nerves. He looked up to see the beleaguered ship shuddering from impact. For one dreadful moment the men onboard stood still and wondered at the damage, but soon a cry from beneath the deck brought forth the news they'd all been fearing: "She's taking on water! She's going down fast!"

From that moment on it seemed to Ptah that the sea exploded in a mad frenzy of fighting. It was as though Octavian's warboats, like the sharks that infested some dangerous waters, had received their first taste of blood and were driven mad with the desire for more. His boats began attacking at a dizzying pace. Their assaults were swift and unexpected, and they came from all sides at once. In many ways they were like the cavalry in a land fight—darting forward to make an attack and then rapidly falling back before Antony's men had time to effectively take aim.

Antony's ships, on the other hand, acted more like cities under siege. Their massive size and weight made it difficult for the rowers to maneuver them for battle. As a result, the soldiers onboard were reduced to merely defending their ship, being limited in their ability to launch any attacks of their own. If they were lucky, the boulders flung down from their catapults would sink the attacking warboats before they came too close, or they would succeed in trapping a warboat between them and then obliterate it with iron missiles hurled down from above. However, if their catapults missed, or if the slender warboats slipped through their deadly trap, then all would be lost, because the enemy's vicious battering rams would shatter the blades of their oars and snap off their rudders, and eventually split open their hulls as their weak spots were found.

As the fighting intensified, Ptah covered his ears to deafen the sounds of men shouting and cursing and screaming; the dull clang of metal hitting metal; and the cracking and splintering of wood—all set to the heavy beat of the steersmen's drums. He also tried closing his eyes, but found this to be unnerving. As terrible as it all was to watch, he decided he'd rather see his demise than to not know it was coming. He took comfort in the sight of the bold, brave figure of Marc Antony standing in the prow, barking out orders while launching his catapult with nary a miss. Despite Antony's efforts, and despite the efforts of his men, Octavian's forces still managed to punch through their wings and were now attacking the weaker ships in the middle. For now, Cleopatra's warships still hovered near the rear, waiting for their chance to escape.

The battle raged on and on. It seemed to Ptah that they'd been fighting all day, but the sun in the sky told him it had been less than two hours when two things happened. Seen together as a miracle at first, they gave reason for Antony's men to draw hope. First, in the center of battle, several of Octavian's warboats went down at once, clearing a wide swath of open sea. Next, a stiff northern wind gusted, signaling the arrival of the afternoon breeze. Seizing her chance, Cleopatra ordered her ships to set sail at once, and before anyone knew it, her fleet had slipped through the opening and was making a run.

Octavian was the first to notice their escape. "After them!" he shouted, but by then it was far too late. His men hadn't bothered to stow their sails, so his fleet couldn't muster a chase, and Cleopatra was already well on her way, running well before the swift summer breeze.

Watching her go, Antony quickly took stock of the situation. While most of his ships were still holding their own, he saw no hope of a victory now. So, grabbing his trumpet, he blew the signal for retreat. Immediately, his men all responded by hoisting their sails. Unfortunately, this action brought forth a terrible response from Octavian's side, as his soldiers unleashed their deadliest weapon of all.

Fire! From iron cauldrons filled with burning embers onboard their boats, the enemy soldiers lit pitch-covered arrows and began shooting them at the sails of Antony's ships. The sails ignited upon impact, the hot, dry days of summer having turned them brittle as papyrus. Horrified, Antony's men began tearing down the sails as fast as they could, but the stiff northern breeze, which earlier had been counted upon to help save them, now proved to be their nemesis, because it caused the flames to roar upward even higher. Before they knew it, the fires had spread to the masts and then leaped to the towers. Terrified, the men began grabbing for buckets and lowering them into the sea, but in their haste to put out the fires they drew up buckets that were only half full, making their situation even worse, because salt water poured on a fire in small quantities makes it burn all the more vigorously.

The flames raged out of control. In desperation, the men began ripping the burning timbers off from their ships and hurling them into the sea. Whole towers were cut down in an effort to halt the destruction. But their efforts were to no avail. The fires leaped and skipped from tower to tower as though charged with a will of their own. In no time at all, the flames had spread down into the holds, where the men who were chained to their benches were powerless to stop them.

Antony's flagship was spared from this blazing assault because it had escaped from the battle before the arrows began. So also were forty other of his ships, which had managed to break free and join him. But the rest of his ships were doomed. Without the use of their sails, they sat crippled before the warboats, which were now pulling alongside them. Eager to claim whatever booty might be found, the enemy soldiers began scaling the sides of the burning crafts while the men onboard fought back with battleaxes and grappling irons.

From the stern of his flagship, Antony stood beside Ptah and stared in stunned disbelief as one after the other of his ships went up in flames. Seeing Theo's ship meet the same fiery fate, Antony screamed for his men to go back, but his men all refused. To turn back now was folly, they cried, and so they fled before the mighty wind.

In shock and in horror, Antony stumbled to the bow and sat down by himself, burying his face in his hands. There he stayed, speaking to no one and eating nothing for the rest of the journey to Egypt. And when, at last, the remains of his fleet reached the Alexandrian harbor, Antony staggered to the lighthouse, a broken man, who with this battle had lost his standing as the greatest general of his time.

48

Ships on the Horizon

Following Antony's arrival, news of the defeat spread swiftly through town. Everyone feared the worst. Some people instantly began packing their bags, and the Alexandrian harbor saw a flurry of activity for a while, but soon an eerie calm settled over the city. Even the sea became calm, the slow-breaking waves lapping against the sea wall like a clock ticking away the hours until doom.

Meanwhile, Cleopatra refused to admit there had even been a defeat. Upon her arrival two days before Antony, she had sailed into the harbor with the music playing and her flags flying high. Once back in the palace, she had arranged for a series of feasts to be held in celebration of a victory, and she had paraded through the streets dressed as Isis. But Antony's very different arrival had forced an end to her charade. Each day the Alexandrians scanned the horizon, waiting for what they knew must inevitably come.

It took Ptah a couple of days to work up the nerve to find Sphinx. Having had participated on the losing side, he'd been feeling ashamed. He felt that he'd let down his friends, and he worried what they might say to him.

When at last he located Sphinx near the base of the stairs to the library, he hung his head. "I failed," were the first words to spring from his mouth.

"What do you mean, you failed?" asked Sphinx. "Did you do nothing to try and help the cause?"

"Of *course* I tried," Ptah answered, "but there were too many forces beyond my control. I found there was only so much one small cat could do."

Sphinx nodded his head knowingly, apparently having encountered a similar situation. "You didn't fail," he said. "To fail would have been to sit back on your haunches and do nothing. You, on the other hand, succeeded in trying, which is the most anyone can ever ask of himself. Do you understand the difference?"

Ptah met Sphinx's eyes and could tell that he meant it. "Thanks," he said, grateful for the encouragement. "So, where will you and your gang go now?"

"Oh, don't worry about us. We'll survive; we always have. Maybe we'll travel to the far reaches of the north and join up with the Huns. If anyone can defeat the Romans, the Huns can do it." Sphinx smiled ruefully, winked his one green eye, and then turned to go.

"By the way," said Ptah, "have you seen Nefertiti?" He'd seen no sign of her since his return from the battle.

"No, I haven't," replied Sphinx. "But you know, I think she'd been missing you while you were gone. The last time I spoke to her, she told me she'd been sleeping inside your urn—found it to be quite comfy. I'm sure she's around here somewhere. She's probably off getting her fur dusted or some such nonsense." He flicked his tail in disgust, then grinned.

Ptah grinned back, but his words caught in his throat as he said, "Okay, thanks. Good luck to you!" Sphinx's statement reminded him that he had yet to locate his urn. An ominous thought popped into his head. Had Nefertiti taken it? Or, a better question, had it taken her? Was he now trapped in this time period forever? He returned to the palace and searched high and low, but found no trace of either.

With each passing day, the news from the war front grew worse and worse. Antony received word that Octavian's forces attacked Darius and his men while they were crossing the mountains into Greece. Darius had been killed and the rest had either died or defected. He also received word that his legions in Syria and Asia Minor had surrendered. Theo aside, these were far worse blows for him than losing a few ships manned mostly by prisoners of war. Antony's feelings of sorrow and hopelessness deepened, and he remained in the lighthouse, imprisoned by his own despair.

Cleopatra waited patiently for him to come down, but after two weeks had gone by, she went to go see him. Ptah accompanied her, sitting on her lap as they rode inside a carriage that took them over the narrow strip of land and across the island of Pharos. When they reached the lighthouse, Cleopatra did not employ a litter, but rather ascended the spiral roadway on foot until she reached the room full of mirrors. There, on the northern side of the room, she found Marc Antony in much the same position as Ptah had seen him last: his body slumped and his vacant blue eyes staring out to sea. He looked as though he hadn't slept for days. He also looked drunk.

Cleopatra's face softened with pity for a moment when she saw him, but then she stiffened. Marching over to him, she demanded, "Antony, snap out of it! It's unfitting for a ruler to be seen this way. There's work to be done. I need you to be strong!"

Antony barely lifted his head before mumbling, "I can't snap out of it. Whenever I close my eyes, I am tormented by the vision of Theo's ship going down, of him being carried to his fiery doom. I will forever be forced to live with that vision . . . or maybe not," he added softly, taking another swig from his wine jug.

"Marc Antony, pull yourself together! You still have men who need you! There is talk of desertion—"

"Let them go!" cried Antony. "Pay them well and then let them go," he repeated. "It is no longer a victory I can count on, but rather an honorable death."

"Stop it. Stop it at once! You can't give up now!" Cleopatra stood with her hands on her hips. "Look on the bright side. We saved my treasure and a hundred of our ships. We may have lost the battle, but we can still win the war."

Antony frowned. "Cleopatra, haven't you heard? It's *over!* My legions in Syria and Asia Minor have surrendered. The majority of my men have defected to the other side. King Herod, who owes his very crown to me, is supplying Octavian's army with weapons and food. The odds against us—"

"Forget about the odds!" snapped Cleopatra. "No one ever achieved *anything* by focusing on their chances for failure!" Pacing the floor, she began to think out loud. "If you refuse to fight, then let us flee. We'll load what treasure we can onto a caravan and destroy the rest. We'll gather our forces elsewhere—in India, perhaps. A dozen of my ships have already been sent overland on rollers to the Red Sea and—"

"They have been burned," Antony finished for her. "They were attacked en route by Arabs who support Octavian. Our escape route has been cut off."

Cleopatra gasped. "And what of Caesarion? He was traveling along with them."

"No word of his whereabouts, I'm afraid. I've already sent our other children into hiding."

Cleopatra doubled over briefly, as though she'd been punched in the gut, but then she straightened back up to her regal position and clenched her fists. "No!" she shouted. "I will *not* give up! I'll order new ships to be built! I'll recruit new forces! I'll . . . I'll—"

"You'll do what?" asked Antony. "You'll go back out to the Egyptian people and ask them to raise their pitchforks and shovels to defend you? Is that what you'll do?"

Cleopatra softened her stance. "No, I would never do that," she replied, "although that offer has already been made. But while I am touched by their loyalty and courage, I could never ask my people to fight. It would be sheer suicide against the highly trained Roman legions." Pausing for a moment, she sighed and then said, "Well, I don't know what I'll do, but I'll tell you what I do *not* intend to do, and that is to sit around here getting drunk while grieving over people and things that are gone."

"You're heartless, woman," Antony said quietly.

"No, I am not heartless. I simply have never been able to afford the luxury of being sentimental," Cleopatra replied.

Antony shrugged. "Do what you will then, but you had better do it quickly." He tilted his head in the direction of the sea.

Ptah followed Cleopatra's gaze as she turned her attention outward. There, on the edge of the horizon, hovered an immense fleet of ships. Octavian's flagship could be seen in the lead.

"They will be here by morning," Antony said flatly.

Cleopatra drew in her breath and stomped her foot. "No!" she cried. "I will *not* give up! I refuse to be chained and dragged through the streets of Rome for people to jear at like a common criminal. That would be Octavian's greatest glory. If I am to die, then I shall die like a queen!"

Antony smiled sadly. "Fine for you," he said, "but as for me, I think I'll just stay right here and drown my sorrows." He took another huge swig of wine.

Cleopatra's face flushed with anger. "How can you say that?" she demanded. "Why don't you just go ahead and kill yourself now, like all good Roman generals who call it *quits* after being defeated in battle."

"I may do that as yet," Antony mumbled, then hung his head in shame, for he had not found the courage to do so.

Disgusted, Cleopatra spun on her heel and left. Ptah scampered after her as she stormed down the spiral roadway and then climbed inside her carriage for the short ride home. Once back in the palace, she began spewing orders. "Man the ships! Assemble the cavalry! Set up the lines of defense!" As she raced about, she carried with her a quill and some sheets of papyrus that she used for issuing commands, one of which was to move her treasure from her chambers to her tomb inside the tower next to the Temple of Isis.

Coming upon Antony's elderly servant, Eros, Cleopatra ordered, "Go to the lighthouse and tell Antony that if he doesn't come down at once I shall end my life! Better yet, take him this note. He will believe you more if it is written in my own hand." The queen scrawled a message on a piece of papyrus and thrust it at Antony's servant, saying more softly, "Oh, and Eros, see that he has something to eat, will you?"

Eros bowed and retreated while Cleopatra hurried off in a different direction. For a moment Ptah stood between them, trying to decide which of the two he should follow, but his decision was not a hard one to make. Cleopatra's distress radiated from her like the heat from a fire—a distress Ptah chose to avoid so as not to get burned.

Catching up with Eros, Ptah followed him into the kitchen and watched as he put together a tray full of meats and cheeses and a small loaf of bread. From the kitchen, Eros went up to Antony's chambers and collected a clean robe and tunic. After that, the two walked side by side to the lighthouse, where they hopped aboard a wagon that was filled with wood for the lighthouse fire.

By the time they reached the room full of mirrors, it was late afternoon. The sun, sitting low in the sky, shone brilliantly against the panels of smooth, polished brass, which reflected the light more than thirty miles out to sea. At first glance the room seemed empty, but on closer inspection they found Marc Antony passed out on the floor, an empty wine jug still clutched in his hand.

Overcome with pity for his beloved master, Eros knelt down and gently shook him on the shoulder, trying to wake him. Getting no response, he set the tray holding the food and Cleopatra's note on the floor beside him. Picking up the wine jug and moving it off to one side, he murmured, "My master knows his true enemy all too well." After that he made a makeshift pillow from the clean robe and tunic, placed it beneath Antony's head, and then sat on the floor to wait for his master to awaken. Ptah, in need of a nap, curled up at his feet.

That night, Cleopatra threw one last party in a grand celebration of life. Desperate to escape from reality, the Alexandrians flocked to the palace, where they ate and drank and laughed until the wee hours of the morning. At dawn, people later claimed, they were awakened in their beds by the sound of music drifting along the streets and out through the gates of the city. It was the sound, they said, of the god Dionysus leaving their town.

49

In True Roman Style

The morning after the party Ptah was awakened by the light-house bell ringing in alarm. He jumped to his feet and ran past the slumbering figures of Eros and Marc Antony to the window, where he swallowed hard. Not only was Octavian's fleet stationed less than a mile outside the harbor, but his troops coming in from Judea had positioned themselves outside the city walls. Alexandria was surrounded.

Running halfway around the mirrored room and gazing across to the palace, Ptah could see Charmian and Iras standing beside Cleopatra at the window of her chambers. The women's eyes were riveted to the harbor, where the remains of Antony's navy were rowing their battleships for the exit. Although their numbers were few and the odds were slim, the women looked hopeful. Encouraged by their confidence, Ptah watched excitedly as the navy reached the open waters, then sailed out to meet the enemy fleet. However, his excitement turned rapidly to dismay when Antony's men drew near, because rather than firing their catapults, they raised their white flags instead. Then, saluting Octavian's fleet with their oars, they sailed on over to his side.

The three women rushed from the window. Ptah scanned the palace, searching for their whereabouts. Suddenly, a loud commotion at the city gates distracted him. He turned his head, and to his astonishment he saw Antony's cavalry bursting through, waving their white flags above them. They, too, galloped over to Octavian's lines. Soon afterwards, Ptah heard a voice cry out, "The Romans have entered the city!"

At once people began streaming from the palace. Among them, Ptah spotted the three women running across a deserted courtyard toward Cleopatra's tomb, a slender, pinkish stone tower situated next to the elegant Temple of Isis. As he looked on, they barreled through the entrance, then shut and bolted the massive wooden doors behind them.

A deep groan behind him startled Ptah. He whipped around to see Marc Antony rise to his feet, then wander to the window, where he observed both his navy and his cavalry having taken position on Octavian's side. He did not seemed angered by this turn of events; rather, he merely sighed and looked around the mirrored room as if acknowledging the now-limited extent of his territory. Seeing the note lying on the tray, he picked it up and read it. Turning sharply and running over to Eros, he shook him on the shoulder and cried, "When did this note arrive?"

Groggily, Eros sat up. "Last night, General. I tried to wake you but—"

"Then the deed has already been done," said Antony. "Fate has taken away the only thing I had left to live for." Crumpling the note in his fist and letting it drop to the floor, he cried, "End my life, Eros! End it now. I beg of you!" Antony's burly arm took hold of his sword, then thrust the handle toward Eros, who instantly shrunk back.

"Oh no, master . . . I couldn't!" he stammered.

"You must! I order you to! Here, take my sword. Take it!" Reaching out, Antony seized Eros's wrist, then forced the handle into his hand, wrapping his fingers around it. "Go on now, do it!" he shouted, taking a few steps back.

Eros flinched. Rising to his feet, he held the sword lightly, as though it was made of snake venom. He looked with anguish upon his beloved master, seeing the boy he once knew now standing before him as a man. Slowly, he raised his arm to strike, but then cried out, "No, master, I simply *cannot!*"

What happened next, happened so fast that it caught both Antony and Ptah by surprise. Eros lowered his arm, then tilted the sword upright so that the tip of the blade touched the base of his rib cage. Grabbing the handle with both of his hands, he drove the blade upward, deep in his chest. Antony and Ptah stared dumbfounded as Eros collapsed on the floor, and with a great rush of breath, died.

Antony dropped to his knees. "No!" he cried. *"No!"* Cradling Eros's head in his lap, he sobbed, "With this action you have placed another death on my hands. And yet . . . and yet you have shown me how to do what it was you could not do yourself. Well done, Eros. Well done."

Wiping the tears from his eyes, Antony pulled the sword from his servant's chest. Then, while still on his knees, he tilted the blade upright and positioned the tip just below his rib cage. After that he steadied himself and took several deep breaths.

Knowing what he was about to do, Ptah darted between Antony and the sword, trying to push them apart, but Antony grabbed him and tossed him aside. And then, in true Roman style, the general threw himself onto his sword so that the blade sliced right through his guts.

Ptah watched with horror as Antony hung suspended on his shining weapon for a moment before he rolled to his side and crumpled to the floor.

Ptah panicked. He had to get help! Antony was still breathing! Desperately he sprinted down from the lighthouse, across the island of Pharos, and over the narrow strip of land. He raced through the city in search of Sphinx, but instead he found chaos. Roman soldiers were storming the streets, smashing statues and looting shops. Anyone who tried to stop them was immediately killed. Ptah ran helter-skelter through this madness, and was coming around a corner when he collided with two Egyptian slaves, who immediately dropped to their knees before him.

"Ptah! Save us!" they cried.

"Help me!" he yelled in return.

One of the slaves, a bright young man with keen black eyes said, "I think he's trying to tell us something. I think he wants us to follow!"

Both slaves leaped to their feet and began running after Ptah, who led them back to the lighthouse. There they found Marc Antony, still alive but barely breathing.

"Cleopatra," he uttered weakly.

The slaves responded quickly. They removed the sword from Antony's chest and bound his wound tightly with his clean tunic. Next they assembled a makeshift stretcher and placed him gently upon it. Covering his face with his robe so the Romans wouldn't see him, they carried him down from the lighthouse and through the streets of the city, while Ptah padded along beside them.

It was common knowledge where Cleopatra had gone. By the time they reached the slender pink tower next to the Temple of Isis, a large crowd had gathered. Calling up to the lone window above, they shouted, "Ho, there!"

Charmian's head instantly appeared. "What news do you bring?" she cried.

Shaking their heads sadly, the slaves replied, "Only death and destruction. The city of Alexandria is in ruins. The Library has gone up in flames! Octavian is being merciless! People have nicknamed him 'the Executioner,' while at the same time he has renamed himself Augustus Caesar and has given himself the title of Emperor of Rome! We come bearing Marc Antony. He still lives!" The slave with the keen black eyes pulled the robe from Antony's face.

Charmian gasped and disappeared from the window. In a moment, Cleopatra's head appeared. "How did this happen?" she cried.

"We know not. We found him in the lighthouse this way."

Cleopatra looked thoughtful. "Stay there. We'll unlock the doors so you can bring him up."

Behind her, Ptah could hear Charmian warn, "Oh, no, mistress, it may be a trick! There may be Romans hiding behind the door of your tomb this very minute!"

Immediately, Cleopatra countered, "On second thought, we'll pull him up by rope. Send the cat up with him!"

She disappeared from the window, returning shortly with Iras and Charmian and three long ropes. The women let down the ropes, upon which the slaves wrapped them around Antony's ankles, waist, and shoulders. Ptah was placed gently on his lap. After that, Cleopatra,

Iras, and Charmian slowly began pulling him up. This was no easy task. Even with three strong women straining as hard as they could, it took quite a while before they were able to haul Antony up to the window and drag him inside. When they were finished, Cleopatra tossed a handful of gold coins down to the slaves, who gratefully scooped them up before running off.

Ptah hopped off Antony's lap as soon as he had reached the sill. Looking around, he decided that Cleopatra's tomb looked very much like a storage room except that it was larger and more fancifully furnished. Silver and gold tapestries adorned the pinkish stone walls, and couches and low tables sat off to one side. Pushed against the back wall between a pair of oil lamps was a huge bed with a golden canopy on top.

But—what was that? Ptah breathed a sigh of joy when he noticed his urn sitting on a table beside the bed. He scampered over and peered inside; sadly, no Nefertiti.

The rest of the room was taken up by the stacks and stacks of wooden chests containing Cleopatra's treasure, still wrapped in the ropes used for hauling. Around the base of these chests were heaped rough timbers and crumpled pieces of papyrus, which confused Ptah until he realized what they meant: Cleopatra intended to burn her treasure rather than let Octavian have it.

The three women carried Antony to one of the couches, where they gently laid him down, placing a pillow beneath his head. Gingerly, Cleopatra lifted the blood-soaked tunic that covered his chest. She sucked in her breath. It was clear to her that he had done this to himself and that his wound would be fatal. "Oh, Antony," she said with a sigh.

Upon hearing her voice, Antony opened his eyes. He seemed not to know where he was at first, nor even to recognize his own wife sitting sorrowfully beside him. But then a glimmer of understanding passed through his eyes, and he whispered, "My lady, I thought you were dead." Reaching for her hand, he whispered, "Come closer. The bright light is making it difficult for me to see your pretty face."

The three women exchanged glances. The couch where he lay was dim. Cleopatra softly began wailing. "Oh, Antony, I'm sorry for getting mad at you at the lighthouse, and I'm sorry about the note I sent, and—"

"Hush!" Antony said softly. "There is no need for you to be sorry, my dear, for I die a noble death: a Roman conquered by a Roman."

Cleopatra was about to respond when Antony put up his hand for silence. "Shhh," he said, "just listen. While at the lighthouse, I came to realize that had we won this war, the Romans never would have accepted it without another fight. They would have insisted on battling us again and again, and the peace so longed for by the people of this region would have continued to elude them forever. And I predict that Octavian will be an able ruler, once he has rid himself of all his enemies. But I will not live to see it, for I must leave you now." Antony sighed deeply, then closed his eyes.

"No, please don't go!" Cleopatra felt for his pulse. Turning quickly to Charmian, she whispered, "He must not take his own life. Hurry, pour me the wine!"

Charmian rushed to the bedside table where, sitting beside Ptah's urn, rested a small decanter of wine and a jeweled wine glass. Pouring some of the wine into the glass, she carried it to the queen, who emptied a vial of dark-looking liquid inside. Turning to Antony, Cleopatra said soothingly, "Here, drink this wine. It will help to ease your pain." Lifting his head and cradling it in her palm, she brought the wine glass to his lips. Antony swallowed some of the dark red liquid and then coughed, upon which Cleopatra gave him some more. After that she laid his head back onto the pillow and set the wine glass on the floor. Then she waited.

It didn't take long for the poison to begin taking effect. Antony's body started to quiver and then it turned tense. A look of pain passed across his face. He opened his eyes and parted his lips, as though he intended to speak, but then his face relaxed and his body went limp. A few moments later, he died.

50

Favored Creature of Isis

Upon Antony's death, Charmian instantly threw herself onto the floor and began weeping and tearing her hair out in the Egyptian style of mourning. Iras crumpled to her knees while fat tears rolled down her face. But Cleopatra just sat there, her body listless, her expression forlorn.

Ptah felt heartsick. Hopping down from the table, he crept to the couch where Antony lay and jumped up beside him. Placing his paw over Antony's heart, he wished more than anything right then that he had the power to heal. But unlike the dream he had had, in which Osiris rose up from the dead, Antony remained motionless.

After several minutes Iras stood and wiped away her tears, then tottered to one of the low tables, on which sat a basket of figs. Picking up the basket, she carried it to Cleopatra, saying, "Here, mistress. Have something sweet. It will help make you feel better."

Cleopatra reached out her hand, but then changed her mind and shook her head no. Iras shrugged and thrust her own hand deep in the basket, rummaging around until she found a plump one near the bottom. She bit into it.

Charmian stared up at her in disbelief. "How can you eat at a time like this?" she wailed, and then cried, "Oh mistress, you've lost *everything!*"

Cleopatra stiffened. "No, dear Charmian, not everything," she replied. "There is one thing I still have that no man can take from me, and that is my dignity. I will choose my own fate, which is all I have ever really asked." Picking up the wine glass from which

Antony had drunk, she slowly raised it to her lips.

Beside her, Ptah yowled in alarm. He had already seen more than enough death for one day and was not about to witness another. "Don't do it!" he cried.

Startled, Cleopatra dropped the glass, which instantly shattered into a hundred pieces on the floor. Very quickly, the dark red liquid seeped into the stone, leaving behind a stain the color of blood.

"The poison . . . it's gone!" she gasped, and then softly began keening, "Oh, Isis, do not let it end this way for me! Send me your scorpions, seven and deadly! Send me your snake so that I may live forever!" Getting up from the couch, she stumbled to her treasure pile and combed its surface until she located a long gilded box. She carried it over to the foot of the bed and then sat back down, her movements as stiff and as wooden as the box she was holding.

Cleopatra opened the lid. Inside the box was a shining flute, a marvelous instrument of silver and bronze, meticulously detailed and finely crafted. Carefully lifting it out, she held the flute lovingly in her hands. A faraway look came into her eyes. Then, smiling a bittersweet smile, she said, "This one's for you, Father." She raised the flute up to her lips and began playing a mournful tune that pierced Ptah's heart with sadness. *Were her father, 'the Piper,' here,* he thought, *he certainly would have loved this.* When she finished that song, she played another, equally as sad. Her body seemed to relax as she played, and Ptah thought she looked to be the picture of calm until he studied her fingers, which trembled ever so slightly.

The music flowed through the room like a river of honey, soothing Ptah's spirit. For a while he just sat there and listened, while outside the tower the screaming and shouting and the sacking of the city seemed to fade away in the distance. Letting go of his sorrow, Ptah was just beginning to relax himself, when suddenly, out of the corner of one eye, he detected a movement near his urn. He turned his head, then froze, stunned. An immense cobra was rising over its rim! The snake stared unblinkingly at the queen as it slowly undulated to the music.

Charmian gasped when she saw it, and Iras backed away, but Cleopatra merely lowered her flute and said, "You have come. I knew you would." Then, addressing the women, she said, "It is time. Light the fire." She resumed her playing.

Charmian balked at her order, but Iras responded. Without taking her eyes off the snake for even one moment, she skirted the perimeter of the room until she came to an oil lamp. Removing it from its bracket, she carried the lamp to the treasure pile, then smashed it onto some crumpled papyrus. The flames caught rapidly, their amber brilliance sending tiny tendrils of smoke dancing into the air.

Cleopatra quickened her tune, her body now dipping and swaying to the music as the notes flitted out from her flute like a hummingbird's flight. The cobra responded by raising itself higher, and then curling over the rim. A few moments later, it dropped heavily onto the floor.

Ptah cowered in terror. The snake had to be at least twelve feet long! Brownish-green in color, and with pale yellow crossbands running down the length of its back, the cobra began slithering across floor toward Cleopatra. Taking advantage of the situation, Ptah leaped from the couch, then ran for the windowsill, where he peered at the ground below. Were he to jump, the fall would surely kill him. He was considering making this move anyway, and was wondering if cats did indeed have nine lives, when suddenly a loud commotion broke out beneath him. A group of Romans had arrived at the tower and were pushing their way to the front of the crowd. One of them called up, "Cleopatra, I command you to surrender at once!" It was Octavian and his guards!

Charmian shrieked when she heard him, and Iras began to cry, but Cleopatra ignored him completely and kept on with her playing. Meanwhile, the cobra had slithered to the foot of the bed and was winding itself into a coil at her feet.

Outside the tower, Octavian hollered up again. "Cleopatra, open the door this minute!" Then Ptah heard him say to his guards, "I smell smoke. Hurry, get the battering ram! *I want that treasure!*" His guards raced away, returning several minutes later carrying a long, squared timber. A series of thunderous crashing blows followed as they began ramming the timber against the bottom set of doors.

Inside the tomb, the flames climbed higher and higher. Smoke billowed upward, blanketing the ceiling with a thick gray cloud. Iras and Charmian coughed and sobbed. Utterly terrified, Ptah considered jumping again, and was actually feeling quite good about this plan, when suddenly he detected more movement near his urn. He turned his head, and to his absolute horror he saw *more* snakes rising over its rim. These snakes were different from the first—they were smaller and coppery-red in color, and they had blackish zigzags running down the length of their backs. As more and more snakes emerged, Ptah realized that these were asps—deadly venomous snakes, feared more than even cobras, because their bite brought about a long, painful death as opposed to a death that felt much like falling asleep. Slow moving but aggressive, the asps began dropping onto the floor and slithering around the room in a whirlwind-like motion. A low hissing sound—somehow familiar to Ptah—accompanied them.

Iras started whimpering, and Charmian nearly fainted, but Cleopatra ignored the asps and focused her attention solely on the cobra while she played at a dizzying pace. The monstrous snake reared upward, then fanned its neck out wide to form a sort of hood with a double chevron on the back. As it swayed back and forth, it opened its mouth up wide, revealing a deadly pair of fangs.

Suddenly, a tremendous crash reverberated beneath them as Octavian's guards broke through the bottom set of doors. There was a loud commotion on the stairway, then scuffling noise outside the door of the tomb, after which Octavian's voice boomed out, "Cleopatra, I command you to surrender at once! You will *not* deny me this triumph!" Next he could be heard shouting, "Quick, get the battleaxes! Break down this door! I *must* have that treasure!"

Charmian picked back up on her wailing as the guards began hacking away at the door with their axes. Still on the sill, Ptah gazed again at the ground below. No matter that there was an asp on the floor just beneath him, and another one inching its way upward, he simply could not bring himself to jump. Frantically, he began searching the room for a place he could hide. The asps seemed to be everywhere—swarming all over the floor, on top of the couches, around the bed. The only place that they *didn't* seem to be anymore was inside his urn. So, just as the asp that was inching its way upward crested the sill, Ptah took a deep breath and plunged to the floor. Racing to the bedside table, he leaped to the rim of his urn. That very same moment, Cleopatra hit a high shrill note on her flute, and then threw her flute down, upon which the cobra lunged, striking her on the arm. The queen let out a cry and fell back on the bed.

Immediately Iras ran toward them, sobbing. "Take me! Take me, too!" She barely made it across the room when the cobra lunged again, biting her on the leg. With a yelp Iras fell to her knees, then crawled the rest of the way to join Cleopatra, who lay dying on the bed. Reaching up, she straightened the crown in the queen's hair before slumping to the floor.

The cobra then turned its attention to Charmian, whose brown eyes had grown wide with fear. "No!" she whispered hoarsely. "No! I am too *young* to die!" She took a step back, and then another, and then kept on stepping backward with her eyes riveted to the cobra, which was slowly slithering toward her. Meanwhile, the hacking noise continued, the blades of the axes now visible through the door.

And then it happened. Charmian took another step back, and her foot came down upon an asp. Ptah gasped as the asp reared upward to bite her, and would have, but the cobra streaked across the room and bit her first instead. Charmian screamed and fell to the floor.

The cobra then coiled about and fixed its beady black eyes on Ptah. Petrified with fear, he met its gaze, and in that moment he could have sworn that he saw a look of both sadness and resolution in its eyes, as though it knew it was about to do something unpleasant but was determined to go through with it anyway. Ptah's breath fell short and his heart felt weak. He dove to the base of his urn and scrunched into a ball, waiting for what he knew must come.

He saw its tongue at first, flickering above the rim. Then he saw its head, followed by its long, thick body. Ptah cringed as the cobra dipped down inside his urn. A low hissing sound, like the rush of the wind, accompanied it. He squeezed his eyes shut. Any second, he knew he would feel the deadly fangs sink deep in his hide.

Suddenly, Ptah heard the door to the room crash open, and shouts of, "Hurry; put out the fire!" and "The queen is dead!" followed by

"This one's still alive!"

Above the din, Ptah could hear Octavian shout, "Was this right, young woman?" upon which Charmian responded weakly, "Yes, it was very right and fitting for a queen who has descended from so many kings." With that, she spit on Octavian's feet, then died.

The hissing sound inside Ptah's urn grew louder and louder, as though a thousand snakes were now circling around him. He began to feel dizzy, then woozy, and he assumed that the cobra had bitten him. A strong sense of vertigo seized hold of his gut. His senses reeling, Ptah felt himself teetering on the brink of despair, when all at once the hissing, the shouting, and the vertigo stopped, and the room he was in grew quiet.

Epilogue
A Friend from the Past

I must be dead, thought Ptah, *but if I'm dead, then where is the light? Where is the beautiful music Horus spoke of?* Ptah strained his ears to listen for it; but instead he heard voices speaking in hushed tones.

"Congratulations on receiving your medal of honor today," a woman was saying. "Your discovery that the great god Ptah also came to earth in the form of a cat has revolutionized ancient Egyptian studies! Imagine, after all of these years, finding the images of him on the temple walls of Hoot-Ka-Ptah, and riding high on a chariot basket during the Battle of Kadesh, and in the tomb of the official palace scribe named Nebre. I just don't see how everyone could have missed seeing them all before."

"Neither do I," a man replied, "although I might have missed them, too, had I not become more sensitive to cat images as a result of having lost my own dear cat. Funny how the cat in those pictures looks just like him—blue eyes and all."

Ptah's ears perked up. There was something familiar about that voice! Stretching up and placing his paws on the rim of his urn, he poked his head outside.

It was Professor Mariette! In three seconds flat, Ptah leaped from his urn, dashed across the museum room floor, and was purring loudly at the professor's feet.

"Ptah!" cried the professor with a start. "Oh, Ptah! I can't believe that you're back! How I've missed you! Where have you *been*?" Just as fast, the professor scooped up Ptah and cradled his cat in his arms.

"Oh, professor," Ptah began excitedly. "You won't believe where I've been and what I've seen. Or who I met! I was in ancient Egypt, and together with Imhotep, we traveled into Nubia in search of gold! Then I joined Nebre and Ipuwer, who taught me more things than I can possibly say. After that I was with Ramses, and we battled the Hittites near the town of Kadesh! Then I met Marc Antony and Cleopatra, and we sailed around the Mediterranean Sea on our way to battle Octavian, but his navy trapped us, and—"

"Ptah, settle down, kitty! Just listen to you! You must be starved! When we get home, I'll fix you a nice bowl of cat food—canned salmon, your favorite." Professor Mariette happily turned on his heels and began heading for the museum exit. "Speaking of home," he said, "so much has changed in the year since you've been gone. I've moved to a house in the suburbs. It's a nice house, filled with all the things you know, plus we'll soon have some lovely Italian antiques! And because of the prize I just won, we'll be traveling to distant lands. I know you're not used to that, but I'm sure you'll adjust."

The tall, dark-haired Italian woman trailing after him tugged on his sleeve.

"Oh, forgive me! This is my fiancée, Isabella," the professor added with a shy smile.

"I'm very pleased to meet you, Ptah," said Isabella, gently shaking Ptah's paw. Leaning closer to the professor, she whispered, "Do you think that he'll mind? About the other cat, I mean? She's in the car now."

"Oh, yes . . . thanks for reminding me." The professor paused while he opened the museum door and stepped out onto the sidewalk. "I hope you don't mind," he said hesitantly, "but after Isabella and I are married, you'll be having a roommate—a stray, actually. She turned up here at the museum a couple of weeks ago. She's really quite beautiful, probably the prettiest cat I've ever seen! No one knows where she came from, although we assume her owner must be very rich, because her fur was dusted with gold and she was wearing a solid gold medallion etched with the profile of a woman's face."

Ptah's heart started to race and his face felt flushed as they halted beside an Italian sports car, red with leather seats. "It's the strangest thing," the professor continued, bending down low and tapping on the glass, "but the woman on her medallion looks just like an ancient Egyptian queen. Anyway, to make a long story short, we've named her—"

"Nefertiti!" Ptah shouted, spying his friend sleeping on back seat of the car. He noticed her glamorous gold dusting was gone, but still she looked every bit as beautiful to him.

In response to the noise, Nefertiti lifted her head. She gazed out the window, her turquoise-green eyes widening with delight at the sight of Ptah's blue ones.

And in that moment, they smiled.

About the Author

Kathryn DeMeritt is a graphic designer living in Seattle, Washington. In this, her debut novel, she has combined her fascination with history and her love of literature to create a work she hopes will teach, inspire, and entertain children the world over.

This book is dedicated to my son, Max.

Special thanks to my husband, Mark, and my daughter, Hannah; to Carol Gaskin and Val Paul Taylor for joining my team; to teachers Dennis Simpson and Jan Laskelle for their encouragement; to Stephen Marafino for his guidance; and to T. Harv Ecker for starting me on a path I might not otherwise have followed.